Praise for Karen Rose

Nothing to Fear

"A pulse-pounding tale that has it all: suspense, action, and a very hunky private investigator." —*Cosmopolitan*

"Phenomenal . . . Filled with heart-stopping suspense and graphic terror . . . In the pantheon of horrific killers, [this one] surely ranks near the top." —*Romantic Times BOOKclub Magazine*

"Readers can always count on Rose to deliver an action-packed book, and this one is no exception." —*Southern Pines Pilot* (NC)

"An absolute gem . . . it's definitely earned a place on my keeper shelf, and I look forward to reading it again and again. This is what true romantic suspense is all about, and I thank Ms. Rose for such a wonderful read." —RomanceJunkies.com

"A tense, chilling suspense that readers will appreciate from start to finish." —*Midwest Book Review*

"Rose's well-crafted story sets pulses pounding and pages turning." —*BookPage*

"A caring women's advocate heroine, a determined, gritty hero, and a diabolical villain drive the plot of Rose's riveting story." —*Library Journal*

I'm Watching You

"TOP PICK! Terrifying and gritty." —*Romantic Times BOOKclub Magazine*

Please turn the page for more rave reviews . . .

Praise for Karen Rose's Previous Novels

"The suspense unfolds right up to the last page."
—*Southern Pines Pilot (NC)*

"A sensual, riveting book that kept me on the edge of my seat."
—*Rendezvous*

"Action-packed . . . a thrilling police procedural romance . . . fans will enjoy this tense thriller." —*Midwest Book Review*

"It's perfect . . . Love the characters, loved the side stories. It doesn't get any better than this!" —*Romantic Review*

Have You Seen Her?

"Heart-racing thrills . . . showcases her growing talent . . . readers will . . . rush to the novel's thrilling conclusion."
—*Publishers Weekly*

"Terrifying and gripping." —*Romantic Times BOOKclub Magazine*

Don't Tell

"As gripping as a cold hand on the back of one's neck . . . and tempered by lovable characters and a moving romance."
—*Publishers Weekly*

"One of the best suspense novels [I've] read this summer . . . one hot author you don't want to miss."
—*The Belles & Beaux of Romance*

"A well-written thriller—a definite page-turner that never lets up until the last page."   —*Romance Reviews Today*

"Action-packed [with a] story line [that] is character driven."
                                        —*Midwest Book Review*

"A stunning tour de force that readers won't want to miss . . . *Don't Tell* belongs on the keeper shelf."   —WordWeaving.com

"A fantastic job of telling a tale . . . touchingly narrated."
                                        —Bookloons.com

"A truly spectacular example of romantic suspense."
                                        —ARomanceReview.com

"*Don't Tell* is a seat-of-your-pants tale, dragging the reader deep into the characters and wringing emotions from all concerned."
                                        —ScribesWorld.com

"Couldn't put it down."   —Bookhaunts.com

"Karen Rose's nail-biting delivery is unique . . . *Don't Tell* is the harbinger of great things to come."   —Heartstrings.com

"Excellent romantic suspense . . . will keep you on the edge of your seat . . . excellent writing and storytelling by Karen Rose."
                                        —RoadtoRomance.ca

"A story that satisfies on every level . . . vivid and memorable."
                                        —TheWordonRomance.com

ALSO BY KAREN ROSE

Don't Tell
Have You Seen Her?
I'm Watching You
Nothing to Fear

ATTENTION: CORPORATIONS AND ORGANIZATIONS:
Most WARNER books are available at quantity discounts
with bulk purchase for educational, business, or sales
promotional use. For information, please call or write:

Special Markets Department, Warner Books, Inc.,
1271 Avenue of the Americas, New York, NY 10020
Telephone: 1-800-222-6747 Fax: 1-800-477-5925

SSIHM LIBRARY/
RESOURCE CENTER
610 W. ELM AVE.
MONROE, MICHIGAN 48162

YOU CAN'T
HIDE

KAREN
ROSE

WARNER
VISION
BOOKS

NEW YORK   BOSTON

If you purchase this book without a cover you should be aware that this book may have been stolen property and reported as "unsold and destroyed" to the publisher. In such case neither the author nor the publisher has received any payment for this "stripped book."

Copyright © 2006 by Karen Rose Hafer
Excerpt from *Count to Ten* copyright © 2006 by Karen Rose Hafer
All rights reserved. No part of this book may be reproduced in any form or by any electronic or mechanical means, including information storage and retrieval systems, without permission in writing from the publisher, except by a reviewer who may quote brief passages in a review.

Warner Vision is a registered trademark of Time Warner Book Group Inc.

Cover design by Diane Luger
Book design by Giorgetta Bell McRee

Warner Books

Time Warner Book Group
1271 Avenue of the Americas
New York, NY 10020
Visit our Web site at www.twbookmark.com

Printed in the United States of America

First Printing: April 2006

10 9 8 7 6 5 4 3 2 1

To Martin for loving me just the way that I am and for buying me M&M's when I needed them most. I love you.

To my children who understand when I hid in my office writing and who create such incredible stories of their own. I'm grateful and very, very proud of you both.

To Karen Kosztolnyik and Karen Solem for continuing to make all my dreams come true when I thought all the dreams already had.

Acknowledgments

Carleton Hafer for all the technical advice on surveillance and computer networks. And for everything else.

Marc and Kay Conterato for all things medical and pharmaceutical and for the Minnesota Buzz. Love you guys.

Niki Ciccotelli who shared her wonderful family with me and for making me hungry with all the talk of ziti and "flying saucers."

Shannon Armstrong for the vivid pictures of Chicago and all the chichi things therein.

Danny Agan for answering all my questions on detectives and homicide investigations.

Sam Basso for helping me profile Dolly the rottweiler.

All my pals—Terri Bolyard, Martha Wile, Kathy Caskie, Jean Mason, and Lani Rich—for putting up with me! Thank

Acknowledgments

you. Oh, and to Lani for helping me remember the "wire thing" in the oven is called an "oven rack."

The SPCA for giving me my own sweet kitty, Bella. And Bella, for making sure I never sleep past 6:00 A.M. (That was sarcasm.)

Megan Scott for teaching me the fundamentals of newspaper journalism.

The Florida Department of Law Enforcement Crime Lab for answering all my questions on fingerprinting and crime scene investigation.

Frank Ahearn for teaching me how to hide behind corporations. Wherever you are.

To all of these people (and pets)—I thank you for all the wonderful and thorough information. Any mistakes in this book are entirely my own.

Prologue

Chicago, Saturday, March 11, 11:45 P.M.

Cynthia." It was the barest of whispers, but still she heard.

No. Cynthia Adams clenched her eyes shut, pressed the back of her head into her pillow, its softness a mockery to the rigidity of her tensed body. Her fingers dug into the sheets, twisting until she grimaced in pain. *Not again.* A sob rose in her throat, wild and desperate. *Please. I can't do this again.* "Go away," she whispered harshly. "Please, just go away and leave me alone."

But she knew she was talking to no one. If she opened her eyes she'd see nothing but the darkness of her own bedroom. No one was there. But still the hideous whisper taunted, as it had for weeks. Every night she lay in bed . . . waiting. Waiting for the voice that was her worst nightmare. Some nights it spoke. Some nights she merely lay tensed, waiting. It was wind, it was shadows. It was nothing at all.

But it was real. She knew it was real.

"Cynthia? Help me." It was the voice of a child calling for comfort in the night. A scared little girl. Who was dead.

She's dead. I know she's dead. She placed the lilies on Melanie's grave herself every Sunday. Melanie was dead.

But she was here. *She's come for me.* Blindly she grabbed the bottle from her bedside table and dry swallowed two pills. *Go away. Please, just go away.*

"Cynthia?" It was real. So real. *God, help me, please. I'm losing my mind.* "Why did you do it?" The whisper drifted. "I need to know why."

Why? She didn't know why. Dammit, she didn't know why. She rolled over, burying her face in her pillow, drawing her body into the smallest possible space. She held her breath. And waited.

It was quiet. Melanie was gone. Cynthia let herself draw a breath, then sprang from the bed as the scent assaulted her senses. *Lilies.* "No." She backed away, unable to take her eyes from the pillow where just the tip of a single lily was visible.

"It should have been you, Cynthia." The whisper was harsher now. "I should be putting lilies on your grave."

Cynthia drew a breath. She made herself repeat what her psychiatrist had told her to say when she was afraid. "This isn't real. This is not real."

"It's real, Cynthia. I'm real." Melanie was no longer a child, her voice now that of an angry adult. Cynthia shuddered at the sound. Melanie deserved to be angry. *I was a coward.* "You ran away once, Cyn. You hid. You won't hide again. You'll never, ever leave me alone again."

Cynthia backed away slowly until she came up hard against her bedroom door. She closed her eyes tight as she gripped the hard, reassuringly real doorknob. "You aren't real. You are not real."

"It should have been you. Why did you leave me? Why

did you leave me with him? How could you? You said you loved me. But you left me alone. With him. You never loved me." A sob shook Melanie's voice and tears burned Cynthia's eyes.

"It's not true. I loved you," she whispered, desperately. "So much."

"You never loved me." Melanie was a child again. An innocent child. "He hurt me, Cyn. You let him. You let him hurt me . . . again and again. Why?"

Cynthia yanked the doorknob and tumbled backward into the hall where a single light burned. And stopped short. More lilies. Everywhere. She turned slowly and could only stare. They mocked her. Mocked her sanity.

"Come to me, Cyn." Melanie coaxed now. "Come. It's not so bad. We'll be together. You can take care of me. Like you promised you would."

"No." She covered her ears and ran for the door. *"No."*

"You can't hide, Cyn. Come to me. You know you want to." She was sweet now, so sweet. Melanie had been so sweet. Then. Now she was dead. *It's my fault.*

Cynthia jerked open the front door. And stifled a scream. Then slowly leaned over and picked up the picture at her feet. She stared in horror at the lifeless figure hanging from the rope, and remembered the day she'd found her. Melanie had just been . . . dangling there. Swinging . . .

"You made me do that," Melanie said coldly. "You don't deserve to live."

Her hands shook as she stared. "I don't," she whispered.

"Then come to me, Cyn. Please."

Cynthia backed up again, groped for the phone. "Call Dr. Chick. Call," she muttered. *She'll tell me I'm not crazy.* But the phone rang and startled, she dropped it. Stared at it as if it were alive. Waited for it to sprout fangs and hiss. But it just rang.

"Answer it, Cynthia," Melanie said coldly. "Now."

Hands shaking, Cynthia bent over and picked up the phone. "H-hel-hello?"

"Cynthia, it's Dr. Ciccotelli."

Gasping in relief at the solid, familiar, *live* voice, Cynthia's shoulders sagged. "I hear her, Dr. Chick. Melanie. She's here. I hear her."

"Of course you do. She's calling you, Cynthia. It's what you deserve. Go to her. End it. End it now."

"But . . ." Tears welled, spilled. "But . . ." she whispered.

"Do it, Cynthia. She's dead and it's your fault. Go to her. Do what you should have done years ago. Take care of her."

"Come," Melanie ordered, her voice again adult and full of authority. "Come."

Cynthia dropped the phone, backed away, wearily now. *I'm tired. So tired.* "Let me sleep," she whispered. "Please let me sleep."

"Come to me," Melanie whispered back. "Then I'll let you sleep."

Melanie had promised it so many times. So many nights. Cynthia turned and stared at the window. Dark night was outside the glass. But what else? Sleep. Peace.

Peace.

The living room was empty. Cynthia Adams was no longer in view of the camera. The feed to the laptop no longer showed the pacing, frantic woman. She was going to do it. The excitement was building with each moment. After four weeks, Cynthia Adams was finally going to do it. After four weeks of intense effort, she'd been driven to the brink of sanity. Just a little nudge would send her flying. Hopefully quite literally.

"She's at the window." The woman seated in the passenger seat was pale as she murmured the words. Her hands trembled as she carefully set the microphone in her lap. "I can't do this anymore."

"You'll do it until I say otherwise."

She flinched. "She's going to jump. Let me tell her to stop."

Stop? The girl was as crazy as Cynthia Adams. "Tell her to come." She did nothing. Temper bubbled. "Tell her to come or your brother dies. You should know by now I'm not bluffing. Tell her to come. Tell her you need her, you miss her, she owes you. Tell her it will all be better when you're together. Tell her now. And do it with feeling." Still she sat, unmoving. *"Now."*

She picked up the microphone, her hands shaking. "Cyn," she whispered, "I need you. I'm scared." She was. Nothing like reality to fuel great drama. "Please, come." Her voice broke. "It will be better this way. Please." She ended on a pleading whisper.

The view of Adams's window from the driver's seat was superb. The plate-glass door slowly slid open and Cynthia Adams appeared, her sheer nightgown whipping in the cold March wind. She'd make an attractive corpse. Very Gloria Swanson. What a great movie that was, *Sunset Boulevard.* Hollywood just didn't make them like that anymore. It would be a great way to celebrate. Popcorn and an old movie. But the celebration would never happen if Adams just stood on her balcony. *Just jump, dammit.*

"Tell her to come. Make her jump. Show me your stuff, sweetheart."

She swallowed hard at the sarcastic endearment, but nevertheless complied. "Cynthia, just another step. One more. I'm waiting."

"Do it like a child now. Like a little kid."

"Please, Cynthia. I'm scared." The girl's command of

voices was good. She could go from adult to child, from dead Melanie to psychiatrist Ciccotelli in a blink. "Please come." She drew a deep breath, shuddered it out. "I need you."

And then . . . success. A horrified cry rasped from the girl's throat as Adams came plunging down. Twenty-two floors. They could hear the thud of her body striking pavement even through the closed car windows. Maybe her corpse wouldn't be so attractive after all. But beauty was in the eye of the beholder and the sight of Adams sprawled dead on the pavement was . . . breathtaking. The girl in the passenger seat was crying hysterically.

"Pull yourself together. You need to make another call."

"Oh, God, oh God." She turned her face away from the window as the car passed within feet of Adams's body. "I can't believe . . . God, I'm going to be sick."

"Not in my car you're not. Take the phone. Take it."

Shuddering, she took the phone. "I can't."

"You will. Hit speed dial number one. It's Ciccotelli's home phone. When she answers, tell her that you're a concerned neighbor of Cynthia Adams and she is standing on the ledge, threatening to jump. Do it."

She dialed and waited. "She's not answering. She's asleep."

"Then call again. Keep it ringing until the princess answers her phone. And put it on speaker. I want to hear."

The third try yielded results. "Hello?"

She'd been asleep. Home alone on a Saturday night. It was satisfying, knowing that aspect of Ciccotelli's life was also well under control. A nudge to the girl had her stuttering her lines. "Dr. Ciccotelli? Dr. Tess Ciccotelli?"

"Who is this?"

"A . . . a neighbor of one of your patients. Cynthia Adams. Something's wrong. She's on the ledge. She's threatening to jump." With her eyes closed the girl ended the call and let the cell phone drop to her lap. "I'm finished."

"For tonight."

"But—" She jerked around, her mouth open. "You said . . ."

"I said I'd keep your brother alive if you assisted me. I still need your assistance. Keep practicing Ciccotelli's voice. I'll need you to do her again in a few days. For tonight, we're done. Say one word and you and your brother die."

Ciccotelli was coming. *Let the games commence.*

Chapter One

Sunday, March 12, 12:30 A.M.

Normally a suicide drew a bigger crowd, even in a high-priced neighborhood like this one, Detective Aidan Reagan thought grimly as he slammed his car door and flinched at the bite of the cold air blowing in from the lake. But most people with any sense were inside on a night like this. Aidan couldn't afford the luxury. Dispatch called and he and his partner were next in the barrel. For a damn suicide.

This was a distraction from the child homicide he'd spent the last two days working. He hated child homicides but he thought he might hate suicides just a little bit more. He could only hope he could get this jumper off his desk quickly so he could focus on finding who'd broken a six-year-old's neck like a dry twig.

The people who watched from the curb appeared to be twenty-somethings coming home from a night on the town. They waited silently, eyes fastened to the scene with a morbid mixture of horror, fascination, and sympathy. The horror Aidan understood. No body was a pretty sight, but a plunge twenty-two stories was a step beyond generic gruesomeness. As for the sympathy . . . Aidan would save his for the real victims. Whoever said suicide was a victimless crime had obviously never notified a family.

He had.

He wished the morbid curiosity-seekers could see that part of it. They might not find such a scene so damn fascinating after all. But they were well-behaved at least, standing silently behind the yellow tape strung between two light posts by the officers first on the scene. An occasional stamp of cold feet broke the unnatural silence. One of the two uniforms stood by the yellow tape at the curb, the other on the sidewalk, facing away from the body.

Aidan approached, his shield in his hand. After four months it still felt strange, approaching the uniform, not wearing one. "Reagan, Homicide," he said crisply, then stopped short, first at the stench, then at the sight. The stomach he'd have sworn was seasoned after twelve years on the force took a nasty lurch. "My God."

The uniform nodded, his jaw tight. "That's what we said."

Aidan's eyes took a quick trip up the wall of identical balconies and back down to focus on the iron spike protruding from what had been a woman's chest. Now her chest was ripped open, revealing shattered bone and . . . insides. For just a moment he stared, remembering the other time he'd seen such a sight. He steeled his spine. This was nothing like the other. That other victim had been an innocent. This woman lying here . . . she was dead by her own hand. *No sympathy,* he told himself.

This woman had thrown herself twenty-two stories to concrete—and onto a decorative wrought-iron fence. The fence was only about a foot high, mostly inverted "u"s, but every four feet or so a spike jutted upward. The force of her impact on the spike had literally split her wide open, geysering blood to splatter a dirty pile of snow three feet away. "She hit it dead on," he murmured.

The uniform winced. "So to speak."

Aidan dragged his gaze back to the cop's drawn face. "You are?"

"I'm Forbes and that's my partner, DiBello, over there doing crowd control." Forbes grimaced. "I lost the toss."

Aidan scanned the faces of the silent crowd that needed no control, but hell, a toss was a toss. He'd lost his fair share during his years in uniform. "Anybody see anything?"

"Two seventeen-year-olds say she jumped from the twenty-second floor at about midnight." Forbes pointed a black gloved finger upward. "It's that balcony up there, the one with the curtains blowing in the wind, third from the left."

"Nobody pushed her?"

"Kids didn't see anybody. They said she kind of glided up to the railing."

Aidan frowned. "Glided up? Like a ghost?"

Forbes shrugged. "That's what they said. Kept repeating it, again and again. I put 'em in the back of the squad car until you could talk to them. They're pretty shook up."

"Poor kids." They deserved the sympathy. This sight would haunt them for a long time. They were only seventeen, just a year older than his own sister. He shuddered at the thought of Rachel seeing such a grisly sight, then jerked a nod toward the crowd. "Any of them know her?"

"DiBello asked, but nobody did."

Aidan looked at the woman's face, her features now loose and spongy. Blood seeped from her ears, nose, and her open mouth. The iron fence had taken the brunt of the force of her fall, but any fall from that height smashed the skull, the scalp basically containing the mess. The features kind of liquefied, giving the face a macabre, melted wax look. "Nobody would recognize her now, even if they did know her. We'll need to get into the apartment she jumped from. Is the super around?"

"I knocked but he's not home. A neighbor says he's at a Bulls game."

"The game was over two hours ago. Where is he now?"

"I paged him once. I'll see if I can find out where he hangs."

"Thanks, man. Also, can we move this crowd to the other side of the street? And make sure nobody in the crowd takes any pictures. Have your partner keep his eyes open for camera cell phones." Aidan pulled out his own cell and called in for a warrant and a medical examiner, then crouched down to take a closer look at the body. She was wrapped in black lace and silk and he wondered if she'd dressed especially for the occasion. If she had, the effect was ruined by the spike. And the guts oozing onto the concrete. He swallowed hard. It was a hell of a mess for someone to clean up. That was the problem with suicides, he thought bitterly. They wanted to go out with dramatic flair but they never thought about the consequences to anybody else. To the people they left behind. To the people who had to clean up.

Selfish. So damn avoidable. *Goddammit.*

He realized he'd clenched his fists and deliberately loosened them. *Get a grip, Reagan.* The deep breath he drew filled his senses with the metallic scent of warm blood and foul stench of busted bowel, but underneath he caught a hint of cinnamon as footsteps crunched the snow behind him. His partner was here.

"Hell of a way to go," Murphy stated in his quiet way.

Aidan shot a harsh glance over his shoulder. "Hell of a thing to do to her family. Can't wait to make that visit."

"One thing at a time, Aidan," Murphy said evenly, but his eyes were kind and understanding and made Aidan feel small. "So what do we know?"

"Only that she jumped from the twenty-second floor. Two witnesses say she 'glided' up, whatever the hell that means. I haven't talked to them yet. As for her, she was young. Her arms look well-toned." He focused in on her limbs, the only body parts that remained reasonably unscathed. "Maybe in her late twenties or early thirties." He pointed at one hand that draped over the inverted "u"s of the decorative fence. "Big rock on her right hand, no sign of any rings on her left, so she's probably unmarried. Somebody has some money. That ring costs a hell of a lot of green. Her arms and hands don't appear to have any defensive wounds."

Murphy crouched down next to him. "Snazzy colors."

Her two-inch long nails were painted bright bloodred. "I noticed. The red against the black lace does make a real statement."

Murphy shrugged. "It wouldn't be the first time a jumper wanted to leave a lasting impression. Nobody knows her?"

Aidan pushed to his feet. "No. I'm hoping the apartment she jumped from was hers. I called in for a warrant and the ME's on his way. Let's go talk to the kids who—"

"Let me pass." The voice cut through the night—soft, yet ringing with authority.

"Ma'am, you can't go through here. Please stay behind the tape."

Aidan looked up in time to see Officer DiBello's arm come up to block a woman in a tan wool coat, her dark hair whipping in the wind, covering her face.

Again she spoke, her voice calm and quiet but commanding. "I'm her doctor. Let me pass, Officer."

"Let her through," Murphy echoed and DiBello did, but Aidan stepped into the woman's path, blocking her once again before she could contaminate his scene. She lifted on her toes, but still wasn't quite tall enough to see over his shoulder. Aidan put his hand on her shoulder and gently pushed her back down. She stiffened, but cooperated.

"Ma'am, we're waiting for the ME. There's nothing you can do now."

She took a step back, going very still. "She jumped?"

Aidan nodded. "I'm sorry, ma'am. Maybe you can tell us . . ." But the words just trailed away as she pushed her hair from her face and instant recognition sent a new wave of anger to boil his blood. "You're Ciccotelli." Dr. Tess Ciccotelli. This woman was no doctor. She was a shrink. That alone would have been bad enough, but *Miz Chick* had made quite a name for herself.

She wasn't just a garden variety do-you-hate-your-mother shrink. She was a bleeding heart shrink who'd thrown weeks of solid police work in the chipper-shredder when she'd sat on the stand and calmly testified that a known, *confessed* killer of three children and one cop was unfit to stand trial. Four grieving families were denied justice because a "doctor" said a killer was insane.

Of course the bastard was insane. He'd confessed to brutally murdering three little girls. Babies. With his bare hands he'd strangled a seasoned cop that was trying to take him down. That he was crazy didn't make him an iota less guilty. Now the bastard was sitting pretty in a Chicago psychiatric hospital making pot holders all day instead of in a six-by-eight waiting for a needle in his arm. It wasn't fair. It wasn't right. But it had happened. And this woman had allowed it to happen.

Aidan had been there, sitting in the courtroom with the other cops, hoping against hope that Ciccotelli would change her mind, hoping she'd do the right thing. He remembered how the girls' parents had wept quietly in the courtroom, knowing they'd find no justice that day. How the cop's wife had sat front and center, surrounded by a sea of supportive uniforms. Ciccotelli hadn't blinked, just continued looking straight ahead with cool brown eyes.

Just like she was looking at him now. "And you are?" she asked.

"Detective Aidan Reagan. This is my partner Detective Todd Murphy."

Her eyes narrowed slightly as she studied his face and it was all he could do to maintain his glare. From his seat in the courtroom she'd been sleek, sophisticated. Unapproachable. Up close there was a wild beauty to her features, yet she was still unapproachable. His own eyes narrowed as she turned to Murphy. "Todd, please ask your partner to step aside. I can at least give you a positive ID."

Murphy grasped her arm gently. "Tess, you don't want to do that. She's . . . She's really messed up."

Aidan stepped aside, holding out his arm in mock gallantry. "If she wants to see, by all means let the good doctor look."

Murphy shot him a warning glare. "Aidan."

"It's all right, Todd," she murmured and stepped forward without a flinch. She stood looking down at the body for a good minute before turning back to them, her face perfectly composed, her eyes still cool. "Her name was Cynthia Adams. She has no next of kin." From her coat pocket she pulled a business card and handed it to Murphy without a tremor. "Call me if you have questions," she said. "I'll answer what I can."

And with that she turned away and started walking toward a gray Mercedes parked behind Murphy's plain Ford. Aidan's annoyance bubbled over.

"And that's it?"

"Aidan," Murphy cautioned. "Not now."

"If not now, when?" He controlled his voice, conscious of the crowd camped nearby. "She waltzes in here and IDs the victim, cool as a damn cucumber. And then she just walks away? How about what made her jump twenty-two stories, *Doctor*? You should know, shouldn't you?" *And you should care, dammit,* he thought viciously. *You should care about* something. "What the hell kind of doctor are you?" he finished on a hiss and watched her pause, her hands deep in her pockets.

She pulled a glove from her pocket and tugged it over her fingers, her back to them. "Call me if you need me, Todd," was all she said before walking away.

Murphy's eyes flashed as he sucked in both cheeks. "Aidan, I told you *not now.*"

Aidan turned on his heel, dismissing her. "What does it matter? It's not like she gives a damn anyway."

"You have no idea what you're talking about. You don't know her."

Aidan looked over his shoulder. Murphy was watching Ciccotelli cross the street, his face one big, wholly uncharacteristic scowl. "And you do?" He wouldn't have expected it. The venerable Todd Murphy, fallen prey to the charms of a cold piece of work like Miz Chick. *Well, I won't.*

Murphy blew out an angry breath that turned to vapor, a barrier hovering between them for an instant of time. Then the barrier was gone as was the scowl, leaving Murphy staring at Ciccotelli with a sadness that gave Aidan serious pause. "Yeah. As a matter of fact I do. Go talk to the teenagers, Aidan. I'll be back in a minute."

Aidan shrugged away his uncertainty. Let Murphy deal with the icicle. He had other things to do, like process a crime scene so the ME could scoop up what was left of Cynthia Adams and they could all go home. He'd take the teenagers' statement, check her apartment for ID, and then he'd get the hell out of here.

* * *

Another minute. Just another minute. Tess Ciccotelli chanted the words in her mind, a mantra to keep her composure until she was alone. Cynthia was dead. Dear God. Lying on the street, ripped apart . . .

Don't think about her. Don't think about her dead and mutilated. Just run. Run fast. Just another minute. Then you can fall apart, Tess. But not yet.

She fumbled the key in the car door lock, conscious of Todd Murphy and his partner behind her, watching. Todd and his very angry partner, whoever he was. He said his name was Aidan Reagan, she remembered, finally getting the key to slide into the lock, pulling the door open. She made her mind focus on the picture of the man's cold blue eyes. He'd been so angry. No, he'd been furious. *Just another—*

"Tess?"

Dammit. She bobbled her keys, dropping them to the dark street where they skittered underneath her car. She drew a deep breath. So close. "I'm all right, Todd. Go and do your job."

"I am. Tess, you're shaking."

"Todd, please." Her voice hitched, humiliatingly. "I need to get out of here."

He took her arm and guided her into the driver's seat. "You shouldn't drive, Tess. Let me call somebody to get you home."

"There isn't anyone," she said numbly. "That's what took me so long to get here. I called my partners, my friends. I never come to a patient's house alone. Not done. Not ethical." She was rambling now and couldn't seem to stop herself. "Nobody was home, so I came anyway." She closed her eyes. Opened them again when all she saw was Cynthia . . . lying there. "And I was too late."

"This isn't your fault, Tess," Murphy said gently. "You know this."

A sob was building. Resolutely Tess shoved it back. "She's dead, Todd." How stupid was that? Cynthia Adams lay gutted on the street, her head a ball of Jell-O, her guts hanging out for all to see. Yeah, she was dead all right.

"I know." He took her hand, gave it a squeeze. "How did you know to come tonight, Tess? Did she call you?"

Tess shook her head. "No. I got an anonymous call from one of her neighbors."

"Why did she jump?"

His voice was calm, so gentle, battering the dam that kept her tears at bay. "Dammit, Todd, let me go. Please. I'll talk to you tomorrow, I promise."

"I won't let you go until I'm sure you're all right."

Tess drew another deep breath and let it out slowly. Gripping her steering wheel with both hands, she lifted her gaze over Murphy's shoulder to where his partner stood next to a squad car, his hard face illuminated by its bright flashing lights. He was looking at them. Watching her. Even from this distance, she could feel the man's piercing stare. His animosity. Those intense blue eyes were narrowed, his jaw tight. "You have a new partner," she murmured, holding her gaze steady, as did Reagan.

"Yes. Aidan Reagan."

Aidan Reagan. "He's related to Abe?" She knew Abe Reagan, trusted him. Trusted his wife Kristen. They were good people.

"Aidan and Abe are brothers."

"That makes sense then." Aidan Reagan mirrored his brother's dark good looks. They had the same dark hair, the same blue eyes, although Aidan's were harder, starker than his brother's. His face was sharper, his jaw a little squarer.

His mouth . . . softer before he'd realized who she was. He had the capacity for compassion. *Just not toward me.*

"Tess, he—" Murphy's voice stumbled to a halt.

"Doesn't like me," she said levelly. "It's all right, Todd. Not many of them do."

His sigh was deep and sad. "He was there, Tess, in the courtroom that day."

Murphy didn't have to say which courtroom. They both knew. Harold Green had murdered three little girls, brutally. But the homeless man hadn't seen little six-year-old girls with blond pigtails and toothless grins. He'd seen demons with bloody fangs coming to devour him. She'd been skeptical at first, but after hours of observation and consultations with the free clinic doctors who'd treated Harold Green's acute schizophrenia over so many years, she believed him. He was quite truly insane. And so being, according to the law was not responsible for his actions. So she'd testified, barely managing to keep her eyes cool, her voice level, despite the dozens of faces who stared at her with contempt.

They thought she was cold, all the cops who'd packed the courtroom that day. They thought she was easily duped by a killer. They thought she'd sat unmoved while the mothers of those little girls wept so pitifully.

They'd been so very wrong.

That Detective Aidan Reagan had been among them explained a great deal. Across the road, Reagan still stood, still stared with a disdain he didn't try to hide. Tess was the first to break eye contact, returning her gaze to Murphy's worried face. "I see."

"No, you don't. Not entirely. He found the third girl."

She gripped the steering wheel tighter. She'd been the one with Green that day, the one to extricate the location of the third little girl. He'd said the child was alive. But when the police had arrived, they found she was not. She hadn't known who found the child. She hadn't really wanted to know. That she had been too late for that little girl had been a bitter pill to swallow.

How much more so for the man who'd found that baby's lifeless little body? "Then that really does explain a great deal. He's entitled to his anger."

"He's a good man, Tess. A good cop."

She nodded. "It's all right, Todd. I really do understand." And she did. More than anyone realized. "Can you get my keys? They fell under the car."

Murphy sighed. "Okay. I'll call you tomorrow. I'm going to need access to Cynthia Adams's file." He felt the pavement under her car and came up with her key ring.

Tess nodded, feeling some small measure of relief when her engine reliably roared to life. She started to close the door, then stopped. "Tell your partner . . ." Whatever she might say would make no difference. "Never mind. Thank you, Todd. As usual."

Her hands trembled as she pulled from the curb. She gave herself three blocks, then pulled into a side alley, let her forehead drop to the wheel and let the tears come. *Dammit, Cynthia. Why didn't you call me? Why did you do this to yourself?*

But she knew why. Just as she knew there was nothing she could have done to stop the woman. She helped the clients that wanted to be helped. The others would do what they would do. She knew this. But the knowing never stopped the grieving.

Cynthia Adams had led a life of pain and twisted guilt for events over which she'd had no control. But she'd controlled her own death. There was irony in that.

Drained and exhausted, Tess pulled away from the alley and pointed her car toward her apartment. There would be no rest tonight. Cynthia's file was inches thick. It would take more than a few hours to pull out the relevant facts for Todd

Murphy and his angry partner. It was the least she could do, for Aidan Reagan and for Cynthia Adams.

And maybe for herself.

Sunday, March 12, 1:15 A.M.

Aidan had watched Murphy stare after Ciccotelli's car for a long moment before he'd turned back to the job at hand, professional once more. Murphy had dealt with the ME and the Crime Scene Unit while Aidan had interviewed the teenagers.

The kids said nothing new, just that Adams had glided up to the railing, stood for a minute then turned backward, both arms out, and fell. He'd sent the kids home with their parents, knowing they would never be the same after witnessing such a sight.

Now he and Murphy stood outside Cynthia Adams's apartment door watching as the building super tried his drunken best to get his master key in the lock. Jim McNulty had apparently celebrated the Bulls' win by getting totally shit-faced in his favorite bar. They'd just about given up on him returning for the evening when he'd staggered up, his master key in his hand, just as the ME techs were lifting Cynthia Adams's body onto a gurney. The MEs hadn't been able to separate her from the spike, so they'd taken eighteen inches of wrought-iron fence with them. The super bellowed about the missing fence until his eyes dropped to Adams's body.

He hadn't said a single word since.

"How long did you know Miss Adams?" Aidan asked him and winced at the stench of the man's sigh. It was a good thing there were no open flames around. McNulty was completely pissed. "Three years. She moved in three years ago." He pushed the door open and Aidan was immediately struck by two things. First, the apartment was ice cold, which he'd expected. The patio door had been open for over an hour. But the second, the overpowering scent of flowers, made him blink. Cynthia Adams's living room floor was covered with more flowers than he'd ever seen outside a flower shop.

Murphy was frowning. "What the hell?"

"Lilies." Aidan stepped inside Adams's apartment and tentatively plucked one of the flowers from the floor. "Death flowers."

"My God," Murphy murmured, his eyes searching the living room. "She must have a hundred dollars worth of flowers here."

Aidan raised a brow. "Try three times that." When Murphy gave him an inquisitive stare, Aidan shrugged. "I took a horticulture class when I was getting my degree." He picked up the top envelope of a three-inch pile of mail that littered the foyer table. "She's got a stack of mail." He turned to the super. "Has she been out of town?"

The super shook his head. There was a fine sheen of sweat on his upper lip and his eyes darted from side to side. "No, but she was a month behind on her rent. First time she'd gotten behind in the three years she lived here. The manager had me watching her place to make sure she didn't try to move out on the sly."

Aidan carefully stepped around the flowers as best he could, walking out to the balcony. "Step stool," he called back to Murphy. "The teenagers said she glided up. She walked up a step stool."

"Convenient."

The super stumbled to the glass door. "That wasn't there before. I was up here a week ago to fix a leaky faucet and this step stool wasn't here."

"If you were fixing the faucet, how did you notice the balcony?" Murphy asked mildly.

The super's face paled. "I came out for a smoke."

"She put it there especially for the main event," Murphy murmured, then his voice abruptly sharpened. "Aidan."

Aidan's head whipped around. Murphy was holding a printed paper between two gloved fingers, his mouth gone grim. It was a photo, printed on glossy paper. It was of a woman, hanging from a rope, her toes a good foot off the ground. The woman's face was grotesque, her eyes bulging, mouth open as if gasping for air.

"Who is this?" Murphy asked the super.

The super took a step backward, his face gone even paler. "I don't know. I never seen that woman before. I need to go."

"In a minute, Mr. McNulty." Aidan stepped in McNulty's path, stopping him. "Please. You say you've been watching the place for the manager. Did you see who brought in all these flowers? Was it Miss Adams?"

"I don't know. Sorry," he mumbled.

"It doesn't matter. We can get the tapes from the security cameras." He'd noticed the camera eye pointed at the elevator exit as soon as the doors had opened.

McNulty shook his head. "No, you can't. Camera's broken."

"Convenient," Murphy muttered. "For how long?"

McNulty shuffled his feet. "A few weeks."

Aidan looked him in the eye. "Weeks?"

McNulty looked away, his pale cheeks now mottled with color. "Okay, months."

Aidan was sure McNulty knew a great deal more than he was saying. "Has anyone been here to visit Miss Adams recently?"

McNulty looked miserable. "She gets a lot of visitors."

Aidan's ears perked up. From the corner of his eye he could see Murphy had picked up on it, too. "What kind of visitors, sir?"

McNulty's attempt at nonchalance fell flat. "Lots of people liked Cynthia."

"You mean lots of men?" Aidan asked sharply.

McNulty closed his eyes, guilt clear on his face. Had he been sober, Aidan didn't think he'd have been nearly so transparent. Or cooperative. Go Bulls. "Some. Yeah."

"Some or yeah?"

He opened his eyes, panicked. "Listen, if my wife finds out . . . She'll kill me."

Murphy blinked. "You mean you were having an affair with Miss Adams?"

"No." McNulty shook his head hard. "Not an affair. Just once."

Aidan raised a brow. "Once."

McNulty took another step back. "Twice. Three times, tops."

"Did she . . . charge you, Mr. McNulty?" Murphy asked quietly.

Aidan doubted the look of sheer horror on the man's face could have been faked. "No! God, no. She was . . . appreciative. That's all."

This was getting interesting, Aidan thought. "Appreciative. For?"

"I turned off the camera on this floor, okay? Some of her friends didn't want to be seen. I don't know any names. Didn't want to know any names. She did her own thing and I looked the other way, I swear to God. Please, just let me go."

Aidan shot a look at Murphy. "We done with him?"

"For now," Murphy said mildly and they watched as McNulty clumsily picked his way across the strewn flowers, anxious to be as far away as possible. "We'll be in touch, Mr. McNulty," he added. McNulty gave one last shaky nod and was gone.

Aidan pushed the door closed. "Now I wonder what kind of friends those could be."

"And I wonder if any of them could have given her this." Murphy held up the photo of the dead woman dangling from the noose. "Autoerotic asphyxiation?"

Aidan grimaced. "I wouldn't know. I've never come across it."

"I have," Murphy said, moving into the bedroom. "When something goes wrong, it's not pretty. See if you can find a picture of Adams's face so we'll at least know what she looked like while I search in here."

Aidan listened to Murphy opening drawers in Adams's bedroom while he went through her purse, pulling her driver's license from her wallet. He felt an unwelcome tug of pity for the somber face that stared back from the license picture. This woman looked put together. Very proper. Very restrained.

Now she was lying on the sidewalk, twenty-two stories down. Very dead. Why had she done it? What had happened in the last month to make her late on her rent and ultimately so depressed she thought taking her own life was the only solution? But then, that was ultimately the problem with suicides, he thought bitterly. They didn't stick around long enough for the people that loved them to get answers to those questions. "She was thirty-four, Murphy. She wore corrective lenses and she was an organ donor."

Murphy appeared in the bedroom doorway, furry handcuffs in one hand, a small leather whip in the other. "She was also into some pretty kinky shit. There's a pulley rigged in the corner. Looks like she's hoisted herself a time or two."

Aidan blinked at the paraphernalia in Murphy's hands then looked again at the solemn woman on the driver's license. "You wouldn't guess it by looking at her."

"You can't always. What does she have in her purse?"

Quickly Aidan sorted through the small bag. "Four credit cards, a cell phone, various and sundry lipsticks, and a key ring." He held it up. "One Honda key, one key to the apartment door, and one very little key."

"Safe-deposit box?"

Aidan bagged the keys while Murphy bagged the whip and cuffs. "Maybe. Was there a bank statement in all that mail?"

Murphy went back to the table, sorted through the pile. "Doesn't look like she's opened any of this mail. Here's her bank statement. We can check it . . . Hell." Murphy frowned at the envelope in his hand. "She opened this one. No stamp, no return address." He pulled a picture from the envelope, his expression grim. "Another dead woman. This one's in a casket." He passed it to Aidan. "Check out her hands."

A small tingle raced down Aidan's back. "She's holding a lily. She looks like the same lady that's dangling from the noose." He took half the pile of mail and began sorting. Within minutes they'd found ten such pictures, equally grisly. All the same woman. All disturbing. Not one signed with a name or return address. "Somebody was playing with Cynthia's head."

Murphy picked up a framed picture from Adams's desk. A young girl with hair in her eyes skulked behind the glass. "This is the woman. Adams obviously knew her." He slipped the picture from the frame. "But there's no name written on the back."

"She's younger there than in these pictures. Maybe sixteen? Looks like a school picture to me. My sister Rachel's pictures have that same gray background." He stooped and picked up a long thin box that lay under the table. It was the right size for a dozen roses. Somehow that's not what he thought he'd find inside.

"Open it," Murphy said tersely.

Carefully Aidan lifted the lid. "Shit." A rope twisted into a noose lay nestled on a bed of bright white tissue paper. A small gold gift tag dangled from the looped end. "'Come to me. Find your peace,'" he read, then looked up to meet Murphy's grim stare. "Let's get CSU up here."

Murphy called them, then sighed as he slipped his cell phone back in his pocket. "I think Tess has a lot of questions to answer tomorrow."

Aidan's jaw tightened at the thought. "I think you're right."

Chapter Two

Joanna Carmichael watched as her photographs were methodically studied, the text she'd spent the wee hours of the morning refining, carefully read. After what seemed like an eternity, the managing editor of the Chicago *Bulletin* lifted his head.

"How did you get these?" Reese Schmidt asked, gesturing to the pictures.

"Right place, right time." Joanna shrugged. *Karma,* she thought, but didn't think Schmidt would appreciate the sentiment. "The victim lives in my apartment building. I walked around the corner toward my building just after she jumped. I heard a scream and started running, along with about three other people. Two teenagers had seen her fall." She laid a finger on the corner of the first picture, a stark study of a woman gutted and bleeding with two teenagers standing to one side, their shock completely captured in black and white. "I started snapping away."

He looked skeptical. "In front of the cops?"

"They weren't there yet," she said calmly. "When they got there, I kept snapping, but less obtrusively."

"You didn't use a flash?"

"I have a good camera. Didn't need one." She lifted a brow. "I like to be able to keep my pictures."

His mouth bent in a wry smile. "I understand. What about the story?"

"I wrote it."

He shook his head. "That's not what I meant. How did you get this information? 'An unnamed source confirms that police found evidence indicating the victim had been coerced into jumping twenty-two stories.' Who is your unnamed source?"

When she said nothing, Schmidt's eyes narrowed. "You don't have a source. You either made the whole murder angle up or you overheard the cops. Which is it?"

Joanna sucked in one cheek in frustration. "The second one."

"I thought so." He sat down in his chair, his fingers lightly steepled. "You get me corroboration inside CPD, someone I can contact for verification, and I'll run your story."

Yes. The words she'd been waiting to hear for two long years. "Where?"

His grin was quick and slightly mocking. "Don't be greedy, Miss . . . Carmichael, wasn't it? You get me a statement I can verify and we'll talk."

It was fair, she decided. Not ideal, but fair. For a split second she considered using the other trump card she carried. Her father. But that would not be fair, to Schmidt or to herself. She gathered her pictures, frowning when he put his hand on the first one, the one with the teenagers and the body taken just moments after impact.

"I don't want to get sued for false information," he said smoothly, "but I still can use the pictures. They don't lie."

Joanna gritted her teeth. "Neither do I. I'll be back." She hit the street at a brisk walk, headed for the police station. She had no idea how she'd get corroboration. But she would. Fate had tossed a story into her front yard, so to speak. Now she had to make good on the gift.

Sunday, March 12, 12:30 P.M.

Aidan hated the ME's office. Even on a good day the smell was enough to turn his stomach. This was proving not to be a good day. For anyone involved.

He stopped just inside the door, his gaze resting on the body on the exam table. Least of all for Cynthia Adams. If she had committed suicide, it was assisted. They knew that now. Someone had systematically tortured this woman with pictures and gifts. Anything bearing a signature was signed "Melanie." Murphy thought she was probably the woman in the casket picture and Aidan was inclined to agree with him.

The ME hadn't heard him come in, so engrossed was she in her study of Cynthia Adams's hands. Mercifully she'd covered Adams's torso with a sheet. He cleared his throat and Julia VanderBeck looked up, her eyes covered by plastic glasses. He didn't see how she could stand the smell, especially being so obviously pregnant. His regard for Julia climbed a notch or two. "You rang?" he asked and her lips quirked up.

"I did. Where's Murphy?"

"Listening to the victim's voice mail and watching security

video of the victim's apartment lobby." Apparently building super McNulty's appreciation hadn't extended to disabling every video in the building. "He's trying to find who carried up all those lilies."

Julia nodded briskly. "Remind me of the lilies before you leave," she said, "but first you'll want the tox screen."

"Which one was it?" Aidan asked, reaching for the clipboard she passed over Adams's body. They'd found seventeen different prescription bottles in the woman's apartment. Four were prescribed by Dr. Tess Ciccotelli. The other thirteen bottles bore the names of other doctors, the dates going back more than five years.

Julia stretched, supporting her lower back. "You're lucky I owe Murphy a favor. I wouldn't come in in the middle of the night for just anybody." She blew out a breath and lowered herself onto a stool next to the exam table. "Her urine tox screen didn't show any of them. The most recent prescription was through Ciccotelli for Xanax. It's used to treat anxiety and depression. It's what I should have found in her urine tox. What I actually found was high levels of PCP."

Aidan frowned. "She could have been a user."

She pushed herself to her feet. "Come here. I want to show you something."

She led him out of the morgue and into the lab itself. The smell was better here. Aidan sucked in a deep breath, ignoring her wry chuckle. "So show me."

She shook a few capsules from two different bottles onto a white piece of paper. One of the bottles he recognized from Adams's apartment. The other bore the label of the hospital pharmacy. "Xanax from the pharmacy on the left and the pills you took from Adams's nightstand on the right," she said.

Aidan frowned at the pills. "They look the same."

"That's what somebody wanted her to think. Somebody emptied the capsules and refilled them with PCP."

Aidan met her troubled gaze. "Somebody went to a hell of a lot of trouble."

"Somebody wanted her to be out of her mind and totally suggestible."

Aidan thought about the pictures, the noose in the gift box. The loaded gun they'd found in a second gift box, stuffed in a closet. The step stool on the balcony that hadn't been there the week before. The lilies. "Hell."

"Eloquently put," Julia said. "Come back to the exam room. I want to show you something else." He followed her and watched as she lifted Adams's right arm. Deep, jagged vertical scars lined the inside of her wrists.

"She's tried to kill herself before," he murmured.

"At least once before."

"We found a loaded gun and a noose in her apartment." Both in gift boxes, both with the same little gold gift tag. Both tags said "Come to me."

Julia sighed. "Somebody really wanted her to take her own life."

"So it would seem. You told me to remind you about the lilies."

"Yeah. She had pollen from the lilies in her nostrils."

"We found one of the flowers under her pillow."

"That makes sense then. I didn't find any evidence of the pollen on her hands."

"Could she have washed it off?"

"Perhaps, but with as many lilies as you said you found, it's unlikely she wouldn't have some under her nails if she'd handled all the flowers. Especially with those nails."

Aidan stared at Adams's long bloodred nails. "So she didn't touch the lilies."

"Probably not."

"So somebody else brought them in." His cell rang and he pulled it from his pocket.

It was Murphy and he sounded . . . furious. "Where are you, Aidan?"

"In the morgue. What's wrong?"

"Latent came back with an ID on the prints CSU pulled from Adams's apartment."

Aidan waited but Murphy said no more. "And? Murphy, what did Latent find?"

"Just get up here," Murphy bit out. "Now. Dammit."

SSIHM LIBRARY/
RESOURCE CENTER
610 W. ELM &
MONROE, MICHIGA.

Sunday, March 12, 12:30 P.M.

Tess studied her reflection in the mirror next to her front door. A good bottle of concealer was worth its weight in gold, the dark circles under her eyes all but invisible. It was the second Sunday of the month, time for brunch with her friends at the Blue Lemon Bistro. After studying Cynthia Adams's file for hours followed by a short, unrestful sleep, she was tempted to call her friends and beg off but resisted. The loss of a patient could not be allowed to derail her life. She should know this by now. It was a routine lecture from her friend Jon, a surgeon who lost patients on the table. Hopefully not too routinely.

Pushing the pendulum the other way, she'd decked herself out this morning, spending extra time on her hair, her makeup, even pulling the price tag off the red leather jacket she'd been saving for a special occasion. Amy would swallow her tongue when she saw it, Tess decided. She'd beg to borrow it and as usual Tess would relent and let her. And as the sister she'd never had, Amy would keep the jacket until Tess raided her closet on a commando hunt to retrieve her things. It had been that way since Amy had come to live with the Ciccotelli family almost twenty years before.

Tess closed her eyes. Just the thought of her family stung, especially on Sunday. They'd be gathering around the table right about now, back home in her parents' old house in South Philly. It would be loud and noisy and wonderful, packed to bursting except for her own chair in the corner of the dining room. In the old tradition of remembering the family dead, her chair would remain empty. Because in her father's eyes, she was dead to the family.

Most days she could shove the hurt back. Today it seemed worse, perhaps because she'd been reminded again and again throughout the night of Cynthia Adams's solitary existence. No family. No one significant. No one to miss her now that she was gone. It reminded Tess that with the exception of her brother Vito who'd defied their father's decree, she had no family either. And Vito was so far away. South Philly. It reminded her that she had no one significant because Phillip, damn him to hell, was a lousy two-timing weasel.

But she did have friends. She glanced away from the mirror, to the last group picture they'd had taken at the Lemon. Amy and Jon. Robin, who owned the bistro. Jim, who'd left them recently for humanitarian work in Africa. Her heart squeezed as she studied his face, hoping he stayed healthy and safe. There was Gen and Rhonda and all the others that were probably already gathered at the Lemon wondering where the hell she was.

She straightened the picture on the wall and turned back to the mirror, quickly slashing her lips with Ravishing Red. It matched the coat and was the final touch to a look she hoped would raise a few brows. Maybe drive some interested men from the bushes. Her love life could use shaking up. Hell, her love life could use a complete blood transfusion. Or perhaps a medium, because it was all but dead. Jon told her that, too. Routinely. She really was grateful for her friends. Sometimes she just wished they were selectively mute.

Bypassing the elevator, she took her normal skipping jog down the ten flights to the lobby where Mr. Hughes stood guard at the lobby desk as he always did. Seeing him seemed to return a sense of balance to the morning. "Good morning, Dr. Chick."

Tess smiled at the doorman. "Good morning, Mr. Hughes. How are you?"

The old man's chuckle was musical. "Can't complain. Well I could, but Ethel says nobody wants to hear it." Mr. Hughes was studying her through narrowed eyes. "You don't look well, Dr. Chick. Are you sick again?"

She hefted her briefcase on her shoulder. It was heavier today, filled with Cynthia Adams's file. "Just tired."

"Riggin said you came in late. That you'd been crying."

Riggin was the night man. That they'd been discussing her was annoying. It was nobody's damn business what time she came in or her state of mind when she did. But one gave up privacy in exchange for security. She knew that. The puff of annoyance blew away on a sigh.

"Mr. Hughes, I'm fine. Can you just flag me a cab? I'm already late." A cab would get her to the Lemon a lot faster than driving and looking for parking.

Mr. Hughes still looked concerned. "Where you going this morning, Dr. Chick? No wait. It's the second Sunday, so you'll be going to the Blue Lemon for brunch."

Her brows bunched as she passed through the door he opened. "Am I that predictable, then?" There'd been a time when she hadn't been.

"I can set my watch by you," Hughes said cheerfully as he flagged the cab. "The Blue Lemon on the second Sunday, the hospital on Mondays, dinner with the doctor on Wed—" He cut himself off abruptly, his back going stiff. With a guilty look he met her eyes. "I'm sorry."

With an effort she made her lips smile. "It's all right,

Mr. Hughes." Her Wednesday dinners with the doctor were a thing of the past. Because the doctor himself was a thing of the past. That thinking of Phillip could still hurt made her angry, but she shoved both the anger and hurt back down as a cab stopped at the curb. Neither emotion was healthy. Neither would undo the past.

"The cab won't be necessary," said a hard voice behind her and Tess turned on her heel only to find herself staring up into the same cold blue eyes that had held so much contempt for her the night before. Eyes that hadn't softened in the light of day.

"Detective Reagan," she said, annoyed that he'd come *here,* invaded her space looking like he owned the damn world. Annoyed that in the light of day he was even more compelling. Annoyed that she'd even noticed. "How can I help you?"

Murphy appeared at Reagan's side. Together the two of them formed a wall that blocked her view of the street. "We need to talk to you about Cynthia Adams, Tess."

"I have her file right here," she said evenly, patting her briefcase. "I honestly expected you to call hours ago." She looked from Reagan's stony face to Murphy's carefully expressionless one and her annoyance rapidly slid into apprehension. Something was very wrong. Still, she kept her voice cool. "I'm rather busy now, gentlemen. I'm on my way to a lunch meeting. Can I call you when I'm finished?"

His jaw hard, Reagan offered her his cell phone. "Cancel it."

Tess's eyes flew to Murphy's face. There wasn't a whisper of familiarity or softness in his eyes. "What's going on here, Todd?"

"We need you to come with us, Tess," he said quietly. "Please."

She tilted her head toward Murphy. "You gonna cuff me, Todd?" she murmured.

Reagan opened his mouth, but Murphy gave him a sharp look and he closed it. "Tess, let's just get this over with, okay? Then we can all go on with our day." Murphy took her elbow and led her to his beat-up old Ford. "Please."

She slid in, conscious of Mr. Hughes still standing at the curb, his mouth agape. Ethel would have an earful of this before they hit the next block, she knew. "Can I make a phone call?" she asked acidly as Murphy pulled into traffic.

He met her eyes in the rearview mirror. "To who?"

To whom, she thought, but bit back what would have been a snarled correction. "To cancel my meeting, as Detective Reagan so hospitably requested."

Reagan turned, pinned her with his angry eyes, even bluer in the daylight. "Just one call." He lifted a sardonic brow. "Thank you for your cooperation, Dr. Ciccotelli."

She closed her fingers around her cell phone, fighting the urge to throw it at him, unsettled by the flash of pure fury that left her white hot and trembling inside. "Anytime, Detective Reagan." She focused on punching numbers, wishing she weren't visualizing punching Reagan's stony face. Last night she'd felt sympathy for the man who'd been so obviously scarred by finding Harold Green's last little victim. That was before he'd pulled the bad cop routine on her. *He can just go to hell and take all his issues with him.* His eyes watched her as the number she'd called rang in her ear.

Thankfully Amy answered on the third ring. "Where are you?" she asked without preamble. "You're late." Tess could hear the activity of the Blue Lemon in the background as well as Jon's worried voice asking what was wrong.

"I'm not going to be able to join you," she said formally. "I've got an emergency."

"Tess." Amy stopped just short of her predictable whine. "We all said we'd hold this time sacred. We all have client emergencies."

Tess met Reagan's eyes in a stare of pure challenge. "Not like this one," she said. "I'll come by if I can, but just go on without me."

"Tess, wait." Jon had taken Amy's phone. "I got your message last night but I was out and didn't get home until after three. Are you all right?"

She'd called him to go with her, to be a witness to what she'd hoped would be a consultation with a live patient. "I'm fine. The issue has been resolved." By Cynthia Adams herself. It was only Reagan's cold stare that enabled her to control the shudder at the memory of Cynthia's body on the sidewalk the night before. She'd be in the morgue now, on a cold slab, a number on a toe tag, but at least she'd found some peace. At least Tess hoped so. "Jon, I've got to go. I'll call you later, okay?" She flipped her phone shut. "One call, Detective. Per your request."

His eyes flashed at her sarcastic tone. "Thank you."

"When will you tell me what this is all about?"

"We'll talk downtown, Doctor." Reagan shifted in his seat, dismissing her.

Downtown. It had an ominous ring, just as he'd intended. The bad cop was playing mind games. *He'll find he's met his match.* She turned to the good cop. "Murphy?"

Murphy stared straight ahead, not meeting her eyes and for the first time she felt a twinge of alarm. "We need to do this officially, Tess. We'll talk downtown."

Sunday, March 12, 1:25 P.M.

Aidan studied Ciccotelli through the two-way glass. She sat staring straight back at him, even though he knew she saw only her own reflection. She'd been on both sides of the glass often enough to know she was being watched. She knew what would come next, but she wasn't flinching. Her eyes never wavered. She was a cool one, for sure. But it would take a cool one, to do what she'd done.

If she'd done it. All the evidence said she had.

It was improbable. Totally impractical. Damn near impossible.

Murphy was sure she had not. But Murphy didn't seem to be completely objective when it came to Dr. Tess Ciccotelli. It was hard to blame the man, Aidan had to admit. Sitting on the other side of the mirror was a knockout in tight, low-riding jeans, a turtleneck sweater that fit her curves like a glove, both black. Her black hair curled wildly. Today she looked like a modern day gypsy, masquerading as a "respected doctor." She'd been going to a meeting, she'd said. *Ha. Nobody went to a meeting dressed like that.*

Hell, nobody he knew dressed like that. Or looked like that when they tried to. He gritted his teeth, annoyed at himself for his body's reaction to the sight of what Ciccotelli had hidden under that conservative tan coat. She was a suspect, no matter how improbable. And if she turned out not to be a suspect, she was still a cold bitch. That she was a remarkably sexy cold bitch was just one of those little quirks of fate with which decent men had to deal.

Beside him, Murphy dragged the heels of both hands down his face. "She's got circles under her eyes. Looks like she had a sleepless night."

"That makes three of us," Aidan returned evenly. He looked over his shoulder to where their lieutenant leaned against the back wall of the small observation area, a scowl bending his salt-and-pepper mustache straight down. "You still don't agree."

Lieutenant Marc Spinnelli shook his head. "I've known Tess Ciccotelli for years. She's a good person. A good doctor.

She may not always diagnose the way we'd like, but she's not capable of driving that woman to the brink of sanity."

"And shoving her over," Murphy muttered. "Let's get this over with."

Aidan watched Murphy go in the interview room, take the seat farthest from Ciccotelli. Her gaze snapped to Murphy briefly, then returned to the glass, no longer cool. Now her dark brown eyes flashed with anger. Good. Angry was better than cool and collected any damn day. "He's involved," Aidan murmured, his hand on the doorknob, his eyes on Murphy's expressionless face.

"We all are," Spinnelli shot back, frustration in his tone. "Any cop in the city would be. There aren't many that don't know about Harold Green but most of them don't know Tess. Go in there and do your job, Aidan. So will Murphy."

"And if he doesn't?"

Spinnelli huffed a sigh. "Then I'll step in."

With that promise, Aidan walked into the interview room. Her eyes followed him, narrowed and . . . dangerous.

"I'm here, Detective Reagan, just as you wanted me to be. You've watched me for fifteen minutes. When are you going to tell me what the hell is going on here?"

He sat down next to her, at the end of the table. "Tell me about Cynthia Adams."

She blinked and drew a breath, visibly fighting for control. And degree by degree achieved it, while he watched, totally fascinated. "Cynthia Adams was a complicated woman," she finally answered, looking at Aidan directly, ignoring Murphy completely. "But you know that if you've been in her apartment."

"Have you?" Aidan asked. "Been in her apartment, that is."

"No. I've never been inside her apartment."

The woman could lie without blinking. From the corner

of his eye he could see the muscle in Murphy's jaw twitch as his partner clenched his teeth. Aidan felt pity for Murphy, and for Spinnelli, too. They obviously cared for Ciccotelli. This was going to be difficult for them, he knew. *So I'll do it for them,* he thought. "But you have been to her apartment, Doctor?" he pressed. "Outside?"

She regarded him warily. "Once. She'd missed an appointment. I was concerned. I called and only got voice mail, so my partner, Dr. Ernst, and I went to check on her."

She'd been in practice with Dr. Harrison Ernst for five years. Nearing retirement age, Ernst was highly respected. This Aidan knew from his quick search on Ciccotelli before picking her up for questioning. "You normally do that? Make house calls?"

"No, I don't. Cynthia was a bit of a special case."

"Why?"

Her jaw cocked slightly to one side, she laced her fingers together tightly in her lap. Her expression was unreadable now. "I cared about her."

"When was this? The visit," he clarified and watched her jaw clench reflexively. His presentation of a question followed by a clarification annoyed her. Good.

"About three weeks ago."

"Did she call you back?"

"Eventually."

"And?"

"And she set up another appointment with me." She was playing the game now. Admirably so. Answer only what was asked, revealing nothing more.

"Did she show up? To the new appointment."

"No." Any caginess disappeared, replaced for a fraction of a second with a look of such acute sadness, he found himself mentally circling back around. If she was innocent, she really cared. If she was guilty, she was damn good. "No she didn't," she murmured. "I called her again, left her another message, but she never called me back. I never talked to her again."

Aidan took his pad from his pocket. "Why was Miss Adams seeing you, Doctor?"

The wary look was back. "She was depressed."

"About?"

Ciccotelli closed her eyes. "Were she alive I couldn't tell you any of this. You understand that. It would be privileged."

"But she's not alive," Aidan said silkily. "She's lying on a slab in the morgue, eviscerated, by her own hand." Her eyes flew open and in them he saw shocked outrage. But she carefully banked it.

"I began treating Cynthia about a year ago. She'd been to perhaps a dozen doctors before she came to me."

Aidan thought about all the prescription bottles they'd found in her medicine cabinet. So many doctors. And yet Cynthia Adams was still dead. "You obviously helped her so much she killed herself," he said sharply. Her eyes flashed then calmed while Murphy shot him a warning glare.

She pulled a folder from her briefcase and set it on the table between them. "Cynthia suffered from severe depression stemming from abuse she suffered as a young girl. Her father molested her from the time she was ten until she ran away from home at seventeen." She leveled him a steady look. "I imagine you found evidence of . . . extreme sexual behavior in her apartment, Detective."

"We found cuffs and whips, yes. A few pictures."

She continued looking at him steadily. "Cynthia hated herself, hated her father for his abuse. Sometimes victims of abuse turn to the thing they hate the most. They become defined by that one hated thing. Sometimes victims of sexual abuse become addicted to sex. Cynthia was. She would have sex with as many men as she could in one night, then despise herself the next day. She'd promise to stop but it got worse."

"So you were treating her for her sex addiction," Aidan said, but she shook her head.

"No, I was treating her for depression. I met Cynthia almost one year ago. She was in the hospital recuperating from a suicide attempt. She'd slit her wrists, the way a person does when they really want to die. You'll find deep scars on the inside of her wrists if you haven't already."

He thought about the jagged scars he'd seen, ironically one of the only identifying marks to survive Adams's jump. "What made her try suicide a year ago, Doctor?"

"I told you. Self-loathing."

"But she'd hated herself for some time. Why did she pick then to slit her wrists?"

"She underwent another trauma at that same time."

He was starting to get annoyed now. "Which was?"

"Her sister hanged herself and Cynthia found her."

He controlled his sudden flare of interest. "Why did she hang herself? The sister."

"The sister was younger. When Cynthia ran away from home, her father started on the younger sister. When she'd grown up, the sister couldn't take the memories and hanged herself. Cynthia felt an enormous guilt for leaving her sister alone with their father. Her sister's suicide sent her over the edge."

"What was her sister's name, Doctor?"

She opened the folder, searched its contents. Most of the pages were typed, but a few were written in a neat, confident hand. She pulled out one such handwritten page and scanned it. Upside down, he read an April date from the year before on the top of the page. "Her sister's name was Melanie. She killed herself . . ." She stopped, her wide eyes fixed on the page. "A year ago today. Oh, God. I should have seen this coming." Her throat worked as she tried to swallow and for that moment Aidan was ready to believe Murphy was right.

Murphy rubbed his mouth with the back of his hand. "We found medication in her apartment. A lot of medication."

She lifted her eyes to Murphy, stark and stripped of any belligerence or anger. "I prescribed Xanax."

"The ME found PCP in her tox screen, Tess."

Taken aback, Ciccotelli shook her head hard, eyes narrowed. "She was using PCP? I never saw signs of illegal drug use."

"Only of the drugs *you* gave her," Aidan said, his tone a few shades too agreeable.

Her head whipped around to stare at him, twin flags of color riding high on her cheekbones. "What the hell is that supposed to mean?"

Aidan didn't answer. Instead he began laying out the pictures they'd found in Adams's apartment the night before.

And watched as all the color drained from her face. "Oh my God," she whispered, hands trembling as she picked up each one and stared, horrified. When she reached the last one, the one of Melanie hanging from a noose, dead, a muffled whimper broke through her lips, now an unnatural red against her pale face. "Where did you find these?" she asked in a strangled whisper.

Murphy met his eyes, his look clearly saying, *I told you so.* He tapped the corner of the noose picture. "This one I found near the sliding glass door to her balcony last night. Some of the ones of her sister in the casket came in the mail, no return address."

Her attention was still focused on the pictures, her voice still a haunted whisper. "Who would do such a thing?"

Aidan raised a brow. Once again he thought if she was innocent, she really did care. If she was guilty, she was one of the best liars he'd ever met. As long as Murphy was sold on the former, he'd have to protect the possibility of the latter.

"Some came as e-mail attachments. Do you know Cynthia's e-mail address, Doctor?"

She turned to him, slowly, her dark eyes wary now. "I have it somewhere. It's one of the questions on my new patient form." She turned back to Murphy. "Why?"

Murphy pursed his lips. "Play it."

Aidan ducked from the room long enough to grab the cassette player he'd left on the floor outside. He set the machine next to Ciccotelli, waited for her eyes to lift to his before he hit the PLAY button.

"Cyn-thia." It was a childlike wail, oddly haunting. Ciccotelli flinched as the message continued. "You didn't come again. You promised you wouldn't leave me. Check your e-mail, Cynthia."

Aidan stopped the tape and pulled a casket picture from the pile on the table. "That was on her voice mail. This was the attachment to the e-mail. Last night the floor of Cynthia's living room was covered in flowers like the one the corpse is holding."

"Someone was forcing her to relive Melanie's death," Ciccotelli said slowly, closing her eyes. "The PCP in her system would have made her believe it was true, that she was hearing ghosts. Who would do such a thing?" she repeated.

Who indeed? Aidan started the tape again, watching every nuance of her expression. He didn't have to wait long. At the first words her eyes flew open. She was . . . truly shocked. Horror had her eyes glazing over as she listened.

"Cynthia, this is Dr. Ciccotelli. I've missed you. Melanie's missed you, too. It's one year today. It's her birthday, Cynthia. Melanie's left you presents. Isn't it time to give her what she wants? Isn't it time to keep your promise? Keep your promise, Cynthia."

Aidan stopped the tape and the interview room was suddenly silent. She said nothing, just sat looking at the tape recorder as if it were a cobra, poised to strike. He put two more pictures on the table in front of her, the noose and the gun. "These were Melanie's gifts to Cynthia," he said flatly.

He watched her eyes drop to the pictures.

And began to believe Murphy was indeed correct. Her total and complete shock was utterly convincing. But then again, this woman knew the human mind. She'd know exactly how to play a scene like this. Wouldn't she?

"Tess," Murphy said, his voice gone rough. "The security tapes of Adams's apartment lobby show a woman with black hair and a tan coat carrying a large bag onto the elevator." He hesitated, then blurted the rest. "We found fingerprints on the boxes that held the rope and the gun. On the bottle of Xanax, too."

Slowly she pulled her gaze up to Murphy's face. "Whose?" But the look of dread in her eyes said she knew, even before she heard the answer.

Murphy swallowed hard. "Yours, Tess. Your fingerprints were on the medicine and the rope and the gun. They matched your prints we lifted from the card you gave me."

She leaned back in her chair, carefully. Then she looked up at Aidan with the same calm he'd seen the night before, after she'd turned from viewing Adams's mangled body on the street.

"I think I'm going to call my lawyer now, Detective. This interview is over."

Chapter Three

Sunday, March 12, 2:43 P.M.

It was simply unbelievable. But it was real. *And it's happening to me.*

Cynthia was dead. *And I am sitting on the wrong side of the glass, needing a defense attorney for the first time in my life.* There had been only one choice, one lawyer Tess trusted enough to call. Her best friend Amy was a civil defense attorney, but Tess knew Amy did pro bono work in the criminal courts from time to time. So where the hell was she? The Blue Lemon was less than twenty minutes from the police station, but Tess was certain she'd been sitting here alone twice that amount of time. Waiting, as the minutes ticked by. Still, she fought the urge to look at her watch, keeping her eyes straight ahead.

They were watching her. Behind the glass. She knew it as well as she knew her own face staring back at her from the mirror. Todd Murphy and his arrogant asshole of a new partner with his stony face and cold blue eyes. She didn't break her gaze, didn't look away. *Let the bastard watch me. Let him wonder.*

They thought she'd done it. Driven Cynthia Adams to take her own life. They actually thought she'd done it. The notion left her coldly furious.

Even Murphy. Her heart hitched while her eyes stayed locked on her own reflection, connected to the cops behind the glass. Reagan she would have expected to be aggressive with this kind of evidence. But Todd Murphy? That he could even imagine her doing such a thing left her . . . hurt.

They'd been friends. A breach of trust like this . . . It could never be fixed. This she knew from personal experience. Trust was a fragile commodity and only idiots gave it blindly. Only bigger idiots tried to humpty-dumpty it back together when it was crushed and shattered. And Tess Ciccotelli was no idiot.

Neither am I crushed and shattered. She narrowed her eyes at the glass, visualizing Reagan standing on the other side, arms crossed over his wide chest. Glowering at her. He used his size effectively. The way he'd leaned over her, studying her as he'd played that damn tape recorder. She'd expected him to try to intimidate her. He'd tried. Unsuccessfully.

But he had managed to shock her. That she could readily admit. To hear her own voice, saying such obscene things . . . To know her fingerprints were on instruments of Cynthia's mental torture . . . She was still shocked, underneath. But quickly the wave of rage had overtaken the shock, jarring her senses back to life.

Someone had done this. Someone had orchestrated what was nothing less than the murder of Cynthia Adams. *And that someone set me up for the fall.*

Quite skillfully, too. That she could admit as well. She'd never been in Cynthia's apartment. Never touched her belongings. Never had cause to touch her medication. Never sent her any gifts that could have been perverted to such an end. Yet her fingerprints had been found, as had her own voice.

Reagan had been quite serious. He'd believed she'd done this terrible, vile thing. He'd all but accused her with words, but his eyes had said what his words had not.

And in so doing, he'd stood up for Cynthia Adams.

Tess's quiet sigh seemed to roar through the silent interview room. Aidan Reagan had stood up for Cynthia Adams's rights even as she'd lain dead on the pavement. *What the hell kind of doctor are you?* he'd asked. There had been anguish under his rage last night. He'd cared about Cynthia, when he thought she didn't. He was a good man, Murphy had said. A good cop.

Tess certainly hoped so. She hoped he was the kind of cop who would see past what was obviously planted evidence, who could look beyond his own preconceived notions about what the hell kind of doctor she really was.

Her anger now ebbed enough to focus, she dropped her eyes from the mirror to the pictures Reagan had so conveniently left on the table. He probably hoped she'd break down under the weight of her own guilt and confess what she'd done.

Sorry, Detective. Not today. Tess picked up the picture Murphy had found on Cynthia's floor. The last picture Cynthia received, its timing impeccable. She'd heard the story of Melanie's suicide from Cynthia, of course. Many times. Melanie had threatened to kill herself, but Cynthia had not honestly believed her sister would actually do it. Then one year ago today, Cynthia had arrived at Melanie's apartment to take her sister out for her birthday dinner only to find Melanie dead. Swinging from a noose, a note pinned to her white blouse. Tess brought the picture closer, turned it to eliminate the reflection of the overhead lights on the photo's glossy surface.

Ah. There it was. The note pinned to Melanie's blouse. So this picture was taken before the police took her body down, she thought. Taken by whom? The police? It didn't have the look of a police photo. Cynthia? Unlikely. The report had her well into a breakdown by the time the police arrived on the scene of Melanie's suicide. Melanie herself in some bizarre last kick at her older sister? It was possible, especially as Melanie had been very specific as to the time Cynthia should arrive that night a year ago. It was as if she planned for Cynthia to find her hanging that way. That she set up a camera to flash her picture minutes after her death was not so inconceivable after all.

But who could have gotten their hands on this picture? Who would know this much about Cynthia's past? Cynthia had been very clear on the need for total confidentiality, worried that any leak of her sexual compulsions would cost her her job at an upscale financial planning firm. Cynthia would not have shared any of this information willingly.

Who would want Cynthia dead? And why? But perhaps the most pressing question of the hour kept circling her mind. "Why use me?" she murmured.

Tess blew out a breath and gave in to the urge to check her watch. She'd been sitting alone for sixty-three minutes, dammit. Where was Amy?

Aidan stood on the other side of the mirror, watching her. After that one moment of gross shock, she'd regained her composure and hadn't lost it again.

Behind him, the door opened, then closed and Aidan smelled faint cinnamon and strong cigarette smoke. Poor Murphy. He'd been chewing cinnamon gum the entire four months they'd been together as a stop-smoking aid. Looked like the stress of the last few hours had knocked his partner off the wagon. "You smoke the whole damn pack, Murphy?"

"Half." Murphy cleared his throat roughly. "How's she doing?"

"Seems to have recovered well enough." She'd been staring at the mirror with steadfast calm mixed with defiant challenge for the better part of an hour. He could have, should have let her go. He knew that. They didn't have enough to hold her, that was for damn sure. Yet still he stood, frozen in place.

Watching her as she watched him right back.

She stirred him, Aidan had to admit. He didn't think there was a man alive who could look at that face, that body, without being stirred, and Aidan was certainly alive. But there was more to his response than the outer package. There was a quiet dignity in the way she waited.

She's a psychiatrist, he told himself. Trained in hiding her emotions. Trained in waiting out long periods of silence. Kind of like cops. He had something in common with Dr. Tess Ciccotelli. He didn't like that.

On the other side of the glass there was sudden movement as she sighed, her shoulders slumping for the briefest of moments. She dropped her eyes to the pictures he'd left on the table and calmly placed the police photos of Cynthia Adams's impaled body to one side. She then chose the picture of Cynthia's sister hanging for closer scrutiny, her black brows drawing together as she stared.

"Why use me?" she murmured, barely loudly enough for them to hear.

"That's a damn good question," Aidan murmured back.

"You know she didn't do this," Murphy said quietly.

Aidan sucked in one cheek. "I don't *know* anything yet, Murphy. And neither do you. But I do appreciate you giving me the time to come to my own conclusions. You could have pulled rank and dismissed her already." If the tables had been turned, had Aidan been the trainer and Murphy the new kid on the block, Aidan probably would have done just that. "Why didn't you?"

Murphy sighed. "Maybe because, until I saw her face when you confronted her with the tape, I wasn't entirely sure either. She's angry with us both, but I hurt her and that she won't forgive easily. Is her lawyer coming in from another planet, or what?"

"I expected her to get here a half hour ago. Her lawyer's name is Amy Miller." Murphy stiffened, almost imperceptibly. "So you know the lawyer?"

"I've met her before," Murphy said briefly. "Never worked with her."

Aidan turned his attention back to Ciccotelli who was studying each picture with single-minded focus. He'd left the pictures with her on the off chance they might break her down, but he hadn't really thought they would. "I'm willing to admit she's unlikely as a murderer, Murphy. But it's possible she was shocked because we caught her."

"You believe that?"

"No. I think she's too smart for that. I think she's too smart for all of this. But we have evidence that says otherwise and we just can't ignore it. What'd the SA say?"

Calling States Attorney Patrick Hurst had been Murphy's excuse for stepping out, but Aidan suspected it was just as much the need to escape Tess Ciccotelli's hard stare. And to smoke half a pack of cigarettes.

"He was torn." Murphy huffed a mirthless laugh. "Patrick knows her, too. He couldn't believe any of this. He said he wants more of a motive. More proof a crime actually occurred."

Aidan frowned. "A woman's dead. Since when is that not a damn crime?"

The door behind them opened, letting in a breeze and the heady scent of expensive perfume, followed closely by a thirty-something woman in a professional navy suit. Her blond hair was swept into a neat twist and small diamonds twinkled in her ears. Her green eyes were hard, her mouth unsmiling, giving her an overall dour appearance. "Since nobody pushed the dead woman off that balcony, there's no damn crime," she said. "I'm Amy Miller, Dr. Ciccotelli's attorney and I'm taking her out of here. Now." Then she stopped and blinked at Murphy. "I know you."

Murphy nodded once. "I'm Detective Murphy. This is my partner Detective Reagan. You and I met at the hospital last year, Miss Miller."

Her eyes narrowed in speculation, then widened in recognition. "You sat by her bed." Her head shook in disbelief. "You *know* her. How you could possibly believe she had anything to do with this? You should be ashamed. Why aren't you out finding out who really pushed that woman to jump, because it sure as hell was *not* Tess Ciccotelli. Now if you'll excuse me, I'd like to talk to my client." She stared pointedly at the switch on the wall. "In private."

Murphy flipped the switch to the speaker. "Why didn't I think of that?" he muttered sarcastically. "Finding the real killer. Hell."

Aidan watched as Miller perched on the corner of the table and Ciccotelli tapped her wristwatch, her brown eyes snapping mad. He turned to Murphy, wanting an explanation of how he'd come to sit next to Ciccotelli's bed in the hospital, but his partner shook his head wearily.

"Not now. I'm going home to catch some sleep. Tomorrow we can check the safe-deposit box and poke around to see who wanted Cynthia Adams dead."

Aidan stood another minute, watching Ciccotelli with her attorney. The Miller woman was talking, asking questions but Ciccotelli just pointed to the mirror. Miller threw an annoyed look over her shoulder and moved her body to block Aidan's view. Of course a defense attorney would champion her client. No shock there, but it looked like Murphy's involvement went a lot deeper than he was willing to say. Aidan wondered if they'd been romantically involved, Murphy and Ciccotelli. He'd never heard any stories about Murphy's love life, no girlfriends, current or past.

It was possible and the notion disturbed him. Murphy's easy-going veneer hid a deep concern for the people, the dead he represented. Still waters ran deep, Aidan's mother used to say. The right woman might find that depth . . . attractive.

Aidan clenched his teeth, watching as Ciccotelli gathered all the photos, tapping them into a neat stack. He pictured how all those curves would fill a man's hands. His partner's hands. He didn't like the picture at all.

He watched as she gathered her things and came out of the room, her lawyer at her side. She didn't look at all surprised to see him standing there and he didn't like that, either.

"Detective," she said in the same even voice she'd used the night before. "I know you were in court the day Green was tried and I know what you think of me. To say you are wrong would do no good at this time."

The even keel of her voice made the hackles on his neck stand straight up. He held her eyes and nodded. "I'd have to say you're right, Dr. Ciccotelli. It would do no good. We have to look at the evidence we've gathered. For Cynthia Adams's sake."

"Tess." Her attorney pulled at her arm. "Let's go."

"No, Amy. Wait." She looked away for a brief moment, then back up, her gaze penetrating and . . . sad. It threw him. Just a little. "Detective Reagan, somebody wanted Cynthia dead and it wasn't me. Please." Then she did the unexpected, grasping his forearm, making his entire arm jolt. His heart took off at a gallop and there was suddenly not enough air in the room. He couldn't seem to look away from her dark eyes. "Find out who did this," she whispered fiercely. "They used me to hurt one of my patients. Cynthia died thinking she'd lost her mind. That I'd forsaken her, too. I know what you think of me. But last night you cared about her. Please make whoever did this pay."

Then her hand was gone and so was she, leaving him to stare after her. And wonder.

Sunday, March 12, 3:30 P.M.

Just another minute. The elevator bell dinged and before the doors were fully open, Tess was through them and into the police station lobby, breathing hard, Amy following at a more leisurely pace. Being shoved into a suffocating elevator had put a cap on an otherwise sucky day. Tess flicked a glance at the glass doors that opened to the street. *Another minute.* In another minute she'd be out of the police station and . . .

And she'd still be in an inconceivable predicament. Tess smacked Amy's helping hand out of her way, shoving her arms into her coat on her own as she walked. "You let me sit in that interrogation room for an hour because you went home to put on your damn suit?" she hissed.

Amy lifted a single brow, managing to look affronted and dignified at the same time. "I thought it better to show up looking like a professional and not a street hooker."

Tess buttoned her coat with jerky movements. "I do *not* look like a street hooker," she bit out from behind gritted teeth, then saw one corner of Amy's mouth quirk up and knew her oldest friend had met her objective. For a few seconds she hadn't been thinking about that stark room with its two-way mirror or Aidan Reagan's accusing eyes. Or Cynthia Adams lying dead in the morgue. Or the fact that her own fingerprints existed in a place she'd never been. She blew out an exasperated breath. "You're just jealous I found this red jacket before you did."

Amy chuckled. "You're right. Macy's?"

"Marshall Fields, sixty percent off."

Amy's grin went cagey. "And you'll let me borrow it?"

"Sure, why not? As long as you let me borrow your black sweater." Tess passed the main desk, ignoring the desk sergeant's blatantly curious stare. She'd come in between two grim detectives and was now leaving with a known defense attorney. Hell. It wouldn't take a genius to put two and two together. By shift's end it would be all over the precinct and she knew no cop here would shed a single tear. Instead they'd toast Reagan and Murphy for giving the shrink her just desserts.

Amy lightly grasped her elbow and propelled her toward the front door. "My new cashmere sweater?" she asked, but the cheer in her voice was strained and Tess knew she was keeping up the routine for any ears that happened to be listening. "Your boobs are bigger than mine. You'll stretch it."

Hearing her best friend strive for merriment served to sour Tess's mood further. The situation was very serious. When this got out, her reputation as a psychiatrist would suffer and in turn, so would her practice and her patients. That it would get out she had no doubt. There wasn't a cop around that wouldn't jump for joy to see her private practice dashed on the rocks. After Harold Green, they'd seen to it that her contracts with the states attorney's office had not been renewed. And seeing her charged and tried? That would just be icing on the cake. "Don't be selfish, Amy," she said caustically. "Not only will your black sweater keep me warm, it will complement the black prison stripes. Which, thank God, at least are slimming."

"Tess, hush," Amy murmured. "This looks bad now, but we'll work this out. You'll see. Let's go get you something to eat. You haven't eaten today, have you?"

"No." Murphy had offered to get her a sandwich while she'd waited for Amy, but she'd refused. Her stomach had been too upset to eat, but even if it hadn't been she wouldn't accept any help from Todd Murphy. Not again.

"Well, I'll take you to my place and make you some soup."

The thought of Amy's soup made Tess queasy all over again. "No thanks. Just take me home. I'll be fine."

Amy bit her lip. "Tess, if you don't eat, you'll make yourself sick again."

Tess felt her temper simmer and clamped it down. Amy meant well. She always meant well. "I'll eat. I promise. Now leave it alone."

"Doctor? Dr. Ciccotelli?"

Tess stopped, not because she wanted to talk to the woman who'd called her name, but because the woman had stepped in front of the glass door, blocking her way. She was young, twenty-five maybe. Studious-looking with her wide gray eyes and narrow glasses. A long blond braid hung over one shoulder and a slight dent creased her chin. The drawl in her voice said "southerner." The gleam in the girl's eye screamed "reporter." *Here we go,* Tess thought and wondered which of the cops in the precinct had set aside his distaste for the press and sicced this piranha on her tail.

"My name is Joanna Carmichael. I'm covering the Adams case for the *Bulletin*. You were at the scene of the Adams's jump just after midnight last night. Can you comment on the police's position that Miss Adams's fall was coerced?"

Amy's arm came down in front of Tess. "No comment," her friend growled. "Step out of the way. Now."

Tess regarded the young woman's eyes thoughtfully and made an instant decision. Joanna Carmichael didn't know she'd been questioned or she would have asked her question very differently. When this got out, it might not hurt to have a mouthpiece in her own corner. "Give me your card," she said. "If I have something to say, I'll call you."

Carmichael dug in her pocket and came up with a card. "Thank you."

Outside, Tess dragged the cold, fresh air into her lungs. The gray sky was almost exactly the same color as the reporter's eyes. But the thought of eyes brought Aidan Reagan's to her mind, piercing blue and accusing.

She was free to go. That she might not have been was a thought she hadn't allowed while sitting in the interrogation room. She'd channeled her emotion into the cold fury that sustained her for most of the hour she'd sat there, feeling Reagan watch her through the glass. Anger was a safer emotion than fear. But now that she was out under the open sky, the fear hit, sending a shiver down her rigid spine.

This nightmare wasn't over. Not by a long shot. "I need to go home," she murmured. *I have work to do.*

Chapter Four

Sunday, March 12, 6:30 P.M.

Aidan stepped out of the cold evening rain and into his parents' warm laundry room. He shivered even as the smell of something delicious teased his nose. It would be the pot roast his mother had made for Sunday dinner and . . . he sniffed again with appreciation. Pie.

Let it be cherry, he thought, stripping off his drenched overcoat. He grabbed a faded towel from a basket and briskly whisked his head dry before going into the kitchen where his mother stood at the sink loading the dishwasher. From the stack of plates they must have had a full house, he thought wistfully, wishing he'd been there, too. It had been some time since the whole family had been together on a Sunday afternoon. They were all so busy with their lives.

Becca Reagan looked up and a smile lit her eyes, for some reason making his heart squeeze in his chest. The picture of Cynthia Adams lying dead on the street filled his mind, along with Ciccotelli's voice. *She has no next of kin,* she'd said. No mother to smile when she came home and only monstrous memories of a father that abused her. Then the mental image became that of a child homicide he'd been working before taking the Adams call. A six-year-old boy killed by the boy's own father. After Ciccotelli and her lawyer had gone, Aidan had visited the boy's mother. The mother knew where the father was hiding, but she protected the brute when she hadn't protected her own son.

If he tried to understand, he'd lose his mind. So he focused on his own mother's voice, warm with welcome.

"Aidan! I was wondering when you'd come by."

Aidan kissed her cheek. "Hi, Mom. Anything left?"

She looked him up and down, carefully scrutinizing. It was a familiar look, the one she'd given his father every day after he'd returned home from a day on the streets. After a career of CPD service, Kyle Reagan now enjoyed his retirement. She dried her hands and cupped Aidan's cheek in her palm, her eyes understanding. She'd ask nothing unless he offered. It was one of the things about her he loved most. One of the things he'd never found in another woman. God only knew he'd tried. Which was why he was still single at thirty-three, he supposed.

"There's a plate of leftover roast in the fridge. Pie's still cooling." She lifted a brow. "Your timing's as perfect as ever it was."

He managed a tired smile. "Excellent."

"Your head's all wet, boy. You'll catch pneumonia, you know."

He opened the refrigerator door. "That's because it's raining, Mom. And the Camaro top sprang a leak on the way home."

She sighed. "It would do no good to tell you to get a sensible car."

He just grinned and sat down at the large kitchen table. "The Camaro's got two hundred and ninety horses."

She rolled her eyes, accustomed to his response. "Your father has some duct tape in the garage. Eat your supper then go fix that heap of yours."

"Already did," he said with his mouth full. "Stopped by the store for tape on my way over here." When he'd cleaned his plate she took it away and deposited a new plate filled with a large wedge of pie.

"You missed Sean and Ruth and the children. Abe and Kristen are still here," she said. "Your father's trying to teach the baby about point spreads."

His fifteen-month-old niece, Kara. His goddaughter. His heart squeezed again, thinking of the happiness his brother Abe had finally found. "I know. Abe's SUV's taking up the whole driveway, which is why I'm parked in the street. Where's Rachel?" His sixteen-year-old sister was growing up entirely too fast for his liking.

"She's at a friend's house. She'll be home by nine. I think she's got some boy trouble, but she hasn't told me." She lifted a brow. "Maybe you can talk to her."

Aidan grunted. "About boys? Hell, no. If I was Dad I'd keep her locked in her room till she was twenty-five then nobody would have to worry about those boys."

"You were one of *those boys* once."

"My point exactly."

She sipped at her coffee, her eyes sobering. "I saw Shelley's mother last week, in the beauty parlor."

Aidan's jaw clenched. Shelley St. John was an off-limits topic. "Mom, today is not the day for this."

Becca nodded. "I know. But I didn't want you to hear this from somebody else and be unprepared. She's getting married."

Once he'd felt hurt. Now he felt only disgust. "I know."

His mother's eyes flew open. "You do? How?"

"She sent me an invitation." One final, well-placed jab in a line of so many. Shelley had been well-versed in the art of backstabbing and betrayal. "Now drop it, please."

Becca sighed. "Eat your pie before your brother realizes I've cut it for you."

"It's too late," Abe growled from the doorway. "Dammit, Aidan, you're eating it all."

"You snooze, you lose," Aidan replied smoothly.

Grumbling, his brother snatched a plate and sat down at the table. "What happened to you? You're all wet."

Becca set the coffeepot between them. "It's raining, Abe," she said and Aidan smiled in spite of himself.

But Abe wasn't smiling. "You haven't slept, have you? You still working the Morris boy?"

Aidan shook his head. "Me and Murphy spent all yesterday afternoon tracking the slimy SOB of a father, but he's gone under. We picked up a new case just after midnight. Kept us busy all day."

Abe frowned. "The only new case on the board from last night was a jumper."

Aidan focused at his dessert. "It wasn't a suicide. Not really."

"How can it not really be a suicide?" Becca wanted to know. "Isn't that like being a little bit pregnant?"

"Who's pregnant?" His sister-in-law, Kristen, entered the kitchen, holding a baby with red curls. She narrowed her eyes at the remaining slice of pie, then at Abe. "Hey."

"Talk to Ma," Abe said with a shrug and reached for the baby.

"Who's pregnant?" Kristen repeated, joining them at the table.

Abe bounced Kara on his knee. "Nobody. Aidan grabbed a jumper last night."

Kristen grimaced. "Tough night." His sister-in-law knew all about tough cases. A prosecutor for the states attorney's office, Kristen saw her share of bodies daily.

Aidan sighed. "You don't know the half of it. This woman was being treated by a psychiatrist who—" He stopped when Abe and Kristen flashed each other a look.

"Tess Ciccotelli," Kristen said flatly. "So *you're* the one who dragged her into Interview this afternoon. Hell, Aidan."

Aidan looked from Kristen to Abe. Kristen looked furious and Abe was fiercely concentrating on retying the bow in Kara's curly hair. Aidan knew he was on his own. "How did you know?"

"My boss called me this afternoon. Told me the basics and asked me to take the case, to talk to the cops who'd brought her in for questioning. I told him I couldn't. Tess and I have worked together for years. We're friends."

"You and everybody else it seems." Aidan jabbed at the pie, annoyed. The woman had more allies than NATO. "Wasn't anybody else sitting in that courtroom when she absolved Harold Green of all responsibility for murdering three little kids and a cop?"

Kristen went still. "She did not absolve him of responsibility, Aidan."

"You weren't there, Kristen," Aidan said, warning in his voice. "I was."

"Not in the courtroom, no. Before, after, yes. She came to me, Aidan, torn up about what she had to do. She knew what the backlash would be. She could never have testified to Green's incompetence to stand trial if she hadn't believed it completely. That's not the kind of woman she is. You spent hours with her this afternoon. Surely you saw that."

Aidan shifted in his chair, uncomfortable because he still was unsure exactly what he'd seen and heard. "She's a shrink, Kristen. She can make people see what she wants them to see."

Kristen shoved her plate away. "She's a psychiatrist, not a witch doctor. You're wasting your time, Aidan. Find out who else wanted that woman dead. And find out who hated Tess enough to drag her into the middle of it." She stood up, breathing hard. "You'll find out the list is a hell of a lot longer than you think."

Aidan rubbed his tired head. "Kristen, please."

"Please, what, Aidan? Please look away while you indulge your petty prejudice? I don't think so. Did you know that Tess Ciccotelli lost her contract with the city because the cops' union protested her?"

He thought about the Mercedes she'd driven the night before. "No, but she doesn't appear to be hurting for income."

Kristen's eyes narrowed, dangerously. "Well, then, did you know that she nearly lost her life because some cop didn't act fast enough to protect her from one of those nutcases in Interview?"

Aidan flinched. "No. I didn't know that."

"Ask Murphy. He can tell you what happened. Tess Ciccotelli has paid enough for doing what was right. I won't sit by and see her charged for this. There is no fucking way she did this and you know it as well as I do."

Becca gasped and Aidan blinked, shocked at the word that rarely came from his sister-in-law's mouth, while Abe's hands came up to cover Kara's ears. "You said the f-word," Abe said slowly. "In front of the baby."

Kristen pursed her lips, visibly trembling, her cheeks red. "I'm sorry for that, Abe. But I'm not sorry for any other part of it. Talk to Murphy, Aidan. Then run a list of all the criminals Tess has helped us put away. Then you look me in the eye and tell me that there's no one who wants to see her suffer enough to set her up like this."

"Kristen," Abe murmured. "Calm down. Aidan will get to the bottom of this." He sighed and jiggled the baby on his knee. "You are going to take this case, aren't you?"

Kristen shook her head. "No. I can't be objective when it comes to this. I think the whole business has been so patently unfair. Patrick said he could be objective, so he'll take it from here." She leveled a serious look at Aidan. "Unless the investigation absolves her from responsibility."

Aidan met her gaze. He'd never known his sister-in-law to be wrong about someone she fought for so passionately. She, more than anyone else, lent weight to Ciccotelli's innocence. "Before I left today, I asked Records to run the list of offenders she's testified against. I should have it tomorrow morning."

She drew a breath. "Thank you."

"And I'll ask Murphy about the . . . nutcase that tried to hurt her."

"Who succeeded," she said quietly. "Check Tess out, Aidan. You'll find you're wrong about her."

"I hope so, Kristen. But either way, I'm going to do my job."

She lifted a brow. "I'm counting on it."

Sunday, March 12, 8:30 P.M.

Ciccotelli was home now, safe and sound. Clearly visible through her window. With binoculars of course. Such an important tool of the trade. Never leave home without them. People would notice a gun or a knife, but no one questioned a person walking the street with binoculars around the neck and, if anyone asked, it was simple enough to claim a fascination with birds.

As if. Annoying little chirping creatures. Except for the birds of prey that silently watched from the skies, swooping down on unsuspecting marks, talons ready to tear into flesh like paper. Birds of prey were creatures to be admired. And emulated.

The unsuspecting mark was sitting at her dining room table, working on her laptop, headphones covering her ears. Occasionally looking up to stare out the window that put Chicago at her feet. It was an interesting fact, truly. Given a high enough window most people never considered that as they looked out, someone else could just as easily be looking in. And really it was so very easy. And at the moment, boring.

She wasn't in jail. And while disappointing, it was to be expected. Enough people still thought enough of Dr. Tess Ciccotelli to defend her against what appeared to be ludicrous charges. Where was motive? they would ask. An upstanding psychiatrist, awarded citation after citation . . . A chuckle broke the silence. By this time tomorrow, the police would have their motive and the number of her staunch defenders would soon dwindle.

But just in case, there should be more. There would be more.

One touch of the speed dial had Nicole's phone ringing and like the smart girl she was, she answered on the very first ring.

"What?" her voice was raw and hoarse.

"What the hell have you done to your voice?" It was expected that an actress would take better care of her voice, but it sounded as though Nicole had been crying. She was a weak woman. She'd need to be watched closely. Perhaps another visit to Nicole's little brother was required to ensure her continued compliance. "You better still be able to perform."

Nicole cleared her throat. "It's nothing. I'm fine."

"You'd better hope so. I've invested a great deal of time and money on your voice, Nicole. Please don't forget that your brother's health depends on you and you alone."

"What do you want?" Nicole asked, her words sounding as if they were being yanked from between clenched teeth.

"Be at the corner of Michigan and Eighth by eleven. Bring the wig."

There was a beat of silence, then the sound of Nicole's voice, choked and afraid. "You said it would be a few days."

"I changed my mind. Eleven, Nicole." *We're going to pay a visit, you and I. To Mr. Avery Winslow.* Winslow's face with its sad, basset-hound droop stared up from the photograph lying on top of the pile. Little Avery Junior's face was next in the stack. Poor Mr. Winslow, losing his infant son like that. That a father would feel guilty was utterly understandable. That he would seek the help of a psychiatrist, rational. That his psychiatrist was Tess Ciccotelli, his doom.

Avery Winslow had been on the juice for three weeks now. His apartment was prepped. It was time for Act Two.

Poor Mr. Winslow. It really was nothing personal. Not against him, anyway. But Ciccotelli . . . she was different. *She* was personal.

Soon enough, she'd be dead. But she'd suffer a great deal first.

Sunday, March 12, 11:30 P.M.

Too late. Too late. I'm too late. The refrain ran through Tess's mind again and again as she pushed her way through the crowd. She couldn't see. Couldn't see past all the men. Tall men. Dark hair. All so angry.

Angry with me. She pushed past the last man and stopped. At her feet lay Cynthia Adams. Dead. *Too late.* One of the men stooped down and scooped Cynthia's heart from her broken body and held it out, still pumping in his hand.

"Take it," he commanded, his blue eyes glowing in the night.

"No, no." She stepped back. The heart still quivered, blood dripped between his fingers to fall on Cynthia's pale face. And as the blood made little drips on Cynthia's face, her eyes popped open and stared. Dead and empty.

She spun around, a scream trapped in her throat. And froze where she stood. Police. *Coming for me.* Uniforms as far as her eye could see. Accusing eyes. *Run. Wake up. Dammit, wake up and run.*

"Tess. Dammit, Tess, wake up."

She could hear a scream, shrill and terrified. Realized it came from her own throat. Tess whipped her head up from the dining room table, her eyes wide, her vision still blurry. She blinked hard and a face came into focus. Familiar. Brown eyes, sandy hair cut short. Fingers pulling the headphones from her ears. Strong hands on her face. Live and warm.

Jon. Jon was here. She was all right. They wouldn't get her. Not today.

Her pulse still raced to beat all hell, but she could breathe again. "God, Jon."

Jon Carter held her face between his surgeon's hands, his capable fingers cradling her skull, his thumbs stroking her cheekbones, waiting till she got hold of herself. Tess gave him a shaky nod and settled back into her chair. He grabbed another chair and straddled it, watching her carefully.

"I'm all right. It was just a bad dream."

"Uh-huh." He slipped his fingertips to her carotid, held them there as he counted.

"I said I'm all right." She pushed her hair away from her face. "Just a bad dream."

"You were screaming so loud I could hear you in the hall. Scared the shit out of me, Tess. Good thing I had a key. I might have called the cops otherwise." He shuddered. "Sounded like you were being disemboweled in here."

She jerked back, the heart dream still vivid in her mind. "That's not funny, Jon."

"It wasn't meant to be." His sandy brows knit in concerned confusion. "That must have been some dream. What happened?"

Tess stood, pissed when her knees felt like rubber. "Why are you here, anyway?"

"I was worried about you. You called Amy away from lunch and never let me know you were all right. I tried calling all afternoon, but you didn't answer so I came by after I finished my shift."

"I turned the ringer off so I could sleep."

"You're not sleeping," he pointed out.

She'd tried, several times. The damn dream kept waking her up. To her knowledge she hadn't screamed before, though. "Actually, I was just now."

"Uh-huh. At the table, your face in your laptop keyboard. I'm certain drool is not good for all the electrical thingies in there. What's going on here, Tess?"

His eyes followed her as she took one experimental step toward the kitchen, then another. "Didn't Amy tell you anything?"

"Nope. All she would say is that you were stranded so she went to get you and took you home and tucked you into bed. I take it there's a bit more to it than that."

"Ah. Attorney-client privilege. So she *can* keep a secret. Good to know." Tess made it to the refrigerator and held on to the door, still shaky. "I'm going to have a glass of wine. You want one?"

He'd followed her and now stood in the kitchen archway, frowning. "No. What are you talking about, attorney-client privilege? Amy said your car broke down."

"Amy was being discreet as I have retained her for her services." Tess found the corkscrew, grateful for something to keep her trembling hands occupied. "I appear to be a suspect."

His frown deepened. "Like, in a crime?"

Tess huffed a nervous laugh as she pulled the cork from the bottle. "Like, in a dilly of a crime, Jon. Pour this, will you? My hands still aren't steady." He poured the glass, which she drained in three noisy gulps. "More."

Silently he obeyed and she took the glass back to the dining room table and sank back down into her chair. "One of my clients committed suicide last night."

"This was the call you got last night? The one you needed me to go with you?"

She fluttered her hand. "Yeah, but this would have happened regardless, so don't feel guilty. Have a seat, my dear. I'll tell you a story."

He sat and she told him everything, down to Reagan's accusing blue eyes and the young reporter by the police station door.

For a long moment he said absolutely nothing. Then he snorted. "That's insane."

Tess laughed. "I suppose that's as good a word as any." She pushed her glass so that it clinked against the bottle he'd set on the table. "More. Please."

He poured what would be her fourth glass. "Did they charge you?"

"Not yet. You should stick 'round town. I might need you as a character witness."

He scowled. "That's not funny, Tess."

She tilted her head. "It wasn't meant to be. I'm in some serious trouble here." She gestured to the stack of cassette tapes next to her boombox. "And not a clue in any of those. Nobody specific Cynthia mentioned in any of our sessions. Not in five hours of tape. I transcribed every spoken word."

Jon drew a breath, contemplating. "What next?"

Tess shrugged. "First I have to finish this wine. Then I have to sleep. Really sleep. I'm hoping enough wine will knock me out so that I don't have that damn dream again. Tomorrow I take these transcripts in to Reagan. Then, if he hasn't found something to arrest me over during the night, I go to the hospital and do my rounds." She shrugged again. "After that, it's anybody's guess."

"Are you sure you want to do that?"

She tipped up one corner of her mouth and tapped the nearly empty bottle with her fingernail, feeling just woozy enough to be pleasant. "I already did. Four glasses."

"Tess." Jon shot her a warning glare. "I meant do you think it's wise to voluntarily give the detective this information. He could have been one of the ones to get your contract yanked."

"He might have been. Probably was. Still, he and Murphy are my only chance to get this resolved, right now. If they fuck it up, I'll take it higher. Spinnelli still likes me. For now, I'll cooperate with the detectives." She leaned her head on the chair back and closed her eyes. "Jon, somebody killed Cynthia Adams, just as sure as if he'd pushed her off the balcony himself. If I can help Reagan figure out who, I can make this go away and get my life back." She struggled to her feet, grateful this time for his guiding hands. "Now, I need some sleep." Leaning heavily on his shoulder, she made her way back to her bedroom.

She chuckled when he pushed her to bed and pulled off

her socks. She leaned back on her elbows and grinned up at him. He was a handsome man and she'd heard more than one whispered conjecture regarding the skill of his hands outside of surgery. But they were just friends, she and Jon. Not a spark of chemistry between them. After Amy, he was her closest friend, and monogamously attached, to boot. Still, she couldn't resist the temptation to tease. "It's been a long time since I've had a man in my bedroom, Jon. Sure you don't want to stay?"

He smiled down at her. "It's an intriguing offer, Tess. But what would Robin say?"

She closed her eyes. "Not to worry. You're safe from my evil clutches." She chuckled again, her senses warmed and dulled just enough to be comfortable. "Tell Robin I kept my hands to myself." She snuggled into the pillow, sighing when his hand pushed the hair from her face. Started to drift. "Fell asleep all alone. Again."

Jon's hand hesitated. "Tess."

She opened one eye. His expression was pained and in turn sent an unexpected wave of longing crashing into her heart. It was the wine, she told herself. *Because I'm over that cheating sonofabitch.* She'd slept alone in this bed without Phillip Parks for more than a year. She didn't miss him. He could fry in hell for all she cared. But she did miss . . . having someone, she supposed. She gave herself a little shake that sent the bed floating. There would be plenty of time for self-analysis tomorrow. *Especially if Reagan actually manages to arrest me.* "I'm fine, Jon. Go home to Robin. Just lock the door and don't let Bella out." As if she'd heard her name, Tess's tortoiseshell cat sprang onto the bed and curled up on her pillow next to her face, purring loudly.

"Call me tomorrow, Tess."

Sleep was coming. Finally. Mercifully. "Okay."

Chapter Five

～

Monday, March 13, 7:40 A.M.

Daniel Morris, age six years, two months. Cause of death, asphyxiation. Fibers found in the lungs, consistent with a foam pillow." *Shit.*

Aidan threw the ME's report on his desk, swallowing the bile that rose in his throat. The bastard father had suffocated that baby with a pillow, then broken his neck and tossed him down a flight of stairs to cover up his crime. Aidan gritted his teeth. And that little boy's mother had gone along with the story. Somehow that made it even worse. He closed his eyes, drew a breath through his nose. *Calm down. You won't get justice for that boy if you lose your head.* He could hear Murphy's voice in his mind, soothing and steady, just as he'd been when they'd stood shoulder to shoulder and watched the ME tech zip that little body into a bag Friday evening.

Damn. He swallowed hard, pursed his lips. Cursed the stinging of his eyes. *Think about something else. Anything else.*

Cynthia Adams and Tess Ciccotelli. Today he'd keep his promise to Kristen. Focus on Adams herself, on finding out who would have wanted her dead. He'd visit the brokerage house where she worked, find out who she hung with. He winced. Very bad choice of words. He would follow up on the lilies. Surely someone buying that many flowers would be remembered, and—

"Detective?"

The voice came without warning, had him shooting to his feet, opening his eyes to Tess Ciccotelli who stood at the corner of his desk, a look of thoughtful concern on her face. The pulse that had started to quiet took a racing leap and for a moment all he could hear was his own blood pounding in his ears. But the pounding subsided as he looked her up and down.

She was professionally dressed today, a tan coat draped over her arm. The tight jeans and red leather jacket were gone, replaced with a conservative, tailored look, charcoal slacks and jacket. Her hair no longer curled wildly. She'd somehow straightened it and pulled it back at her nape, leaving a few wisps to soften her face. Her makeup was more subtle. Gone was the bright red lipstick. Her only color today was provided by a red silk scarf, lightly tied around her neck. Her stiletto-heeled boots were now sensible flat loafers, polished to a gleaming shine. She looked liked a cover model for Businesswoman of the Year and had he not seen the gypsy yesterday, he'd never have believed such a transformation was possible.

Still, conservative or not, cold bitch or not, suspect . . . or not, she made his mouth water. Which meant she was a dangerous woman, one to watch. Never to touch. No matter who her allies were. He brought his eyes back up to meet hers. "Dr. Ciccotelli. I didn't hear the elevator bell."

She'd borne his scrutiny without protest. "That's because I took the stairs. Detective Reagan, I'm sorry to disturb you this early," she said quietly. "I've got rounds this morning, but I wanted to drop this off for you first. I wasn't going to come up, but the desk sergeant said you were in and sent me up." One shoulder lifted, her expression gone wry. "I guess he hadn't heard the news."

He gestured to the chair next to his desk. "Would you like some coffee?"

"From your pot?" One corner of her mouth twitched and he found himself charmed and trying very hard not to be. "Now you're trying to poison me. No, thank you, Detective." Sobering, she pulled a manila envelope from her briefcase. "I spent the evening transcribing my last five sessions with Cynthia Adams. I thought maybe they might provide some . . . insight as you investigate Cynthia's death."

It wasn't what he'd expected her to say. Still, he took the envelope, shook its contents onto his desk. A stack of neatly printed pages fell out, along with five cassette tapes. "You tape your sessions?"

"Not all of them. Only certain clients, and only with their permission."

"Cynthia Adams gave her permission, then?"

"Not at first, no. When we first started meeting, Cynthia was in denial about the more deviant aspects of her behavior. She'd tell me about her episodes."

"Her affairs."

"Her one-night stands," she corrected. "Then the next session, she would deny she'd said any such thing. I persuaded her to allow me to tape our conversations so she could hear what I heard." A shadow passed over Ciccotelli's face. "She was . . . devastated. But it ultimately helped us focus on the real problems."

She was not what he expected at all. Although Kristen, he supposed, would not be surprised. Nor would Murphy or Spinnelli. "You mean her depression."

"Yes. She needed to get that under control, because it influenced all her other behaviors."

"Like her attempted suicide a year ago."

"And her sexual paraphilia—her addiction," she clarified. "It was a compulsion for Cynthia. Possibly a way to control men and her own body at the same time."

"Because her father abused her."

"Yes. She rarely brought home the same man twice, even if they begged."

Aidan picked up the sheaf of papers and started to skim. "Who begged?"

"A few. I highlighted the names I knew had become persistent, but Cynthia never gave me last names. Half the time I think she made up the first names."

"Then how do you know she was telling the truth at all?"

Ciccotelli sighed. She looked weary. "One of her medications causes possible liver toxicity, so she had to have regular blood tests. She came back negative for liver damage, but positive for gonorrhea, contracted from one of these one-night stands. Passed it on to God knows how many more. By law I had to report her to the health department. I spoke with a Miss Tuttle, Cynthia's case worker. We agreed I'd tell Cynthia about the STD and that I'd reported her." She drew a breath, let it out. "Cynthia was explosively angry that day. I'd violated her privacy. She ranted that she'd lose her job at the brokerage. It was our second to last session. She swore she'd never come back."

"But you had one more session, so she did."

"She did. She'd woken up with a man she didn't remember picking up."

"She didn't control that man."

"Exactly. It scared her enough to come back. I changed her medication and she was supposed to come back a week later for a recheck. She didn't show up."

"That's when you went to her apartment."

"Yes, but she either wasn't home or wouldn't answer." She narrowed her eyes slightly. "My fingerprints would be on her doorbell. Possibly on the outside frame, but I didn't even touch the doorknob that night, Detective. I brought a colleague with me, just in case there was an issue."

So she'd said yesterday in Interview. "Do you normally do that? Bring a colleague."

"Yes. Always. I bring a colleague, or I don't go." She closed her eyes. "Except for Saturday night. No one I usually call was available."

He took out his notepad. "Who did you call last night, Doctor?"

She opened her eyes. "I first called Harrison Ernst, my partner, but he wasn't home. Then I called Jonathan Carter, but he wasn't home either. He's a surgeon at County. He won't want to talk to you. He's a good friend and a bit angry about all this."

Aidan wrote down the man's name, ignoring the twinge of jealousy that pricked his gut. So she was through with Murphy and now involved with this Carter. Not that it mattered. Right. "Tell me about the phone call you got Saturday night."

"It came in at 12:06. I checked my caller ID last night, but it listed the number as unknown. You can check my home phone records if you like. It sounded like a cell phone, a little scratchy. The caller was a woman, young."

"How young?"

"Not a teenager, but not middle-aged, I didn't think. She didn't give her name, just said she was one of Cynthia Adams's neighbors and that I needed to come because Cynthia was standing on her ledge, threatening to jump."

Aidan frowned at his notes. "She said Adams was threatening to jump?"

"I think those were her exact words, yes. Why?"

"Because I have witnesses that say she didn't talk to anyone. She just walked up to the edge of the balcony, turned around, and fell."

Ciccotelli's face tightened, almost imperceptibly. If he hadn't been looking for it, he would have missed it. He hadn't been looking for it Saturday night. He'd been too angry for too many reasons and assumed that her expressionless face spoke her mind. He should have known better than to take anyone at face value. Hell, he did know better. Still, there was physical evidence. "How do you think your fingerprints got in her apartment, Doctor?"

She slowly shook her head. "I don't know. I have wracked my brain, trying to figure it out." She glanced down at her watch. "I have to make my rounds now, Detective. Here's my card. I wrote my cell number on the back, but I won't have it with me while I do rounds. If you need to talk further today, my secretary will be able to reach me." She stood up, pulled a little at the scarf around her neck. She hesitated, then caught his eyes once more. "I didn't mean to look at your desk, Detective Reagan, but I did see the ME report you were reading when I came in. On the little boy."

His eyes narrowed. He could feel the blood heating his cheeks. "It wasn't your business, Doctor. It's still not."

"I know. I just wanted to say . . . I'm sorry. You see a great deal in your job. I imagine it leaves you angry when you might not want to be."

She was absolving *him* of responsibility. How ironic. "You see a lot, too."

Her smile was both self-deprecating and sad. "Not the same. Not little kids. I tried to work with the abused kids once, when I first started out. I couldn't." She tilted her head, her regard steady. "That surprises you."

That he was so transparent was more than a little annoying. "A little, yeah."

"You don't trust psychiatrists."

"You have your function, Doctor, and I have mine."

Her lips curved. "Meaning, go treat the sick people, but stay out of my head. Fair enough, Detective." She pulled on her coat while he watched, his fingers itching to assist, his brain telling him to stay back. "I'll be in touch if I remember anything new. You'll let me know if my fingerprints turn up anywhere else?"

He smiled in spite of himself. "I will. Thanks for coming in. And . . . my sister-in-law sends her regards."

She nodded. "Kristen is a good friend. Tell her I said right back at her." She started for the open doorway leading to the stairs and stopped. Murphy stood there, his hands in his pockets, his brows crunched together.

"Tess. I didn't expect to see you here."

"I didn't intend to come up." She edged past him and Murphy turned with her, gripping her arm, his eyes intense.

"I'm sorry, Tess. I should have never even considered it."

Even from across the room Aidan could feel the chill as her eyes shuttered and her voice stilled. Once again he could see the woman who'd sat in the courtroom, pronouncing the words that set a killer free. Carefully she rotated her arm, pulling free of Murphy's grip. "No, you really shouldn't have. I've dropped off some reading material. Have a good day, Todd." Then she was gone, leaving Murphy's hand outstretched, his face grim.

Turning on his heel, Murphy dropped in his chair and stared at his desk for a minute before seeing the ME's report on little Danny Morris. He swallowed hard. "Fuck. That's just a fuckin' perfect way to start the day."

Aidan got them both coffee, perching on the edge of Murphy's desk, which butted up against his own. "Murphy, tell me what happened between you and Ciccotelli. Kristen says you know something about an attack last year."

Murphy cradled his cup in his hands. "It's cold out there."

"It was cold in here a few minutes ago."

Murphy grunted. "Fuck that, too." But he blew out a breath and settled deep into his chair. "About two weeks after Green's day in court Tess was asked to evaluate another suspect."

"This must have been before she lost her contract with the city."

Murphy looked up sharply. "Yeah, before then. This guy she was supposed to evaluate was a bad actor, murdered his landlady and her bedridden husband. He claimed to be schizo, but the SA thought he'd just been high. His lawyer was going for the insanity defense. Really big guy." Murphy went quiet for a moment then shook his head. "They brought him in wearing shackles, hands and feet. Tess sat as far away from him as she could. Guy was my collar, so I was sitting on the other side of the glass with the SA—Patrick Hurst. But there was a guard in the room with her. Guard gave Tess a look." Murphy looked away, his lips twisting in a grimace. "Slimy bastard. Like he hated her, you know?"

"Yeah. I know." And felt some shame because he did. "What did the suspect do?"

"Bided his time, then lunged over the table, grabbed her." He set his coffee on the table. "Got the wrist shackle chain around her throat and threatened to break her neck."

Aidan winced. "What did the guard do?"

Murphy tucked his tongue in his cheek. "After a half beat, he jumped in, but the big guy had Tess. I was in there in less than fifteen seconds but he'd already hurt her. Spun her around and slammed her head into the concrete wall, then held her there, choking her. I'll never forget the look in her eyes. She thought she would die that day."

"You pulled the guy off her?"

"Me, the SA, and two guards. She was passed out by then.

He broke her arm and fractured her skull. She has a scar around her neck from the chain."

Aidan thought about the colorful scarf she'd tied around her neck that morning and understood. He thought about a murderer's hands around her throat and was coldly furious. "So you went and sat with her at the hospital."

"Yeah. I called her brother for her. He was on the plane from Philadelphia that night. I went back the next day to see how she was doing and we started talking. She couldn't talk, actually. She had to write on a notepad because he'd damaged her voice. But after a few days she could talk." His mouth bent up. "She reminded me of my little sister, sassy as hell. And we became . . . friends."

"Does she still?"

Murphy's brows lifted. "What? Remind me of my sister? Yes." He sat back in his chair, thoughtfully studying Aidan's face. "Does she remind you of your sister, Aidan?"

Aidan considered lying, decided against it. "No."

Murphy laughed softly. "Well, I'll be damned."

"Mention it again and you will be."

"Why? She didn't do this, and you know it. We'll clear her and then you'll be clear."

"Doesn't matter, Murphy." Because women like Tess Ciccotelli were extremely high maintenance. Aidan reached backward and grabbed a sheet from his printer. "These are all the florist shops within a five-mile radius of Cynthia Adams's apartment. I thought we could find out if anybody's been buying lots of lilies lately."

"Give me half the list." Murphy waited until Aidan was sitting back behind his own desk before adding, "She's unattached."

Aidan paused midway through dialing his first number. "What?"

"She's unattached. Was engaged, now she's not."

Leave it alone, Reagan, his sensible brain warned. The stupid brain did not concur. Shifting in his chair, he glared across the desk at Murphy who was ignoring him, having already dialed the first number on his list. Aroused and pissed off about it, Aidan made it through calls to five different florists, then smacked the receiver down. "Why?"

"Why what?"

"You know damn well why what," Aidan hissed. "Don't be an asshole."

Murphy looked up, smiling. Smug bastard. "She broke it off with the guy two weeks from the altar." His smile faded. "Rumor had it her fiancé cheated on her."

Aidan shook his head, floored. It would seem he and Tess Ciccotelli did have more in common than he'd originally thought. "Then he was an idiot."

"On that we agree. You got any lilies yet?"

"Roses, carnations. No lilies, at least not in the quantity we saw in that apartment."

"Probably bought from at least a few different places. Let's keep calling until ten. Then we'll go visit the brokerage house where Adams worked."

"Sounds like a plan."

Monday, March 13, 8:30 A.M.

Abandoning her umbrella with a growl, Tess pulled her cell phone from her pocket after it rang for the third straight time in as many minutes. Somebody was persistent. A glance at the caller ID revealed that somebody to be her secretary.

"Yes, Denise?" she asked more sharply than she'd intended, grimacing when her foot sank into a pothole, soaking her up to the ankle. She ducked beneath the overhang in front of the psychiatric hospital and shivered, shaking the cold dirty water from her right shoe that was probably ruined. It was a miserable morning, cold and rainy. So totally in sync with her mood. "What's happened?" she asked more calmly.

"You've had some calls this morning, Dr. Chick."

A shiver that had nothing to do with the icy rain raced down Tess's spine and she swallowed what was sure to have been a very bad word. "From?"

"A few reporters. One from the *Trib,* one from Channel Eight. They want a comment on the story in this morning's *Bulletin.*"

A sharp pain arced through her head. "The *Bulletin.*" Visions of a gray-eyed young woman with a long blond braid came to mind. "Let me guess. Joanna Carmichael."

"No, Cyrus Bremin is the byline, but . . . yeah. Carmichael's name's on the photos. You haven't seen the article, then?"

Photos. The pain trebled. "No. How bad is it?"

"Real bad. You also got two calls from a Dr. Fenwick from the state licensing board. He says you have to call him back immediately." Denise rattled off the number. "I told him you were consulting this morning, but he insisted."

Tess's stomach rolled as she committed the number to memory. "Any other calls?"

"Mrs. Brown is having panic attacks. I referred her to Dr. Gryce. Mr. Winslow has called three times, demanding to see you and no one else. He sounded hysterical so I penciled him in for three."

"Thanks." She dropped her phone in her pocket, her heart beating so hard she thought it would pound straight through her chest. Quickly she scanned the area. There was a bank of newspaper vending machines across the street.

She crossed against the light, earning her blown horns

and irate shouts. Her hands trembled as she pulled the paper from the machine. *The front page.* She was on the front page.

The rain pounded her uncovered head, soaking through her coat, but she couldn't move. Her own face stared up from the page, next to an obscene picture of Cynthia Adams lying impaled on a Chicago street. And the headline that had her heart beating in her throat. NOTED PSYCHIATRIST IMPLICATED IN PATIENT'S SUICIDE.

Her cell phone rang and woodenly she answered it. "Ciccotelli."

"It's Amy. Have you seen the *Bulletin* this morning?"

"Yes."

Silence buzzed between them as the rain continued to pour. "Where are you, Tess?"

Reality somehow reconnected in her mind and propelled by another one of those bursts of white hot fury, Tess shook herself and tossed the newspaper in the nearest garbage can. She had patients to see and she was wasting time standing in the rain like she had no sense at all. "I'm at the hospital." Briskly she started back across the road, this time waiting for the light, not caring about the rain. She was already soaked to the skin. "I have to make my rounds now, Amy, but afterwards, it looks like I'll be meeting with the state licensing board. I'll need my attorney with me, I think."

"Tell me when and where and I'll be there."

Tess's throat tightened and she resolutely cleared it. "Thanks."

Monday, March 13, 8:30 A.M.

"I'm home."

Joanna Carmichael looked up from the sports page and

nearly choked on her Cocoa Krispies. Her boyfriend stood in the middle of the living room, dripping wet from the rain, one hand clutching a bound stack of newspapers, the other an enormous bouquet of yellow flowers. He wore that big sloppy grin that normally appeared only after sex. "What have you done, Keith?"

"Souvenirs." The pile of newspapers landed on the table with a thud, sending the milk sloshing from her bowl. He had to have bought twenty copies of the *Bulletin,* each one of them evidence of her editor's treacherous deceit. Each one bearing Cyrus Bremin's byline on her story. *My story.* Schmidt had promised her a story. He'd never promised her a byline, she thought bitterly.

Keith shook like a wet dog then presented the bouquet with a regal flourish. "Thought you might want to send a few clippings home."

Like hell she would. She gritted her teeth. "Keith, it's not my story."

His smile faded and he stood there, still holding the flowers she refused to take. "Of course it is. And on the front page, too."

"It's Bremin's story," she spat. "He got my byline because he's the senior investigative reporter at the paper. That asshole Schmidt gave him my story."

"Your name's next to the pictures," he said quietly, putting the flowers aside, all the happiness gone from his face.

"A photo credit." She sneered at it. "I'm not a photographer. I'm a journalist and if you had any sense at all you'd see the difference."

He slicked back his wet hair. "I think I have a great deal of sense, Jo. I see the difference. I also see your name in a major paper, on the front page. It's what you wanted. What you wanted to prove to your father you could do. On your own. Now we can go home."

She shoved the papers to the floor, mention of her father and his infuriating condescension bringing her blood to a boil. "I'm nowhere close to being ready to go home, Keith. Not until I have a byline above the fold on page one. Not before."

He stood there for a moment, just looking at her with that expression that had always made her want to squirm. "You've done something good here, Jo. You've exposed a doctor who hurt her own clients. Maybe if you could see around your own ego, you'd see it was true. I've been patient with you, but your name is on page one. You said when that happened we could back to Atlanta. Jo, I want to go home."

"Then go." Disgusted she got up to put her bowl in the sink. "But go alone. I'm not leaving this town until I'm above the fold." She glared at Cyrus Bremin's name, mocking her from the stack of papers on the floor. "I've got to have some leverage with Schmidt." A thought formed amid the bubbling fury. "An exclusive with Ciccotelli would do it. She told me to give her a call." She looked over to see Keith's back as he retreated to the bedroom and felt a sudden surge of guilt. "Keith, I'm sorry I snapped at you. I was just so disappointed."

He nodded without turning around. "Don't forget to put the flowers in water. You always forget and then they die."

Joanna shrugged away her uneasiness. Keith would come around. In the six years they'd been going steady, he always had. Now she had to focus on what was really important. Getting Ciccotelli to agree to an exclusive. After this morning's article it wouldn't be easy, but she could blame the debacle on Bremin, clearing her own way. It could work. Then she'd be able to prove her father wrong. She could make it in journalism without his help. She'd be able to take her place in the family news business with a credential she'd earned herself.

Monday, March 13, 9:15 A.M.

Aidan blinked when a newspaper landed on his desk midway into his tenth florist call. He glanced up to see his lieutenant's face, tight-lipped and stern, then dropped his eyes back down to the page. And stared as the florist's voice became just a buzzing in his ear. "Um, ma'am, I'll have to call you back." He hung up the phone and picked up the paper. It was the *Bulletin,* one step up from a supermarket tabloid.

And Ciccotelli's face stared up at him from the front page. "Murphy, look at this."

Murphy lurched to his feet, his eyes hard and cold. "Who printed this shit?"

"Cyrus Bremin," Spinnelli bit out, his mustache quivering in bottled rage. "He says he has an anonymous source inside CPD. Find out who corroborated his story. I want him in my office, ASAP." The door to his office slammed, sending window blinds rattling.

Murphy still stared at the black-and-white page. "I'll talk to Bremin," he said, very quietly. "He'll identify his source fast enough."

"And get us in deeper with the press. You're always telling me to keep my head. This time, preach to your own choir, Murphy." Aidan studied the picture of Adams. "This must have been taken before I got to the scene, because I pushed the crowd across the street and told Forbes and DiBello to watch for cameras." He squinted at the photo credit. "It says Joanna Carmichael took the picture." He typed Carmichael's name into his computer. "Well, well. Look where Miss Carmichael calls home."

Murphy looked over his shoulder. "Cynthia Adams's building. She walked right into that story, lucky bitch."

"She gets a date with us, so maybe she's not so lucky."
Aidan printed the address just as Spinnelli's door opened.

"Conference room in thirty," Spinnelli barked. "Call Jack
Unger down in CSU and get him there, too. The SA wants
to talk."

Monday, March 13, 9:30 A.M.

Witnesses had been expected. Photographers had not.

Merry Christmas to me. Cynthia Adams lay right on the
front page, her heart on her sleeve, so to speak. But even better was the sight of the ever-popular Tess Ciccotelli, looking
worried and worn. A person couldn't buy that kind of publicity. All in all, a very good day so far.

Mr. Avery Winslow was progressing right according to
schedule as well. All afternoon he'd alternated between pacing his living room, rocking himself in the nursery and frantically calling his trusted psychiatrist.

He was much more mentally unstable than Cynthia
Adams had been. She'd been resistant. Very adept at denying
the very thing she feared the most. Frustrating business, it
had been. Seemed like every time Adams came close, she'd
pulled herself back, denying she'd heard a thing. Sometimes
even denying she'd had a sister at all. Her "medication" had
to be upped three times before she was sufficiently unhinged.
Ultimately the use of unnatural chemicals had been required.
PCP pushed her over.

The lilies had been a masterful touch, the picture of her
sister hanging from a noose, the icing on the cake, as it were.
The birthday cake. The calendar had been very cooperative
in the mental decomposition of Miss Cynthia Adams.

The calendar would be the key to turning Mr. Avery Winslow as well.

That and the nonstop crying of an infant. Masterful.

And, if pretty little Nicole was fulfilling her responsibilities, at this very moment poor Mr. Winslow was receiving one more candid photo that should push him over the edge.

Dragging his trusted Dr. Ciccotelli with him.

Monday, March 13, 9:45 A.M.

States Attorney Patrick Hurst tossed the newspaper to the table in disgust. "Dammit. This is bad, Marc. Really, really bad."

Jack Unger from CSU pulled the paper to his side of the table and studied it. "Who is Bremin's anonymous source?"

Murphy scowled. "We don't know. He wasn't there last night. The photographer was. The two uniforms first on the scene remember seeing Carmichael in the crowd, but deny having said a word to her."

"Anyone on shift yesterday could have seen Ciccotelli come in with us." Aidan shrugged uneasily, remembering how angry he'd been. One look at his own face would have given her away. "Her attorney signed in downstairs, so anybody looking at the log knew she was here. Lots of people would have seen them leave together. None of them will admit to talking to the press, Marc, but we all know that any of them would have been more than happy to do it."

Spinnelli folded the paper so that Ciccotelli's face no longer stared out at them. "True enough. But we'll investigate the leak along with everything else, just like we always do. So why are we really here, Patrick? Your visit seems a bit . . . premature."

The SA sighed. "I'm here because this has implications far beyond Tess Ciccotelli's innocence or guilt or even beyond finding whoever did this to that poor woman."

"Cynthia Adams," Aidan said softly, then lifted his brows when Patrick frowned at him. "That was the poor woman's name."

Compassion flickered in the SA's eyes. "I know that, too, Detective. But right now we haven't even ruled Miss Adams's death a homicide." He lifted his hand before Aidan could argue. "You'll investigate. You'll find who did this. I'm not telling you to stop. In fact I'm telling you to hurry. The big issue here is Dr. Ciccotelli's credibility on past cases. That you've brought her in for questioning is public knowledge now, thanks to Bremin and the *Bulletin*. Every defense attorney who's lost a case where Ciccotelli has testi-fied will be citing grounds for appeal. This could be devas-tating for my office. Do you know how many cases she's been involved in over the last five years?"

Yes, Aidan thought. Now he knew exactly how many. And Kristen had been absolutely right. Harold Green was an aberration. Tess Ciccotelli had done more than her share to put some very bad guys away. The knowledge left him sub-dued. "Forty-six," he murmured.

Spinnelli's mustache bunched over his pursed lips. "What?"

Aidan cleared his throat. "Dr. Ciccotelli's testified in forty-six cases. Yesterday I requested Records run the list. I picked it up on my way in here." He tossed the printout to the center of the table.

"How many convictions, Aidan?" Spinnelli asked.

"Thirty-one of the forty-six."

Murphy let his head fall back against his chair. "Oh, my God."

Patrick grabbed the printout, his face grim. "Thirty-one

possible appeals. Do you know how long that will tie up my staff?"

"I don't even want to think about it," Spinnelli said. "So let's clear Tess and let your staff focus on convicting all the new assholes. What do we have other than her prints in Adams's apartment?"

"Her voice on Adams's voice mail," Aidan answered.

"I sent the tape to the electronics department to have a voice print made," Jack said.

Patrick shook his head. "Not admissible."

"But we can exclude her if the prints are different," Jack argued. "Our guy is good, Pat. It's worth the time."

"Do it then," Patrick agreed.

"Then we'll need Dr. Ciccotelli to come in and give them a live voice sample for comparison." Aidan jotted it down. "She's being very cooperative, so I don't think she'll have a problem with that. What about the gun with the gift tag?"

"Wiped clean for prints. Serial number was sanded down, but I think I can raise it." Jack looked at Spinnelli. "I assume we're bumping the priority to high?"

"You assume right. What else?"

"We're tracking down the lilies," Murphy said. "So far we have three stores that made big lily sales on Saturday. We'll visit them this afternoon. First we want to visit Adams's office. Somebody hated that woman enough to want her dead. We know she had many sexual partners and that she probably gave a few of them a nasty little parting gift. Maybe one of those somebodies hated her enough to want her dead."

Aidan looked at the list of trials in which Ciccotelli had testified, remembering her sitting alone in Interview the day before. *Why use me?* she'd asked. Maybe they had it backward. "Or maybe Cynthia Adams was just the pawn. Maybe somebody really wanted an appeal."

Patrick's brows lifted in surprise. "Seems there are easier ways."

"Too many maybes," Spinnelli said. "Let's get some definites. What about the e-mails with the attachments? Have we traced them?"

"Request is in to Electronics. Again, I'll bump it up." Jack frowned and opened the paper again. "This picture was taken right after this woman landed. I mean *right* after. Thirty seconds maybe. One minute, tops."

Aidan leaned closer. "How do you know?"

"Look at the concrete next to her head. No pool of blood yet."

Aidan's pulse quickened. "Ciccotelli said she got an anonymous call saying Adams was about to jump at 12:06. The teenaged witnesses said Adams jumped at 12:05."

"Specific," Patrick commented, but his eyes had also grown bright.

"They were late for curfew. The girl said she had to be home by midnight and that she'd just looked at her watch, afraid she'd be in trouble with her parents." Aidan looked over at Murphy. "Ciccotelli said the call sounded like a cell phone."

Murphy narrowed his eyes. "The caller was there, watching her fall. Sonofabitch."

"Ciccotelli also said the caller was a woman claiming to be Adams's neighbor and—"

"Carmichael lives in Adams's building," Murphy finished. "Wouldn't be the first time a reporter made their own news." He shrugged. "It's worth putting on the list."

"Certainly worth seeing if she took any other pictures," Jack added. "If your perp was there, maybe Carmichael saw him. Or her."

Aidan sat back in his chair. "So our suspects right now are thirty-one potential prisoners seeking appeal, any number of sleazebag sex addicts with an STD, one young camera-happy reporter, and, unfortunately, still Tess Ciccotelli."

Patrick stood up. "Rule Tess out before you do anything else. I do not want to have to deal with appeals."

"Understood," Spinnelli said. "Gentlemen." He pointed to the door. "Go get me some definites. Today. I still want that 'anonymous source.' Get to work."

Murphy gave a salute. "We're off to check the flower shops. You in any present, past, or future hot water with your wife, Marc? We could pick you up some flowers. Small carrying charge. Wives like flowers."

Spinnelli's mouth tipped up. "I'm always in hot water with my wife. Unfortunately her tastes run more to big shiny rocks. Go."

Aidan gave Murphy a sideways look as they left the conference room. "You been married, Murphy?"

"Was. Not anymore. What's the first florist on your list?"

It was obvious the topic had been changed. "Josie's Posies. She sold some lilies on Saturday." Aidan studied the list of Ciccotelli's trials as he walked. "You drive. I want to look through these names. Some of these prisoners have been released." He glanced at his watch. "Before we hit Adams's brokerage house, let's stop by the Health Department and see if Adams and Tess Ciccotelli pissed off any of the same people."

Monday, March 13, 10:30 A.M.

A middle-aged woman, Miss Tuttle frowned up at them from a large wooden desk. "Any information we get from our clients is confidential, Detectives. You know this."

"We're investigating a murder, ma'am," Murphy returned

mildly. "One of your clients is dead. Her privacy is no longer at issue."

"But the privacy of her partners *is*. I can't help you."

Aidan pulled a picture from his notebook. "This is Cynthia Adams, ma'am. After she fell twenty-two stories."

Miss Tuttle looked at the picture, then looked away, her eyes clenched shut, the color drained from her thin face. "Go away, Detectives. I can't, nor will I, help you."

"Somebody made her fall, ma'am," Aidan said quietly and having made his point, put the picture away. "That somebody could have been one of her partners. Somebody with a grudge. Would you remember anyone who threatened Miss Adams when they were notified of possible infection?"

"Detective," she began, directly meeting his eyes. "If I revealed anything about our clients, nobody would come here. My job is to protect the public. Just your being here is making that difficult. If I told you what you want to know, my job would be impossible."

"We don't want to keep you from doing your job. Truly we don't." Aidan gave her what he hoped was his most persuasive look. He hadn't thought this would be easy. Tuttle actually was being more helpful than he had expected. "Her doctor's records list you as Miss Adams's contact. Can you tell us if you at least remember her?" He pulled another photo of Cynthia from his notebook, this one taken from her drivers license. "She looked like this. She would have come in about six weeks ago."

Tuttle bit her lip. "I remember her. Yes."

"Can you tell us if any of her partners expressed any kind of threat, any kind of anger when they were notified? No names, just tell us if we're going in the right direction."

"No names, Detective?"

Aidan shook his head. "No, ma'am."

She drew a breath. "One. He was livid. He threatened to make her pay."

Aidan took a step back. "Thank you, Miss Tuttle. We'll leave now."

Murphy waited until they were outside on the street before pulling a stick of cinnamon gum from his pocket. "You didn't get a list of names."

"Didn't expect one." Aidan slid into the passenger seat of Murphy's car and waited for his partner to take the wheel. "But now we know that it's worth the trouble of getting a subpoena, which is all I really expected."

Murphy pulled into traffic. "Then you did good, kid. Let's grab some lunch then head over to the brokerage house where Adams worked. Then Josie's Posies."

Chapter Six

❧

Monday, March 13, 3:15 P.M.

Amy closed the door to Tess's office. "It could have been worse, Tess."

Tess slumped in her chair. Her meeting with Dr. Fenwick, the head of the state licensing board, had not gone well. "It could have been better."

"They didn't pull any sanction shit. You still have a practice."

"Because I didn't do anything wrong, dammit," Tess snapped, then rubbed her forehead where a migraine brewed. "I'm sorry. Thanks for coming. It took the edge off, having you here." Tess suspected Dr. Fenwick would have done more than "disapprove" had her attorney not been present. But disapprove he had. The board, he'd declared, did not find accusations against their members acceptable. The board did not appreciate not having their calls returned while she finished her rounds. The board would be watching the investigation and her. When she was cleared by the authorities, she was to present an affidavit to the board stating same. "Fuck the board," she muttered.

"I don't think it will come down to that," Amy teased lightly. "I don't think most of them can anymore, not without a healthy dose of Viagra."

Tess shot her a scathing look. "Not funny. This is my career here."

Amy sat down on the arm of the sofa and crossed her arms over her chest, sobering. "So what are you going to do about this, Tess?"

"What do you mean?"

"I mean you can't let this accusation slide unchecked. It could ruin your career."

"Duh."

"Tess, I'm very serious."

Tess stood up and began packing her briefcase. "I'm going to work with the police to find out who really did this."

Amy leaned forward, her brows lifted, her expression sarcastic. "News bulletin, kid. The police think *you* did this."

Tess studied the contents of a folder, then tossed it in the briefcase with the others. "I don't think they do."

"Todd Murphy might not, but that Detective Reagan sure as hell does."

Tess thought about Reagan, about the way he'd asked his questions that morning. "No, I don't think he does either. Regardless, they won't be able to charge me because I haven't *done* anything."

Amy's laugh wasn't pretty. "Like that will stop them. Wake up and smell the damn coffee. I defend people every day that think they won't be charged because they haven't *done* anything. What makes you think you're different?"

Tess slammed the lid of her briefcase down, a cold shaft

of fear shooting her pulse like a rocket. "Because I'm *innocent*, that's what."

Hurt flashed through Amy's eyes. "I don't represent people I think are guilty, Tess."

Tess's shoulders sagged. "I'm sorry. I didn't mean to hurt your feelings." She laid her hand on Amy's arm, felt her friend tense. "I know your ethics are just as important to you as mine are to me."

Amy's nod was tight. "It's okay." But it wasn't. It was plain to see. Nevertheless, Amy squared her shoulders. "Look, I think you should attack this head on. Call the newspaper and give them your side. Make Bremin look foolish for jumping the gun."

Tess had considered a similar plan throughout the day. "All right. Do you have a contact at any of the papers? Somebody you trust to be fair?"

"Yeah, I do. Let me take care of making the arrangements. I'll let you know who and when." Amy pointed a warning finger. "Don't talk to anybody else except for the interview I set up. Promise me."

"All right." She looked at her clock with a frown. "I had a three o'clock session scheduled. Who was that with?" She bit her lip, then remembered. Mr. Winslow. Such a sad man. His story nearly broke her heart. "Amy, I have to see this patient. I'll call you at your office when I'm finished."

Amy was buttoning her coat when a soft knock sounded at the door. Denise stuck her head in. "Doctor, I've got about twenty messages for you. Mostly from reporters, a half dozen from patients." She frowned. "Three canceled their sessions for tomorrow."

Tess sighed and took the stack of messages Denise offered and scanned each one. "I suppose some attrition is to be expected."

"A Detective Reagan called twice. He asked you to call

him as soon as you were free. It's urgent. He left his cell number. Oh, and you have a call on line one. It's about Mr. Winslow. Somebody claiming to be Mr. Winslow's neighbor. She insisted on talking to you. Wouldn't leave a message."

Tess's head whipped up, the word "neighbor" sending her heart plunging to her gut. "What?"

"A neighbor of Mr. Wins—"

Tess leaped to the phone. "Shit. Oh, shit." Tess ran to the phone at her desk and picked up, her hands shaking. "Hello?"

"Dr. Ciccotelli?"

It wasn't the same woman. This woman sounded older than the woman who'd claimed to be Cynthia Adams's neighbor. *Dammit.* She waved Denise and Amy to silence. Took a deep breath and willed her voice to be steady. "This is Dr. Ciccotelli. What seems to be the problem?"

"I'm a neighbor of one of your patients, Avery Winslow. I'm worried about Avery. He's been in his apartment all day, crying. I knocked on his door to check on him but he told me to go away. He . . . he had a gun in his hand, Doctor."

Oh, God. "Did you call the police?"

"No, just you. Oh, dear, I suppose I should have called 911. I'll do that now."

"No. I'll do it. Thank you, Miss—?" The phone clicked in her ear. "Shit." Hands shaking, she sorted the messages until she found Reagan's. "Shit. Goddammit. Denise, call 911. Have the police go to Mr. Winslow's apartment. Tell them he's suicidal. Then get me his address. I'll call you to get it when I get down to my car. *Move, Denise.*" White-faced, Denise disappeared to do as she was told. "Dammit, where's my cell phone?"

Amy reached into Tess's jacket pocket. "Right here. Calm down, Tess."

"I can't calm down." A terrified sob rose in her throat and she pushed it back as she dialed Reagan's number. She'd grabbed her coat and was out the office door when he answered.

"Reagan."

"Detective Reagan, this is Tess Ciccotelli."

"Dr. Ciccotelli, I've been trying to reach you all afternoon." His voice sounded tense, angry once again. "We—"

"Whatever it is, it needs to wait." She bypassed the elevator and took the stairs at a run, barely aware of Amy following close behind. "I need your help. I got another call."

"Who?"

"Avery Winslow. My secretary is calling 911 now. Call her if you need Winslow's address. I'm on my way. Please meet me there."

"We will."

"Hurry, Detective." She snapped her phone closed and burst into the parking garage. "My car's over there."

"We're taking mine." Amy grabbed her arm and steered her the opposite direction. "You're in no condition to drive." They reached Amy's Lexus in a minute that seemed like a year. Tess was trembling as Amy pulled out of the garage and into traffic.

She jumped when Amy's hand closed over hers. "Breathe, Tess. Just breathe. I'll get you there as fast as I can."

Monday, March 13, 3:45 P.M.

"Does it have a gift tag?" Murphy asked.

Aidan stood up, holding Mr. Avery Winslow's Colt .45 between two gloved fingers.

Mr. Winslow wouldn't be needing it anymore.

"No gift tag." Just brains and fragments of skull all over the man's living room. The wall behind his computer desk bore the most debris, but Winslow's computer monitor was covered, the keyboard red and gray and sticky. The monitor was knocked askew. Behind the blood and tissue matter the screen brightened and darkened as a series of pictures scrolled.

Murphy got close enough to the screen to study the slide show through the mess. "Baby pictures. A little boy."

A chair with wheels lay on its side, next to Winslow's body. "He was sitting in his computer chair with his back to the screen," Aidan said.

Murphy grunted. "The force of the shot must have thrown him into the monitor."

Aidan crouched down beside the body. "He's holding a bear." For some reason it made his throat tighten. Swallowing it back, he looked up at Murphy. "A stuffed teddy bear with a gold gift tag. Same kind as before. 'Happy Birthday, Avery, Jr.'"

Murphy grimaced philosophically. "But no flowers," he observed.

"Obviously not his trigger."

"Here's the box the bear came in." Murphy picked it up from the coffee table, along with a notepad. "He was meeting Tess today at three."

"Looks like he got distracted," Jack Unger said from the doorway. "Spinnelli wanted me here, just in case." He took in the scene with a critical eye. "I'll get my team over here and we'll get started."

Aidan pointed him back to the bathroom. "See if he has any medication. Tag and bag everything, even the aspirin."

Jack tossed a look of mild impatience over his shoulder. "Don't worry, Aidan. We'll go over this place with a pair of tweezers."

Murphy moved beside the computer desk, nudging the mouse with one gloved finger. "The computer is stuck on this slide show. Moving the mouse doesn't stop it."

"Could be mucked up with brain mush."

"You don't think so, do you?"

Aidan shook his head. "No. Let's have the hard drive hauled in, too. You want the bedroom or the kitchen?"

"I'll take the bedroom."

Leaving Aidan to search the kitchen. It was dirty, stacks of dishes in the sink. He touched the oven. It was hot, the dial turned to its highest setting. But he wasn't prepared for the sight that greeted him when he pulled the door down. Gagging, he took a giant step back as full comprehension sank in. "Murphy! Come and see this."

Murphy wasted no time, hurrying to look over his shoulder. "What the hell?"

"It's not real," Aidan said grimly. He pulled out his handkerchief and tugged on the oven rack until the roasting pan was clear of the oven. "Just a doll, but it looks damn real." The doll's fingers, toes, and nose were melted and the stench of burning hair burned his nose and eyes. "Real hair and everything."

"Close it up," Jack ordered behind them and the Aidan quickly obeyed. "We may be able to figure out how long it's been in there based on the inside temperature." Jack flipped the oven light on and peered through the glass. "That's . . ." He shook his head. "Inhuman. What's this guy's story, anyway?"

"Tess can tell us," Murphy said, opening a drawer. "Aidan, look."

Aidan looked down at the revolver that lay on top of a pile of oven mitts with disgust. "They were hoping he'd find the doll, get unhinged, then find this."

A voice came from the living room. "Detectives?" Aidan stepped back into the living room where the ME tech stood frowning over Winslow's body. "I'm Johnson from Vander-Beck's office. Julia said this guy gets the royal treatment. What am I looking for?"

"Time of death for starters," Aidan said. "Tox screen, for sure."

Johnson crouched next to the body. "He's still warm. Blood hasn't started coagulating. I'd say he pulled the trigger an hour ago, tops. What's with the bear? Oh, man, look at this," he continued, not waiting for an answer. He looked up, stunned surprise on his face. "My mother always used to say we drove her to pull her hair out, but I never saw anybody who really did."

Aidan bent over for a closer look. In his left hand Winslow clutched a handful of dark brown hair, threaded with silver. The same hair that straggled from a hunk of scalp still loosely hanging from the back of his head.

Johnson gently removed the bear from Winslow's hand and held it up for inspection, rotating it slowly. "His hair's on the bear, too. He must have pulled it out with both hands before grabbing the bear."

"What did they do to you, Winslow?" Aidan murmured.

"Sorry, Detective, I need a little space here. Can you back up?"

Aidan carefully stepped aside, his focus on the ME's movements until a strangled cry jerked his gaze to the open door.

Where Tess Ciccotelli stood, coatless, her hair and suit jacket soaking wet. Her face utterly bloodless. One hand covered her mouth and her dark eyes were wide with horror. She took a single stumbling step into the living room and stopped.

"Oh, no," she whispered. "Oh, Avery."

A uniform stationed in the hallway grabbed her arm. "Sorry, Detective. She got by me." He pulled her, but she struggled, her eyes never leaving Avery Winslow's body. The cop yanked again, harder this time. "Come on, *Doctor*." The term was not respectful and, together with the sight of the man's hands on her, set Aidan's temper to boiling.

"Take your hands off her, Officer." Despite his efforts to keep his voice calm, it still came out as a growl.

The cop blinked, genuinely surprised. "This is Tess Ciccotelli, Detective. She—"

"We know who she is," Aidan said acidly. "Let her go."

His face darkening, the officer complied, stepping back with a look of complete contempt at Ciccotelli, which she never even noticed. Murphy peeled off one glove, took her by the shoulder and tugged. "Come on, Tess," he murmured. "There isn't anything you can do now. Let me call somebody to take you home."

She shrugged free of Murphy's grasp. "He lost his son," she said as if none of them had spoken. "His baby." She lifted her eyes to Aidan's and in that moment any vestiges of doubt as to her innocence were . . . simply erased. There was anguish in her eyes. And truth.

"How did he lose his son?" Aidan asked quietly. And watched her throat work beneath the colorful silk scarf she wore. He'd been very wrong. He could see that now.

"It was last summer," she murmured. "It was so hot, remember? He was running out the door to go to work that morning when his wife reminded him that it was his turn to drop their son off at day care." Her eyes dropped back down to Winslow's body, pursing her lips when they trembled.

From the corner of his eye he saw Johnson's hands still and Jack watching from the kitchen archway. Ciccotelli just went on, oblivious to all of them, her voice taking on an ethereal quality that raised the hair on the back of his neck.

"He didn't want to. He was busy. And running late. His mind was filled with appointments, but he did what his wife asked because they shared the baby duties equally and . . ." Her throat worked again. "And because he loved his son. He strapped the baby into his car seat and settled in for the drive. Traffic was bad and he became even later. He flipped on a CD to calm down. Finally he got to work and ran inside. He had clients waiting. Somewhere along the way he'd forgotten about his son. Until a few hours later when he heard a disturbance outside. There was a police car in the parking lot, and an ambulance. One of the officers was breaking a car window."

She closed her eyes. "It was his minivan, Mr. Winslow's, the baby still inside. They said the temperature inside the van had reached a hundred and ten. His baby's brain . . . was . . ." She trailed off shaking her head, unable to continue. Not needing to. The picture she'd painted was vividly clear. Aidan could only imagine the scene, the frantic helplessness of a father, standing there, knowing he'd done such a terrible thing. The image of that father discovering a doll baking in the oven became even more horrific.

"They tried to revive the baby while Avery stood there and watched but it was too late," she finished heavily. "His son had been dead for at least two hours."

Aidan drew a breath. This was not the time to think about all his nieces and nephews, about how busy his own brothers so often were. How such a tragic mistake could happen to even good parents. But he did anyway. And because he did, he cleared his throat roughly. "When did he come to you?"

"After he tried to commit suicide the first time. His wife had left him by then. He . . . hated himself. And everyone he knew blamed him." She opened her eyes, met his gaze. "It was an accident, Detective. Just a horrible accident."

Johnson had quietly begun to work again. "Detectives, there's something underneath him," he said, pulling a flat box the size of a small plate from beneath Winslow's body.

Murphy took the box and lifted the lid. He looked up with a puzzled frown as he tilted the box so they could see the contents. "It's a CD. The soundtrack to *Phantom of the Opera*. Why?"

She'd flinched as if she'd been shocked with forty volts. Her fingertips pressed her lips as she stared at the CD in the box. "It was the music he listened to that day. He'd been caught up, he said, singing 'Music of the Night.'" Again she swallowed hard. "After that day, it was all he could hear. That and his baby crying. He couldn't sleep, couldn't function. He lost his job, his wife. His guilt drove him to the edge."

"Well, somebody just pushed him over," Aidan said and she nodded woodenly.

"Yes. They did."

Murphy replaced the box's lid and gave it to Jack. "Bag it. Please."

"Detectives." Johnson rolled the body onto its side, exposing a color photo, eight-and-a-half-by-eleven and glossy. And more horrible than Melanie hanging from a noose. Aidan's stomach turned over, wanting to avert his eyes, somehow unable to. A baby wearing a blue playsuit sat in a rear-facing car seat, his face red and bloated, his features barely recognizable.

Her movements stiff, Tess Ciccotelli walked from the doorway to Aidan's side and looked down. "That's his son." Her voice was harsh, trembling now with rage. "That's how the police found him that morning." Her eyes slid closed and her lips twisted bitterly. "You want to know the ironic thing? Whoever sent this didn't need to. Avery Winslow saw this picture every damn time he closed his eyes."

No one said a word for a few beats. Then Murphy blew out a breath. "There's an envelope here on the desk, same size as the picture." With a grimace he grasped the one corner not covered by blood and brain. Then hissed out the return address. " 'Dr. T. Ciccotelli, MD.' It's embossed, Tess. It's one of yours."

Her mouth dropped open, her body frozen. Her horrified gaze flicked from the envelope to the picture to Avery Winslow's body, where she stared, a storm raging in her eyes. "I'm sorry. I need to go." She spun on her heel and ran for the door.

Murphy started after her, but Aidan shook his head, pulling off his gloves. "I'll go." She was headed for the stairwell door. "Dr. Ciccotelli, wait." She kept going, her face resolutely turned away. He followed her through the door, seeing the top of her head halfway down the first flight. "Doctor, stop." She hesitated for the briefest of moments, then charged faster, grabbing onto the handrail for balance as she careened around a corner to the next flight down.

Tess ran, the stairs a blur under her feet. Reagan was still coming, his footsteps echoing behind her, getting louder. But she couldn't stop, couldn't breathe. She needed a minute. Just a minute to get her breath, her composure.

That picture . . . dear God. Who would do this? Who could be so cruel? That picture . . . that hideous obscenity had come in her envelope. *With my name embossed into the corner.* Avery had opened the envelope because he trusted her. Her throat closed. What he must have thought . . . felt. *The pain of seeing his son like that . . . and thinking it came from me.* Then putting his gun in his mouth and pulling the trigger.

He was dead. Avery was dead. But as bad as that was, the bigger reality was far worse. Even an hour ago she'd been able to tell herself that she wasn't to blame, that she'd been merely a tool used by someone who wanted Cynthia Adams dead.

Now she knew that wasn't true. Now she knew that Cynthia and Avery had been the tools. The real target . . . *Is me.* Two innocent people were dead. *Because of me.*

She dragged in a sobbing breath and abruptly stopped, hanging on to the handrail while her heart pounded in her ears and her knees gave way. She lowered herself to sit on a step, each breath she drew harder than the last.

The sound of Reagan's footsteps slowed, then ceased. He was right behind her. Now the only sound in the stairwell was that of her own ragged breathing.

"Tess," he said. Nothing more. Just that.

But the one syllable of her name seemed to hover between them, pulsing with a life of its own. She fixed her eyes on the wall in front of her. "I won't leave town," she said and rose to her feet. "You have my word. I'll cooperate in any way I can." Woodenly she began walking again and she'd made it down another half flight before he passed her on the left. He stopped on the landing, blocking her path with his big body. Tess stopped on the last step, her knees shaking.

He can't arrest you, she told herself. *You haven't done anything.*

But she knew he could if he chose and there wouldn't be a damn thing she could do about it. "I'm sorry, Detective." Her voice shook and she cursed her own weak fear. This should be about Avery and Cynthia, but she was enough of a pragmatist to admit it was not. It was all about her. "You've been trying to reach me all afternoon. What have you found?"

He was standing so close she could feel his sigh against her cheek. He was strong and solid, his eyes sharp and fierce, yet she'd seen the compassion there. For Cynthia. For Avery. And for just a moment she let herself wonder what would it be like to be the recipient of his protection instead of his accusation. The moment was short-lived.

"We found three florists who'd sold lilies to a young woman on Saturday," he said grimly. "She paid them all with a credit card."

Tess didn't have to ask. She already knew. Gathering her courage, she lifted her eyes to his. They were serious, but not accusing. "Mine," she said flatly.

He nodded once. "Yes."

She pressed her lips together. "I didn't do this, Detective. Any of this." She looked away. "I don't expect you to believe me."

"I didn't expect to believe you, either."

Stunned, she jerked her eyes back to his unsmiling face as her pulse spiked once again. "You do believe me?"

His brows knit, as if his path to this point was a complete mystery. "Yes."

"Then . . ." She was almost afraid to say the words aloud. "Then you're not going to arrest me?"

"No." He grabbed the end of the handrail and took a step back on the landing, his intense eyes troubled. "But I need to understand why *you*."

"I don't know. I thought I was just a tool. A pawn. But I'm not."

"I thought you might be the target this morning. I wasn't sure until now."

She tilted her head. "Why this morning? What changed?"

He looked away for a few seconds. When he looked back his eyes were subdued. "Yesterday afternoon I requested a list of the cases in which you'd testified for the prosecution. There were a lot of them, a lot of people who could gain from setting you up. I owe you an apology, Dr. Ciccotelli. I was wrong."

His use of her title served to reerect the wall between them. Still, formality beat accusation any damn day of the week. "Thank you."

"We have to decide where to go from here." He checked his watch. "I've been gone too long. I have to get back upstairs and finish processing the scene. Come on, I'll walk you up and you can go back down the elevator."

Tess shook her head, her stomach clenching at the thought. "That's all right. I'll take the stairs."

His look said he thought she was crazy. "It's nine floors."

Nine floors or nineteen, it didn't matter. Tess only took elevators when it was completely unavoidable. That usually required a destination twenty floors or above. In her current state, she didn't even want to think about being trapped in an eight by ten box, even for only nine floors. "I ran down a flight and a half, so it's only seven and a half floors now. Go on up and finish your job, Detective. It's the least we can do for Avery Winslow now. I'll be fine. Call me when you're ready to sit down and talk. I'll go back through my notes on my court evaluations. Maybe it will help shake loose one of the names on your list." She looked down, then back up to meet his eyes. "Thank you, Detective, for believing me."

He nodded once and walked up two steps, while she walked down two. Something prickled at the back of her neck and she looked up, only to find he'd stopped and was looking down. His mouth was a grim line, his blue eyes bright and focused on her face, which heated under his scrutiny. It wasn't the same accusing look as before, but this new expression was every bit as intense. Her pulse scrambled.

"You're welcome, Doctor," he finally said, very soberly. Then he took the stairs two at a time and less than a minute later a door above her head opened and closed, the sound echoing through the stairwell.

Tess exhaled a huge lungful of air, feeling lightheaded. Detective Aidan Reagan was a potent man. Her skin tingled with the aftereffects of that long look that she refused to even try to categorize. *Just be grateful he isn't arresting you, Tess,* she told herself. She started down the stairs, relieved and guilty at the same time. She wasn't going to be arrested.

But two people were still dead. That she could not change.

Still weak-kneed and lightheaded she managed the remaining seven and a half flights, exiting the first-floor stairwell just as Amy stepped off the elevator, Tess's tan coat over her arm. Her friend's eyes immediately narrowed. "What happened up there? I finally found a parking place and went up to find you, but they wouldn't let me off the elevator. There was a snotty cop standing guard that said Detective Reagan chased you down the stairs. I thought I'd have to meet you downtown again."

"It wasn't like that. Avery Winslow is dead."

"I figured that much," Amy said. "Cops and CSU everywhere."

"There was another picture." The thought of which sent her stomach pitching. "The picture came in an envelope from my office, Amy."

Amy's brows snapped together. "Well, that's not good, but anybody could steal an envelope. It's not the end of the world."

"It is for Avery Winslow."

"You didn't cause that, nor can you change it. Take your coat. I'll take you home."

Tess took it with a small smile of gratitude. She'd bolted from Amy's car half a block away when traffic had snarled to a halt, leaving her coat in the backseat. "Thanks. The only good thing is that Reagan knows I didn't do it."

"He does, does he? And the grand detective told you this?"

Tess shifted on her feet, uncomfortable at her mocking tone. "Yeah, he did."

Amy's laugh was just shy of a sneer. "And you believed him?"

Tess nodded. "Yeah, I did."

"Hell, Tess, don't be an idiot."

Tess straightened her spine, affronted. "I'm not."

Amy pushed through the door to the street. "If you believe anything any cop tells you, you're an idiot. My car's parked two blocks away." She studied Tess's face critically. "You're pale. Do you want to wait here while I get the car?"

Tess shook her head, still stinging from the insult. "The walk will be good for me."

Amy shrugged and started walking. "Whatever. Look, I'm sorry I called you an idiot, but you're scaring me here. The police want you to trust them. It's part of the scam. Reagan's got incredible blue eyes that I'm sure beamed total sincerity, but bottom line is that he's a cop. Cops lie to get you to confess." She shot her a sharp look. "You talked to him in the stairwell, didn't you?"

Tess kept her eyes forward. "Only to say I didn't do it."

"And he asked you to get together later to talk."

She lifted her chin, unsteady under Amy's verbal assault. "Actually, I offered."

Amy's scornful laugh grated. "How much did I say I was going to charge you? I'm going to have to double it."

Tess gritted her teeth and said nothing.

Amy huffed impatiently. "Now you're mad at me because *I'm* the only one telling you the truth. Tess, do not trust the police. Reagan's going to bat those long eyelashes and flash that movie-star smile to get you to tell him everything. And honey, anything you say, can and *will* be used against you. Don't make me work so damned hard. Keep your mouth shut and everything will be fine. Do not talk to any detectives without your attorney being present. Last I checked, that was me. Do I have your word?"

Tess shoved her cold hands in her pockets, not certain which irked her more—Amy's ultimatum or her rather disparaging view of Tess's ability to judge character. *It's not like I'm a psychiatrist or anything,* she thought sardonically. Working with the police was not a mistake. It very well might be her only hope of ending this before anyone else died. "And if I say no, Counselor?"

Amy stopped in the middle of the sidewalk, forcing Tess to do the same. Her friend was totally serious, her eyes sharp as razors, her cheeks red with ire. "Then you'll need to hire yourself another attorney, *Doctor,* because I won't represent you." Then she started walking again, leaving Tess standing on the sidewalk staring at Amy's back with her mouth gaping open. As Amy disappeared into the crowd, Tess realized it was the second time in an hour someone had called her "Doctor" in that nasty tone.

The first had been the cop outside Avery Winslow's front door whose grip on her arm had probably left a bruise. But Aidan Reagan had confronted him. Told the cop to take his hands off, and he hadn't said it nicely, either. Reagan had stood up for her. But, she told herself, it was in his nature to do so. It appeared to be the way he was wired.

It was sobering, as were her current options for getting home. Amy was long gone and Tess couldn't catch up even if she went running after her, which she wasn't about to do. But she'd left her office without her briefcase or her purse. Her pocket held a dollar fifty in change, some lint, and her cell phone. *If I were home, I could call Vito and he'd come without blinking.*

The thought was just unexpected enough to make her blink. And clench her teeth. Home was Chicago now, not South Philly. And her brother Vito was hundreds of miles away. *I miss him.* She could admit it to herself. *I miss them all.* She knew Vito would come if she called. But it would cause her brother trouble with their father and she didn't want that.

Now if she'd actually been arrested . . . *Yeah, I would have called Vito then.* But she hadn't been, so it was moot.

Jon would be in surgery right now and Denise would be gone. She glanced up the height of Avery's building. They were still up there, Murphy and Reagan.

As was what was left of Avery Winslow. She closed her eyes against the memory, opened them quickly at the pictures that flashed against her eyelids. Avery lying there, his head blown half off. Cynthia, her body ripped wide open. And the sound of her own voice goading Cynthia to her death. The images would haunt her forever.

She couldn't go back up there, couldn't face it again.

And as much as it galled, Amy's warning was rolling around in her mind. Reagan was a good man, a good cop. Murphy had said so. And yet Murphy had allowed her to be brought in and grilled. Logically she knew he'd been doing his job. But it still hurt. And it illustrated just how quickly a cop's trust was set aside.

She'd help Reagan and Murphy. But carefully. For now, she needed a place to sit down and get out of the cold. She glanced around, got her bearings. She was only a few blocks from the Lemon, a place she knew she'd be welcome without a dime.

Monday, March 13, 4:45 P.M.

Joanna side-stepped a lady walking a lumbering basset hound, murmuring apology as she hurried. Tess Ciccotelli, like everyone else on the street, had her head down against the wind and rain. Made for smooth tailing. She'd been following the woman all afternoon and now knew another of Ciccotelli's clients was dead. That would be another front-page story.

With Cy Bremin's byline. *Over my dead body.* No pun intended.

Her eyes narrowed, still focused on her subject who had turned a corner and was now heading west. She needed exclusivity to guarantee that bastard Schmidt wouldn't throw her story to Bremin.

She needed unencumbered access to Tess Ciccotelli. It looked like she'd be able to get her wish. In a move that still had Joanna scratching her head, Ciccotelli had all but fired her defense attorney. Right out there on the street. Because the shrink actually wanted to cooperate with the cops.

Personally, Joanna agreed with the lawyer. Ciccotelli was an idiot. Or, and it *was* a consideration, maybe she really hadn't done anything wrong and this was one really elaborate setup. Frankly, it mattered little which one was true, as long as the byline said "Joanna Carmichael."

Chapter Seven

Monday, March 13, 4:45 P.M.

Aidan got back just as ME tech Johnson zipped Winslow's body bag. He stepped out of the way of the gurney and walked over to Murphy's side. "She's all right," Aidan said, his voice low. "I told her about the credit cards. I didn't have to tell her they were hers. She already knew."

"Spinnelli called me while you were with her." Murphy showed him his notepad, on which he'd scrawled the address for a mailbox store on the other side of town. "He traced the billing address of the credit card to this place. They're open till six."

Aidan glanced at his watch. "We'll just make it."

"Spinnelli also said he'd heard from Patrick. He's gotten notice from five different lawyers who are filing appeals."

"Shit."

"Just hit the fan," Murphy finished. "Where's Tess?"

"Said she was heading home to start going through her old court evaluations. I told her we'd call her later tonight."

"Murphy!" Jack emerged from the hallway that led to the bedrooms, motioning them to come. "You, too, Aidan. Come on. You'll want to see this."

They followed Jack back to what had been the Winslow baby's nursery. The crib still stood in the corner, the changing table still stocked with disposable diapers and baby powder. A thick layer of dust covered everything. One of Jack's men stood on a step stool, his face in an open air vent, the vent cover propped up against the wall.

"This is Rick Simms. Show them what you found, Rick."

Rick turned around, his thumb and forefinger gripping a small black box, an inch wide and half an inch thick.

Aidan stepped up on the corner of the stool to get a better view. An inch-long cable protruded from one end of the box and he suddenly knew exactly what Rick Simms had found. He looked back at Murphy, both stunned and angered, surprised he could still feel either after all he'd seen this afternoon. "It's a camera."

"Good eye," Rick said. "Wireless camera, high res." He twisted the box slightly. "And capable of transmitting sound. Here's the mike."

"Sonofabitch likes to watch," Murphy muttered. "How did you know it was there?"

"Rick saw that there was no dust on the corner of this one vent cover," Jack said, a twinge of pride in his voice. "Nice job."

Rick's smile flashed. "Thanks."

"How many more of these cameras are there?" Aidan asked, stepping off the stool.

"We wondered the same thing." Jack led them back into the living room. "They wouldn't want to miss the grand finale," he said and pointed to the vent cover over the desk, now empty as the computer had been taken back to the lab. "Try that one."

Rick grimaced as he strained to reach the vent cover, which was spattered with blood and brain matter. "Man, this is nasty, Jack."

Jack chuckle was dry. "Do you good to get your hands dirty for a change. Rick is one of the unit's electronics experts," he told Aidan. "Normally he's in the lab, but I called all hands."

Rick handed the vent cover to Jack who carefully set it aside. "You were right," Rick said. "Another camera with a mike and . . ." He shone his flashlight into the dark opening, then turned around, perturbed. "And a speaker mounted to the inside of the wall." He pulled it loose so they could see it—a small box the size of a plum. "Why a speaker?"

"A neighbor came by while you were with Tess, Aidan," Murphy said. "She said she heard a baby crying all day. I thought he might be watching a video. Now we know."

Rick frowned at the speaker in his hand. "We've got ourselves one sick bastard."

"Where does the video feed go?" Aidan asked.

"I'll have to find the receiver," Rick said, "but my first guess? It goes to the Ethernet. And then . . ." He waved his hand. "Out there."

Murphy blinked. "Ethernet?"

"It's a way to get to the Internet," Aidan murmured, his mind racing, the implications too overwhelming.

Rick nodded. "Streaming video. It's all the rage, man. Normally I see the cameras pointing straight up through the floor or on their shoes so that pervs can look up women's dresses. This one was meant for surveillance."

Murphy was shaking his head. "So this is on the *Internet*?" he repeated. "Like on a Web site or something? You're telling us anybody could have been watching Winslow blow his brains out?"

"Maybe." Rick lifted one shoulder. "Depends on what

your perp is looking to do. If this is a private show, it's not going to show up on your standard Google search." He lifted his brows. "But if it's not private . . ."

Aidan's stomach gave a sick twist as Rick's meaning hit home. "Oh my God. Like pay-per-view?" He looked at Murphy, saw he'd arrived at the same conclusion.

"Twenty-first century snuff movies." A muscle in Murphy's taut jaw twitched. "This is unbelievable."

"Any idea how long these have been there?" Aidan asked.

Jack crouched down to inspect the vent cover. "There's dust on the vents themselves, but hardly any around the screws. Maybe a week or two?"

"So we need to find out who's had access to this apartment in the last two weeks," Murphy said. "What kind of person are we looking for? Would they need special tools?"

Rick stepped down. "Honestly, any teenage hacker could do the job."

Aidan blew a weary sigh up his forehead. "Jack, we need to check Cynthia Adams's apartment for the same devices."

Jack looked up at Rick. "Can you do it tonight?"

Rick nodded. "To catch this guy? Oh, yeah."

"We've got to follow a lead on the flowers from Adams's place," Murphy said. "Can you finish up here, Jack?"

Jack dismissed them with a flick of his hand. "Go. Let's meet in Spinnelli's office at eight. Tell Spinnelli to order Chinese. It's going to be a long night."

Monday, March 13, 8:30 P.M.

She was still here. Sitting at her dining room table in a red silk robe and white sweat socks, half a glass of red wine at her elbow, browsing through files.

She was still here. Not where she should be—cowering in a holding cell surrounded by unwashed vermin, waiting for one of her so-called friends to post bail, or standing before a judge.

.But patience was a virtue. And Ciccotelli's face was showing evidence of strain. Her hand trembled when she picked up the wineglass and occasionally a look of sheer horror would turn her skin pale and her eyes glassy. She was remembering the way the bodies looked. She was thinking about how they'd felt just before they died, thinking she'd betrayed them. She was wondering who'd be next.

That would have to be enough for now.

As for the police, they'd be lucky to find their asses with both hands. Eventually they'd go through the victims' financial records and find the nails that would secure Ciccotelli's pretty little coffin. Until then, there was the angle of the state licensing board. They'd stepped in earlier than expected, thanks to Cy Bremin and his front-page spread. How entertaining it had been.

Well worth a replay. A mouse click on the sound file brought the scratchy voice of Dr. Fenwick to life. *The board finds such allegations both serious and unacceptable.*

No. *Really?* Not both serious *and* unacceptable. It was one of the more asinine comments the microphone had recorded in the weeks since it had been hidden behind a filing cabinet in Ciccotelli's office. The board had nothing on Ciccotelli and everyone in the room had known it. Fenwick, Ciccotelli, and her attorney, who'd dispensed with old fart's threats handily.

But the visit itself left a foundation on which to build. The imperious Dr. Fenwick would likely find the death of Mr. Avery Winslow even more serious and less acceptable. Strike two, as it were. The third pitch would be aimed at the licensing board, not the police. It wasn't the ultimate payoff, but might relieve the boredom while the police bumbled around.

And it would, above all, be so much fun to watch.

Monday, March 13, 8:30 P.M.

"Well?" Spinnelli sat at the head of the table, frowning as they ate. Around the table were Aidan, Murphy, Jack, Rick, and Patrick, who had glumly informed them the number of appeal notices was now up to eight.

"Give us a minute to eat, Marc," Jack protested. "I haven't eaten since lunch."

"We didn't eat lunch," Aidan muttered. They'd been too busy with the florist shops. "But we can show you some video while we eat." He stood up and grabbed the disc they'd taken from the mailbox store's security camera, then grabbed his carton of General Tso's when Murphy cast a greedy eye at his food. "We didn't have to go back too far." He inserted the disc, hit PLAY, then stepped back so the group could see the TV screen. "This was last Thursday afternoon." A woman walked into the picture, wearing a tan coat. Her black hair fell in waves around her shoulders. She was roughly the same height as Tess Ciccotelli but the bulk of her coat disguised her build.

The woman appeared to be Latina. And her face, while slightly thinner than Ciccotelli's, was similar enough that she could pass for Italian in the memory of a harried desk clerk or the poor quality store video.

"Tess wears that same color coat," Murphy said. "This part really steamed me," he added. "Watch her unbutton her coat, just enough to show off the scarf around her neck. She wanted to be sure the clerk saw the scarf because Tess always wears one."

Unless she's wearing a black turtleneck that fits her like a second skin, Aidan thought, then shoved that mental picture as far away as he could.

Spinnelli's jaw tightened. "Because of her scar from that attack last year."

Now the mental picture Aidan shoved away was his own hands around the throat of the con who'd nearly killed her.

"Damn," Patrick murmured, staring at the screen. "She looks like her."

"No way in hell she looks like Tess," Murphy shot back. "What, are you blind?"

Patrick shook his head. "No, I'm not, but a judge might see enough resemblance to let those appeals go through. Especially with all the other physical evidence that's piling up. Without motive, there's not nearly enough to charge her," he added, "but plenty enough to muddy the waters. Shit. This is not good."

Aidan was watching the woman walk to her box, lean over, and insert the key. "Nobody in their right mind would think that was her. This woman doesn't move anything like Tess Ciccotelli."

"I can't quite see myself using that argument in front of a judge, Aidan," Patrick said, wry humor in his voice. "Although I will give you that few women move quite like Tess."

Aidan looked over his shoulder to where Patrick sat, wearing as close to a smile as he'd ever seen. Murphy had developed a sudden interest in the bottom of his carton of twice-cooked pork. Jack was openly grinning and Rick looked like he wanted to. Feeling his cheeks heat, Aidan rolled his eyes. "I meant she . . . Never mind."

Spinnelli's mustache twitched. "We *all* know what you meant, Aidan." He cleared his throat, sobering. "But regardless of the fluidity of this woman's movement, Patrick's right. We still have to prove she's not Tess. Can we get any prints off that mailbox?"

"I'll send a team over there, Marc," Jack said. "But it looks like she kept her gloves on the whole time."

The woman in the video shoved the mail from the box into the side pocket of the briefcase she carried. "So could this be our mastermind?" Patrick mused.

"I don't know," Aidan said. "She looks awfully . . . nervous to me. Twitchy."

Patrick shrugged. "I might be twitchy if I was planning to kill two people. But it doesn't feel right to me, either. She's too out in the open. She knows she's being taped and she's posing. We need to find out who she is."

Murphy crossed his arms over his chest, his brows crunched. "She was on the tape from the lobby of Adams's building, too. The building super disengaged the camera at the elevator on Adams's floor, but not the one at the first-floor elevator. We'll find out if anyone saw her in Winslow's apartment."

Spinnelli steepled his fingers under his chin. "What about the cameras you found in the apartments themselves?"

Rick pushed the remnants of his dinner aside. "I found the same camera system in Adams's apartment. One above her bed, one in her living room. One in her bathroom, too," he added, puzzled.

"She slit her wrists the first time she attempted suicide," Aidan said, taking the mailbox store security disc out of the machine. He sat down next to Rick. "People usually do that in the bathtub. Maybe our guy thought she'd try that again."

"Maybe. At any rate, I found similar setups in both apartments. Wireless cameras and speakers. Everything was wiped clean and whoever installed them didn't leave any prints behind on the vent covers, either. And before you ask, it would be nearly impossible to trace the parts themselves to point of purchase. They're generic surveillance systems. Good quality. You can buy them in any electronics store or off the Internet, and they're leaping off the shelves. It's a needle in a haystack."

"What about the transmissions?" Aidan asked. "Can we trace them?"

"As long as the feed stays live we can try. The feed at Adams's apartment isn't live anymore, but the cameras in Winslow's apartment are still transmitting. I found the router that the wireless camera is feeding into. I can put a packet sniffer onto the network and read the IP address it's going to."

Patrick blinked. "English, Rick."

Rick chuckled. "Sorry. Internet transmissions get broken into packets, sent to wherever they're going, and get reassembled on the other end. Packet sniffers break each packet into its component parts. One of those parts is the IP address—where it's headed. I can read IP addresses on my screen as the messages pass across the network. There are two big problems, though. The first one is you guys," he said to Patrick. "It's like wiretapping a phone. I'll need a warrant to even get started."

"I figured you would." Patrick drummed his fingers on the table. "What else?"

"This is the bigger problem. Once I find the IP address, there's no guarantee that it's real. Any hacker worth his salt isn't going to send this video to himself. He's going to send it to a zombie computer somewhere. If he's smart, he'll have the first zombie send it to a second." He shrugged. "By the time I find the final IP address, I still have to connect it to a person and ISP providers don't cooperate. It'll mean another warrant."

"Sniffers and zombies," Spinnelli muttered. "How long's this going to take, Rick?"

"A few days, maybe. But you need to know that some of these ISP's are run through foreign holding companies. The smart ones are."

"This looks pretty damn smart to me," Patrick grumbled. "If it's foreign, it's like hitting a brick wall."

Aidan rubbed his temples. "You've done this a lot, Rick."

"Unfortunately, yeah. One of the big areas for us right now is Internet crime, kiddie porn being at the top of the list. These pedophiles know the system, man. They can spin your wheels till you're too dizzy to see straight. And by the time you get to the end, you're screwed because they've picked up and started all over again somewhere else. I'll do what I can. Be assured of that."

"But you don't hold a hell of a lot of hope," Aidan said.

Rick shook his head. "Nope. I wish I could say otherwise."

Patrick blew out a breath. "But it's all we have to start with. I'll have your warrant in less than an hour, Rick. Get back over to Winslow's apartment and wait."

Rick gathered his things and waved. "Thanks for dinner, Lieutenant. Oh, and one other thing. Your guy turned off the juice to Adams's cameras. I expect he'll do the same to Winslow's pretty soon. Once that happens, I got nothin'."

Spinnelli made a frustrated noise as Rick left the room. "He always so optimistic?"

Jack shrugged. "He deals with kiddie porn peddlers most of the time. How optimistic do you expect him to be?"

Patrick pushed himself away from the table. "I've got to go get that warrant," he said. "Keep me up to date. Marc, call me as soon as you have anything I can use to refute this and get those damn appeals off my back."

When the SA was gone, Spinnelli looked at Aidan, Murphy, and Jack, his eyes weary. "We can try to prove it's not Tess or we can find out who's really behind this. So far, we're not doing too well with the first one, so let's focus on the second. Who do we like for all this?"

Murphy glanced at Aidan. "We thought it might be one of

Adams's irate lovers, but given Winslow, it doesn't make sense to subpoena the Health Department's records."

"No," Aidan agreed. "You're right. Right now we could take this two different directions. Option A, somebody wants to discredit Tess Ciccotelli."

"Why?" Spinnelli asked. "What's the motive? This is elaborate. Somebody would have to have one hell of a grudge and the intelligence to pull this off. Most of the people she evaluated aren't bright enough to pull off a setup like this."

"An appeal is a good motive," Murphy said. "And these people have families."

Aidan pulled the trial printout from his notebook. "Then we're back to one of the names on this list. I haven't had time to check them out, but Tess said she'd go through her old files tonight. Maybe she's found something." He stared at the printout, then shook his head, still troubled by something Rick Simms had said. "But there's an Option B that's nagging at me. What if she isn't a personal target? What if somebody figured she's a good source of people who can be manipulated to kill themselves? Her specialty is people who have attempted suicide. What if somebody is picking victims from her patient list and juicing them up, tormenting them with their own guilt until they kill themselves?"

"And then catching the whole thing on streaming video," Jack finished grimly.

Spinnelli looked unconvinced. "Seems like a whole lot of trouble."

"Somebody enjoys their work, Marc," Aidan said sharply. "And given the right audience willing to pay the right price . . . The motive could be simple greed."

"There's nothing simple about this," Spinnelli said. "But you've made your point, Aidan. We've all dealt with sociopaths who wouldn't bat an eye to abuse another person for profit. So who are we talking about here?"

"If Tess is just a conduit and her patients are the real commodity . . ." Aidan shrugged. "Then we don't have a connection. We could be talking about anyone."

Spinnelli blew out a breath. "You're as optimistic as Rick Simms. Give me some better news, gentlemen, before *I* become suicidal."

Jack pushed a sheet of paper to the center of the table. "I went by to check on Julia on my way over here and she had your tox report on Winslow." Julia Vanderbeck, the ME, was also Jack's wife. "She found PCP in his blood, same as Adams," Jack went on.

"The pills switched?" Murphy asked and Jack nodded.

"Yep, and Tess's name was on the Xanax bottle as prescribing physician and her fingerprints were on the bottle, same as Adams."

Spinnelli scowled. "I said *better* news, Jack."

"Patience, Marc. What was outside the bottle isn't as interesting as what was inside. I had a spectral analysis done on the residue in the bottom of the bottle. It was just dust caught in the crease of the bottle's base. You couldn't see it with the naked eye. The better news, Marc, is that it wasn't either Xanax or PCP. It was Soma. Julia says it's a muscle relaxant. And it's in both bottles."

Spinnelli nodded slowly. "Then somebody reused the bottles."

"And since her prints are on the bottle, maybe they were Tess's to begin with," Murphy said. "But that doesn't clear her, Jack. In fact, it makes it worse."

Jack lifted a brow. "Unless they were stolen."

Spinnelli shook his head. "Too many maybes, people. Find out if Tess ever took Soma and when. We'll put it in the pile with the rest of the maybes. What else do you have, Jack?"

"We're checking to see how long that doll was in the oven based on how much of it melted and we vacuumed both apartments. We'll look for common fibers to put the perp in both places."

"Assuming there's just one," Aidan said. "Tess said the caller today sounded different from the one Saturday night. Older."

"You pull her LUDs?" Spinnelli asked.

"We got her home phone LUDs. The call on Saturday night looks like it came from a disposable cell. Today's call was to her office phone, so I requested those LUDs, too. The report wasn't ready before we came down. I'll let you know. What about the serial numbers on the guns, Jack?"

"My people couldn't raise the number on Adams's gun so I sent it to the Bureau lab. Their equipment's better, but it'll be a few days before they get to it. Winslow's is filed down, too. Same story. Sorry." Jack slid another sheet of paper and a stack of photographs in front of Spinnelli. "Here's an inventory of what we took from the two apartments. The teddy bear Winslow had in his hand is a standard model. Nothing special about it. We found it in Wal-Mart and Toys "R" Us, so that's likely a dead end."

Aidan leaned across the table, bothered by the memory of the bear in the dead man's hand. "Let me see the picture of the bear." When Spinnelli had passed it over, Aidan opened the folder he'd retrieved from Records on his way to the conference room that evening. "Damn. It's special all right. This is the police report from the Winslow baby's death." He pushed a photo from the folder next to the picture of the bear so everyone could see it. It was a wider view of the death scene, showing the entire backseat of the minivan. A diaper bag rested to the left of the car seat, a plush bear to the right. "It's the one found next to the baby's car seat the day he died."

"Bastard doesn't miss a trick," Murphy muttered. He looked up from the pictures, disgust on his face. "Do you have the file on Melanie Adams?"

"Yeah. I had them both pulled." Aidan slid the police photo taken at Melanie's death scene to the middle of the table, while Murphy searched Jack's stack for a copy of the picture he'd found in Cynthia Adams's apartment.

"They're the same," Murphy pronounced. "Same pose, same clothing. Same shoes. Only thing different is the background. The one the police photographer took looks flatter. This one," he tapped the new photo, "is glossy. Bolder."

"You can do that with Photoshop," Aidan said, then met Murphy's puzzled look. "I took a graphics class for my degree. It's a software program. You can take a picture, crop it, change colors, even. Somebody with experience could make this picture look like Melanie had hanged herself from the Eiffel Tower if they wanted to."

"So somebody has access to our files," Spinnelli murmured. "Sonofabitch." He leaned back in his chair, jaw taut, clearly unhappy with the implication.

There was absolute silence for a very long moment. Then Aidan spoke the words nobody else seemed willing to say. "There is one other group that could have a grudge motive against Tess Ciccotelli."

Spinnelli met his eyes and Aidan could see his boss had already reached the same conclusion. "Us," he said.

Aidan nodded. "Us."

Spinnelli looked away, closing his eyes with a brief shake of his head. "Murphy, go to Records, pretend like you and Aidan got your signals crossed and you're there to check out the files. Ask to see the logs. We need to find out who's viewed those files." He looked at the three of them, his eyes sharp. "And for now we keep this to ourselves. I'll give Internal Affairs the heads up when I have to."

"They might not stop at two," Murphy said quietly. "Her other patients are at risk, no matter who's behind this. We're going to need to see her patient list."

Jack winced. "She won't give it to you. Doctor-patient privilege."

"Let's show her the courtesy of asking first," Spinnelli decided. "She'll say no, then we'll get a subpoena. For now, we're looking for someone who has a knowledge of medicine and electronics, who may or may not be the woman in the video. Now go and get me something to work with. We meet back here at oh-eight-hundred tomorrow."

With that, they were dismissed. Murphy cast Aidan a sideways look as they walked back to their desks. "Call me after you're done talking to her."

"What do you mean, after *I'm* talking to her? You're coming with me."

Murphy shook his head. "You heard him. I have to go to Records."

"Fucking coward," Aidan grumbled. "You just don't want to face her."

"She won't talk to me yet. She's still hurt. Besides, you're the one who likes to watch her move."

"Shut up, Murphy." They'd reached their desks and Aidan grabbed his coat from his chair. "I haven't done a thing on Danny Morris all day. His scumbag father is still out there somewhere while Danny's in the morgue."

"So stop by the bar where Morris hangs out on your way to Tess's. Maybe you'll get lucky and he'll have dropped by for a brew."

"While you hang out in Records. Not fair, Murphy."

"Seniority, Reagan. See you tomorrow."

Monday, March 13, 11:15 P.M.

Tess leaned over the stack of folders on her dining room table to fill Jon's glass with a nice merlot. "You don't have to keep checking on me, you know. I can take care of myself." Although after hours of reading court-ordered evaluations and knowing one of the names in one of those files could be responsible for the deaths of two of her patients . . . well, she was grateful both for the break and Jon's company. Her apartment was too quiet. Normally she could make herself comfortable with the quiet, sometimes even enjoy it, but tonight every little creak, bump, and rattle of the wind against her window made her jump.

Jon scowled at her over his wine. "Of course you can take care of yourself. You just choose not to. You walked ten blocks to the Lemon in freezing rain. Dammit, Tess, Robin said you were frozen solid when you got there. You didn't even have a hat, much less an umbrella."

She'd headed to Robin's Blue Lemon Bistro after Amy had exited stage left and Robin had welcomed her with open arms, just as she'd expected. "I left my umbrella at work along with my purse. Look, I run in worse weather all winter. I was cold, but I warmed up easily enough. Robin clucked over me, gave me soup. I was fine." She tossed him a cheeky grin she hoped would erase the frown from his face. "Then Thomas gave me a shoulder massage. Robin's wasting that man's talents in the kitchen. He has wonderful hands."

Jon's lips twitched. "So I've heard." He shook his head with an overly patient sigh. "Just next time you find yourself on the street with no money, call me, okay? I'm allowed to worry about you."

"Well, you can stop for tonight. Robin loaned me cab fare and I went back to my office for my things and drove myself home. Took a nice long soak and got cozy. See?" She stuck out her sweat-sock covered feet.

Jon laughed. "Only you could make silk and sweat socks work." But the smile quickly faded from his eyes. "How much trouble are you in, Tess? I worried about you all day. Then when that story broke about the second suicide . . . It was all over the TV news and each reporter made sure to mention your name."

Tess swallowed hard, the levity they'd shared gone, the horror of the afternoon back in its place. "The police say I'm not a suspect anymore."

"That's good. But?"

"But it was awful. Him lying there, holding that bear. Half his head was gone, Jon."

He covered her hand with his. "Not your fault, Tess."

She dropped her eyes to his hand. "Everyone in his life had left him. His wife couldn't forgive him. He couldn't forgive himself. Most of their friends couldn't look him in the eye anymore. I was the only one he had to talk to." Jon's hand grew blurry as her eyes filled, the first time that day she'd allowed them to do so. All she could think about was how he must have felt, seeing that picture. "It was hideous," she ended in a hoarse whisper. "Obscene."

"Tess, look at me." Jon's voice was so rarely sharp she did as he asked. His expression was a mix of fierce loyalty, anger, and worry. Gently he wiped at her wet eyes with his thumb. "You can't do this to yourself, honey. How many times have we talked about your getting too involved with your patients?"

Her temper roused itself, just enough to give her tongue some edge. "It's different for you. Your patients are out cold the whole time. They might as well be slabs of beef."

Jon took the criticism with equanimity. "Which is the way I like it. I can't think about them the way you do, Tess. It would tear me up. And the next time I picked up a scalpel, I might hesitate. That hesitation could cost a patient his life."

She sighed. "I know. Professional distance. You can, I never could. You win."

His smile was rueful. "There are some that would say you win. My point is, you have to play to your strengths, kid. You're a good doctor because you care, but what's it costing you? Too much, I say. Maybe you should rethink the population you deal with. All these suicidal patients eat at you." Suddenly he brightened, adorably, Tess thought. Until he went on. "What about treating some nice phobias for a change?"

She gave him a narrow look. He was one of a handful who knew of her embarrassing phobia. "Like claustrophobia?"

One side of his mouth lifted and she knew it was as much of a smile as he dared. "Perhaps. Hell, maybe you just need a vacation. When was your last one?"

Her jaw automatically clenched. "My honeymoon." The cruise she'd taken with Amy because she'd have walked across hot coals to China before letting that sonofabitch Phillip take his little floozy tramp and because the tickets were, of course, nonrefundable.

Jon winced. "Sorry. Robin and I are going to Cancún next month. Come with us."

Her laugh was hollow. "No thanks. The only thing worse than going on your honeymoon with your best friend is being the *trois* in your *ménage*."

Jon grinned, waggled his brows. "C'mon, Tess. Live a little. Robin won't mind. We could find somebody for you."

She smiled back in spite of herself. "Go home, Jon. I'm exhausted."

He set his glass aside and stood up, pulling her to her feet. "Walk me out and—"

"Bolt the door." She opened the door. "You're worse than Vito ever was."

Jon stopped in the doorway, his eyes wide. "You called home?"

Her smile disappeared. "No."

"Tess—"

"Go home, Jon," she repeated, serious now.

He hesitated, staring at his toe. "There's another reason I stopped by, besides Robin's worrying." He blew out a breath and looked up from beneath lashes that most women would kill for. Aidan Reagan's were longer. And darker. His eyes much bluer.

Tess blinked hard, bringing Jon's face back into focus. *Whoa. Where had that come from?* Too little sleep and too much stress, she decided. And too many nights of sleeping alone, with only the cat to keep her warm.

Jon was leaning closer. "Tess, what's wrong? Your face just went pale."

"It's nothing. I'm just more tired than I thought. What were you going to say?"

"Just that Amy called me a few hours ago."

Tess's lips thinned. "Oh? Did she tell you she fired me as a client?"

"She said that she'd said some things she wished she hadn't. She'd been so scared that you'd been carted off to jail by that detective, that she wasn't thinking straight. She wanted me to find out if you're still mad at her."

Tess shook her head. It was like they were still sixteen and sharing a room in her parents' house. "It didn't occur to her to call me herself?"

"She thought you'd hang up."

"I might have."

"And she said she did call to make sure you got home all right, but you didn't answer. I don't want to be the go-between guy, so call her, okay? Tell her you want to kiss and make up. And listen to her, Tess. She knows more about this than you do. And even though she acted like a jerk, she's a well-meaning jerk who doesn't want to see you go to jail."

He was right. Amy did mean well. Tess had come to that same conclusion as she'd walked the ten blocks to Robin's bistro. "Okay. We'll kiss and make up and take you out of the middle." But she wouldn't promise to do what Amy said. She'd thought a great deal about it in the hours since leaving Winslow's apartment and was more convinced than ever that her cooperation with the police was vital. But Jon did worry so. Impulsively she rose up to kiss his cheek. "Thanks." The instant her lips touched his cheek, his back straightened and his arm went around her shoulders protectively. She followed his gaze and her heart took a leap.

Detective Reagan stood in the hallway outside the elevator. And he didn't look happy at all. She grasped the sides of her robe, pulling the silk up and over her throat. It was purely instinctive. Jon had seen her scar. Very few others had.

Slowly Reagan approached, his eyes on her shoulder where Jon's hand still clenched, his own hands shoved deep into the pockets of his overcoat. He stopped far enough away to just be respectful. Still close enough that she could smell his aftershave. Because he'd shaved just before he'd come. His face was shiny smooth where this afternoon his cheeks had been dark with stubble. "Dr. Ciccotelli."

"Detective Reagan. This is Dr. Jonathan Carter, the colleague I mentioned."

His nod to Jon was curt. "If I might have a word with you, Doctor."

Jon's fingers dug into her arm, his warning about as subtle as the ferocious frown on his face. "Not without her lawyer here."

Reagan's eyes rose to meet hers, his gaze unreadable. "If that's what you really want, Doctor, we can call your attorney." His voice was cold enough to send a shiver of apprehension down her back. "But I need some answers to some questions tonight."

Tess patted the middle of Jon's chest. "I'll be fine, Jon. I'll give Amy a call. I promise. Go on home."

"I don't kn—"

"I'll call you when he leaves so you'll know I still live and breathe," she interrupted, purposefully keeping her tone light. "I won't say anything he can use against me in a court of law." She slipped from his grip and gave him a nudge, her robe still tightly clutched around her throat. "Go home, Jon."

Jon's parting glare was as sharp as one of his scalpels. But he said nothing and a minute later, he was on his way down the elevator.

She was alone. With Aidan Reagan and his long eye-lashes. "Where is Todd?"

"Following some other leads."

"I see. Well, are you comfortable talking in my apart-ment, or would you prefer to stand in the hall?"

"That would be up to you, ma'am."

So I'm a "ma'am" now. Reagan's "ma'am" sounded remark-ably like an insult. "Let's go in then. I prefer not to stand in the hall in my robe."

He closed the door behind them. "I apologize for the late hour," he said stiffly. "I was hoping you'd still be awake."

She waved her free hand at the stacks of folders on her dining room table. "I've been going through my files. Let me change my clothes, if you don't mind. I'll be just a few minutes."

She was back in less than three, her robe traded for a thick turtleneck and jeans. The sweat socks stayed. She found him standing in her living room, examining the framed pen-and-ink sketches on her wall. "Can I take your coat, Detective?"

He shook his head. "No thanks."

"Then can I get you some wine, or are you still on the clock?"

He turned around, his eyes lingering on the two wine-glasses on the dining room table before moving to her face. "No thank you." His voice was polite, but coldly distant. "Are you going to call your attorney now? I'd like to get this done."

"No. Go ahead and ask your questions, Detective. If I can answer, I will."

The flicker of surprise in his eyes was so brief she wondered if she'd imagined it. "You told your boyfriend you were calling her."

"And I will. After you've gone. My attorney and I don't have the same working relationship with the police, Detective." Her mouth bent in a rueful smile. "And I don't think she's my attorney anymore, anyway. We kind of had a fight." She lifted a brow, watching his face carefully. "And Dr. Carter is not my boyfriend."

This time the flicker in those blue eyes was a flash, unmistakable. Intense. His gaze caught hers and for a long moment it was like they were in the stairwell all over again. Then the moment was over.

He looked away, pinning his gaze on the stack of folders on her table. "Did you find anything?" he asked, his voice rough.

Tess drew a breath. The sudden spike of oxygen served to kick her brain back into gear. Amy's warning crawled back into her mind, that Reagan would use his looks to get her to drop her guard. For that one moment, her guard had been annihilated and the notion left her shaken.

"Before I answer, Detective, I have a question of my own." She waited until he once again met her eyes, his brows raised, waiting. "Do I need a lawyer?"

He didn't flinch. "No."

She weighed the risk, then went with her original plan. "Okay. I went through the files. I was primarily looking for the trials where a conviction hinged on my testimony. Of the thirty-one convictions, there were five. All male. Four of them were homicides, one rape." She shook her head, pragmatically skeptical. "But none of them struck me as having the intellectual capacity to stage something like this. These guys were thugs, not criminal geniuses by any stretch of the imagination. And, besides, all five should still be in jail unless some parole board really f— I mean messed up."

She thought she saw his lips twitch at her near slip. "We'll look at their families," Reagan said. "See who's been actively campaigning for a new trial."

Tess's stomach clenched. "So we're looking at appeals?"

"Yes."

She sighed. "I'll bet Patrick Hurst is not a happy man tonight."

"You'd win that bet, Doctor. Have you heard of Soma?"

His sudden change of topic had her blinking. "Yes. It's a muscle relaxant."

"Have you ever taken it?"

She nodded slowly. "Yes. I had an accident last year." A con with a chain, the memory of which still had the power to turn her gut to water. She focused on Reagan's eyes, willing the panic back. "My back went out and my doctor gave it to me then."

"How long did you take it?"

His expression was once again unreadable, and once again Amy's voice loomed. *Don't be an idiot, Tess.* "Off and on for about six months. Why?"

"Do you still have it? The prescription."

"No. I didn't want it anymore. It made me too groggy to work." Even though the pain had been excruciating and at times still was. "Why are you asking about Soma?"

He hesitated, then shrugged. "Because traces were found in the bottles we found in both victims' apartments."

Her knees simply failed her. Clutching the table's edge, Tess lowered herself to the dining room chair, unable to look away from his face. "The ones with my prints."

"Has your apartment ever been broken into?"

She shook her head, eyes widening at the thought of that sadist in her own apartment, her own space. "No. No, I would have reported it."

"What happened to the bottles?"

She stood up, suddenly restless and cold. She paced from the table to the window, rubbing her arms, blindly staring at the traffic on the street below. "I can't remember. I must have thrown them away."

She heard him moving and then he was behind her, his hands on her shoulders, warm. Strong. Warmth moved down her arms and back and for one weak moment she wished she could turn and feel his arms close around her. Wished she could lay her head on his wide shoulder. But wishes were just that. Reality was this . . . a nightmare that got worse with every new piece of information.

"Sit down," he murmured. "You're pale." He gently pushed her back down in the chair and crouched in front of her, blue eyes narrowed. "Are you all right?"

Numbly she nodded. "This makes it look like I did it even more."

He stood up and said nothing.

Swallowing hard, she lifted her eyes to his. "I didn't."

He didn't blink. "Has anyone ever threatened you, Doctor?"

"When do you mean? Like, ever?"

"In the last . . . year."

His meaning hit her like a brick. "You mean since the Green trial. You mean . . . cops." Her gut churned at the very thought. "Oh my God."

Again he said nothing, which said more than a simple confirmation ever could.

"I got some letters," she said. "None of them signed. Most of them were personal insults, a lot of name-calling. 'Baby killer.' 'Cop-killer.'" The names had hurt at the time. They still did. "There was one person who wrote more than one. Said I'd be sorry. A month later I got a letter saying my contract was not being renewed. I thought that's what they meant. Somebody threw a brick through my car window when I was in the mall, but they never caught the person. I thought that might have been part of it, too."

Reagan looked angry. "Did you report any of this?"

"The broken window I did. Not the letters. There was no physical threat."

"Do you still have the letters?"

"Somewhere. I'm sorry. I'm having trouble thinking right now."

"It's all right," he said quietly. "Take your time." He picked up the wine bottle. "Do you want some of this?"

"No." She focused on her thoughts, willing them to slow, picturing herself receiving the letters and filing them in the cabinet in her office. "Wait here. I remember what I did with the letters."

Aidan watched her retreat, clenching his hands into fists at his sides. Knowing he'd smell her on his palms if he gave into the urge to drag them down his face. The last fifteen minutes had certainly proved beyond a shadow of a doubt that he was a man of self-control. Coming off the elevator, seeing her in that red silk robe had sent a jolt of pure lust to his groin. Seeing her rise up and kiss that blond doctor's cheek had sent a surge of jealous fury that for a split second had hazed his brain.

Hearing her say the blond guy wasn't her boyfriend made him want to drag her against him and find out if that long look in the stairwell had affected her as much as it did him.

Just putting his hands on her shoulders made him want more. If he'd touched her like he'd wanted to . . .

But he hadn't and he wouldn't. He looked around at her apartment. Situated in one of Michigan Avenue's ritzier neighborhoods, her apartment alone would run a cool mil, not including the furnishings and the art that would send his interior designer sister Annie into spasms of delight. A woman accustomed to living like this wanted more than Aidan Reagan was prepared to give. This Aidan had learned the hard way. Fool me once . . .

The thought evaporated, along with every drop of moisture in his mouth.

"I found them." Ciccotelli emerged with a large envelope, her tongue licking at the adhesive strip, and his system went into overdrive.

Willing his hand to take only the envelope, he reached— and was stopped.

Her exclamation caught him by surprise as did her hand on his. "What did you do?"

Aidan drew a breath. His knuckles were raw and scraped, compliments of one of the lowlife friends of Danny Morris's father, the man they suspected of smothering his son then tossing his body down a flight of stairs. Aidan had stopped in Morris's main haunt after leaving the office. Morris's lowlife friend was now in a holding cell after throwing a drunken punch at Aidan's face. Morris himself was still nowhere to be seen. Morris's wife sported a new black eye but still denied her husband's involvement in her little boy's death.

And Tess Ciccotelli was still holding his hand.

"I hit a brick wall," he said, shocked his voice was still level. His heart sure as hell wasn't. He tried to tug his hand free, but she held firm. She looked up, her dark eyes filled with concern.

"Was that wall somebody's face?"

"No. It really was a brick wall. A suspect resisted and I scraped my hand trying to cuff him." He gave another tug and she let him go.

"Was that suspect on this case?"

"No, another one I'm working."

She nodded, subdued. "The little boy whose autopsy report I saw this morning."

"Yes." He managed to get the word past what felt like a wad of paste in his throat.

Her lips drooped and Aidan clenched his teeth. The woman had lips that just begged a man to find out if they were as soft as they looked. "I'm sorry," she said quietly. "Will you let me put something on your hand? It's a nasty cut." When he hesitated, she forced those full lips to smile. "I am a doctor you know."

He should go. Right now. But his feet wouldn't move. "I guess you are. I always forget psychiatrists are MDs, too."

"Most people do." She went into the kitchen and came back with a first aid kit. "But I went to medical school like all the other doctors. That's where I met Jonathan Carter, actually, in med school. We've been friends a long time." Her head bent over his hand, her hair forming a dark wavy curtain that hid her face. Her hair was still damp where it parted at her neck, the fragrance of her shampoo drifting up to torment him. It didn't take supreme detective prowess to assume she'd been in the shower, which meant she'd likely been naked beneath that red robe. He gritted his teeth against the picture of those curves, wet and soapy.

"He's protective of me," she went on, then looked up, her hair sweeping back from her face. Her cheeks flashed hot and whatever words she'd been about to say were lost. Abruptly she dropped her head and cleared her throat.

"Well . . ." Her shoulders rose and fell as she drew a deep breath. "At least it's not dirty. This might sting."

It did, but the sting was centered somewhere else entirely. "The guy tossed a beer in my face so I had to take a shower once I brought him in. I cleaned it up."

Her throaty chuckle sent a shudder down his spine and his hand jerked reflexively. She stilled, then continued dabbing his knuckles. "Well, they say beer is good for the complexion." She wound some gauze around his knuckles and taped the end. Stepping back, she looked up, her eyes cool. Two days ago he'd mistaken it for no emotion. Now he knew it was her shield. The knowledge that she needed one made him want to do everything he shouldn't. "Keep it dry," she murmured. "I think you'll live."

Aidan held up the envelope in his left hand. "I'll check these letters out. Have you had any more calls?"

"No."

"Would you be willing to let us tap your line so we can listen in case you do?"

She was quiet a moment. "Yes. Go ahead. I'll sign a release. For my home phone only. Not my office line."

It was more than he'd expected. "We'll also need a sample of your voice, to compare to the message on Adams's voicemail."

"I'll come in tomorrow morning. My first two appointments canceled."

"I'm sorry."

She lifted a shoulder. "It was to be expected after that article in the *Bulletin*."

He'd put off the patient list long enough and with a sigh damned Todd Murphy to hell once again. "This could happen again. You know that."

Her chin came up but her eyes stayed cool. "I know."

"We need to be able to anticipate his next move. I have to ask for your patient list."

She didn't blink. "You know I can't do that. Patient confidentiality isn't just a 'nice-to-have.' It's the law, Detective."

She didn't sound angry, he thought. Instead she sounded resigned, as if she'd expected the question all along. "You told us about Adams and Winslow."

"I'm permitted to disclose when it's critical for the detection of a crime or when the client is at risk and not able to consent. In both situations I judged the requirements for disclosure were satisfied. Besides, I didn't tell you much more that you couldn't get from your own police reports if you dug deep enough."

"You told me that Cynthia Adams had contracted an STD."

Something moved in her eyes, elusive and brief. "That was when I thought she was the target and that knowing that would give you a motive. And you would have learned it from the autopsy report anyway." She drew a breath. "I was visited by the state licensing board today. They did not concur with my judgment."

Aidan frowned. "How did they know you'd talked to me?"

"The case worker from the health department called them. Don't apologize, Detective," she said sharply when he opened his mouth to do just that. "I understood the risks when I disclosed."

But it had been another blow, he could see that. He wasn't certain what form any licensing board censure might take. "Did they . . . do anything?"

"Not this time. My attorney was there and that seemed to diffuse the situation a bit."

"But they'll be back tomorrow. Once they've seen the news about Winslow."

"Probably. As will the reporters that were camped around the door of my apartment building when I got home tonight." Her voice softened marginally. "Don't worry about me, Detective Reagan. I can take care of myself."

He wondered if she could. Wondered how she would take the news that her patients' suicides had been recorded, perhaps for profit. Remembered the look in her eyes as she'd stared at Winslow's body and wished she wouldn't have to find out about the cameras, but knew that sooner or later she would. But it didn't have to be tonight. "Then I'll let you go to sleep, Dr. Ciccotelli." He lifted his bandaged hand. "Thank you."

She smiled, sadly. "Thank you for not hauling my ass downtown again." She winced. "Sorry. When I'm tired my vocabulary deteriorates."

There were a lot of other, better places he'd like to haul her ass. He turned away before his straining libido made any of them a reality, and found himself once more looking at the pen-and-ink sketches he'd studied earlier to keep his mind off the fact she'd been changing her clothes in her bedroom. " 'T. Ciccotelli,' " he read in the bottom corner of each one. "You did these?"

"No, my brother Tino did."

Surprised, he turned to look at her. "You have a brother named Tino? Really?"

This time her smile showed actual amusement. "I have four older brothers—Tino, Gino, Dino, and Vito. And no, none of them are Sopranos, so don't ask."

Four older—and more than likely very protective—brothers. It was nearly a deflating thought. Nearly. The red robe was still too close to the front of his mind. "Any of them live around here?"

Her smile went sad again. "No, they're all back home."

"Philadelphia."

Her eyes widened. "How did you—? You checked up on me."

He nodded, levelly. "Which is why your ass is in your posh apartment, and not sitting in a hard chair downtown."

She stared at him for a second, then surprised him with a laugh that seemed to fill every corner of the room and sent his pulse scrambling once again. "Touché, Detective. And good night."

He let himself smile back. "Good night, Doctor."

He waited until he heard the deadbolt fall, then turned for the elevator. He'd go home and get some sleep himself. But first he'd need another shower. And this time a very cold one.

Chapter Eight

Monday, March 13, 11:55 P.M.

Tess let her body fall back against her front door and pressed the heel of her hand to her heart. Unsmiling and angry, Aidan Reagan was the most potent man she thought she'd ever met. But smiling . . . he was quite simply beautiful. And the last distraction she needed right now.

Or maybe not. It had been quite some time since her heart had beaten so fast, since her skin felt like every square inch had fallen asleep and was now just waking up. Since she'd been so aroused. She'd been starting to fear she never would again.

"Go ahead and say it, Chick," she murmured aloud. *You need to get back on that bike. You need to get laid.* But she couldn't say it. She had trouble even thinking it. Phillip's betrayal had scarred her deeper than any con with a chain ever could. She'd told herself she'd get over him, that his cheating was no reflection on her. What a joke. Of course it had been a reflection on her. She picked a man incapable of keeping his promises. At least that she'd come by honestly. Like mother, like daughter.

And at least she'd had the pride to throw her cheater out on his ass. Unlike her mother. But pride was a poor substitute for the human touch she craved in the night. There had been men who'd tried to catch her eye since Phillip. Unfortunately, her eye hadn't been interested.

Until now. Her eye was interested, along with the rest of her. He was interested, too. And if she was any judge of character, he didn't want to be any more than she did. But what kind of character judge could she be? She'd picked Phillip after all.

Cheerful thought. Perhaps Amy was right. *I should call her now. Kiss and make up and all that shit.* She had promised Jon, a fact that Reagan seemed to think important. Score one for the good guys. She pushed away from the door, then jumped a foot when her doorbell rang. A look through her peephole had her hissing an oath. Little Miss Carmichael stood outside her door, holding a pizza box.

"I know you're in there," Carmichael said loudly. "I just saw the cop leave."

"Go away, Miss Carmichael. I have no comment for you."

"I have a proposition for you."

Tess opened her door a crack. "Your propositions require Vaseline, Miss Carmichael. Now please go away before I call the police."

Carmichael eyed her through the crack in the door. "I want an exclusive."

Tess laughed at the sheer absurdity of the statement. "You're out of your frickin' mind. And, trust me, I know of what I speak."

"I'll write an article with or without your help, Doctor. If you give me an exclusive, the words will be yours."

Tess shook her head. "Like I can believe anything you say. How the hell did you get up here anyway?"

"Told your doorman I was delivering a pizza to your neighbor. Your building security sucks, by the way."

She was right about that. "Good to know. Go away." Tess shut the door with a snap and flipped the bolt, then aimed her parting shot through the door. "If you're still there in five seconds I'm calling the cops and you can do your story from a holding cell. Five, four, three—"

Joanna stepped back with a grin. She hadn't expected Ciccotelli to agree to an exclusive, but hadn't expected such an acerbic tongue, either. When Ciccotelli finally gave in, the copy would be exceptional. For now, she'd go back to her apartment and eat the pizza herself.

She had a lot of work to do before morning. Her mamma always said you caught more flies with honey than with vinegar. Her father had always insisted that flypaper was the smartest way to go. As much as she hated to admit it, this time Daddy was right. She'd just have to see how many flies Ciccotelli could stand to see writhing on the flypaper before admitting defeat.

It wouldn't be pretty and Ciccotelli wouldn't cooperate quietly.

But cooperate she would. *And when the dust clears, the byline will be mine and Cy Bremin will just be an annoying little buzz in my ear.*

Happily munching a slice of pizza, she went down the elevator and waved at the sucky doorman on the way out.

Tuesday, March 14, 12:35 A.M.

Aidan was back in control by the time he pulled into his driveway, which was a good thing because cold showers hurt and weren't particularly effective anyway. He hoped Dolly hadn't made a mess in the living room. She was a good dog, well-trained, but he'd left her for a long time today. He had an arrangement with the twelve-year-old next door who let Dolly out when he was gone for long periods, but Aidan had forgotten to call the kid. He went in through the kitchen and was greeted by ninety-six pounds of body-wagging rottweiler.

Aidan dropped to one knee to scratch behind her ears and laughed when Dolly's tongue bathed his face. "You're a tart, Doll-face." Giving her side an affectionate slap, he stood up and grabbed the leash from its peg on the wall. It was late, but Dolly liked to walk and Aidan still had a lot of residual stress to work off.

"I walked her already."

Startled, Aidan spun toward the sleepy sound, weapon in hand before recognition kicked in. He smacked the wall switch, flooding the room with light.

His sister Rachel stood in the doorway, her eyes wide with groggy terror, one hand splayed against her chest.

"What the hell are you doing here?" he demanded. "Don't you know better than to sneak up on me? I might have shot you."

"I'm . . ." She blew out a shaky breath. "I'm sorry. I didn't think."

Aidan shoved his gun back in his holster. "Damn right you didn't think." But she was pale and shaking so he walked over and put his arms around her. "Are you okay?"

She nodded against his chest. "Yeah. Just give me a minute." She stepped back and slumped against the wall, her dark brows bunched in a frown. Like Aidan, Rachel had their father's hair and eyes, but her delicate size was purely their mother's. As was the imperious expression on her face. "You're late."

"You're AWOL," he snapped back. "Why aren't you home in bed? Mom and Dad'll be worried sick if they wake up and find you gone."

"No, they won't. They think I'm at Marie's."

Aidan stared down at her. "You lied to them? Rachel."

"I didn't lie. I was at Marie's. She had a party that I decided . . . not to attend."

Still glaring, Aidan grabbed a jug of milk from the refrigerator. "You want some?"

She wrinkled her nose. "Yuck."

"You need milk, kid. You'll get osteoporosis, then you'll be sorry." He mimicked their mother to make her smile, but her mouth stayed firmly pressed in a hard line. "So why did you decide against the party? Besides the fact it's a school night," he added, then narrowed his eyes. "Mom and Dad let you out on a school night? They never let us go out on a school night."

She shrugged. "We were going to study for a history test."

"But you're not."

"I thought we were there to study, Aidan," she said quietly. "I really did. Then Marie's boyfriend showed up and . . . things got out of hand."

Aidan downed a glass of milk and wiped his mouth with the back of his hand. "Out of hand, how?"

"Never mind. The important thing is I didn't join in." She lifted her sleeve and sniffed. "Although it sure smells like I did."

Aidan leaned in, sniffed, then leaned back with a frown. "Beer and pot? Rachel, who are these kids? And where were Marie's parents?"

Rachel sat down on one of his garage sale kitchen chairs. "They weren't home." She held up her hand when he would have scolded. "Just don't. I should have left right away, but for the first two hours it was just me and Marie and we did study." Her eyes implored. "I swear, Aidan."

"I believe you, Rachel." He sat down next to her. "What happened, honey?" Then he was startled when her blue eyes filled with tears. "Rachel?"

"I'm all right," she said and wiped her eyes with the heels of her hands. "It got scary there. A bunch of boys came and . . ." She shuddered. "I slipped out the back door."

His heart was skipping every other beat, able to visualize all the possible outcomes only too well. "Why didn't you call Mom and Dad?"

She shook her head. "One of the guys spilled beer on me and I . . . I didn't want them to think I'd lied to them. So I walked here."

"You *walked?*"

She nodded. "Three miles." The smile she managed was pathetic. "So no more cracks about video games making me soft. I wasn't going to stay here. I just needed a place to hang and get this smell out of my clothes. But Dolly was begging to be walked, then I sat down to rest for just a minute and fell asleep on the couch."

"You should have called me, Rach. I would have taken care of things."

She rolled her eyes. "Sure, my big cop brother rushing in to save the day. Aidan, I don't go to keggers, but I would like to retain *some* portion of my social life." Her face fell. "So don't tell Mom and Dad, please?"

He considered it. Abe and Sean had covered for him plenty of times when they were younger. "Is the party still going on?"

"No. Marie's parents were due home by twelve, so everybody's long gone by now."

"You promise to not see Marie anymore?"

She shuddered again. "Oh, yeah."

"Then we have a deal. Go take a shower. I'll find you some sweats and we'll see if we can get the beer out of those clothes." He shot her a grin. "I've got beer clothes to wash, too, so we can save water."

Her brows lifted. "You been partying, Aidan?"

"Nope. Bar fight."

Her lips twitched. "You win?"

"Honey, I always win." He touched her nose with his fingertip and both their gazes fell on his bandaged hand. *Well, not always,* he thought. Not when it came to one Michigan Avenue doctor who was out of his price range. Even though she'd been interested. Very interested.

Rachel sniffed, then brought his hand to her face. "Forevermore."

"Excuse me?"

"The fragrance on your hands. It's called 'Forevermore.' It's also mega-expensive." Her eyes went sly. "You *have* been partying. So dish, Aidan."

He laughed, oddly embarrassed. "Go take your shower, squirt."

She got up, but paused at the doorway, a sober, old look in her eyes. "Thanks, Aidan. I didn't know where else to go tonight."

His heart turned over in his chest. His baby sister had been his parents' late-life surprise and they all had spoiled her rotten. But she was a good kid. A really good kid. He hated the thought of her seeing the uglier side of life so soon. "You can always come here, Rachel. Just don't sneak up on me again, okay?"

"Okay."

Tuesday, March 14, 8:09 A.M.

Aidan slid into the chair next to Murphy, avoiding Spinnelli's annoyed glare.

"You're late, Aidan."

"I'm sorry." He'd gotten caught up in the drop-off traffic

in front of Rachel's school after sneaking into his parents' house to get his sister some clean clothes. The beer on her clothes was gone, but the pot lingered.

Jack slid a half-empty box of doughnuts across the table. "You snooze, you lose. Murphy and I ate all the jellies." He eyed Aidan speculatively. "You get her client list?"

"Nope." Aidan picked out a glazed cruller and licked his fingers. "She refused, very politely. But she did get threatening letters after Green. They're in here." With his clean hand he pushed the envelope across the table. The envelope that smelled like Forevermore. He'd felt ridiculous, sniffing an envelope, but somehow he hadn't been able to resist. "And she confirmed she'd been on Soma. Again, after Green. She didn't have any of the bottles anymore and couldn't remember if she'd thrown them away or not." He looked at Spinnelli. "She's coming in this morning to give a voice sample and to sign a wiretap release for her home phone."

Spinnelli sighed. "She's cooperating, as best she can. If she gives over her patient files, she'll lose her license."

"The licensing people already are on her back. They visited her yesterday." Aidan glanced at Murphy. "That lady at the Health Department squealed."

Murphy winced. "Damn. It just keeps getting better."

"Did you find out anything in Records?"

Murphy looked at Spinnelli who nodded soberly. "Go ahead, Todd."

"Both the Adams and Winslow files were checked out three months ago." He blew out a breath. "By Preston Tyler."

Aidan shook his head, stunned. "No way. He's—" *Dead.* But of course they all knew that. He'd been killed by Harold Green's bare hands. Which was a hell of a lot more merciful than the bastard had been to the three little girls. Aidan's teeth clenched as he fought to stem the rage that threatened to consume him every time he thought about that little girl's mangled body.

And that fact that Harold Green had escaped justice. Thanks to Tess Ciccotelli. *Who had put away thirty-one other very dangerous men.* He made himself remember that. Made himself remember the agony in her eyes as she looked at Avery Winslow's body, that behind the cool facade was a woman who cared. Because she was human. And being human she'd made a mistake. A terrible, tragic mistake.

He realized everyone was silently watching him and hissed out a breath. "Who would allow anyone to sign out a report using Preston Tyler's name?"

"A new clerk. She didn't know, Aidan," Murphy said. "I had her in here this morning and she said it was a cop and that he had ID. She also said the report didn't even leave the counter, but the cop came back on her next shift to look at it again."

"Internal Affairs has her now," Spinnelli said grimly, "taking her through photos."

Jack's expression hardened. "And if she can't or chooses not to make an ID?"

"It's a possibility," Spinnelli admitted. "But IA has their ways."

"Security videos?" Aidan asked.

Murphy shrugged. "Conveniently missing."

"So much for Records keeping records," Jack muttered.

"IA's looking into that, too." Spinnelli looked weary. "There'll be a probe."

"You're right, Murphy," Aidan said. "It does just get better and better. Any good news from Rick?"

Jack shook his head. "He worked it all night, but our guy is smart. Transmissions are practically routed to Mars. But I do have some other news. One of my guys found black fibers on some of the lilies. They're nylon. We found what look like the same fibers on the doll from Winslow's place, but the heat of the oven had melted the nylon fiber into the doll's plastic skin, so we can't separate them for a certain analysis."

"A bag maybe?" Murphy asked. "Something somebody used to carry them in?"

Jack nodded. "That's what we thought. It's not going to lead you to the bag, necessarily, but if you find the bag, you'll probably find pollen from the lilies inside."

Aidan remembered the sheer number of lilies that littered Adams's floor. "Somebody would have had to make a lot of trips if the lilies were in just one bag. We can canvass Adams's building with a picture of the woman at the mailbox store, see if anybody saw her. Maybe while we're there we can find Joanna Carmichael and see if there are any more photos of the Adams scene. She wasn't there yesterday afternoon."

"Sounds good," Spinnelli said. "Anything else?"

Murphy munched on his doughnut thoughtfully. "We have Adams's safe-deposit box key."

"And a list of the five convictions Tess thought her testimony clinched." Aidan caught Murphy's look of surprise. "She gave it to me last night. But all five are still in jail." *Because no parole board had either fucked up or messed up,* he thought, remembering the way her cheeks flushed at her near slip. Murphy was still looking at him. "What?"

Murphy looked away. "Nothing. Who's going to subpoena her patient list, Marc?

Spinnelli's mustache bent down. "I'll tell Patrick to go ahead ASAP."

"Have him get a warrant for Adams's safe-deposit box, too," Murphy said.

Spinnelli wrote it down. "Anybody else have an order before the kitchen closes?" he asked sardonically. "Aidan, when's Tess coming in?"

"Sometime this morning. I'll call you when she gets here."

Jack stood up. "I'll get everything ready in the sound booth."

Spinnelli watched him go, still frowning. "We have too many possibilities. Go narrow them down."

Murphy stopped at the door. "We all know IA's not going to tell us who the Records clerk IDs, Marc."

"Go do your job, Murphy." Spinnelli's voice was sharp. "I'll deal with IA."

Murphy was shaking his head as they headed back to their desks. "Better him than us. You okay?"

Aidan frowned at him. "I'm fine, why?"

"Your knuckles are a mess."

And she bandaged them was all he could think. Then forced himself to focus. "Morris's pal decided to be a hero last night. Now he's cooling his jets in lockup. I still have to finish the paperwork. Resisting arrest and striking a cop."

Murphy studied him as they walked. "Your face is still pretty. Where'd he hit you?"

Aidan grimaced. "Got one in the gut. Man has one hell of a left jab."

"You'll live."

Exactly what she'd said.

Murphy sat behind his desk, still studying him and the scrutiny made Aidan want to squirm so he turned his attention to finding an empty wiretap release form. A minute later he looked up with a snarl. Murphy was still looking at him. *"What?"*

"You called her 'Tess.' "

Aidan opened his mouth to deny it, but Murphy was right. "So?"

"So she's growing on you, too."

Aidan thought about the dream that had waked him just before dawn. She'd been in his bed, the dark waves of her hair spread across his stomach as she kissed her way down his body. All those curves, and that busy mouth . . . The phone on his desk rang, saving him a reply. "It was the desk downstairs," he said curtly. "Dr. Ciccotelli is here."

A corner of Murphy's mouth lifted. "Then by all means escort Dr. Ciccotelli up. I'll call Jack and let him know we're coming."

Tess sat in the lobby of the police station, vividly aware of every cop eye watching her every move. Before, there had been hatred and contempt. Now, she had to wonder if anyone wearing a badge was aiming for a more personal revenge. The thought had kept her awake most of the night. As had the speculation on which of her patients might be next.

One part of her had desperately wanted to give Reagan the patient list he'd requested last night so that they could be protected. So that she wouldn't have to look into the dead eyes of another patient. But it wasn't ethical. Reagan had known it. The privacy of the patient must be protected. There was a stigma associated with seeing a psychiatrist. Many of her patients believed their lives would be ruined if anyone knew they needed help.

She prayed their lives wouldn't be ended instead. She couldn't give Reagan their names, but she could call each one herself. This she would do once she'd met her obligations here. One release to tap her phone and one voice sample.

The elevator door slid open and Reagan stepped out. Predictably her pulse kicked up a notch. He was an incredible-looking man. She could admit that now. He walked with a kind of coiled power that said he was a force to be reckoned with. She was sure he would be. He scanned the room as he approached, met her eyes. He was assessing, as was she. Then his eyes dropped to the scarf around her neck and her mood flattened. He knew. And it bothered her that he did.

"Dr. Ciccotelli," he said, his voice smooth. "Thanks for coming down."

"I said I would." She gathered up her things. "I do what I say." She followed him, her stomach quailing when he stopped at the elevator. "I missed my run this morning." She grimaced. "Reporters all over. Do you mind if we take the stairs?"

He looked down, his brows slightly furrowed. "It's four floors to the technology division where you'll be giving your voice sample."

"That's okay."

His eyes softened. "Then let's take the stairs."

"Did you call your attorney?" he asked when they'd cleared the first flight.

That he cared so much that she kept her promise was enlightening. "I did." Amy had been waiting up for her call and had apologized more than once. But the conversation had been awkward and neither of them brought up reinstating their attorney-client relationship. Perhaps it was better this way. She and Amy had been through so much together. Their friendship had taken a battering and was ultimately too precious to risk. There were other defense attorneys if she ended up needing one after all. "I called her after I chased that *Bulletin* reporter away."

Reagan shot her a surprised look. "Cyrus Bremin went to your apartment?"

"Nobody so famous. Her name was Joanna Carmichael."

"Ah. The photographer. Can I carry your briefcase?"

She shook her head. "No thanks. You mean you know Carmichael?"

"Not yet. We checked her out when we saw the article in the paper yesterday morning. We went by her place trying to see if there were any other pictures of Adams's jump." He hesitated, then shrugged. "She lives in Cynthia Adams's building."

"So she stumbled onto the big story, only to have Cy Bremin get the byline. No wonder she wanted an exclusive."

"An exclusive?" His short bark of laughter bounced off the walls as they steadily climbed. "She's crazy." He winced. "Sorry. That wasn't very sensitive."

Tess chuckled. "It's okay. I told her the same thing, only a little more colorfully."

"More vocabulary deterioration?"

"I believe I used the word 'Vaseline.'" She grimaced. "I'll probably regret that."

They reached the fourth floor and he held the door open for her. A short walk led them to a sound studio where it seemed the entire cast of players waited. Spinnelli, Patrick Hurst, and Murphy stood outside the studio window while Jack stood inside, talking to the technician. "So I'm playing to standing room only," she said lightly and Spinnelli smiled. "Where's my name on the marquee?"

"We want to do this completely by the book, Tess. For your good and ours."

"And I appreciate it, Marc. I hear you're fighting appeals, Patrick."

Patrick scowled, but he always seemed to be scowling whenever she was around. When he'd first taken the office after the last SA resigned in scandal, she'd wondered if she'd offended him. Now she knew that was his normal expression. "There were two more waiting for me on the fax this morning," he complained.

"I'm sorry. I wish I had a way of making this all go away. For all of us." She swallowed. "Especially for Cynthia

Adams and Avery Winslow. But you know I can't hand over my client lists, Patrick."

He nodded. "And you know I'll subpoena you."

"I'm obligated to fight it."

Patrick shrugged. "So goes the game. I hope no one else dies while we duke it out."

She flinched. It was a low blow, carefully aimed. "So let's find out who's doing this before that happens."

Spinnelli stepped in. "That sounds like a good idea. They're ready for you, Tess. Let's get this done."

Jack came through the door. "You know what you'll have to do, don't you, Tess?"

She drew a breath. "You want me to say the same message you found on her voice mail. I know how this works, Jack."

"Then you know it's not an exact science. We'll compare the printout visually then have our expert do an auditory analysis. You'll need to say a variety of sounds, also. Even when we're done, we may have nothing definitive."

"I thought you said your guy was good," Murphy said, his voice tight.

"I am." The voice came from inside the booth, making them all turn to look. The man inside opened the door and leaned against it.

"This is Sergeant Dale Burkhardt," Jack said. "He's my counterpart in the Technology Unit. They do R and D on all the new gadgets and gizmos. Dale exceeds the FBI standards for voice assessment. He's the best we've got."

Burkhardt's lips quirked. "Ass-kissing won't wipe the slate, Jack. You still owe me." He turned to Murphy. "The theory is that no two voices are exactly alike. Voice comes from the voice cavity, throat, vocal cords, and the movement of the mouth during speech. Imitators can be difficult to detect because even though it's unlikely they have the same vocal cavity dimensions, they study lip and tongue position and . . . imitate it. Those aspects will be the same. We'll play it by ear." His pun was good-natured and on any other day, Tess might have smiled. But not today. Too much was riding on this analysis. "Dr. Ciccotelli, if you're ready, let's get started."

She followed Burkhardt inside and sat down in the chair he indicated. A stack of index cards lay next to a mounted microphone on the shelflike table that ran the length of the room. Printed on the top card was the message from Cynthia Adams's voice mail. With a shaky nod, Tess picked it up. "Start now?" she asked him.

"Wait until I'm outside." He sat at the console outside the booth and motioned her to begin. She tried, but closed her eyes when her voice broke. Hearing those hideous words aloud again made her picture Cynthia Adams listening to them, and in her drugged state, believing them.

Burkhardt's voice sounded scratchy over the intercom. "Start again, Doctor." There was quiet, then Burkhardt's voice again, kinder this time. "Try not to think about the victim. Try to do it like it was in the message. Kind of silky."

Silky. Tess straightened her shoulders and read it again.

"Better, but again. And silkier."

She read it again, looking up midway through to find Aidan Reagan's eyes fixed on her face. He nodded. "You're doing fine," he mouthed.

Her nerves still jittered, but the sick feeling in her gut calmed enough for her to manage the tone of the caller before going on to the other cards, which were a series of random words, chosen for the sounds they required the speaker to make. She read them all, then read through the stack again. And every few minutes she'd look at Reagan. Each time he'd nod. He never smiled, never said another word. Still, she felt a little less alone on her side of the glass.

Finally she was done. Burkhardt stood up, his face giving away nothing. "Thank you, Doctor. You can come out now."

Tess came out of the booth, her hands and knees steady through sheer will. But nobody said a word. The men were looking at Burkhardt's computer screen. Not one of them would meet her eyes. Finally she could take it no longer. "Well?"

Jack shook his head. "It's close, Tess. Real close."

Slowly she exhaled. What had she expected after all? The voice on the machine was close enough to her own to fool her own mother. "Well, then. What next?"

Burkhardt's look was a mix of respect and sympathy. "I haven't even started to analyze, Dr. Ciccotelli. I figured they'd be this close. Don't give up yet."

Patrick draped his coat over his arm. "Call me when you have something. It would be nice if it were by noon. I have a lunch meeting with Judge Doolittle then and I'd like not to look like a complete idiot."

Burkhardt snorted when the door closed behind Patrick. "Noon? Is he kidding?"

"No," Spinnelli said. "We'll get to the bottom of this, Tess. Try not to worry."

She nodded stiffly. "Right." She'd be more successful trying not to breathe.

Spinnelli left shaking his head. "Damn. I was hoping."

Tess shrugged into her coat and picked up her briefcase. "Thanks for trying. I need to sign that wiretap release and let you gentlemen get to work." She walked past Murphy, who'd said precious little throughout the test. He looked nearly as devastated as she felt and she was suddenly too weary to be angry with him any longer. She stopped so that she was inches in front of him and couldn't see his face. "I understand, Todd," she murmured. And she did. "It still hurts that you didn't believe me, but I do understand. I might have thought the same thing given the evidence."

She heard Reagan and Murphy talking softly as she made her exit, then Reagan was behind her. She knew it was him, just from the way he sounded, the way his aftershave smelled.

They walked to Reagan's desk in silence. Wordlessly he handed her the wiretap release form and she stared down at it. The only words she could hear were Amy's. *Don't be an idiot, Tess.* She was willfully signing away her civil right to privacy. But if the woman called back, they'd have her voice. *And not mimicking mine.* Assuming the same woman made all the calls, which at this point seemed fair. It would have to be worth the risk. Quickly she signed the form, then when she was sure her eyes were even, looked up at Reagan. "Thank you. You made it easier for me in there."

His smile was brief, but still it sent a shiver down her back. "You've had a hard few days, Doctor. I'm not sure I'd have held up as well."

This made her smile. "Have a good day, Detective. I can see myself out."

Tuesday, March 14, 11:55 A.M.

After dealing with bank officials all morning, Aidan now understood the ever-increasing popularity of ATMs. They were impersonal, true, but the machines were prompt and didn't have sticks stuck up their asses.

Even with a warrant it had taken some time to determine which branch Cynthia Adams had chosen to house her safe-deposit box. Finally, they were being escorted into the vault by a thin-faced woman named Mrs. Waller. She vaguely reminded Aidan of his eighth-grade algebra teacher. It was not a pleasant memory.

Mrs. Waller pulled a medium-sized box from its slot and placed it on a tall table. "You have the key?"

Murphy produced it. "This could be Geraldo breaking into Capone's safe, you know," he muttered while unlocking it and pulling back the lid. "Some stock certificates. Her will." He handed it to Aidan who skimmed it quickly.

"Bulk of her estate goes to her sister."

"Must not have updated it recently." Murphy looked over at Mrs. Waller. "When was the last time she was in the box?"

The woman folded her thin hands primly. "This past Friday."

"Really?" Aidan frowned. "Did she take something out or put something in?"

"We don't keep that information. We uphold our clients' privacy."

"You know I'm getting a little tired of everybody's privacy," Aidan grumbled.

"Then I'm glad you're not defending my fourth-amendment rights." Murphy rattled a small envelope. "I'd say she put something in." He slit the end of the envelope and shook two microcassettes to the table. "Tiny."

"They go in dictating recorders," Aidan said. His sister-in-law never went anywhere without her little recorder. "Kristen is always muttering into one. One of the secretaries in Patrick's office should have a machine that will play it."

Murphy gathered the contents of the box. "So should Burkhardt."

"You just want to see if he's made a decision on the voice-print."

Murphy's smile was fleeting. "The thought had crossed my mind. Let's go grab something to eat, then go to Burkhardt's for a listen."

Tuesday, March 14, 12:35 P.M.

"Are you planning to stand me up?"

Tess looked up from the file and blinked to focus on the man standing in her office doorway, then the clock on the wall. The clock was an antique and so was the senior doctor of their practice, Harrison Ernst. They had a standing Tuesday lunch date. "Harrison. I'm sorry, I lost track of the time. Would you mind if we didn't go to lunch today?"

Harrison pulled her coat and purse from the coat tree. "I would indeed."

"I need to finish going through these files." She'd been at it for hours, trying to figure out which of her current clients were most at risk for mental manipulation. Now she pushed away the one she was reading with just a hint of petulance.

"You need to take a break, Tess. Your eyes are . . . twitching. Humor an old man." He took her hand and pulled her up. "See, that wasn't so hard."

"Harrison, please."

He flicked a glance at her desk. "You're trying to figure out who's next, aren't you?"

His slightly indulgent tone had her back up. "I was."

"Would you have suspected the two who died would be so susceptible?"

Tess closed her eyes and held on to his gnarled old hand. "No more than about half of my other patients. I can't find any obvious link other than they both had suicidal tendencies stemming from trauma."

"Like half of your other patients. May I suggest a different course of action?"

Somehow he'd put on her coat and had her headed for the elevator. It was only three floors down, but Harrison was no longer able to take the stairs. She could handle it for three floors. She forced a smile. "Can I stop you?"

He chuckled and hit the button for the parking garage. "Probably not. Tess, stop trying to be a mind reader. Be a psychiatrist."

The doors closed and her pulse quickened. *Two floors. One floor more.* The elevator doors opened and she took a deep breath, not caring that the air was oily and dank. "What do you mean?"

"If you hadn't been a suspect, and these two detectives had come to you for a consult, what would you have done?"

He helped her into his car. "I would have prepared a profile," she said when he slid behind the wheel.

"Then do that," Harrison said mildly and pulled from his parking space. "And I'll help you. Oh, I anticipate there will be reporters waiting at the exit."

"I'm sorry."

His glance was reproachful. "Hush, Tess. Look inside the bag."

Tess opened the brown paper sack that lay on the seat between them and had to laugh. Inside were a black felt hat and Groucho glasses, complete with nose and mustache. "My disguise?"

His lips twitched. "I thought you might want to go incognito."

"Do you have a fake passport and ten thousand dollars in here, too?"

"We're not going to Mexico, Tess. Just to lunch."

Her heart squeezed. "Harrison, have I ever told you that I love you?"

He patted her thigh. "No, but I'd figured it out myself. Eleanor wouldn't want you to be sitting around beating yourself up."

Tess thought about the woman who'd taught her so much.

Eleanor Brigham had been her mentor and Harrison's best friend. Together Eleanor and Harrison had started the practice nearly twenty years before. Tess knew she'd been chosen as the heir apparent, but had been unprepared when Eleanor died of a stroke in her sleep three years before. "I miss her. I wish she was here. I'm glad you are."

He pulled out into traffic, never blinking at the reporters that tried to stop them. "I truly have grown to hate the media of late."

"I know what you mean. So who is this monster, Harrison?"

"You tell me. You know more of the facts than I do."

"I don't know them all. Detective Reagan keeps a great deal from me." She settled back in the seat and bit at her lip. "But I know enough to form an impression. This is a person with a need to control and a flair for both detail and drama. There is an ability to understand vulnerability and the capability to ruthlessly exploit it. They have access to my patients' names and their police reports."

"Male or female, Tess?"

"I don't know. The person who's called me twice now is definitely female. The person who imitated my voice was definitely female."

His quick glance was shocked. "Someone imitated your voice?"

"On Cynthia Adams's voice mail. I went in this morning to give a voice sample, hoping to exclude myself from the investigation, but so far that doesn't look likely."

"This somebody has planned this for some time, then."

"Looks like."

"How did they know your patients' names?"

"I've been thinking about that, too. One thing both Winslow and Adams had in common was that both were referred by the hospital when they were admitted for suicide attempts. But then again, so are half my patients."

"But the hospital would have records of those referrals."

"They would, yes. Technically, those records are private, guarded, just like we protect our records. But . . ." She shrugged.

"Are your records intact?" he asked carefully.

"I thought of that, too. Nothing is out of place and my electronic records haven't been accessed by anybody except me and Denise."

He frowned. "She's been with us for five years. Since you joined the practice."

Tess sighed. She'd never been comfortable with Denise, but Harrison was quite fond of her. "I know. Besides, this person has access to police records as well. They knew about Cynthia's sister, had a copy of her death scene photos. Winslow's baby's death photos, too. I certainly didn't have those things in my records. There were also lilies in Cynthia's apartment. I didn't know anything about that."

"So somebody has a cop in their pocket?"

"Or a cop's holding the reins."

Harrison drew a deep breath while pulling the car into the restaurant's parking lot. "Revenge then?"

"Detective Reagan seemed to think it was a possibility."

He put the car in park. "So we have an organized, theatric sociopath."

"Who knows about meds."

"Ah, now that's interesting."

She thought about the tragedy of the two deaths. Suicides when both had fought so hard to dig themselves out of the mire. There was a cruelty here that went beyond mere violence. "And who doesn't like to get his hands dirty."

"Who has a hard-on for you."

Tess's eyes widened at the uncharacteristic vulgarity. "Harrison." He said nothing and she shrugged. "I guess so."

"Sounds like you have the beginnings of a profile, Doctor," he said with a smile. "And I have a taste for roast pork."

There was one good thing to be said for Chicago traffic midday, Joanna thought as she pulled the lens cap from her camera. Nobody went so fast that a biker couldn't keep up with them. Straddling her bike, she snapped ten good pictures of Dr. Ciccotelli and her companion.

After tailing Ciccotelli for a day her camera's memory card was nearly full and her flypaper was getting good and sticky.

Chapter Nine

❦

Tuesday, March 14, 12:35 P.M.

It's not finished," Burkhardt snapped before Aidan or Murphy could say a word.

"We didn't come to harass you," Aidan said and produced a white paper bag from his coat pocket. "But we'd be willing to bribe you."

Burkhardt lifted a brow. "What's in the bag?"

Aidan held it just out of reach. "Baklava. The really good stuff." He'd intended to keep it for his own midafternoon snack, but Burkhardt looked frustrated, his hair standing up in spikes as if he'd pulled at it repeatedly. Aidan's mother had always said you catch more flies with honey and baklava was dripping with it.

Burkhardt scowled. "You fight dirty, Reagan. Okay, hand it over." He snagged the bag and opened it, sniffing in appreciation. "There are nuances."

"What does that mean, 'nuances'?" Murphy asked.

"It means that I see some differences in certain sounds, but they don't occur frequently enough on the tape to be sure. This impressionist is very, very good." He hesitated, looked at Aidan, then Murphy. "Are you sure your shrink's not guilty?"

Aidan could hear Murphy's teeth grinding. "We're sure," Murphy bit out.

Burkhardt shrugged. "Well, she's got your shrink down pat."

The term "impressionist" had struck a chord and visions of bad Richard Nixon impressions were flickering through Aidan's mind. "You think she could be a pro?"

Burkhardt shrugged. "Maybe. It's certainly worth a try. The best impressionists usually end up on the comedy circuit. Some are voice actors for cartoons, but you're not going to find too many of them in Chicago."

"Theater actresses do voices too," Murphy said slowly. He pulled the envelope holding the microcassettes from his shirt pocket and handed it to Burkhardt. "But we really didn't come to harass you or bribe you. Can you play these for us?"

Burkhardt shook the microcassettes onto his palm. "Not on this equipment." He went to a filing cabinet and rummaged until he straightened, a small dictating recorder in his hand. "This is the best I can do for now." He slipped one of the cassettes in the recorder and pushed play.

Aidan frowned at the high-pitched keening cry. "What the hell is that?"

Burkhardt put the machine to his ear. "Sounds like 'Cynthia, Cynthia, why did you do it?'" He handed the recorder to Aidan, a disturbed look on his face. "It sounds creepy. Like a little kid, but it's hard to pick up. These little machines don't produce the greatest quality."

Aidan listened, rewound, and listened again. "Cynthia

Adams put these tapes in her safe-deposit box two days before she died." He caught Murphy's eyes. "The speakers."

"You're right," Murphy said grimly. "Taunting Adams into believing her sister was calling her from the grave. Why would she make a tape?"

"Maybe she thought she was losing her mind and was afraid to tell anyone. Tess said Adams was good at denying what she didn't want to believe. She didn't want to believe she heard voices and the tape would have been proof she wasn't imagining it."

Murphy looked at Burkhardt. "If this is the same impressionist, can you compare it to the imitation of Tess Ciccotelli's voice?"

Burkhardt nodded. "The tape's lousy, but I'll do my best."

Aidan looked at the tapes. "You know there was one other taped message. The one urging Adams to check her e-mail. Have you analyzed that?"

Burkhardt frowned. "I didn't know about it."

"We were so focused on Tess's message that we forgot about it," Murphy scowled.

"Well, at least I know about it now. I'll get it from Jack and maybe all together I can get you something definitive."

Tuesday, March 14, 3:15 P.M.

Mrs. Lister was crying, wild wracking sobs of grief and rage. But it was beautiful music to Tess's ears. For three months this woman had been coming to therapy for symptoms ranging from chest tightness to insomnia. The underlying reality was that she had been unable to deal with the sudden suicide of her thirty-year-old son. She'd gone through the motions, burying him, mourning him. But her rage ran so very deep.

Somehow, some way, the public deaths of Cynthia Adams and Avery Winslow had served to unlock all that rage and now, finally, Mrs. Lister was admitting how very angry she was. How much she hated him for leaving her that way. How much she loved him and wished he'd come home. She should have protected him, but she hadn't known. Never suspected. Until it was way too late. Now there would be no second chance.

It was a common enough theme among those left behind, but it never failed to make Tess's eyes sting, her throat close. For now, she pressed some tissues into Mrs. Lister's hand and let her cry it out. She'd be hollowed out afterward, Tess knew, but not necessarily ready to take the next step. Every patient was different, their needs unique.

While Tess quietly waited, the pager in the front pocket of her slacks buzzed silently against her hip. It was Denise. No one else had the number. The pager was the discreet way Denise would contact her when she was in session. *Not now, Denise.* Thirty seconds later the pager buzzed again. Tess rose and surreptitiously pulled it from her pocket under the guise of staring from the office window down at the street.

Her heart skipped a beat, then two. A series of "911"s filled the little message screen. A single "911" was their emergency code. Her hands trembling, she slipped the pager back in her pocket. Forcing her voice to remain steady, she turned to the weeping woman on her couch. "Mrs. Lister, I'm going to step out for a moment, to give you some time."

Tess slipped out and her skipping heart dropped to her gut. Denise sat behind her desk, her face totally white. "I'm sorry, but there's another call. Line two. She'll only talk to you and she says you'll want to talk to her."

Tess picked up the phone, squared her shoulders, and gave Denise a brisk nod. Denise punched the button for line two and Tess's ear was filled with the staticky sound of a cell phone with a lot of background noise. A horn blared and a second responded in kind. Fiercely she wished she'd allowed Reagan to tap her office phone even though she knew she could never do so. "This is Dr. Ciccotelli. How can I help you?"

"Dr. Ciccotelli, I'm a neighbor of one of your patients."

Cut the bullshit, lady, was on the tip of Tess's tongue, but she bit it back, not wanting to antagonize the woman into hanging up. "Which patient, ma'am?"

"Malcolm Seward."

Tess drew a deep breath and gestured for Denise to hand her a pen. She wrote the name on the pad and Denise typed Seward's name into the computer.

This was going to be very bad indeed. "What is Mr. Seward's difficulty?"

"He's having a violent argument with his wife," the woman said diffidently. "Looks like . . . yes, he just slapped her to the floor. Says he's going to fucking kill her," she added, as if commenting on the weather. "I'll let you take it from here, Doctor."

The woman hung up and Tess looked at the door to her office where Mrs. Lister still sat, knowing what she had to do. "Call Harrison, tell him to come and do something with Mrs. Lister."

"Do what?"

"Hell, I don't know!" Tess's hands were shaking. "Wrap up the session. Reschedule her for tomorrow. He'll know what to do. Give me Seward's address." She grabbed the notepad on which Denise had jotted two addresses. "What?"

"He's got two homes," she said helplessly. "One in the city and one out past North Shore. Where do you think he is?"

"There was traffic in the background," Tess said. "It'll be the city address." Less than three blocks away. "Call 911. Tell them to hurry."

She ran from the office, down the stairwell, praying the

reporters had gone away, knowing it wouldn't mean anything even if they had.

Malcolm Seward was news. Big news. If the media didn't know now, they'd sure as hell know soon. She burst onto the street and took off at a sprint, ignoring the sole cry of an outraged pedestrian. *Reagan.* His face materialized in her mind. *Call Reagan.*

Tuesday, March 14, 3:30 P.M.

Luckily Spinnelli's wife was a patron of the arts in a variety of forms. Luckily she'd dragged Spinnelli to an improv show the week before and their lieutenant had enjoyed it enough to stay awake, which apparently was not the case with every performance she took him to. Within minutes of calling his wife, their lieutenant had been able to hand them a list of contacts at the Chicago Studio Theater, a well-known improv training ground and now Murphy and Aidan entered the theater together, badges out. A rehearsal was in process and all eyes frowned at them.

"I'm Detective Murphy and this is my partner, Detective Reagan."

"What's this about?" an older man on the stage asked.

"We just have a few questions," Aidan said. "We're looking for a woman who imitates voices and we were pointed in your direction."

The older man sat down on the stage's edge and pushed himself to the floor. "I'm the stage manager. Name's Grant Oldham."

"Well, like I said, Mr. Oldham, we're looking for a woman who can imitate voices. She's very good. We were thinking she might be involved in the theater somewhere."

Oldham straightened to his full height of about five feet seven inches. "I'm not going to give you a list of our performers so you can go on a witch hunt."

"This is a murder investigation, Mr. Oldham, not a witch hunt," Aidan returned mildly. "You are, of course, under no obligation to tell us anything. Are they, Murphy?"

"Nope, but I have heard that actors and actresses are terribly bohemian. Who knows what we might find hidden backstage when we come back with a warrant?"

It was hard to tell in the semidarkened room, but it looked like Oldham paled. "You can't get a warrant to search us without just cause. It's unconstitutional."

Aidan sighed. Everybody was an expert on the Constitution all of a sudden. "We're trying to track down a murderer who's already killed twice with no sign of stopping. We'd like to have your help, but this is of a high enough priority that if we took you in for questioning, nobody would fault us. Please. Do the right thing and help us out."

Oldham blew out a breath. "What do you want to know?"

"Women who can imitate voices," Murphy said. "Talented ones."

Oldham rubbed the bald spot on the top of his head. "Let's see, there's Jen Rivers, Lani Swenson, Nicole Rivera . . ." He threw a look over his shoulder at the other performers on stage. "Anybody else?" Oldham asked.

"Mary Anne Gibbs," said a man with a mangy-looking goatee. "She does a great Liza." The others just shook their heads, still frowning.

Aidan wrote down all the names while Murphy pulled from his pocket a picture of the woman from the mailbox store video.

"Do you know her?" Murphy asked.

Oldham squinted. "Hey, Egypt, hit the house lights, will ya?" The goateed performer ambled off-stage and suddenly bright light flooded the theater, making them blink. Oldham took the picture and studied it intently. "Hair's wrong, but . . . It could be Nicole. Then again, it's really grainy. Sorry, Detectives."

Aidan's spine was tingling. They were a step closer. "Do you know where we can find Nicole?"

Oldham looked over his shoulder again. "Any of you know where Nicole hangs?"

"She used to wait tables in a café near the Sears Tower," the goateed man said. "I don't know if she still does. I haven't seen Nikki around in a few months."

Aidan's cell phone rang. "Excuse me, I'll just be a minute." He moved a short distance away as he looked at his caller ID. Tess Ciccotelli.

"What?" he said, skipping salutation.

"I need you to meet me." She was breathless, her voice just shy of frantic. "I got another call."

"Murphy," Aidan called sharply. "We need to go. Who this time, Tess?"

"Malcolm Seward."

Aidan stopped abruptly in the theater's lobby, Murphy right behind him. "The football player?" Not just any football player. He was a legend. Malcolm Seward was one of her clients?

"Yes. Please, Detective, please hurry. Here's the address."

Trapping the phone between his shoulder and ear, Aidan scratched the address on his notepad, below the names of the four women. It was a high-priced address, not too far from Ciccotelli's. "Where are you now?" He heard a car horn and tires squeal and something that sounded like Ciccotelli saying "asshole." "*Tess?* Are you all right?"

"I'm fine, I'm all right. I'm running into his apartment building now. It's on the seventh floor. Hurry."

"Tess, *wait*. Wait for us." But she was gone. "Let's go, Murphy," he said and started to run.

Her heart was pounding. Pounding. Its pace set hers as she hurtled through the glass doors of Seward's apartment building.

The astonished doorman was a few seconds too late to catch her. "Stop. You can't go up there!"

"I'm a doctor," she gasped over her shoulder. "Medical emergency." An elevator door was just sliding open and after a split second of hesitation, she jumped in and hit the button for the seventh floor. The faint wail of sirens pierced the pounding in her head as the doors slid closed. The police were almost here. Just a block away.

Only seven floors. Now six. She fastened her eyes on the digital display, counting her heartbeats as the elevator rose.

Malcolm Seward, a football player with so much pent-up rage. She dragged in a breath, her lungs burning. He was sent to therapy by the team doctor when he pounded another player's face in an off-field and thankfully off-camera dispute. She'd seen his problem quickly, although it had been weeks before he'd been ready to say the words.

The elevator doors slid open and Tess stumbled into the hall. Seward's apartment was easy enough to detect from the rabid cursing, broken only by the terrified screams that chilled her blood.

"No, God, no. Malcolm, please." A woman's screams. *He says he's going to fucking kill her.* But she wasn't dead yet. *I'm not too late.*

The steel door hung on its frame, battered. She stared at it for a moment, gathering her wits. He'd broken the door down. *Where are the cops? They should have been here before me.* But they weren't here and the screaming had stopped. Now there was only terrified whimpering, which was even worse.

"Please, Malcolm." The woman's whisper was strained, hoarse. "Please. I won't leave you. I won't tell."

"You *lie*. You fuckin' *bitch*. Don't you *lie* to me."

"I'm not lying. I'm not—" A muffled shriek.

Unable to wait any longer, Tess pushed the door open and froze. Three feet inside the door stood Malcolm Seward, six feet five inches of solid muscle and boiling rage, holding his petite wife off the ground, his forearm crushing her throat. A gun to her head. *Her name,* Tess thought desperately. *What is her name? Gwen. Her name is Gwen.* Tess made herself breathe, settle. Hard to do as Gwen's eyes popped from their sockets, wide with terror. Her small hands clawed at his arm, to no avail. She was looking straight at Tess, her frantic pleas utterly noiseless.

"Malcolm." Tess said his name calmly. "Let her go. I can help you if you let her go."

Gwen was gasping for air now, her legs thrashing against his. But the man was a rock, capable of running the ball with three two-hundred-fifty-pound men hanging off him. His tiny wife was as much a threat as a bug.

Seward looked up, his eyes wild. Accusing. Sweat poured from his body, soaking the shirt he wore. "You *told* her. You promised you wouldn't, but you *told*."

Tess held her hands up, palms out.

Her heart was pounding again, this time in fear. The woman again. The woman who had left the message on Cynthia Adams's voice mail had imitated her once again. "Let Gwen go, Malcolm."

"No." He shook his head, his movements frenetic. "No. She's going to leave me. She's going to tell." He tightened his hold, jerking Gwen higher off the ground. "Nobody leaves me."

"Nobody's going to leave you, Malcolm." Tess made her

voice soothing, melodious, and watched him start shuddering. "Nobody's going to tell."

He was shaking now, tears running down his face. "You
told her. You called and told her. You promised you'd never
tell, but you did." He sobbed, jerking his wife high then
bringing her back solidly against his chest. Gwen's struggling had stopped. She simply dangled like a limp doll.

"No, Malcolm. I didn't tell."

"She knew. She knew."

Tess's heart stopped. Knew. Not knows. *Knew.* "Don't
hurt her. Please."

"She said she was going to leave me and tell. I'll lose it.
Everything." He stilled. "Nobody leaves me. Nobody tells."
He uttered the words carefully. Precisely.

Then he pulled the trigger. The scream froze in Tess's
throat as Gwen Seward's body jerked, then went limp. Malcolm tossed his wife to the floor and, shocked into immobil-
ity, Tess's eyes followed her down. Blood was seeping from
Gwen's head, soaking the vanilla Berber carpet. Gwen
Seward didn't move. She was dead. He'd killed his wife and
now she was dead.

Sanity returned with a jolt. *Get out. Run.* She turned on her
heel to run, but he was faster and in less than a heartbeat he
had her. Tess thrashed and kicked, but his forearm came
around her throat and the gun ground into her temple. She
could hear his voice at her ear, calm now.

"Nobody tells," he said. "Not her. Not you."

Aidan clenched his fists at his sides. Damn elevator was like
molasses, his stomach like water. Murphy said nothing at all,
but his hands were steady at his sides. His eyes, however, told
a different story. Gunshots. Hostage situation. Tess Ciccotelli.

What if we're too late? Aidan thought. *Dear God, don't let
us be too late.*

Finally the elevator slid open and it was all Aidan could do to approach the scene with calm caution. The layout of the apartment building was like a hotel, its corridors nearly as long. Six uniforms lined the hallway outside an open doorway, weapons drawn. One of the cops walked toward them, his face grim. "I'm Ripley. My partner and I were first on the scene."

"What's the status?" Murphy asked, his voice low and urgent.

"He's shot his wife in the head and won't let any of the EMTs in to check her out. But we didn't see any sign of her breathing."

"And the doctor?" Aidan asked and held his breath.

Ripley's eyes flickered. "He's got her by the throat with a gun to her head."

Aidan flinched, the picture flashing before his eyes all too real.

Murphy swallowed hard. "Like before."

Ripley tilted his head. "Excuse me, Detective?"

"She's been attacked before," Murphy said harshly. "By an inmate she was evaluating." They started walking toward Seward's apartment. "Have you called a hostage negotiator?"

"We called for him but he's a half hour away." Ripley stopped several feet shy of the door, pitching his voice low. "There's a big window behind him. If we could get a sniper in one of the apartments across the street, he might be able to get a decent shot. We've evacuated everybody on this floor and the floors below and above us."

"I'll call Spinnelli," Murphy said and walked off to the far side of the apartment floor where he couldn't be overheard.

Aidan took off his overcoat. "Let me try to talk to him."

The officer shook his head. "I don't think it'll do any good. He's high on something."

"We can't wait a half hour for the negotiator. He's already killed his wife. There's no reason for him to keep the doctor alive. Does anybody know why he's doing this?"

"When we came off the elevator we heard him saying something about how the doctor called his wife and told, that she'd promised not to tell. His wife had threatened to leave him. He shot his wife." Ripley's jaw clenched. "Your doctor was stunned. She turned to run and he ... grabbed her. There wasn't anything we could do."

Aidan looked over his shoulder to the far end of the hallway where Murphy stood, talking on his cell phone. His partner's head raised, his eyes wary. Finally he gave a nod and Aidan moved to the doorway. The steel door hung on its frame. It would have taken two men to kick it in.

Or one very enraged football player. Who at this moment held Tess Ciccotelli in a stranglehold, his gun at her temple. It was a .45 caliber, but still looked like a toy pistol in the man's big hand. Her eyes were closed, her body still, but her chest rose and fell with the even breaths she drew through her nose. Her hands clenched Seward's forearm, pulling herself high enough to breathe. Her toes just touched the floor. One of her shoes had landed in the hallway, the other next to Mrs. Seward's body.

She'd fought him, but now she stood in strained repose.

Seward himself was staring right at him, his eyes unfocused. The man swayed slightly as if to a rhythm only he could hear.

"Seward," Aidan said quietly and the man's eyes immediately focused. "Let her go."

Tess's eyes flew open and in them Aidan saw controlled terror. And pleading. And trust. He had to hold his spine straight to keep his own knees steady. Her life was in his hands.

"No," Seward said. "She told. She broke her word."

There was a shift in Seward's expression and Aidan made a snap judgment. Malcolm Seward was coherent enough to hear the facts, too far gone to accept platitudes and promises. "She didn't tell. Someone else called your wife, Seward, posing as the doctor."

His eyes flicked down to look at his dead wife for just a moment before rising again to meet Aidan's. "You're lying," he said unsteadily. The enormity of what he'd done had begun to sink in.

"You read the papers, Seward? Watch the news? You hear about the two suicides this week?"

Something moved behind his eyes. "Yeah. So?"

"They were her patients, too. Somebody called them. We have evidence that it wasn't Dr. Ciccotelli. Just someone imitating her voice." It wasn't the exact truth, but at this point Aidan didn't care.

Seward's gaze dropped to the floor once again, to his tiny wife who now lay in a pool of her own blood. His hand trembled on the trigger of the gun and Aidan saw Tess draw a deep breath. But her dark eyes stayed focused on him, just as they had this morning as she'd sat in the sound booth, imitating the words of a killer.

"She knew," Seward rasped. "She was going to leave me."

"I'm sorry, Malcolm," Aidan said, still quietly. "But Dr. Ciccotelli didn't tell. Let her go. Do the right thing and let her go."

He closed his eyes. "I killed her. My Gwen."

Aidan said nothing and the big man started to sob brokenly. His hold on Tess tightened, and she grimaced in pain as he ground the gun harder against her temple. "I killed her and it's your fault." He pulled harder against her throat and Tess gasped for breath, straining to get higher on her toes. Unable to. Still Seward sobbed, the tears cutting through the layer of blood and grime on his face.

Aidan fought back the panic, his throat closing. "One innocent woman is dead, Seward," he said sharply. "Don't make it two." He had Seward's attention now and he softened his voice. "She wouldn't have wanted it this way, your Gwen. Please, Malcolm. Let her go before it's too late."

Abruptly Seward straightened and in one motion shoved Tess away and dropped to his knees next to his wife. Tess stumbled forward, gasping, and Aidan grabbed her hand and yanked her out of Seward's reach. She came hard against his chest, shuddering, trembling, shaking like she would shatter.

Or maybe it was his own body shaking. Aidan's arms wrapped around her and he held on as she struggled to get her breath just as Seward lifted his wife in his massive arms and rocked her like a baby. His sobs had quieted, but tears still ran down his face.

The cops behind Aidan had moved into position. Guns trained on Seward who knelt, rocking his Gwen, still clutching his gun in one hand.

Murphy appeared at Aidan's side and by unspoken agreement the baton was passed. Aidan moved out of the way, taking Tess with him, and Murphy took his place in the doorway, his own gun drawn. "Drop the gun, Mr. Seward," Murphy said, his voice level. Aidan wasn't sure his own voice would ever be level again.

Malcolm Seward carefully laid his wife down and with one hand gently arranged her arms at her sides. Then turned the gun to his own mouth and pulled the trigger.

In Aidan's arms, Tess flinched, grabbed the front of his shirt, and held on.

For a long moment nobody said anything. Then Murphy carefully reholstered his weapon and sighed. "Fuck. Goddammit."

The hallway exploded into motion, EMTs rushing into

the Seward apartment. But just as quickly they stood, shaking their heads. "Both dead," one said. "Call the ME."

Tess pulled away and leaning against a wall in the hallway, slid bonelessly to the floor. She looked into the apartment at Seward, then up at Aidan, her face drained of color. Her pulse beat hard in the hollow of her throat, under which ran a wide red scar. "Thank you," she whispered.

Not trusting his voice, he could only nod.

Murphy leaned over to pick up something bright from the floor. Her scarf. But the scarf fluttered back to the floor when Murphy let it go. "It's . . ." He grimaced. "You don't want that one anymore, Tess."

Her voice was wooden. "Do you need me here? Or can I go?"

Aidan didn't think she could stand on her own feet, much less get herself home. "We'll see you home. But first we'll need your statement." He didn't really, not at this moment anyway. He just wanted her to stay where she was until some of the color returned to her face.

Amazing him, she pushed herself to her feet. "Let's get it done so I can go home and clean up." She plucked at her jacket, fouled from Gwen Seward's blood and Malcolm Seward's sweat. Swallowing hard, she swayed. "I think I have her blood in my hair." She looked down at her stocking-clad toes. "And on my feet. Oh, God." She shuddered, her hand coming to cover her mouth before she jerked it back, staring at her bloody palm. "Oh, God." Her eyes flew up, focused on his white shirt, now streaked with red where she'd held on for dear life. "I got it on you. I'm sorry."

Aidan's throat tightened, remembering her hands clutching him as if he were her lifeline. "It's all right. I've had worse." He moved forward to push her back to the floor before she fell over, but one of the EMTs got to her first.

"Let's check you out before you go anywhere."

"I'm fine," she protested weakly.

"Uh-huh," the EMT responded noncommittally and proceeded to do his job. She let him check her pulse, her blood pressure, even flick a light in her eyes. But she drew back when the EMT put his fingers on her throat.

"It's an old scar," she said flatly. "Give me a form to absolve you of responsibility if you want, but I'm fine. I just want to go home."

Two people no longer had heads. It should have been three. But like a damn cat with too many lives, Ciccotelli still lived. She still breathed. It simply was not fair. But perhaps for the best. *When she dies, I want to be there in person.* To savor every moment. Every nuance.

And there was yet another sour cast to the day. Detective Reagan had told Seward that they had evidence that Ciccotelli's voice had been imitated. Reagan was lying. There was absolutely no question that Reagan had lied through his teeth. The match to Ciccotelli's voice was impeccable, confirmed by one of the best sound studios in Germany. Nicole was good enough to fool Ciccotelli's own mother.

Perhaps it had been a miscalculation to leave the voice mail for Cynthia Adams, but without it the police would have taken days longer to compare the fingerprints on the box to Ciccotelli's. If they'd ever made it that far.

No, the real miscalculation was that Ciccotelli still had so many cops willing to believe her. Obviously the hatred within the police department did not run as deeply or broadly as the police had claimed. That Detective Reagan had become one of her defenders was . . . disappointing. *I expected more of him.*

But judging from the way he'd fought for her freedom, he didn't hate her. *Au contraire.* Judging from the way he'd held her while Seward killed himself, he cared more than he'd probably admitted to himself.

It was disgusting. What was it about that woman that had men falling at her feet? Men who should know better than to be fooled by a pretty face and a twitching ass. Most men were weak.

I am not.

Two courses of action were indicated. The first, the elimination of pretty Nicole. If the police suspected Ciccotelli's voice had been imitated, it was only a matter of time before they found Nicole. Luckily she was expendable. Luckily she was of use no longer because the plan now had to change. Ciccotelli would not be going to prison. Not in the traditional sense at least. Not a concrete structure with high walls and iron bars.

It was a bitter disappointment. The setup had been so carefully planned. So much time had gone into each and every step with the express goal of seeing Ciccotelli behind bars. Alone and isolated. No career and no friends. And ultimately, no life.

But there were other kinds of prisons. Other ways of inducing isolation. Fear. Agony. Ciccotelli's prison would have them all.

Because she deserved every one.

Tuesday, March 14, 4:45 P.M.

They hadn't asked Seward's secret, Tess thought numbly, watching Murphy and Reagan direct the activity inside the apartment. A half dozen guys from CSU had come, led by Jack Unger. The ME's office had come with gurneys and body bags. And, except for the EMT, everyone had left her mercifully alone. Not one person had demanded to know what Malcolm Seward had insisted she'd told. Not yet anyway. But they would. They'd have to. And she'd tell them.

It didn't seem to make much difference now. Malcolm was dead. Gwen was dead. They'd had no children together. There was no one left for the truth to hurt.

Tess sat outside in the hall on the floor, one uniformed officer standing by the elevator, another positioned at the stairwell to keep unauthorized people from the scene. And, she supposed, to prevent her from leaving before she'd told the police what they wanted to know. Like that was going to happen. After hearing Seward pulling the trigger on himself, a surge of pure adrenaline had fueled her motions. Now, she wasn't sure if she could move if . . . She swallowed hard as the rest of that time-worn adage flitted through her mind. *If someone held a gun to my head.*

Her hands and feet were now clean, her bloody knee-high stockings removed by an EMT with gentle hands and an encouraging smile. Her feet were bare. The EMT had given her a pair of those footie socks with ribbed soles. Right now she didn't have the energy to lean over and slip them on her feet.

One of her shoes was unusable, covered in both Malcolm and Gwen Seward's blood and brains. The other she'd kicked into the hall and it now sat on the floor by her hip. It wasn't like she'd wear them again anyway. When she got home, every stitch of clothing she wore would go in the garbage. When she got home, she'd shower under a scalding stream of water, scrubbing her hair and skin until every last drop of hot water was gone. But even that wouldn't make her feel clean. When she got home, she just might finish off the bottle of wine Reagan had offered to her last night until the events of the last hour blurred into unconsciousness.

But it wouldn't help. Because when she woke up, she'd

still be in this nightmare. Malcolm and Gwen would still be dead. As would Cynthia and Avery.

Because of me. Logically she knew it was not true, but just as logically, she knew what was true wouldn't really matter when the city read their newspapers tomorrow. When she'd try to sleep tonight. What was true was that these people had trusted her to help them. What was true was that four innocent people were dead. *Because of me.*

The ME techs were now rolling the bodies past where she sat. One large bag, one small. She leaned her head against the wall and closed her eyes. It was an image she didn't want added to the others, but one she knew would linger for a long, long time regardless of what she wished. Regardless of how she commanded her brain to forget.

"Tess?"

She opened her eyes to the sight of Aidan Reagan towering over her. His gaze was watchful, as if he was afraid she would break. She pressed her cold fingertips to her colder cheeks. "You want my statement now."

"If you think you can."

"I can." She struggled to stand, then stared when he crouched down and slipped the socks on her feet as if she were a child. Then he twisted, scooting back until he leaned against the wall to sit beside her. Heat radiated from his warm body and she shivered, trying very hard not to remember how it had felt in his arms. How tightly he'd held her. How good it had felt. How safe. How his heart had thundered hard under her ear. He'd been afraid, too. Yet he'd done his job, with confidence and calm assurance. She owed him her life. The thought of a different end made her shiver once again.

"You're cold," he said flatly. "Good God, woman, did you run all the way from your office without a coat?" He shrugged out of his overcoat and wrapped it around her shoulders before she could utter a protest. "Don't fight me, Tess," he warned when she tried to give the coat back. "You look like a five-year-old could take you out right now."

"It'll get bloody," she murmured and he took her hand between his and began briskly rubbing to get her blood circulating again.

"It's all right. God, your hands are like ice. Why didn't you say anything?"

She leaned back against the wall, suddenly so weary. "You were busy." All the activity around her seemed to meld into a dull buzz she recognized as exhaustion. "Did I say thank you?"

He took her other hand, warming it. "Yeah," he said, gently now. "You did. Tell me about the call."

"I was with a patient." Who had it been again? *Mrs. Lister. That's right.* "Denise answered the phone. The woman would only talk to me. She sounded bored this time."

"Did it sound like the same woman?"

"No. She didn't sound young or old this time. Just bored. She said that Malcolm Seward and his wife were arguing." He'd finished rubbing her hands and now held her right hand loosely. She could pull it away if she chose, but she didn't. She couldn't. "She said Malcolm had just knocked his wife to the floor."

"When was this?"

"A few minutes before I called you, maybe. I told Denise to call 911 as I was running out the door." She frowned. "They took so long to get here. I thought they'd be here long before me." She looked up to find his eyes fixed on her face. *Cop's eyes,* she thought. Carefully expressionless. "I didn't plan to be a hero, Detective. But there was no one else to help. He'd kicked down the door and I knew how violent he could be when he got angry. I knew how afraid he was that someday he'd use his strength on his wife. He had her by the throat . . ." Her voice broke and he squeezed her hand.

"Take your time, Tess."

She straightened her shoulders, forced herself to finish. "He was ranting that I'd called his wife and told his secret. She'd threatened to leave him and nobody left him, he said. Then he shot her." A shudder ripped through her and she tightened her grip on his hand. "Then just tossed her aside. I tried to run. But he was too fast. Then he . . ." Her breath hitched and stubbornly she controlled it. "He put the gun to my head. Right about then the cops showed up."

"Why were you treating him?"

She huffed a mirthless laugh. "Anger management was what he claimed at first. He'd gotten fined for breaking some player's nose in a fight during one of the games."

"I remember that."

"Apparently so did the team management. They insisted he go get counseling."

"So he came to you."

"No, he went to the team doctor, for show. Then he came to me, for help." She met his eyes. "He was gay, Detective. He'd hidden it for years, denied it to everyone, including himself. But his personal needs were becoming too hard to control. He had a wife, a career. He was terrified he'd lose it all if anyone found out. And being Malcolm Seward, he couldn't just take up with anyone. He'd be recognized. Exploited. So he did nothing. And became angrier every day."

His eyes had flickered once in surprise, but were flat again. "Was he being blackmailed?"

"I don't think so, but I doubt he'd ever admit that to me. Frankly, we weren't getting anywhere in therapy. He kept insisting he could deny himself. He'd been able to . . . satisfy his wife often enough that she didn't suspect, but that was changing. She wanted to have a child and Malcolm didn't. She was accusing him of having an affair."

"Ironic," Reagan said quietly.

"Yes. He was getting angrier, lashing out at strangers." She sighed sadly. "Lashing out at Gwen. It was eating him up. He loved Gwen, he really did. He didn't want to hurt her or shame her. They'd been high school sweethearts. She was old-fashioned. She wouldn't have approved of his homosexuality." She swallowed. "I guess it doesn't matter anymore."

He squeezed her hand again, but made no move to comfort her with empty phrases and she appreciated that. "How did Seward find you?"

"Through the Yellow Pages. Malcolm didn't trust any of his friends enough to ask for a referral. He didn't want them to know it was any more than anger management, which most of his teammates could understand. He certainly didn't want Gwen to find out." Tess closed her eyes. The numbness was wearing off and her brain was clicking back into gear, remembering the lunch conversation with Harrison. Three hours ago she'd thought someone could have found her patients through the hospital's psychiatric unit. Now, she had to face the truth. "The only way somebody could have found out about all three is if they were watching the door to my office twenty-four/seven or they somehow broke into my records." The very thought made her physically ill, even to consider. All of her patient files . . . compromised. She gritted her teeth and forced the nausea back. "Based on all the events, I'm inclined to believe the second one."

He was quiet for a moment. "Where do you keep your records?"

"In a vault, along with Harrison's. Dr. Harrison Ernst. He's my—"

"Your partner. So who has access to the vault during office hours and after?"

"Just myself, Harrison, and Denise—our receptionist."

He released her hand and pulled his notepad from his

pocket. Tess stretched her fingers, feeling bereft. "Is this vault like a safe?"

"No, it's like a big walk-in closet."

"Do you keep electronic notes?"

Tess regarded him warily. "Sometimes. Not with every patient." There was probably one patient, five years ago whose files weren't kept electronically so technically she wasn't lying.

He shot her a hard look. "I'm not after peeking in your files, Doctor. Patrick will do that with his subpoena. Where do you keep these electronic files?"

"On my computer at work. I type up my own notes, print them, and put them in the file. In the—"

"In the vault, right. Do you delete these files off your hard drive?"

She hesitated. "Not as often as I should. But the system is password protected."

"Do you back up your hard drive?"

Again she hesitated. "Every Friday afternoon. I keep the records on my thumb drive." He lifted a brow in question. "Which I keep on my key ring," she added, "so it's always with me." *Except yesterday,* she thought. She'd left her keys in the office in her purse. In fact, she thought, growing more nauseous with each passing second, anytime she didn't have her keys in her hand her files were unprotected.

"There's one other option, Doctor," Reagan said, watching her intently. "Somebody could have been listening to your sessions."

Tess's eyes widened. "You mean . . . You mean you think my office is bugged? Oh my God. You do think this." She swung her eyes over to the Seward doorway where Murphy was coming out with Jack Unger. The nod Murphy gave Reagan was barely perceptible. "What?" When Reagan said nothing, Tess grabbed his arm. "Tell me."

Reagan sighed. "We found cameras in all three apartments. And microphones."

Tess fell back against the wall, scarcely feeling her head bump. "Cameras?"

He nodded. "Connected to the Internet."

The lunch she'd barely managed to keep down rose to gag her and she lurched to her feet. "No. You can't be right." He simply stood up, looking at her with sad resignation. "Dear God. Why?" she asked heavily.

"We don't know yet. We were thinking the cameras were installed to record the suicides themselves. Now, we're not so sure. On the way over here, we started thinking he could be using cameras to choose his victims, too. If he's spying on your patients, he could be spying on you. Will you let Jack check your office?"

Tess nodded shakily. "Yes. Yes, of course. Let's go now."

"Not now," he said gently. "Now you go home and clean up. Then we'll go to your office." He slid his hand along her back, turning her toward the elevator, leaving a trail of warmth everywhere he touched, even through the layers of his coat she still wore. His coat dragged the floor and she should have given it back to him, but she didn't. He tipped her chin up, once again studying her face. "You're shaky. Can you handle the elevator, or should we take the stairs?"

She dropped her eyes, embarrassed that he'd met her fear so head-on. "Stupid, huh? A shrink with a common phobia. Physician heal thyself and all that shit."

His hand tightened on her upper arm and gave her a gentle shake. "It's not stupid. It makes you human, Tess."

Her eyes flew up, met his. His blue eyes held only understanding and sympathy. No condescension. No accusation. Unexpectedly her eyes filled with tears. "Thank you," she whispered. "For everything."

He smiled down at her. "You're welcome. I guess I owed you one."

She drew a shuddering breath, got hold of herself. "Then we're even, Detective."

His smile dimmed a shade. "All right then. There's a battery of reporters downstairs. Do you want to walk out on your own, or do you need help?"

Tess straightened her spine. "I'll walk out on my own. But let's take the stairs."

He was silent as they walked down the stairs, stopping when she needed to rest, which was more often than she'd thought she would. The lobby of the apartment was lined with cops, keeping the reporters at bay. Aidan nodded at one of the uniforms.

"You can let the evacuated residents back into their apartments," he said. Then he opened the front door. "Don't make a comment. Don't say a word."

He sounds like Amy, Tess thought. She suspected neither Reagan nor Amy would have appreciated the comparison. But the thought was lost in the sea of faces and flashing lights as she walked into the throng of media. There were at least thirty people, some with microphones, others wielding cameras on shoulders.

Cameras. The sight of them made her think of the cameras the police had found in all the apartments, capturing her patients' last moments. Microphones. There might be one in her office. *Dear God.* It was enough to make her sick again, which was all she needed now. To throw up on what was probably live television. So she steeled herself for the gauntlet.

A microphone was shoved in her face. "Is Malcolm Seward dead? Were you held at gunpoint?"

With one hand she gripped Reagan's coat tight around her throat. With the other she pushed the microphone aside and kept walking, Reagan at her side. She looked to the street where Todd Murphy waited with his car. *Just another minute.*

"Were you shot?"

"Did you see Gwen Seward die?"

"Is it true Malcolm Seward killed himself?"

The barrage of questions melded together in her mind until a perfectly made up brunette stepped into her path. There was a gleam in her eye, a sharpness in her smile that shot warning bells in Tess's ears just a moment too late. "Dr. Ciccotelli, I'm Lynne Pope with *Chicago On The Town*. Did the fact that Malcolm Seward was hiding a homosexual lifestyle lead to this tragedy today?"

Shocked gasps rippled through the crowd followed by murmurs of disbelief.

It was only Aidan Reagan's hand on her arm that propelled her forward as her body seemed to freeze where she stood. Recovering, Tess schooled her face into an impassive mask, but she feared she'd shown her own shock long enough to whet Pope's appetite for salacious gossip. "I have no comment at this time."

Lynne Pope followed, her smile strained. "But Malcolm Seward was gay," she insisted. "You yourself confirmed this fact, just this afternoon, Doctor."

The impassive mask melted from her face as every drop of blood seemed to rush away from her brain. "Excuse me?"

Murphy opened the car door. "Just get in, Tess."

Pope blocked her path. "I don't know what kind of game you're trying to play, Doctor," the reporter muttered through smiling teeth, "but I won't stand for your bait and switch. If you think you can summon me here promising me the story of the year, then give me a 'No comment,' you'd better think again. By eight o'clock tonight my story will air, complete with a recording of you telling me that Malcolm Seward had become a violent and dangerous threat due to his rejection of his own homosexuality."

Tess went still as a new set of implications exploded in her head.

The media. The bastard had revealed her patient's secrets to the media. Her other patients would hear and wonder if their secrets were next.

Dr. Fenwick and the board would not be pleased. *My license will be revoked. My career is over.* Which now appeared to be the prime motive.

Pictures of her dead patients flashed across her mind. Mutilated bodies, sightless eyes. Would more patients die? *Are they finished now? Is the destruction of my career enough or will they keep going?* Who would be next?

Pope was watching her face carefully, one brow lifted sardonically. "Surprised, Doctor? Don't be. I record all incoming calls. For my own records of course."

This had to stop. Now. Her patients needed to be warned, regardless of any consequences to herself. Tess lifted her chin. "No, you do not have a recording of me, Miss Pope. What you have is a clever deception."

"Doctor," Reagan warned under his breath. "No comment."

Tess shot him a look from the corner of her eye. "I can't let this allegation slide, Detective." He nodded once in acceptance before she looked back at Pope who, to her credit, now looked more interested by the turn of events than angered. "Miss Pope, I have no comment other than to categorically deny ever having contacted you in the past on any topic. I am a therapist. It would make no sense for me to contact you in the manner you describe. I'm afraid you have been duped."

Pope's eyes glittered, pleased to have provoked a response. "By whom, Doctor?"

"I don't know." Narrowing her eyes, Tess looked directly into the camera. "But I intend to find out."

Chapter Ten

Tuesday, March 14, 5:10 P.M.

Aidan slipped his cell phone back in his pocket. "Patrick's getting a court order to block Pope from using that recording on the air tonight."

Murphy glanced over, then returned his gaze to the road. "He'll get the tape?"

"Yep. Now Burkhardt will have even more to compare."

"What do you mean, more to compare?" The question came from the backseat where Tess had been sitting silently for the ten minutes it had taken them to move two blocks. Traffic was gridlocked, courtesy of what seemed to be every news van in the city.

Aidan turned around to see her better. She was pale and trembling, her hair still matted, one hand clutching his overcoat around her throat. Her lips were bloodless except for the red marks her teeth had left behind. But her eyes were clear. She'd held herself together with an inner strength he wouldn't have predicted before Sunday afternoon and he found he could now understand how she'd retained such loyalty in the few that seemed to know her best.

"Cynthia Adams made a tape," he said.

She swallowed hard. "Of me?"

"No. It was hard to hear, but it sounded like a little girl's voice."

Tess closed her eyes and looked away. "Torturing her."

"Yes. We gave the tape to Burkhardt so he could compare it to the voice mail."

She opened her eyes at that. "Did you mean what you told Malcolm? That you can prove it isn't me on that tape?"

Aidan glanced at Murphy. She'd seen the glance and sighed. "You just told him that so that he'd let me go." One corner of her mouth lifted in a wry little smile that squeezed at his heart. "Not that I'm complaining, mind you. I'm just disappointed."

"It wasn't a lie," Murphy said, looking in the rearview mirror at her.

"Just not the whole truth," Aidan added. "Burkhardt saw what might be differences, but said he'd need more voice samples to be certain."

"He planned for you to find my voice on Cynthia's voice mail," she murmured. "He wanted to point you in my direction, identify my fingerprints. Make you suspect me."

And it might have worked, Aidan thought grimly, if she hadn't had such stalwart supporters like Kristen and Murphy behind her.

"I wonder if he knows Cynthia and Lynne Pope made tapes," she went on.

"I would imagine not." Murphy cleared his throat. "Tess, Aidan told you about the cameras."

She flinched. "Yes. I told him to sweep my office."

Aidan knew where Murphy was going with this. "We

should probably sweep your apartment as well," he said, as gently as he could.

She froze, her mouth open, her eyes wide and he could see the thought hadn't yet occurred to her. "I'm sorry," he said quietly.

"It's . . . it's all right." But it wasn't all right. He could see the way she struggled for composure. She was rocking unconsciously, her knuckles white as she tightened her grip on his coat until he thought she'd strangle herself. "Oh my God. Oh my God."

"Tess." Aidan barked it out and she looked up, still stunned. "We're almost at your apartment. More media will be there."

She nodded and before his eyes pulled herself together once more. Visibly she relaxed and her pale face became expressionless, her dark eyes cool. "I understand. Perhaps I could gather a few things and go to a hotel. I need to . . ." Her lips trembled for a moment before she firmed them resolutely. "I need to take a shower somewhere. I can still smell the blood in my hair."

"You stay with her," Murphy said to Aidan in a low voice. "Get Jack and Rick to search her place after she's gone. Then drive her car to the impound garage and have Rick go over it, too."

Aidan nodded as Murphy pulled up to the curb in front of Tess's building where a smaller, but persistent crowd of reporters waited. "Where are you going?"

"Spinnelli ran the address on that actress, Nicole Rivera, while I was requesting a sniper. I'll check her out." Murphy brought the car to a stop. "Don't let her out of your sight. Whoever is behind this has just taken this up a full notch."

"What do you mean?" Tess asked.

Murphy twisted so that he could see her face. "I mean that every reporter on the street heard Pope say you spilled the beans."

"But I didn't." She blew out a breath. "It doesn't matter. I'm going to have some angry patients."

Aidan frowned. "Dangerous?"

"Some. Nobody likes to have their deepest secrets revealed on live TV. Everyone likes to think there are some things they can hide, some places where they're truly alone." She straightened her back and opened the car door. "I used to."

Aidan climbed out after her, catching up as she pushed the first microphone aside. He moved ahead of her, clearing a path through the shouting reporters to the apartment entrance where an anxious doorman waited. Aidan recognized him from last Sunday.

Apparently the doorman's memory was quite good as well, because his face filled with a truly formidable scowl as soon as Aidan pushed into the small lobby. The older man rushed forward, then stopped short, his scowl gone, a look of fatherly worry in its place. "Dr. Chick, just tell me you're all right."

She smiled up at him. "I'm fine, Mr. Hughes. It's been quite a day, but I'm fine."

"I wouldn't let them in," he said with an angry look at the media outside. He turned the angry look on Aidan. "I wouldn't let him in, either, if I didn't have to."

She surprised him with a chuckle. "Oh, Mr. Hughes, I'm so glad to see you."

"Ethel says I should tell you she believes none of it, not a single word."

"Tell Ethel I appreciate all the good press I can get. But I don't think you have to worry about the detective." Her expression softened. "He saved my life this afternoon."

Hughes looked Aidan over, then gave him a grudging nod. "All right then. I did let your friends up, Dr. Chick. Dr. Carter and Miss Miller. They're waiting for you upstairs. I'm to call Dr. Carter's cell phone the moment you arrive."

"Well, make your call, Mr. Hughes. And thank you again."

This time Aidan didn't have to ask. He opened the door to the stairs and waited for her to pass through. She stood at the bottom of the stairs and looked up with a sigh. "You have any debilitating phobias, Detective?"

He hesitated. Then shrugged. "I'm not fond of heights." It was a gross understatement. Extreme heights gave him vertigo, a fact he'd never shared with another living soul. "Want to try and cure me?"

Her grin was small and wry, yet it sent a current of electricity across his skin. She appealed to him on too many levels. On Sunday he'd thought her a sexy gypsy with a heart of stone. And he'd wanted her so much he'd ached. Now, standing next to him with dirty hair and a dangerously pale face, she appealed to him even more. She had a soft, caring heart yet her will was stronger than most men he knew. When she'd been at Seward's mercy, a gun to her head, he didn't believe he'd ever breathe normally again.

"Thank you," she said softly. "Even if you're lying, I appreciate the gesture." She made it up half the flight, then turned to sink down on the step, twisting so that her head rested on the iron handrail. Twin flags of red stained her pale cheeks and perspiration dotted her forehead. She breathed heavily and the hand that had clutched his coat around her throat went lax. The coat slipped down to her shoulders, exposing the scar she worked so hard to hide. Now she seemed too tired to notice. "I'm sorry. One lousy flight of stairs should not tire me out."

He sat down next to her. "It's okay. You've had a hell of a day. I think you're entitled to a little combat fatigue. You must have run to Seward's apartment building in four minutes flat."

"I guess I did. I really wasn't thinking about it at the time."

The threadiness of her voice alarmed him. "Did you have lunch?"

"Mm-hmm. I went with Harrison."

"Let me rephrase. Did you ingest food?"

Her lips twitched. "I nibbled on some crackers. Harrison had roast pork, but I was too upset to eat. I suppose I'm a little weak-kneed from lack of fuel."

"You think?"

Her lips curved at that, delivering another sound blow to his self-control. "Give me another minute. I'll be fine." True to her word, she was on her feet a minute later. She shrugged off his coat and handed it to him. "Can you hold it? It's heavy," she said, then took the remaining stairs with the stubborn focus of a mountain climber. Aidan walked two steps behind, intending to catch her if she fell, but was instead treated to a bird's-eye view of her very nice rear end as she climbed.

Very nice, he thought, his hands itching to touch the curves that moved so enticingly with each step she climbed. Instinctively he knew that she'd fit his palms perfectly and for an instant his imagination exploded with erotic pictures of how it would be. How she'd feel when he closed his hands over her ass and jerked her hard against him. How she'd writhe and moan and drive him insane. How she'd feel in his arms when she was mindless with arousal.

Not trembling with fear. Abruptly the image faded and his brain cleared. He already knew how it felt to hold her when she was terrified. *Which is why you're here, Reagan,* he told himself scathingly as they reached her floor. So focus on protecting her and stop dreaming about her ass.

Tess led him to her apartment, then paused, her hand on her doorknob. "My friends will expect me to stay home so that they can take care of me. I'll tell them you think it's safer for me to sleep somewhere else tonight because of the reporters. I won't mention the cameras."

Aidan's mind was suddenly filled with a picture of exactly where she should sleep tonight. *With me.* And to his own surprise, it wasn't wholly sexual. Not nearly. Mostly he just wanted to see her safe. *Then* he wanted to see her naked. He managed to nod soberly. "That would be best."

Her friends were watching the news when they came in. Both instantly jumped to their feet. Jon Carter crossed the living room in two long strides and enveloped her in his arms, his possessive hold making Aidan grit his teeth.

They're only friends. Tess had said so and she might even think it was true, but it was obvious to Aidan that the good Dr. Carter thought something else entirely. Carter drew back, his face bent in a grimace. "God, Tess. You look like you've been in surgery with me and smell even worse. What's in your h—" He broke off when Tess's body stiffened. Carter's horrified eyes lifted to Aidan's and Aidan nodded, confirming what the man had guessed.

Carter blanched. "Then it's true."

"It's hers," Tess said dully. "It was on him and when he grabbed me . . ."

Carter slid his arm around her shoulders. "Let's get you cleaned up, honey."

She pulled away from him, still rigid. "I will, but not here, Jon."

Carter's brows snapped together. "Why the hell not?"

Aidan stepped forward. "What have you heard on the news? Exactly."

"That Tess's third patient killed his wife then himself," Amy Miller provided. She hadn't moved a foot from where she'd been standing. "And that Tess told the press about his homosexuality." She lifted her chin and stared Aidan straight in the eye, challenging him to disagree. "But we know that's not true."

"He doesn't think it is, Amy, but some of my patients might," Tess said, and Miller's eyes shifted to Tess's face awkwardly and Aidan remembered what Tess had said last night. *I'm not even sure she's my attorney anymore.* They'd fought, Tess and her friend, and now the atmosphere in the room was charged with the things they weren't saying to each other. "I'm going to check into a hotel. I'll let you know where I am once I'm settled."

Miller nodded, her jaw tight. "That makes sense, I guess." She glanced over at Aidan suspiciously. "Do you still need a defense attorney, Tess?"

"No." She swallowed hard and cleared her throat. "But I sure could use my friend."

At that Amy followed the same path Carter had taken, throwing her arms around Tess and holding her hard for a long, long minute. "Jon's right, Tess," she said as she broke away. "You jump in the shower and I'll pack your bag."

Tess shook her head. "I really just want to get to a hotel first. Once I'm clean I'm falling into the nearest bed."

Aidan's blood beat a steady drum in his head as she walked back to her bedroom with her lawyer friend, unaware how perfectly she'd voiced every thought his overactive libido had conjured.

"You know she didn't do this," Carter said, dragging him back to ground zero.

"I can't talk to you about what I do or don't know," Aidan said evenly, then something peevish made him throw a live grenade into the conversation. "For all I know, you could be involved."

Stunned, Carter could only stare. "You're out of your mind."

"Then I suppose I'm lucky she's a psychiatrist."

Abruptly Carter threw back his head and laughed. "You're good, Reagan. For a minute you had me there." Still smiling he shook his head. "You think that Tess and I . . . ?" He let the question trail away. "Well, we're not." He went utterly sober. "But she's one of my closest friends in the world and I don't want to see her hurt."

"On that we agree."

"Is she in danger, Detective?"

"Not at this moment, no." Aidan lifted a shoulder. "I'm just being careful."

Carter nodded. "See that you do." Abruptly he turned on his heel and pulled at a drawer in one of the ornate tables that backed Tess's sofa. He was completely at home, Aidan noticed darkly. Carter pulled out a sheet of paper and scribbled a half page before handing it to Aidan. "Here is my home address and some emergency phone numbers. If she needs help, please call me."

Aidan scanned the sheet. "Or Robin?"

"Any time of the day or night. We'll come." Carter hesitated, looking over his shoulder before continuing, his voice low. "Her family's in Philly."

"She told me."

Carter's brows went up, surprised. "She did?" He looked over his shoulder again. "Did she tell you they don't speak?"

Aidan found himself staring back at the bedroom along with Carter. "No. She just said she has four brothers who sound like they could be their own Mafia."

Jon smiled. "Her brother Vito's a Philadelphia cop. The rest are teachers, artists, and architects. Tess is their baby sister. She still talks to Vito." Carter's smile dimmed. "He was the one who came when she got hurt last year."

"Her parents didn't come?" Aidan was shocked at the thought.

"She wouldn't let Vito tell them. Anyway, if she needs help, call Vito. I don't know his number off the top of my head, but if you call us at home, either Robin or I can get it for you. Please take care of Tess, Detective. She's our family."

"I will." And at that moment, Aidan knew he would, whatever it took.

The women appeared from the back bedroom, Miller carrying an overnight bag. Tess wore the same filthy clothes, but the socks were gone from her feet, a pair of canvas sneakers in their place. "The ladies are back," Carter said with a sweeping motion of his arm. "Amy, I'm driving back to the hospital. You want me to drop you off at your office?"

"No, I've got my car." She gave Tess another hug. "Call me when you get checked in." She handed the bag to Aidan and followed Carter out the door.

The door closed behind them and Tess's shoulders sagged. Her mouth opened, then closed firmly as her eyes skittered about, looking for cameras. "Let me feed the cat before we go."

Aidan followed her into the kitchen, gritting his teeth when she bent over to reach the cabinet under the sink, once again unconsciously torturing him with the sight of her round rear end. At his sides, his hands clenched into fists, squelching his need to touch. But he wouldn't.

Not here, where cameras could be watching their every move. Not now, when the shock of the afternoon was still heavy in her eyes. By the time she stood holding a bag of dry cat food in her hands, Aidan had both his thoughts and his body under control.

A pretty little tortoiseshell cat sauntered into the kitchen, lured by the sound of food hitting her bowl. Tess scooped the cat into her arms, pressed her cheeks to its soft fur. "When I was sick this kitty never left my side. I wish I could take you with me, Bella," she said, "but I can't. No hotel will have you. I'll have to find you a kennel."

It was a split-second decision. She wasn't going to a hotel. She wasn't going to be alone. "Do you have a cat carrier for her?"

She blinked at him. "Yes. She hates it.

"Do you want her with you?"

"I can't just—"

"Tess, we're wasting time. Do you want that shower or not?"

She lifted her chin, her eyes flashing. "Don't order me around, Aidan. I've lost enough control over my life in the last three days." She drew a breath, visibly forcing herself to calm. "Yes, I'd like to keep her with me if it's possible. Do you know a hotel that allows cats?"

He'd been unprepared for the wave of possessiveness that consumed him, just hearing her say his name. "Yeah. I know a place. Come on. We'll take your car."

Tuesday, March 14, 6:30 P.M.

Tess yanked the sash of a stranger's petite robe around her waist and stalked the short distance from Aidan Reagan's bathroom to the kitchen where she heard his deep voice. The man was certifiably insane. It would be the only defense that would keep her from killing him.

It was bad enough he'd brought her here, to his house. He'd promised to take her to a hotel. *Actually he promised you a place that would take Bella.*

It was bad enough that he'd brought her here, but to sneak in the bathroom while she showered and steal her robe . . . *To think I trusted him.*

She stopped in the kitchen doorway. "Detective Reagan."

Two heads whipped around to stare at her and Tess let her rigid shoulders relax just a little. "Kristen."

Reagan's sister-in-law set her mug carefully on the table, pursing her lips. "Close your mouth, Aidan, or birds will fly in."

Reagan snapped his mouth shut, but his eyes continued to bug out of his head making him look like he'd swallowed his own tongue. Self-consciously Tess pulled the sash tighter and held the robes lapels closer so that they overlapped at the base of her throat. Although it would serve him right if he choked on his damn tongue.

Kristen was watching them carefully and Tess tried to ignore the blush she knew had turned her cheeks flaming red.

"Did you put this in the bathroom?" Tess asked her.

Kristen sucked her cheeks in. "I did. There are other clothes on the bed in Aidan's room. We put your cat in there, too." She pointed at the rottweiler lying at Reagan's feet. "Dolly's a sweetie, but we didn't want your kitty to be afraid."

Tess nodded, casting a cautious glance at the big dog who'd obeyed Reagan's every command when they'd first arrived. "Thank you. Where is *my* robe? The one I packed in my bag?"

"In the trunk of your car," Kristen answered.

"Why are my clothes in my trunk, Kristen?"

Her friend looked across the table. "Aidan?"

Reagan was intently studying the contents of his mug. "Go change, Tess. Kristen's made you some tea and some soup. When you come back, you need to eat."

She shook her head, dread driving the smile from her face. "Tell me now, Aidan. I need to know."

He sighed. "Then sit down."

Mutely she obeyed, taking the seat next to Kristen, who patted her hand.

Reagan's eyes lifted to hers, solemn and weary. "Jack swept your place after we left."

Tess held her breath. "And?"

"Cameras in every room."

She could feel the blood draining from her face. "Every room?"

He nodded.

She swallowed hard. "Even the bathroom?" He just looked at her, saying nothing. He didn't need to. "How long had they been there?"

"Jack couldn't say for sure. Longer than the others. Maybe a few months."

Someone had been watching her for ... months. Her stomach heaved and she drew a breath to steady herself. "So why are my clothes in the trunk?"

"Jack's search was very thorough," Reagan said. "Some of your jackets had microphones sewn into the lining."

Numb, she could only stare, not believing she'd heard him correctly. But she had. Her lungs jerked and she realized she'd forgotten to breathe. "Are you saying somebody could spy on me wherever I was?"

"Not necessarily," he murmured. "It would depend on how far away you were from their receiver."

Tess looked up at the ceiling. Too many thoughts raced through her head for any one to make sense. Cameras. Microphones. Receivers. And four people dead. The ceiling revolved in a big circle and she closed her eyes, willing the room to stand still. *You will not throw up. You will stay calm.* "So all of my clothes have to be checked."

"I'm afraid so."

Kristen squeezed her hand. "Aidan called me as soon as Jack gave him the news. We put your clothes and your suit-case in your car. Jack's sending a tow truck. They'll check the car and your clothes. I sent Becca to Wal-Mart for some things to tide you over until your clothes are processed."

Gratitude squeezed her heart. "That's nice of her. But who is this Becca?"

"My mother," Reagan answered. He was watching her, gauging her response. His jaw was tight, his eyes gone hard. Almost as if he disapproved. "She's excited to help, so pretend like you're happy with whatever she brings back."

Tess frowned at him. "Why wouldn't I be?"

Kristen pushed away from the table. "I think I'll get your soup now, Tess," she said quickly. "Do you want a bowl or a cup?"

"A bowl, I think," she answered, not taking her eyes from Reagan's face, her temper simmering. "Tell me, Detective, why would I pretend to appreciate your mother's lovely gesture?"

Reagan didn't blink. "I don't doubt you appreciate the gesture. It's just that it's no secret that your tastes run a little more expensive than Wal-Mart, Doctor. That's all."

Her eyes widened. "You think I'm a snob." He said nothing, just sat there looking at her, his blue eyes hard. Clutching the front of the robe, she turned in her chair to where Kristen stood at the stove, ladling soup into a bowl. "He thinks I'm a snob." For some reason, after all the terror and upheaval she'd been through today, this one truth seemed to hurt. To her embarrassment, hot tears suddenly burned her eyes and she dropped her gaze to the bowl Kristen slid in front of her.

Kristen's hand was soothing on her back. "The soup's from a can, but it's better than what I understand you've eaten today, which is nothing. So eat." Then Kristen surprised her by reaching across the table and smacking the top of Reagan's head. "And she's not a snob. Got it?"

He rubbed his head. "Shit, Kristen. That hurt."

"It was meant to. Now I'm going home. Abe's on duty tonight and Rachel's sitting with Kara. It's Kara's bedtime and Rachel has school tomorrow. Tess, eat the soup, then go put on the sweats I laid on Aidan's bed. Becca should be by with some jeans in a half hour or so." She paused at the door, looking back with a worried frown. "Aidan, is Rachel all right?"

From beneath her lashes, Tess watched Reagan flinch, the movement minute. "Why wouldn't she be?" he asked.

Kristen moved her shoulders. "She seemed preoccupied. She said nothing was wrong, but I know something's bothering her."

"I'll talk to her," he said tightly and got up to lock the door behind her. But he didn't turn around when Kristen had gone. In the quiet of his kitchen his emotion seemed to swell. He was angry. He hadn't been this way since that first night, at the scene of Cynthia's . . . suicide.

Tess looked down at her soup. *When he thought I was a murderer.* At least he didn't think that any longer. Now he thought she was an arrogant snob.

What he thought about her shouldn't matter at all. But it did, and she was too damned tired to try to pretend otherwise. She leaned over the soup. Her hand trembled and she realized it had been more than a day since she'd eaten a bite. The last food she'd consumed was soup at Robin's Blue Lemon. Tess was truly growing to hate soup.

The sound of his sharp breath made her lift her eyes. Reagan stood staring, his eyes fixed below her chin. Slowly his gaze rose and her soup was forgotten. It wasn't just anger that flashed in his eyes. It was lust, too, pure and unadulterated. Her pulse pounded in her ears as he stood there, a muscle in his tight jaw twitching. Abruptly he turned his back and when he spoke, his voice was hoarse, his breath labored. "I'll be in the garage. When you're finished eating and dressed, we'll meet Jack at your office. He'll want to sweep all the areas, including the vault. Dolly, come."

Tess blinked at his back as he disappeared through another door, the dog obediently at his heels. The pulse pounding in her head slowed and she looked down, an instant blush heating her cheeks. Leaning over the bowl of soup had parted the robe far past anyone's idea of decency. Not only did he think her a snob, now he thought her a cheap tease as well. He'd seen more of her breasts than she'd shown anyone since Phillip, damn him to hell.

Except for whoever had been spying on her in her own home. They'd seen quite an eyeful. For months. Damn them to hell, too.

But she wouldn't think about that now. Kristen was right, she needed to eat, so doggedly she did so.

Cameras. She shuddered. *In my home.* Visions of herself on Internet porn sites made the soup she'd eaten threaten to make an encore appearance.

Still, that wasn't as bad as cameras in her office. Microphones in the lining of her jackets. The privacy of each one of her patients had been mercilessly violated, personal information used to abuse them.

She pushed the bowl away. The sooner she knew the full range of the truth, the better, she thought, and went off in search of Kristen's sweats, hoping they were bigger than the robe.

Tuesday, March 14, 6:55 P.M.

Beside him, Dolly sat up and growled softly. A half second later Tess appeared in the door from the kitchen. "Can I come in?"

Aidan looked up from his motorcycle with a jerk, relieved that she wore actual clothes. They were Kristen's and they were still way too small, but thankfully the vital parts of her anatomy were covered. He wasn't sure he could survive another eyeful of her breasts. Though they'd been as beautiful as he'd imagined them. Smooth and full and firm. It had taken every ounce of strength he possessed to turn away, to keep his hands from slipping inside the robe and finding out exactly how they felt.

Wholly aroused and utterly frustrated, he hung up the wrench he'd been using to remove a rusty bolt from the bike's chassis. "Sure. Suit yourself, but watch where you touch. It's dirty in here."

From ten feet away she studied his bike. "New project?"

He took an appraising look at the bike he'd bought the week before. Anything to keep from looking at her. "Maybe. Depends on what I find once I get inside her." He winced at his poor choice of words. He'd just have to wince because as much as he wanted her, he wasn't going to have her.

Her face had grown cold when she'd realized he wasn't taking her to a hotel. But she hadn't argued with him, just silently marched into his house and back to his bathroom like she was the queen. It stung, he had to admit. He'd thought she'd appreciate not facing a sterile hotel. He'd been wrong. And still, seeing her in Kristen's robe, he wanted her. So he'd reminded himself once again that she was Michigan Avenue and he was neighborhood Wal-Mart. He'd expected her to be a little angry. But not hurt. He hadn't meant to hurt her.

Her back was to him now, as she stood studying the series of pictures he'd taken of the Camaro in its various stages of restoration. "You fix things." She glanced over her shoulder. "Cars, bikes." She turned to face him, nodded at the bike. "My brother has one like this. Made for speed."

He thought about what Carter had said. That she didn't speak to her family. "Which one? Dino, Tino, Gino, or Vito?"

A forced smile curved her lips. "Vito. He's the family bad boy. My mother always worried about him, racing around town on two wheels like a bat out of hell."

"My mother would worry, too. If she knew."

"I see. Keeping secrets from mama? Shame on you, Detective."

Aidan lifted a brow. "You planning to tell on me?"

"Not me. I can keep a secret." The smile disappeared. "Too bad that by tomorrow nobody else will think so."

He didn't know what to say to that, so he said nothing as he grabbed a rag and wiped his greasy hands.

"Why did you think I'd hurt your mother's feelings?"

Aidan sighed. "I didn't. Not on purpose anyway. Look, you live a different lifestyle. Shop at exclusive boutiques. You drive a Mercedes, for God's sake." *While my Camaro's roof is held together with duct tape.* "Your apartment is worth five houses like this." He spread his arms wide. "My mother knows nothing about fashion and expensive boutiques. But she has a good heart and I don't want to see her hurt."

"Are we talking about your mother, Detective? Or you?"

He tossed the rag in the trash, annoyed that she'd pegged him so well. "You sure you don't want me on the couch for this?" She winced at the tone he hadn't meant to be nearly so caustic. "I'm sorry. That was uncalled for. Are you ready to go?"

"I thought we were waiting for your mother to bring me some clothes."

He scowled. "Fine. You can wait in the kitchen. I've got some things to do out here."

"In a minute." She crossed the garage, picking her way across the parts he'd already removed from the bike, stopping when it was just the bike between them. She was close enough to touch now, close enough that he could smell the sweet scent of her skin over the oily odor of his engines. Close enough that he could see her pulse beating hard at the hollow of her throat.

"I want us to be clear on a few things, Detective. I am not a snob, nor am I in the habit of offending people who try to help me. When I was growing up, I dreamed of clothes from Wal-Mart. My mother worked two jobs to keep five kids in secondhand clothes. Anything new, I made myself. I know the value of a dollar." She paused, her jaw taut. "My Mercedes was an inheritance. So was my apartment. I like to drive it. I like to live there. I have a healthy practice and I make a good living." She gritted her teeth. "I did anyway."

"Tess—"

"I'm not finished yet. I won't apologize to you or to anyone else for the way I live. But I'll be damned before I let you use those things to make me into something I'm not."

He felt compelled to defend himself. "You didn't want to come here."

She rolled her eyes. "Of course I didn't. I was a filthy mess with another person's *blood* and *brains* in my *hair*. You may deal with that every day, Detective, but I sure as hell don't. I couldn't take a shower in my own apartment because some motherfucking murdering peeping Tom is taking pictures of me *night* and *day*. I couldn't even tell you why I wanted a hotel because I was afraid that same motherfucker had bugged my car. All I wanted was a place where I could get clean and not worry about messing up somebody else's bathroom." She shuddered out the breath she'd been holding, regret edging the temper aside. "I'm sorry I was cross before. You offered me the hospitality of your home and I was rude."

Given what she'd been through that day, her actions were completely understandable and once again, he'd been a fool. "I'm sorry. Once again I was wrong about you. I thought you were . . ." He shrugged, uncomfortable. "Looking down your nose at me."

"Well, I wasn't," she said soberly. "I wouldn't."

The fury and confusion and hurt were gone, and in the quiet that followed the awareness grew stronger. "Thank you."

"I liked your bathroom, by the way." Her lips curved up. "The rubber ducky wallpaper is a nice touch."

He felt his cheeks heat. "It came with the house. I babysit my nieces and nephews sometimes. They like it, so I kept it."

"That's sweet." Her smile dimmed. "You really are. I wouldn't have thought it a few days ago."

His chest tightened. "A few days ago I didn't give you much reason to."

"You were doing your job." Her chin lifted. "I understood that."

She'd been honest with him, setting the record straight. He could do no less. "It was more than that. A few days ago I wanted to hate you." She flinched and took a step back but he reached across the bike to grab her forearm and hold her where she stood. "*I'm* not finished yet." He softened his hold until his hand loosely circled her wrist. "I wanted to hate you because you didn't seem to care about anything or anyone. But I couldn't look at you without wanting you, and I hated that even more."

He watched the brash line of her scar move when she swallowed. "I see. Are you quite finished now?" Her tone was authoritative and once I would have mistaken her attitude for haughty disregard.

But he could feel the pulse at her wrist quicken and it gave him the courage to continue. "Not quite. It was easier to hate wanting you when I thought I could hate you for Green. Then I found out how many you had helped put away, some of them even worse than Green."

"I do my job, Detective."

"Then it was easier to hate wanting you when I thought you might be guilty. I got a little mileage out of believing you were cold and heartless. Until you walked in on Mr. Winslow yesterday afternoon, then I couldn't even believe that anymore."

"I'm sorry I'm not more cooperative," she said stiffly.

Aidan smiled and brought her wrist to his lips as her eyes widened. "Your heart is beating fast," he murmured. Her lips parted but no words emerged. Encouraged, he kissed the racing pulse point of her wrist then brought her hand flat against his chest. She pulled back at first, then gave in, spreading her fingers wide over his heart.

A small catlike smile curved her lips. "So is yours."

"I know. It's been doing that a lot lately." He smiled ruefully. "And not always for reasons as pleasurable as this."

"I'm sorry I'm not more cooperative," she repeated, her voice husky this time.

We'll see about that. "My last bastion of hope was that I could hate wanting you because you were an uptown girl."

"What's wrong with uptown girls?"

He met her eyes squarely. "They have expensive uptown tastes. Fancy dinners. Shiny stones."

Her eyes narrowed ever so slightly. "And?"

His jaw clenched. "I can't afford—" He broke off when her eyes flashed a lethal warning and her fingers tightened, gripping his shirt.

"Be careful, Aidan. You wouldn't want to go saying something you don't mean again." She yanked at his shirt, drawing him down until their faces were level. She braced her free hand on the bike and leaned in. "I am not some street hooker that any man *affords*. I afford *myself*. If I want a fancy dinner at a restaurant, I go. If I want to stay home I can cook it just as well *myself*. If I want a shiny stone, I'll buy it *myself*. Are we clear?"

For a moment he could only stare, fascinated. Then he threaded his hand through her damp hair and took what he'd been aching to have, crushing her mouth with his. She met him more than halfway, her hand dropping his shirt and reaching for the back of his neck, pulling him closer. Her mouth was hot and hungry and all he'd dreamed it would be, opening beneath his without hesitation. She made a sound in her throat when he took the kiss deeper, half hum of pleasure, half whimper of frustration. She leaned forward and the bike teetered dangerously, making Dolly edge away.

Tess pulled back, placing both her hands on the handlebars to steady it, her breasts rising and falling with the rapid breaths she drew. Her lips were wet, her nipples visibly erect through the tight sweatshirt. Her chin lifted in challenge as if daring him to stop and Aidan had to struggle to swallow. He crossed around the motorcycle, his gaze locked with hers. He said nothing. He just closed his arms around her, lowered his mouth to hers, and prayed he could take up where he'd left off.

Then he thanked the powers above when her arms wound around his neck and her lips parted for him once again. Instantly the heat was back, intense. Wild. His hands splayed wide across her back, roving up and down as she pressed closer, her breasts flattened against his chest. With a pretty little growl she pulled herself higher, torturing him with the rocking of her hips, still too low to do either of them any good. His body throbbed, his hands too empty.

He pulled back far enough to let them breathe. Her breath

came in hard little pants against his cheek, each one firing his blood higher, hotter. "I want to touch you," he muttered against her lips. "Let me touch you."

Her head fell back, baring the curve of her throat and he took advantage, pressing hot open-mouthed kisses against her skin.

"Where?"

His mouth froze. "What did you say?"

"I said where?" Her murmur was husky. "Where do you want to touch me?"

He pressed his face to the side of her neck and shuddered. "God, Tess."

She unwound her arms from around his neck and captured his face between her palms. "I mean it." He was stunned to see self-doubt in her eyes. "Tell me where. Please." The plea was a hoarse whisper and Aidan remembered what Murphy had said. She'd been engaged and her fiancé had left her. Cheated on her. How was it possible? How could a man even consider it?

But Aidan knew that even more important than the reasons was erasing the vulnerability from her eyes. How he handled the next few moments could bolster her confidence or break her further on a day when she'd already been through sheer hell more than once. Where did he want to touch her? Mother of God. Where didn't he want to touch her?

"Everywhere," he managed. "Anywhere you let me." His hands slid down her back, closed over her butt. "Here." Her eyes drifted closed, her hands resting on his shoulders as his fingers kneaded her firm flesh through the soft fabric of her pants. Although she stood passively, there was a fine tension in her body, a hunger on her face as he layered caress on caress. He brought one hand to cup her breast, testing its weight in his palm. "Here." His thumb swept across one hard nipple and her back went rigid. So did he. And because he didn't trust himself not to take more, he brought both hands up to cup her jaws and placed a kiss on her forehead. "You're beautiful, Tess."

Her eyes opened, dark with unmet need. "Why did you stop?"

He bit back his groan. "Because you've had a hell of a day and I'm not going to take advantage of you. Don't look at me that way," he demanded when the doubt crept back into her eyes. He grasped her butt and pulled her up into him, rubbing her body against the hard ridge of his erection once, twice, three excruciating times before setting her back on the floor away from him. "Trust me," he said ruefully. "Stopping is the last thing I want to do right now. But I don't want to rush you. Not under the circumstances."

She stared up at him, her eyes both aroused and wary, her face flushed. "What circumstances?"

He sighed again. "I'm the first since . . . him. Aren't I?"

"Then you know." Her eyes hardened. "About Phillip, damn him to hell."

"Tess, he was stupid. I don't care what reason he gave." Gently he slid his fingertips down her cheek. "But I have to say I'm glad he's out of the picture. Three's a crowd that way." He pressed a hard kiss to her mouth just as Dolly started to growl.

Aidan came to instant alert. He put Tess behind him as he bent to pull his backup gun from his ankle holster. The door from the kitchen opened and a familiar brown head poked through. Aidan brought the hand holding his gun down. "Dammit, Mom."

She frowned at him. "Don't swear at me, Aidan. And put that thing away."

He dropped his eyes. "Sorry," he mumbled. Behind him he heard Tess snicker and it occurred to him it was only the second time he'd heard her laugh. She'd had too many shocks over the last few days. If she laughed at his expense, that was okay.

His mother smiled broadly. "You must be Kristen's friend. I have your clothes. Kristen looked at your other things and gave me sizes. I only hope everything fits."

Tess stepped around him, a smile on her face. "Thank you, Mrs. Reagan. It was so kind of you to go to so much trouble." She walked over to his mother, careful not to trip on the motorcycle parts. "Aidan was just giving me a tour of the house."

"And showing off his new motorcycle?" she asked tartly and Tess shrugged.

"Just remember I never said a word, Reagan." She opened the door for his mother, throwing a wry smile back at the gun he still held over his groin. "This is like Christmas all over again, Mrs. Reagan."

"He's going to break his neck on that thing," his mother said as Tess herded her into the kitchen.

Aidan stared at the door. Then he laughed as he hobbled across the garage floor. Bending over to grab his backup gun with a raging hard-on had nearly killed him, but hearing Tess laugh made the pain a little more bearable. He headed inside to call Jack Unger, sobering. CSU would need to meet them at Tess's office. The sooner they stopped this killer, the sooner Tess could go on with her life. *Which will somehow be part of mine.*

Chapter Eleven

❧

Tuesday, March 14, 7:45 P.M.

Tess looked up at the duct-taped roof of Reagan's Camaro and prayed the tape would hold because it was raining again. But she didn't dare say a word, worried that he'd once again think her a snob. *Somebody had hurt him,* she thought. Made an issue out of money. Made him feel inadequate. She bit at her lower lip. Any woman who could think him inadequate had obviously never kissed him. Even exerting an iron control, he'd overwhelmed her. He'd been right, of course. It wasn't wise for her to rush into anything physical with him or anybody else. Not today, anyway. But she'd needed him to prove she was desirable. She hadn't known just how much she'd needed it until he'd pulled her into his arms.

She wondered who the woman had been. The one who'd hurt him, who'd valued money more than she'd valued him. But she didn't feel comfortable asking him. Not yet. Still, the quiet was getting to her. "I liked your mother."

Aidan glanced over, then returned his gaze to the wet, dark road. "Everybody likes my mother." A smile curved his lips. "But thank you. She was so tickled that you liked all the things she bought."

Tess fingered the soft sweater she wore. "She picked out the same things I would have. Thanks for telling her to buy turtlenecks."

"You're welcome."

She let out a breath. "And thank you for being the one with self-control. I don't normally throw myself at men that way."

He said nothing, but she could see his jaw tightening in the dim light of passing cars. Then he sighed. "Tess, if you're apologizing, don't. And don't think that because I stopped tonight that next time I will."

Her skin buzzed. "Next time?"

His look was fast, but direct. "There will be a next time, Tess."

She settled back in her seat with a satisfied smile. "Good."

His short laugh was all that passed between them until he parked his car in her space in the office parking garage. Tess got out of his car and frowned. "Harrison's car is still here. He never works this late." Her stomach turned over. "Oh, no." She ran for the stairs, Reagan on her heels and found Jack waiting for them at her office door.

Reagan took the keys from her trembling hands, opened the outer door and flipped on the light, then immediately blocked the doorway with his body. "Don't go in."

She looked around him and the breath left her body in rush. "Oh my God." Denise's office was a shambles, her computer smashed to pieces. Shredded books and magazines littered the floor and the wooden door that covered the vault had been ripped from its hinges. The vault itself was closed.

Reagan and Jack slowly entered, weapons drawn.

"Police!" Reagan's voice echoed against the walls, then there was silence.

Tess pointed to Harrison's door, slightly ajar. He'd never leave it unlocked. "Aidan, please check Harrison's office."

He pushed the door wide open. "There's no one here, Tess. But there's been one hell of fight." Harrison's cabinets were smashed, his sofa ripped to shreds. His computer monitor was on the floor, the screen smashed in.

Jack pushed open the door to her office. "Yours, too, Tess. Somebody was looking for something."

She swallowed. "Cameras?"

Jack shook his head. "Probably not. This is a messy job. Whoever planted the cameras was very meticulous. You say you don't keep any records in your offices?"

"No. Just in the vault."

Which Reagan was studying intently. "Jack, come here." He pointed to one of the heavy hinges and Tess's blood went cold.

The edge of the hinge was dark brown. Dried blood. Jack glanced over at her. "Come here and open it. Just be careful. There's broken glass everywhere."

She nodded shakily and willed her hands to steady as she dialed the combination and pulled the release. She gasped. Every file had been pulled from the shelves, every folder emptied, every box overturned. Paper covered the floor, in some places six inches deep. It was packed under one of the shelves, forming a long mound. The length of a man.

"Harrison." Her heart in her throat, Tess dropped to her knees, pulling the papers away, revealing white hair streaked with blood. She uncovered Harrison's face and pressed her fingers to his carotid. She held her breath until she found his pulse. It was thready, but there.

Reagan crouched beside her. "He's alive?"

She nodded. "Barely. Help me get this paper out of the way. I need to see if he's hurt anywhere else. Careful! Don't move him." Behind her she could hear the crackle of Jack's radio in the outer office as he requested an ambulance while Reagan uncovered the old man down to his toes, sweeping the papers aside. "He's still bleeding from his head," she said. "I need something to stop it."

"Do you have a first aid kit?" Reagan asked.

"In the supply closet." She fumbled for her keys, then remembered he still had them. "It's one of the medium-sized keys. Number sixty. Thank you."

Reagan squeezed her shoulder and rushed off.

Harrison moaned, his eyes fluttering open. "Tess."

She glanced up at his face, her hands still checking for any other bleeding wounds. "Hush, Harrison. I'm here now. We'll get you taken care of."

"Tess." His hand weakly grabbed her sleeve.

Finding no other external bleeding, she crawled up to his head and bent close to his face. "Who did this to you?"

He grimaced. "Patient. Yours. Caught me at my car. Had a knife."

Her heart skipped a beat. "I'm sorry."

"Shut . . . up, Tess. Listen. He took his file. Then he said . . . ," he grimaced again. "He said he didn't want you . . . telling his secrets. Said he'd . . . kill you first."

Her hands fumbled on the buttons of his overcoat. She set her jaw and continued the task. "I'll be careful, Harrison. I promise."

Reagan knelt next to her, opening the first aid kit with steady hands. He handed her some gauze. "Which patient, Dr. Ernst?"

Harrison's lips trembled in a pathetic excuse for a smile that tore at Tess's heart. "One of the crazy ones . . . I expect."

He frowned. "Hadn't seen him . . . recently. Young. Buzz cut. Big ears." His cough was hoarse. "Damn, it hurts."

"Where?" She pushed the description to the back of her mind, focusing only on Harrison. She finished unbuttoning his overcoat, then his shirt beneath, and winced. Ugly bruises darkened his torso. "Where does it hurt?"

Again he attempted a grin. "Where doesn't it?" His eyes slid closed and he moaned. "Ribs. Back. Wouldn't . . . open the vault . . . so he beat me good. Finally had to tell . . ." He drew a labored breath that rattled ominously. "Call Flo. Tell her . . ."

Tess's throat thickened. "I'll call her, Harrison. She'll meet us at the hospital."

"Tell her I love her."

Tears stung her eyes as she pressed clean gauze to the still bleeding head wound. "Don't be silly, Harrison. You'll tell her that yourself. It's just a nasty cut on your head." He just looked at her and she knew he knew that she lied. The dark bruises indicated massive internal bleeding that would be much more difficult to treat.

"Who's Flo?" Reagan asked quietly.

"His wife. Can you call her? My cell phone's in my jacket pocket. It's stored under 'Ernst home.' Tell her I'll meet her at the hospital. You won't be able to get a signal in here." Nodding, he squeezed her shoulder again and took her cell phone.

Harrison's lungs wheezed. "He's a handsome devil . . . your cop."

Tess blinked, clearing her eyes, then swiped at her wet cheeks with her shoulder. "Sshh."

"Saw him with you on the news. Almost as handsome as me," he quipped and Tess let out a laugh that sounded more like a sob.

"Quiet, old man," she said, making her voice light. "Save your charm for Flo."

His eyes opened, urgency mixing with pain. "Tell her, Tess. Please."

She stroked his cheek. "I will. I promise." He settled then, every shallow breath sounding as if he inhaled through tissue paper. It was a very bad sign.

Reagan was behind her again, lifting her to her feet. "EMTs are here, Tess. Let them do their jobs."

Dazed, she watched as they took Harrison away. Reagan stood behind her the entire time, his hands on her shoulders. He turned her to face him and his blue eyes that had once stared at her with accusation now kept her from falling apart. "Not your fault," he said.

"His lung is punctured," she murmured, ignoring him. "Did I tell them that?"

He shook her gently. "You did. Now pull yourself together. I need you to think." He squeezed her shoulders hard. *"Tess."*

She blinked and steeled her shoulders. "What?"

"Who was he talking about? Young, buzz cut. Big ears. Hadn't been here recently."

She closed her eyes, and saw the man's face in the blackness of her mind. It would be so easy. One name and he'd be locked up. Punished. It would be so easy. But it wouldn't be right. "I can't tell you."

"What do you mean you can't tell me?"

She opened her eyes to his expression of stark disbelief. "It means if I'm wrong then I've needlessly disclosed the identity of a patient."

He dropped his hands and stepped back. "You're joking."

Knees weak, she looked around, but there was no place to sit. "I wish I were."

"You heard what your friend said. Whoever did this threatened to kill you."

Weary, she walked over to the wall and leaned. "I heard him." She was almost sure she knew who Harrison meant. Big, young, mean, one of the few patients who had truly terrified her. *He'd kill me without batting an eye.* Tears were forming at the base of her throat and she swallowed hard, unwilling to give in. "I'm scared," she whispered, her voice breaking. "Okay?"

Reagan joined her against the wall and tilted her chin up with his finger. "Then tell me," he murmured. "I won't tell anyone you did. I promise."

She shook her head, so tempted to tell. Tempted to turn into his arms and have him hold her tight. "I can't. Today I was accused of breaking privilege but I knew it wasn't true. If I tell you now, it will be true."

"Tess, no one would know."

"*I'd* know." She looked away. *And so would you.*

Jack's team had arrived and numbly she watched him lead them into the vault. "Jack can't have the records without a court order, Aidan."

His jaw tight, Reagan nodded. "Don't touch any of the paper until we get a court order, Jack," he called.

Jack stuck his head out. "Hadn't planned to. We'll dust all the surfaces in here, shelves and walls. If only three people had access, it should be easy enough to eliminate them."

"If he didn't wear gloves," Reagan said.

Jack shrugged. "I'm an optimist."

Reagan twisted so that his back was against the wall, then turned just his head to look down at her. "Can you at least point me in the right direction?"

She hesitated then nodded. "If you get a print, you'll get an AFIS match."

"He's got a record, then?"

Her smile was void of all humor. "Longer than your arm. If it's the person I'm thinking." She checked her watch. "I need to get to the hospital. How long will Jack need to dust? I have to close up the vault before I go."

His eyes darkened. "Don't trust us to keep our hands off the goodies, huh?"

She clenched her fists at her sides, kept her voice low. "I really want to slap you for that. Dammit, this has nothing to do with me trusting you. It has everything to do with the law. Every piece of paper in there is protected, Detective. I give it to you without a court order and I have broken the fucking law. Does that matter to you at all?"

He gritted his teeth. "What matters to me is that some unbalanced man with a record longer than my arm plans to kill you. That matters to me." He drew a breath, let it out on a sigh. "We'll hurry up here and let you lock it up."

Her own frustration evaporated. "I'm being uncooperative again, aren't I?"

"Yes. But I understand. I don't have to like it, but I do understand." He fished her phone from his pocket. "I noticed you had some missed calls when I called Mrs. Ernst."

Tess looked at her phone blankly then remembered. "I put it on silent when I was in session this afternoon." She flipped it open and gaped. "I missed thirty calls?"

"Most are from reporters, probably."

"How did they get my cell phone number?"

"How do they get any of their information?"

"Good point." She frowned at her phone. "Can this be bugged?"

Now he looked blank. "I haven't a clue. Don't touch the phones here, but you can use mine to call your voice mail if you want." He slipped his hand under her hair and stroked his thumb along the side of her neck, unerringly finding the place her muscles were most tense. A shiver ran down her back. "Try not to worry about your friend," he murmured. "Okay?" He gave her his phone and went to work.

"Thirty messages," she muttered to herself as she dialed her voice mail, hoping it would be enough to keep her mind off Harrison while Jack worked his magic, knowing it would not.

Tuesday, March 14, 8:50 P.M.

Aidan slid into the passenger side of Murphy's car and coughed, fanning the smoky interior. "Hell, Murphy, did you smoke the whole pack at once?"

"Sorry." Murphy rolled down his window, took one last drag on the cigarette between his lips before crushing it in an ashtray that overflowed. "What took you so damn long?"

He'd missed Murphy's first call because Tess was using his cell phone, which was a point he'd keep to himself. "Have you seen her?" he asked instead. *Her* being Nicole Rivera, voice actress extraordinaire.

"No, but she works there." He pointed to a restaurant across the street.

"Expensive." This Aidan knew from experience. The very sight of the place left a bad taste in his mouth.

"Tuxedos and everything," Murphy agreed. "The manager confirmed she works here, though he wasn't too happy about talking to me. He'll be even cheerier now. She's twenty minutes late for her shift."

"Somebody tip her off?"

"Maybe. I was here about two hours ago. That's when I talked to the manager the first time. He gave me the address she'd used on her job app."

"Fake?"

"Old. The woman that answered the door said she'd moved out about two months ago when she couldn't pay the rent."

"If she works here, she's making good money. She leave a forwarding address?"

"Yeah, and I checked it but she wasn't home and I didn't have a warrant for that address yet. I do now."

"You've been busy."

Murphy nodded. "You never told me why it took you so long to get here."

"I had to drop Tess at the hospital." He'd already related the details of the break-in, assault on Ernst, and threat to Tess.

That took a little starch from Murphy's shorts. "Did you inform hospital security?"

"Yeah." Aidan scowled. "Big guy, buzz cut, big ears. Skinned knuckles from beating the shit out of an old man. No damn name." She'd been quietly adamant and while he did understand, it made him frustrated enough to break something—or someone. He hoped he was there when Jack got the name out of AFIS.

"Will Ernst make it?"

"Touch and go. She did a good job of stopping the bleeding before the EMTs got there. Kept her head." He inspected his own knuckles, remembering how she'd bandaged them the night before. "I keep forgetting she's a real doctor."

Murphy's smile was wry. "I wouldn't put it to her quite like that."

He huffed a laugh. "I won't. Look, that restaurant's going to be filling up real soon. If we want to talk to the manager again, we should do it now."

They got out of the car, Aidan gratefully gulping at the fresh air. Murphy shot him a sour glare. "I said I was sorry."

"I didn't say anything."

"Hell," Murphy grumbled. "How do you know this place will fill up soon, anyway?"

"Ex-girlfriend used to drag me here. After the symphony."

Murphy whistled as he opened the door. "Expensive girlfriend."

Tell me about it, Aidan thought grimly, the sight of the pristine tablecloths bringing back a host of memories, expensive in more ways than one. This place had been one of Shelley's favorite haunts. A dinner with cocktails and wine could easily cost two days' salary when he'd been in uniform. So he'd put a stop to it. And she'd pouted.

Shelley could have made a living giving pouting lessons. But she didn't need to now. She'd achieved her goal, marriage to a man who could support her the way her daddy had. Poor bastard. Her future husband, not her daddy. Shelley's daddy was a *rich* bastard. He drew a breath. And Shelley was now somebody else's problem.

Aidan had never felt comfortable in places like this, always afraid he'd use the wrong fork. To pay for the privilege seemed insane. But Tess would be totally comfortable here, he thought, and instantly wished he hadn't. She could afford herself, she'd said and while she'd been mouthwatering as she'd said it, there was no way in hell Aidan was letting the woman pick up the tab.

How chauvinistic, his conscience intoned. *And?* he shot back. *So the hell what?*

"Ancient history," Aidan said curtly, scanning the faces of the scurrying help. "Excuse me." He got the attention of the tuxedoed maître d' who gave him a superior onceover. "We're looking for Nicole Rivera."

"Join the club," the maître d' said with a sneer. "If you find her, tell her she's fired."

"Because she's twenty minutes late?" Murphy asked mildly.

"No, because this is the third shift she's missed in the last two weeks."

"Which days?" Aidan asked.

The man sighed impatiently. "I don't remember."

"Try," Murphy advised. "Or we'll stay much longer."

He rolled his eyes. "Yesterday, and Saturday night, too. Now if you'll excuse me, please." He showed them the door with a disdain that made Aidan want to pound his face. Instead he gave the man a card. "If she shows up, you'll call us."

The man held the card at the corner. "Of course."

Back on the street, Murphy shook his head. "What's a dinner there set you back? A hundred bucks?"

"Each." He had to chuckle at Murphy's boggled-eyed stare. "Times three if you have wine."

"Which is why she's an ex-girlfriend."

"Let's go check Nicole's apartment again. Maybe she was home all along and just didn't answer the door."

Tuesday, March 14, 9:40 P.M.

"Fuck," Murphy muttered. "Goddammit. We were too late."

Truer words were never spoken. Nicole Rivera had been home all right, Aidan thought, surveying the damage. But there was a damn good reason she hadn't answered the door.

They'd found her kneeling beside her bed wearing black slacks and a ruffled shirt that had once been white, her work uniform. Her hands were cuffed behind her back, her torso resting on a bedspread that had once been covered with delicate blue flowers. Now both her white shirt and the blue bedspread were covered in blood.

Aidan slid his phone in his pocket. "ME's on his way." He crouched close to the body, inspecting the single bullet wound in the back of her head. "Execution style." Quick and merciful. More so than Adams, Winslow, and the Sewards anyway. "Looks like a twenty-two did the job. No exit wound, so the bullet's still in her."

Murphy was checking the closet. "She cold?"

Aidan pulled on a pair of gloves and touched her neck. "Lukewarm. She hasn't been dead long." He started opening dresser drawers. "Socks, shirts. Underwear, more underwear . . . Hello. What have we here?" He picked up a handful of receipts that fluttered from inside the cup of a lacy bra, folded and stacked within four others. "They're copies. The Toy Box. One Baby Linda doll." He riffled some more. "And one roasting pan and one teddy bear from Wal-Mart, all dated yesterday morning. She paid cash for all of them." He set them aside to be bagged. "They must have known we traced the credit card."

"Or the card was a one-time decoy," Murphy said from inside the closet. "The lilies were the only charge on that card. Damn, this woman had a lot of shoes for somebody who couldn't pay the rent."

"There could be other cards. I put in a request for all credit-card activity in Tess's name this morning. Hopefully it'll be in my box when we get back."

"Good idea." Murphy emerged from the closet, a black gym bag dangling from his finger. "It was rolled up and hidden inside a shoebox. Smells like flowers to me."

Aidan looked down at the body. "Why kill her now?" he wondered, then blew out a frustrated sigh. "He was watching this afternoon. I told Seward that we had evidence that Tess's voice had been imitated. I tipped our hand."

"You didn't have any choice. Seward had a gun to her head, Aidan. You did the right thing."

"But dead girls don't confess to impersonating Tess."

Murphy shrugged philosophically. "Hopefully the bag and the receipts will be enough here to make Patrick happy. I'll call Spinnelli. You call Jack."

Tuesday, March 14, 10:55 P.M.

Aidan had known how many cameras Jack's team had found in Tess's apartment, but somehow seeing them lined up on Spinnelli's conference room table was a blow he hadn't expected. After a roller-coaster day of adrenaline surges, both personal and professional, his hold on his own self-control was now shaky at best. He'd known better than to take Rick aside and ask where they'd found each camera in Tess's apartment and office and car and clothes, for God's sake, but something in him had to know.

Besides, not asking would make him look too involved, something he'd been cautioning himself about all evening. If Spinnelli thought he was too involved, Spinnelli would assign someone else to take care of Tess.

I am *too involved,* he thought. Because that's what it had come down to. Taking care of Tess Ciccotelli. And because it did, he couldn't take his eyes off the pile of cameras in the middle of the table, especially the one model that stood out from the rest. Waterproof, it bore the signs of slight mildew around the edges. The bastard had installed it in the fan vent in the bathroom ceiling, pointed straight into her shower. The audio would have been destroyed by the fan, but the video had been dead on.

Disgust clenched his gut as thoughts of *him* watching her wound through his mind like a slithering snake. How many other drooling wankers had watched her? He couldn't control his thoughts any more than he could control the slamming of his heart.

She'd been violated and for that alone the bastard should die.

Spinnelli stood over the conference room table, fists on his hips, shaking his head. "My God. We've got more inventory than RadioShack."

It was true. Aidan focused, bringing his simmering rage under control. Jack and Rick had arranged all the cameras and microphones they'd found over the last two days into seven piles. The first three were from the apartments of the three victims—Adams, Winslow, and Seward. The fourth was the biggest pile, taken from Tess's apartment. The fifth was half the size, taken from her office. The sixth was smaller still, microphones taken from her car in Rick's first five-minute search. There might be more and probably were. The seventh was the smallest—microphones the size of sewing needles Rick had found in the lining of every jacket she owned. Even the red leather jacket she'd worn on Sunday. *When I accused her of murder.*

"So talk to me, Rick," Spinnelli said. "What do you know about all this shit?"

Rick stood up. "Not as much as you want me to know, but here it is. First, I've had no success tracking transmissions or the e-mails in Adams's apartment. I left a single camera in each apartment in case they start transmitting again, but they're all dead now. Whoever put them there must know we found them."

"So we're giving up?" Spinnelli bristled.

"It was a long shot to start with." Rick brightened. "But I do have some information on these little babies." He pointed to the first two piles. "The devices I found in Adams's and Winslow's apartments are the same model, consecutive serial numbers."

Spinnelli nodded. "Then they were bought at the same time."

"Probably. Up until two weeks ago, this model was this company's best seller. Two weeks ago they introduced this model." Rick pointed to the Seward pile of circuitry. "Now this one's the best seller. It doesn't mean the camera I found in Seward's place was bought later, but it could be true."

"So Seward wasn't part of the original plan," Aidan thought out loud. *Stay focused, Reagan.* The sight of all those cameras was eating at him. "Adams's boss said she'd been erratic for weeks and Tess said she'd missed an appointment three weeks ago. The camera from Seward's place wasn't available when all this started."

"Maybe." Spinnelli sat down, arms locked across his chest. "But I want to know did our guy get cameras into all these places? Apartments, offices, cars?" He picked up the bag of needle-sized microphones. "Coats? Who had access to all these places?"

"Our best bet is to examine the security disks from Seward's building in the last two days and compare them to Winslow's the day before yesterday," Jack said. "Assuming the same person did both. We have a time frame on Winslow at least. That doll hadn't been in his oven for more than three hours based on the amount of melting that occurred, so we need to check eleven to one."

"How could someone have put a doll in his oven without his knowing about it?" Spinnelli wanted to know. "God, of all of this, that might be the sickest thing."

Aidan vehemently, viciously disagreed. The sickest thing was that waterproof camera, but he wouldn't even think about that right now. He couldn't, and still keep his cool. "If Winslow was asleep, drugged, he might not have heard someone in his kitchen, but now that we have a time frame we'll recanvass the tenants. What about the cameras from Tess's apartment?"

"Older models," Rick answered. "Three different manufacturers."

"How old?" Aidan asked tightly.

"It doesn't mean they've been there that long," Rick cautioned, then shrugged. "They were the best sellers six months ago." He hesitated. "Except for that one." He pointed at the one waterproof model. "This one's about four years old. But it didn't look like it had been in there any longer than the others," he added hastily. "I'd say you're looking at six months, tops."

Aidan's stomach rolled. "Six months? Some pervert's been watching her for six fucking months?"

Spinnelli's brows went up. "How do we know he's a pervert?"

Seething, on the verge of exploding, Aidan reached over and picked up the one waterproof model. "Because this one was in her shower, dammit," he bit out through clenched teeth. He was furious enough to do damage, so he carefully set the camera down, his hand trembling.

Jack frowned at Rick. "You told him that?"

Rick shrugged again, uneasily. "He asked. I didn't . . . Never mind."

Spinnelli looked worried. "Aidan?"

Aidan shook his head to clear his mind. "I'm sorry. You didn't see her face when I had to tell her. I'm sorry." He pulled his palms down his face. "It's been a long day."

"Not for Nicole Rivera," Murphy said quietly. "We searched the whole place, Marc, but we couldn't find anything pointing to anybody who paid her to do this."

"Did you find the coat and wig?" Spinnelli asked.

Murphy shook his head. "No, but we did find tapes of Tess's voice hidden behind some boxes of Hamburger

Helper in the pantry. They were recordings of Tess's sessions with her patients."

"So she could practice." Spinnelli rubbed his forehead. "That should be enough for Patrick to push back the appeals. Maybe ballistics will turn up something on the bullet. So what about her office tonight? What happened?"

"Her partner said it was one of their patients," Aidan said. "Tess thought she knew who it was, but wouldn't say." And damned if he didn't admire her for her principles even as he wanted to shake her for them.

Murphy turned to Jack, his face grim. "Did you identify the asshole?"

"I've got one of my guys running prints through AFIS right now," Jack said. "We should have something in the next hour."

"I want to go when you get a name." Murphy's voice was low, controlled, but beneath it lurked something raw. Aidan knew just how he felt.

"I'm sending somebody else," Spinnelli said giving them both a warning look. "The two of you focus on Spy-guy. Am I clear?"

Aidan nodded briskly. "Crystal. Patrick is going to be unhappy," he said, diverting the subject to give both himself and Murphy time to cool down. "He can subpoena records all he wants, but it'll take days to put all those papers back in the right folders. They must have had twenty years worth of files in that vault and every piece of paper was on the floor. The best he'll do is a patient list but that won't tell him who's most vulnerable for a suicide setup." A thought struck him. "Unless . . ."

Spinnelli leaned forward. "Unless what? Tell me, Aidan."

Aidan drew Tess's keys from his pocket. He'd had them since they'd entered her office and had forgotten to give them back. On her key ring was a small memory stick, no bigger than a man's thumb. "She's got all her files backed up on this."

Murphy narrowed his eyes. "What the hell is it?"

"A thumb drive," Aidan said. "It's like a disk, but it can hold more than . . . what . . . fifty disks? I used one in my graphics class. It plugs right into the computer's USB port."

Murphy shook his head. "Fifty disks on that little thing?"

Rick eyed it. "That one? Try a thousand disks."

"Wow." Spinnelli reached for it, but Aidan shook his head.

"No. This isn't any different from going into her office and taking files. You can't."

Spinnelli's face darkened. "I have five people in the morgue that says I can."

"I want the list, too. I also want it to stick when we catch him. And I want her to have a license to practice once we do. If we look at this, she'll lose her license for sure. It will look like she gave these to us. Just wait until tomorrow. Patrick will have his court order and we'll have our information."

"Tomorrow might be too late," Spinnelli grumbled, then sighed. "Dammit, Reagan. You're right. When did you get to be the calm one?" Not waiting for an answer, he passed Aidan a folded sheet of paper. "Full tox report on Adams."

Aidan read it, then passed it on to Murphy. "Psylocybin? What is that?"

"I called Julia," Spinnelli said. "She said it's one of the magic mushrooms. Very hallucinogenic. The levels in Adams's blood were only about ten percent that of a tripper, but it looked like she'd been taking it for a long time. She also found it in capsule form in one of the prescription bottles you took from Adams's bathroom medicine cabinet."

"Then why the PCP?" Aidan asked, then exhaled, the answer clear. "It was the anniversary of her sister's death. Spy-guy must have been impatient when the mushrooms didn't work. Pushing Adams's sanity on the anniversary was perfect timing."

"And Winslow was riding close to the edge anyway," Spinnelli agreed. "Julia's going to look for the same stuff in Winslow's tox screen."

Aidan thought about Seward, the crazed look in his eye. "What about Seward?"

Spinnelli shook his head. "Julia said they didn't find anything in the initial screen. She put a rush on it, but we'll still need to wait until tomorrow." He hesitated, then turned to Rick. "Rick, I need to talk to these three alone."

Rick stood up. "I don't have to be told twice. Good night."

When the door was closed, Spinnelli closed his eyes wearily. "IA's in."

The very letters made Aidan twitch. Internal Affairs. "Why?"

Spinnelli blinked hard. "Because we got five sets of prints off those threatening letters Tess received after Green. Three were cops. All friends of Preston Tyler."

"What about the Records clerk?" Murphy asked. "Has she identified any of them?"

"No. She insists she can't remember, but IA thinks she's holding back."

"She's young," Murphy mused. "She's afraid to talk."

"If one of them's involved in shit like this, she's got a right to be," Aidan said grimly.

"So who are they, Marc?" Jack asked.

"Tom Voight, James Mason, and Blaine Connell." Spinnelli leaned his head back until his neck cracked. "All perfect records. Not a blemish on 'em."

Aidan shook his head, unable to believe his ears. "No way. I know Blaine Connell."

"He couldn't?" Spinnelli grimaced. "I know." He sighed, heavily. "I know."

Murphy tapped his lighter on his palm methodically. "If one of them is behind this, it means they've done more than set up suicides. Somebody executed Nicole Rivera in cold blood. It's hard to believe it could be a cop, but if it is . . ."

"A cop would know how to set someone up for murder," Jack said.

Aidan gave Spinnelli a hard look. "Now that we have names, what do we do?"

A knock had all four turning toward the door. Rick stuck his head in. "I'm sorry, but Dr. Ciccotelli's out here. She's asking to see you, Aidan. She doesn't look so good."

Aidan came to his feet, worry instantly pushing everything to the side of his mind. "She was supposed to call me when she wanted to leave the hospital. Where is she?"

"Here." Tess pushed past Rick, then froze as her gaze swept the cameras on the table. Her face had been pale, but now every drop of color drained away leaving her ashen. "All those?" she whispered. "Looking at my patients? At me?"

Aidan took her arm and guided her into a chair. He crouched down next to her and tilted her face so that she looked at him, not the cameras. "What happened, Tess?"

She pulled from his grasp, her lips trembling. She looked back at the table, her eyes stopping at her key ring. She turned to Aidan, an immense hurt in her eyes and his heart dropped to his gut. "You gave them my files?" Barely audible, wisps of words.

"I wanted them, Tess," Spinnelli said before Aidan could say a word. "He wouldn't let me have them."

She nodded and the hurt eased away leaving behind a horrible grief, and he knew. Still he asked, hoping he was wrong.

"What happened, Tess?" Aidan asked her again, very gently.

She drew in a shuddering breath. "Harrison died."

Her grief cut at his own heart and he wanted to drag her in his arms and hold her, but he couldn't. Not here. Not in front of his lieutenant who already thought he and Murphy were too involved. If they only knew. So he took her hand only. "When?"

She shook her head numbly. "Thirty minutes ago. He was in surgery, but there was too much internal bleeding. His children came to be with Flo. So I left." She lifted her eyes, dark and haunted. "I finished listening to my voice mail while I was waiting," she went on with a hollow, toneless quality that made his heart start beating faster. "My license has been suspended. And three more of my patients have threatened me if I tell their secrets."

His racing heart stopped. "Do you know who they were?"

"No. I thought about calling all of them, every one of them on my list and tell them I wouldn't say a word, but the ones who'd believe me wouldn't have called threatening me to begin with. And it wouldn't make any difference if *she* tells with *my* voice. The damage is equally done. Harrison died protecting their privacy. Their damn secrets." Her voice broke. "But he died for nothing." Her head bowed, she sat clutching his hand, silently weeping.

His own eyes stung and he blinked as her tears dropped to his hand. "Tess, I'm sorry. I'm so sorry." The words seemed so inadequate, but she nodded and drew another shuddering breath. She pulled her hand free and wiped at her wet cheeks.

"No, I'm sorry. I shouldn't have barged back here. You all are working." She stood up, squared her shoulders. "I'll let you get back to it. I assume I can't go home."

"Not yet," Jack said. "Tomorrow, maybe. I want one more sweep of your place."

She quailed, but nodded. "Thank you. If you'll give me my keys, I'll be on my way."

Aidan put his hand on her shoulder, felt her flinch under the thick turtleneck sweater she wore. "You'll wait for me. Please." He looked over at Rick who stood by the door, sympathy on his face. "Can you wait with her till we're done?"

Rick nodded. "Come on, Tess." He slid his arm around her shoulders. "I'll buy you a cup of coffee."

When the door had closed Aidan turned to Spinnelli. "We need to tell her the Rivera woman is dead."

Spinnelli rubbed the back of his neck. "I agree. We can't get a confession from Rivera now, but it will put Tess's mind at ease to know she won't be making any phone calls using her voice."

"That what he wants us to know," Murphy said slowly. "It was too easy, finding her like that. He could have killed her somewhere else so that it took us a little while to identify her."

Aidan raked his fingers through his hair in frustration. "He knew we'd go looking for her. He was listening when I told Seward we had evidence that someone had copied Tess's voice. So what will he do now? He doesn't have his puppet anymore."

"Maybe he's done," Jack said.

Aidan shook his head. "No, he's not done. He may have accomplished his goal, though. He's riled up God knows how many psychiatric patients. He likes to set things up, keep his hands clean. Now he's got angry crazy people targeting Tess."

"And he could carry a badge." Murphy aimed a hard look at Spinnelli. "What do we do about our letter writers?"

Spinnelli shook his head. "I don't know yet. I just wanted

you to keep your eyes and ears open. Word will get out that IA's involved and things could get ugly." He stood up. "Jack, tell me as soon as you have a match on those prints from her office. We'll pick the guy up for murder of Dr. Ernst. Aidan, get her to a hotel so she can get some sleep. I'll see you all here tomorrow morning."

Chapter Twelve

❧

Tuesday, March 14, 11:55 P.M.

Tess watched as the white highway lines strobed by. She wasn't going back to a hotel. At least not one in the city. Reagan was taking her home. His home.

With its rubber ducky wallpaper and garage strewn with engine parts. She should tell him to take her to a hotel, but she couldn't find the strength. She should thank him. Would thank him. When this horrible weight lifted off her chest far enough so she could breathe.

He was gone. Harrison, who along with Eleanor had taught her so much. Given her so much. It wasn't her fault. She knew it, just as she knew the accusation in his children's eyes was a normal response to grief and pain. But those looks had been like daggers to her heart and combined with the shock of having heard three more threats to her life . . . She'd come to her feet in a daze and walked out of the hospital alone, hailed a cab, and gone to the first place she could think of. She'd gone to Aidan Reagan.

Stupid, it had been. Leaving the hospital alone, that was. Whether gravitating to Aidan was stupid as well would remain to be seen. Wallace Clayborn could have been lurking outside the hospital doors, waiting for his chance to kill her, like he'd killed Harrison. The longer she'd had to think about it, the more she'd been absolutely certain he was the man Harrison had seen. Tess remembered the way Clayborn had sat in her office, looking at his hands with a terrifying combination of pride and fear. His weapon was his bare hands. Which he'd used to kill Harrison Ernst.

"Did Jack get prints?" she asked, her voice flat.

He glanced over, startled. "I thought you were asleep."

"No. Not now." Not later. There was too much bubbling inside her. Grief. Fear. Rage. Hatred. "Did he?"

"When we left he was still running prints through AFIS."

She looked out the window. Weighed her obligations to her patients. To Harrison. To herself. But all she could see was Harrison bleeding. And Flo, and their children, weeping. "Call Jack." She swallowed hard. "Find out if he has a name. Please."

Saying nothing, Reagan pulled his phone from his pocket and dialed. "Jack, it's Aidan . . . No, she's fine. She wants to know if you have a name out of AFIS." There was a slight pause. "He's narrowed it down to fifty men. What do you want to do, Tess?"

Hatred bubbled high, scalding hot. "Any of them start with C?"

He asked Jack. "Yeah," he told her. "Three of them."

It was choking her, the helpless rage. She could say his name so easily. Wallace Clayborn. But if he wasn't one of the three, she'd have disclosed a patient without cause. An innocent man. Aidan wouldn't tell. *But I'll know. And so would he.* And suddenly that was more important than satisfying her anger. She rested her forehead against the cold window glass, so weary. "I'm sorry. I'm not playing games, but can he give me the names?"

Reagan asked Jack, then repeated them back. "Camden, Clayborn, and—"

"Yes." The slap of relief made her head swim. She held up her hand. "Clayborn. Wallace Clayborn."

"It's Clayborn, Jack," he said. "Tell Spinnelli. He's got a team waiting." She heard the snap of his phone as he closed it and put it away.

"Aidan?" She heard the wobble in her voice and didn't care.

His hand came up under her hair to cup the back of her neck, massaging as he'd done before. "It's all right, Tess. We understand that you couldn't just give us his name. Spinnelli's going to send somebody out right now to pick him up."

She shuddered where she sat, his hand felt so good. So necessary. "I want you to make sure you get Paul Duncan to do the psych evaluation. That pissant Clayborn will try to use an insanity defense, but he's not insane. He's just plain mean. Paul will make sure a jury understands the difference."

"You want him to pay," he said quietly. "That's normal, Tess."

"I don't want him to pay," she said savagely. "I want him to *die.* But I know that won't happen. It won't be murder one." His thumb found her taut nerve and applied gentle pressure. "I want Wallace Clayborn to rot in jail until he's an old man." A sob was building. "Then maybe some street punk will show him how Harrison felt today."

The car slowed, then stopped. His hand disappeared and she had to bite her tongue to keep from begging him to put it back. A cold wind hit her as he got out of the car. She lifted her eyes and felt the pressure in her chest abate, ever so slightly. They were in his garage and he was coming around the car to open her door. Without speaking a word he pulled her to her feet and into his arms.

Safe. She felt safe and protected as she hadn't in a year. No, not even then. Phillip had never made her feel like this.

It won't last. The voice of reality was depressing on a night she couldn't stand any more bad news. So she flicked reality off her shoulder and took a deep breath, enjoying the scent of him as she hadn't been able to do earlier. When all she'd cared about was feeling his lips on hers.

His lips now kissed her hair, her temples, and she wound her arms around his body and held on. His heart drummed steadily under her ear and she simply listened to it beat. He let her, holding her until the storm inside her had calmed.

She was still angry. Still hurting. But it no longer choked her. "Thank you."

His arms squeezed. "You're welcome." He tipped her chin up until she looked at him. "I'll take you to a hotel if you want to go."

She didn't want to go. But neither did she want him to harbor any illusions about what would transpire between them. "If I stay, where will I sleep?"

One corner of his mouth lifted. "In my bed. I'll take the sofa. It pulls out." He sobered, his thumb brushing her lower lip. Shivers raced down her spine, even though his expression was very serious. "Tess, you don't have to worry about any more calls to reporters or your patients. At least not using your voice."

"Why not?"

"The woman who impersonated you is dead."

Her eyes widened. "Are you sure?"

"We're sure she's dead. We're pretty sure she's the one who imitated you. I didn't want you to worry. I also didn't want you staying here because you believed there would be any cause for those bastards to make good on their threats."

"I appreciate that." She really did. Aidan Reagan had proved himself an honorable man many times over.

"But I still want you," he added and she sucked in a breath as pleasure fluttered, woman low. "I didn't want you staying here not understanding that, either."

"I . . ." *Can't breathe again.* "I understand. And I thank you for your hospitality."

He grinned unexpectedly and the sight lightened her heart. "The doctor can be taught," he teased.

Her stomach growled, catching her unaware. "The doctor is hungry."

"So am I." He let her go, but kept his arm around her waist as he walked her to the door. It was no longer solely a supportive gesture, she understood. It was possessive. And she liked it. "I seem to recall something from our little discussion earlier." He pointed to the motorcycle and she felt her cheeks heat.

"I recall a great deal from that discussion, Detective."

He stopped abruptly, a frown creasing his brows. "I don't like that."

"What?"

"When you call me 'detective.' My name is Aidan."

She understood his irritation, aware that he'd called her by her first name long before she'd done the same. It had been a way to keep her walls erected. But the walls were down, through fate or circumstance. Maybe those two were the same thing. "I recall a great deal from that discussion, Aidan," she amended.

His frown disappeared. "You said you could cook as well as a restaurant."

Her lips twitched. "I did say that. Does that mean you'd like me to cook for you?"

His eyes flashed, his meaning clear. "Yes. And yes. But first things first. I'm starving. I haven't eaten since lunch." He opened the door to the kitchen, then stopped short making her run into his back. A sheet of paper hung from the doorway above his head and he tore it down. She tensed until he chuckled. "Little squirt," he said affectionately. "Rachel! I'm home."

He stepped into the kitchen, not flinching when the rottweiler bounded in to greet him. He'd called the massive dog Dolly. The thought made her smile. A young girl entered, Tess's cat in her arms. Bella looked right at home, unfrightened by Dolly.

"You're late again," Rachel said, stroking Bella from her head to the tip of her twitching tail.

"And you're AWOL again," he returned. He tossed the paper to the table and Tess could see "Aidan, I'm here" printed in a rounded youthful hand. "Why?"

The girl eyed Tess with some trepidation. "You have company."

"I do. Rachel, this is Tess Ciccotelli. Tess, my sister Rachel."

It was obvious the girl was Aidan's sister. Their eyes were the identical shade of deep blue. Rachel's were shadowed, however, and Tess remembered Kristen saying the girl had been preoccupied. It was Reagan family business, though, so she'd keep her hands out of it. "It's nice to meet you, Rachel. Thanks for taking care of Bella."

Rachel rubbed the cat's cheek against her own. "So that's your name," she said softly. "It suits you."

"It's Italian for 'pretty.'"

"I know." She was scrutinizing Tess's face. "You're the psychiatrist from the news."

"Rachel," Aidan warned.

"It's all right, Aidan." Tess nodded at the girl. "I am. How is the press treating me?"

"My English teacher would say they 'vilified' you. That's an SAT word," she added and Tess found herself chuckling.

"Glad to see you're constantly studying," Aidan said dryly. "You need to talk to me, squirt?"

Rachel looked at Tess uncomfortably. "I can come back tomorrow."

Whatever was bothering the girl was weighty. "Aidan, take her in the living room. I'll stay here and make us something to eat."

He cupped the back of her neck again and it was all Tess could do not to close her eyes and moan. "You sure?"

"Yeah. Go away. Let me cook."

They'd been talking for twenty minutes in hushed whispers. It had been all Tess could do not to listen, but despite banging pots and pans with more volume than necessary, she'd heard enough to know that Rachel Reagan was in serious trouble. Certainly enough not to be surprised when the girl came back through the kitchen, white as a sheet and trembling so hard she nearly stumbled.

Tess's first inclination was to drop her spoon in the saucepan and help the girl to a chair, but the don't-touch-me look on Rachel's face kept her standing where she was. Aidan appeared a few seconds later. If anything, his face was paler than his sister's.

"Rachel, wait for me in the car." He waited until she was gone, then turned to Tess, his eyes hard. "How much did you hear?"

She hesitated. "Not much—I tried not to listen. But enough. There was a party that got out of hand. She left, but afterward things got worse and one of the girls got hurt."

His jaw tensed. "Not hurt, Tess. *Raped*. Repeatedly." He looked away, his throat working. "Brutally."

She nodded calmly. "I thought as much." She laid a hand on his arm, felt his muscles quivering. "You're thinking your sister could have been, too."

His head whipped back and the suffering in his eyes cut at the heart she'd thought couldn't stand any more. "My God," he whispered hoarsely. "I . . ."

She stroked his arm. "She wasn't hurt, Aidan."

He shuddered and dropped his chin to his chest. "I know. I know." He raised his head. "The girl didn't report it."

Tess blinked. "That part I missed. What is Rachel going to do?"

"I don't know. She's scared. Terrified. Hell, so am I."

"How did Rachel know if the girl didn't report it?"

"The girl wasn't in school today, but there were rumors." His lips thinned. "I guess the boys just couldn't keep something like that to themselves. Rachel stopped by to check on her. The girl hadn't even told her parents. They just thought she'd had a wild party and was sick because she drank too much. They've grounded her for a month. Rachel tried to get her to call the police, but she wouldn't. She's too afraid."

"That's not unusual, Aidan. You know this."

His hand slapped down on the kitchen counter, surprising them both. "Dammit, of course I know it." His shoulders sagged. "I also know *I* have to report it."

"And once you do, Rachel is involved."

His eyes fixed on hers. "She's afraid the boys will find out she told. That they'll get her, too."

She could taste his fear, bitter and metallic. She understood exactly how Rachel felt. "Then you have to make sure they don't find out who told."

His nod was jerky. "I have to take her home now. My parents will be worried sick." He reached behind his back and pulled a black semiautomatic pistol from his waistband, smaller than the one he carried in his shoulder holster, bigger than the one she knew he carried at his ankle. "Do you know how to use this?"

Forcing her hands to be steady, she took it and competently set it on the counter next to her homemade salad dressing. "Yes. My brother Vito taught me."

"Dolly will make sure nobody comes in. My parents' house is less than ten minutes away, but I'll need to talk to my dad. I could be a while." He looked at the simmering pots. "I'm sorry. It smells great, but I can't—"

"It'll keep. Aidan, go. I'll be fine."

He zipped up his coat, then paused at the door. "I'll call you on the home phone when I'm coming up to the garage so you'll know it's me. Dolly, stay."

Then he was gone and she heard the garage door open and close as he took Rachel home. Bella came in the kitchen to rub up against her legs and Tess scooped her up, nuzzling her against her cheek. "Bella," she murmured, "remember when Eleanor used to say things went from sugar to shit? This is exactly the kind of day she was talking about." Thoughts of Eleanor inevitably led to thoughts of Harrison and the grief returned. *Start being a psychiatrist,* he'd said.

He'd been right. It was time to stop being a victim. *Get to work, Tess.*

Wednesday, March 15, 6:00 A.M.

His mother was making breakfast and it smelled better than heaven. Aidan rolled over, burrowing his face into the softness of a sofa cushion. He forced his eyes open.

And found himself staring into the yellow eyes of a little brown cat. His mother didn't have a cat. But Tess did. Abruptly he sat up, his brain slogging into motion, and the cat skittered away. He was in his own living room, on his own couch. He'd come home last night after taking Rachel home and talking with his father into the wee hours of the night to find Tess asleep at his kitchen table, her rosy cheek resting on her folded arm, Dolly at her feet.

She'd fallen asleep writing something on one of his notepads, a pen loosely clutched in her hand, his pistol an arm's length away and he remembered his racing heart careening from fear because she hadn't answered the phone when he'd called to an arousal that had stolen his breath. She'd been warm and tousled and it had taken superhuman control not to tumble with her into his soft bed. But he'd tucked her in and bedded down on the sofa alone.

He decided he was a saint.

His stomach growled insistently. A hungry saint. He pushed himself to his feet with a groan, padded into the kitchen and stood mesmerized. Tess Ciccotelli stood in front of his stove wearing a pair of jeans and his old CPD sweatshirt, the sleeves pushed up to her elbows. Her dark hair tumbled down her back in black waves and her sweat-socked feet tapped to the driving beat of Aerosmith, the radio volume turned down low. She did a little shimmy, wiggling that incredible ass as she flipped pancakes on the griddle and Aidan thought he'd never seen a sight more perfect in all his life.

Two long strides carried him to her and before she could say a word he had his hands in her hair and his mouth on hers, hard and hot and demanding. The small squeak of surprise caught in her throat, melting into a low moan that snipped the thin thread of his sanity. His hands streaked under the worn sweatshirt, stroking the silky skin of her back as her arms came around his neck and she opened her mouth, met his tongue full force. She still held the spatula and the handle poked the base of his neck but he didn't care because she was on her toes struggling to get closer, her breasts pressed against his chest, her hips wriggling against his crotch and all he could think was *Now now now*. His hands fumbled for the clasp of her bra, his fingertips skimming the undersides of her breasts when he realized the clasp was in the front.

She whimpered and his hands shook. "Hurry," she whispered against his lips. "Please." He twisted and pulled and the clasp gave way, spilling her breasts into his hands. She went still, rocking back on her heels, her head falling backward. Her lips parted, her eyes closed and he realized she held her breath, waiting. Waiting for him to touch her. And suddenly it was very, very important that her pleasure be worth her wait.

He released her, bringing his hands out from under the sweatshirt. Her eyes flew open, wild and aroused and confused. "What? Why?"

"Because." He kissed her, grabbing the spatula with one hand and shutting off the stove burners with the other. "I want to take my time."

Slowly he walked her backward, out of the kitchen and into the living room until her legs hit the back of the sofa. He lowered her, followed her down, settled her head on the soft cushion. Settled his hips between her thighs. She arched against him and the twist of pleasure nearly undid his resolve. With a laughing groan he pressed his hips against her, effectively pinning her in place.

"Not so fast," he murmured, more to himself than to her. Abruptly he pulled the sweatshirt over her head, trapping her arms, baring her breasts. His breath caught. His chest actually hurt. "My God," he breathed. "Look at you, Tess." And he did, staring at her perfect breasts, round, firm. Her nipples stood erect, begging for his mouth and he bent to sample, but veered off course at the last minute, wringing a strangled cry of frustration from her throat. She struggled to free her arms, sending her breasts jiggling. His eyes nearly crossed.

"Let me go."

"No." He ran his tongue along the underside of her left breast and she shivered. Hard. "Not yet, Tess. Just close your eyes." She did and he repeated the caress on the other side, then buried his face between her breasts and breathed in her scent.

"Aidan." Tess arched her back, but he turned his head, licking her right breast, again stopping too soon. She could feel his breath hot against her skin. She was on fire, every nerve in her body screaming for him to touch her. She wanted to feel his hands, his mouth on her skin. Needed it.

She tried to lift her hips, but he held her fast, his erection throbbing against her. With a jerk she freed her arms, sending his sweatshirt flying across the room. Grasping his head between her palms she pulled him close, crying out when his mouth finally closed over her nipple. And finally, finally he sucked, open-mouthed and hard and the pleasure started to build. "Oh God. Don't stop."

He lifted his head and stared down at her, his blue eyes were black, his lips wet. "I can't," he muttered. "I won't." Then he dropped his head and gave her other breast the same erotic treatment until she moaned, long and low, twisting to get closer to that hard ridge in his pants.

He reared up, holding her head, taking her mouth in a savage kiss. His hips rolled and thrust and she hooked her feet around his calves so that she could thrust back against him. Her breasts pushed against his shirt, the cotton rough against her sensitive nipples. Hands shaking, she pulled at buttons until the shirt separated and there was nothing between them. She twisted sinuously, loving the feel of him. He was breathing hard, sweat beaded on his forehead.

"Do that again," he rasped and she did, watching his face, the way the muscle in his jaw twitched, the way his eyes slid closed. His hips slowed, the motion now deep and rhythmic against her. Without the barrier of their pants, he'd be inside her, filling her to bursting, driving her to the orgasm she'd been so long without.

God, she wanted him to.

His throat worked and he opened his eyes. When he spoke, his voice was husky and sent another shiver radiating across her skin. "What do you want, Tess?" He leaned in, trailing his lips across her jaw. "Do you want to make love?"

More than anything she wanted to say yes, but when it came down to the actual moment, her father's voice echoed in her mind. Despite its hypocrisy, his teaching was firmly planted in her mind, leaving her unsure. She'd dated Phillip damn-him-to-hell for months before they'd had sex and there had been precious few lovers before him. "I don't have anything."

His hips did another roll and she moaned, so torn. "I do," he said in her ear.

Still, she hesitated and his hips stopped. "Don't move," he ordered, his voice shaky now. "Not a muscle." Grabbing the back of the sofa, he pushed himself to his knees, then stopped, his eyes greedily drinking her in. "You're beautiful, Tess."

This from a man who with his muscled torso and gorgeous face could easily have made his living modeling. But he'd chosen to be a cop. To protect. And to serve. So far, he'd done both exceedingly well. She cleared her throat. "So are you."

Carefully he levered himself to his feet and with a grimace bent over and picked up the sweatshirt she'd been wearing. He handed it to her, then turned around with grim resolve, presenting his back as he buttoned his own shirt.

She adjusted her bra, then pulled the sweatshirt over her head. She still tingled, between her legs and everywhere else. "I'm sorry."

"Don't be." He threw a rueful look over his shoulder. "I said I wouldn't take advantage of you."

"And you didn't." She stood up and pressed a kiss to his stubbled cheek. "You made me remember what it felt like to feel wanted. And to want. Thank you."

His eyes flashed. "I think we'd better eat breakfast now." He walked away, muttering something that sounded like "damn saint."

She followed him in the kitchen. "Sit down. I'll get you some pancakes." She surveyed the uncooked mess on the griddle. "Lucky for you this was the last batch. The cooked ones are cold, but I can warm them up in the microwave."

He winced as he sat down. "You didn't have to cook for me." His leg stretched straight out under the table and she bit back a smile as he adjusted himself. "And you don't have to look so damned pleased with yourself." The last, a good-natured grumble.

"I cook when I'm stressed." She set the table and poured his coffee. "My mother does, too." Her mouth bunched in a frown. She hadn't meant to say that.

He shot her a curious look. "Your friend Jon says you don't speak to your parents."

Tess gritted her teeth, annoyed. "My friend Jon has a big mouth." Then she grimaced. "I forgot to call Jon and Amy and tell them I was okay." She picked up her cell phone. "I turned it off last night. I figured you'd call the house phone and I started to get paranoid about the cell being bugged or having a tracking device. Stupid, huh?" The microwave dinged and she put the plate on the table.

Aidan piled pancakes on his plate. "Not stupid. Probably not reasonable, but given everything you've been through, definitely not stupid." He dug in and sighed. "Pancakes, Aerosmith, and a great ass. You're some woman, Doctor."

Tess laughed as she turned on her cell phone. "Such poetry. Oh, shit." She looked up with a frown. "I've got a million messages again. But it looks like most of them are from Jon and Amy." She scrolled through the numbers. "Two unknowns."

His jaw tightened. "We'll try to trace the other threats from last night."

She tried not to panic. "Thanks. And . . ." She blinked at the next number. "Vito?"

"Your brother?"

"Yeah." Hastily she dialed his number. "Vito, it's Tess."

"Where the hell are you?" he roared.

She winced. "Hello to you, too."

"Don't get cute with me, Tess. I've been out of my mind with worry. So has Mom."

"How did you know?"

"Because you're all over the fucking news. CNN and ESPN. You and that football player who committed suicide. Mom saw it last night and called me, desperate. What the hell were you thinking, Tess? My God. You can't be held at gunpoint and not tell us. Mom thought you were dead. We've been trying your home phone for hours."

"I'm not there."

"No shit, sugar." His voice was furious. "I know because I've been standing here in your apartment lobby all night waiting for you to come home."

Her jaw dropped. "You're here? In Chicago?"

"Yes, I'm here. In Chicago. I caught the last flight out of Philly last night."

"Oh, Vito. You didn't have to do that." Memories of the

day before washed over her and her throat thickened. "But I'm so glad you did. There was a break-in at my office last night."

"I know. There's a picture on the front page of the *Bulletin* of the paramedics wheeling your partner out to an ambulance. How is he?"

The rage bubbled up from deep inside her, aimed at both Wallace Clayborn and the newspaper that so callously profited from their misery. "He's dead."

Vito's silence was tense. "What happened?"

"What does the article say?"

"Just that it was an unknown assailant and that the police are working on leads," Vito said. "What happened?"

"One of my patients saw me on the news and . . . ," she drew a breath, "came after me. He found Harrison instead."

"Oh my God." His voice no longer rang with outrage. Now it shook with fear. "Where are you?"

"I'm safe. I'll meet you, but not at my apartment."

"Why?" he asked warily.

"I'll tell you when I see you. Where are you staying?"

"Holiday Inn downtown."

Tess cupped the phone. "Can you drop me off on your way to work?"

Aidan nodded. "Of course."

"Tess?" Vito's voice boomed. "Are you there with a *man*?"

Tess sighed. No matter how old she got, she was still Vito's little sister and they were all still their father's children, like it or not. "Yes, Vito."

"He doesn't just drop you off," Vito growled. "He comes in to meet me."

Tess sighed again. "Yes, Vito. I'll see you in an hour." She hung up and shrugged. "Do you mind meeting my brother?"

Aidan's eyes widened in mock alarm. "Will he hurt me?"

"I don't think so. He never actually beat up any of my boyfriends. Although he did give Phillip a bloody nose."

"Dr. Damn-him-to-hell?" He smiled when she did. "Sounds like he had it coming."

"He did. " She sobered, remembering how worried Aidan had been about his own sister. "What happened last night, Aidan? With Rachel?"

The smile left his eyes. "Dad said he'd take care of it. He's a retired cop, but he still has friends who can receive an anonymous tip."

"And if somebody links it to Rachel?"

He paled. "Then Abe and I will make sure the boys in her school understand that if anybody touches her, they die." He refilled his plate. "These pancakes are incredible. Better even than my mom's, but if you tell her I said so I'll call you a liar to your face."

Understanding his need to change the subject she nodded. "She won't hear a word from me. I made you linguini last night. You can warm it for your dinner tonight."

He lifted a brow. "My dinner tonight? What about yours? I don't think you should be wandering around alone tonight."

Panic fluttered in her stomach again and refusing to give into it, she tilted her head. "You just want me to cook for you again."

His grin was slow and set her heart beating anew. "Yeah. I do."

Disarmed, she looked away and on the corner of the table saw the notepad she'd been using the night before. "I have something for you," she said, leaning over to get it. "I didn't want to use your computer last night without your permission, but I did take one of the blank notepads from your desk. You've got an interesting assortment of textbooks by the way. There's everything from ancient history to calculus."

With a liberal mix of psychology, philosophy, and poetry in between. Scanning the spines of the books on his shelf had been a fascinating look into Aidan Reagan.

He was quiet a split second longer than he should have been. "I just finished my bachelor's degree." He'd shuttered his eyes so that they were flat. Unreadable. Which was readable in and of itself.

Tess's sigh was exasperated. "Dammit, don't do that."

"Don't do what, Doctor?"

"Stick that broom up your ass, *Detective*," she snapped back. "You've assumed I'll look down on your degree because I have a few more diplomas on my wall."

He eyed her coolly, then shrugged. "I'm sorry." But his tone was not one whit warmer, nor were his eyes.

"Why do you do that? Why do you assume the worst of me?" She pushed back from the table on a spurt of anger. "A few minutes ago you had me on my back. Now you've got me up on some pedestal looking down at you. Make up your mind, Aidan. I can look up or down, it's up to you."

Something flickered in his eyes and she narrowed hers, filling the silence when he said nothing. "Okay. Enough said." She flipped past the notes she'd scribbled on the pad. "While you were out last night I worked on a psych profile of the person we're looking for. I'd started it on my computer at work yesterday . . . before I got the call about Seward." Resolutely she pushed back the residual terror, stiffening her knees. "I didn't have it backed up yet and I doubt they'll be able to get it from my hard drive at this point." Because her computer was in pieces on my office floor. "I'm going to change my clothes now. I'll be ready to leave when you are."

"Tess."

Already in the living room, she stopped and turned back to see him reading the page she'd marked. He looked up, his eyes troubled. "Thank you for this."

"It's what Harrison wanted me to do." Her mouth twisted. "We had lunch yesterday. We consulted." She pointed to the pad in his hands. "And there you are. I'd appreciate if you could run me a copy." She'd made it past the sofa and into the hall before he called her name again.

"Tess."

She stopped, but didn't turn around this time. "What?"

"I'm sorry. I was wrong and I'm sorry." She heard him cross the room then shivered when his hands covered her shoulders. "I've got some baggage." He kissed the side of her neck, right above her scar. "Maybe we both do."

"What was her name?"

"Shelley." He paused, then added with a smile in his voice, "Damn-her-to-hell." He pushed her hair aside and feathered more kisses down the back of her neck. "I'll grab a shower and be ready to go in twenty. You can explain your psych profile in the car. There are some terms I don't know."

He pushed by her and disappeared into the bathroom with its rubber ducky wallpaper and she sighed, understanding the admission of ignorance had been harder for him than the apology. She wondered who Shelley was and what she'd done, then shook herself into motion.

She needed to get ready. Vito didn't like to be kept waiting.

Chapter Thirteen

Wednesday, March 15, 7:20 A.M.

It wasn't difficult to pick out Vito Ciccotelli, Aidan thought, instantly finding the man in the crowded lobby of the Holiday Inn. He would be the big guy with the wavy black hair and forbidding glare. Even without the obvious bulge of his shoulder holster everything about the man screamed "cop." Then when his piercing dark eyes saw Tess everything about him screamed "frantically worried big brother."

She took a step toward him, then they were running. Vito grabbed her into his arms and held her there as if she was precious and he'd almost lost her. Aidan's throat thickened. Both of which were true.

She hadn't seen her brother, she'd told Aidan in the car, since Vito had twice rushed to her side ten months before. The first visit was to the hospital after the "con with the chain" as she matter-of-factly referred to her assault. He wondered if she realized she touched her throat when she talked of the experience as if it had happened to someone else. The second time was six weeks later after she'd given Dr. Damn-him-to-hell his walking papers and Vito had given the doctor a bloody nose.

Now Vito frowned at her. "You're still too skinny. Have you been sick again? And why are you not in your apartment?" He looked over her shoulder and gave Aidan a visual third degree, his dark eyes going cool. *It must run in the family.* "He's the cop?"

Tess looked over her shoulder, her lips curved. "No, I'm not, no, I haven't, it's a long story, and yes, he is." She turned so that Vito's arm was around her shoulders. "Vito, Aidan Reagan. Aidan," she sighed, "my brother Vito."

Vito shook his hand, his grip hard but not punishing. "Are you sleeping with her?" he demanded.

"Vito!" Tess's gasp was shocked.

"Not yet," Aidan answered and Vito's jaw tightened. For a moment nobody said anything, then Vito scowled.

"Why is she not in her apartment?"

Aidan looked around. "We can't talk here." He checked his watch. Spinnelli had called a meeting for eight sharp. "I have about ten minutes. Do you have a room?"

"Yeah." Vito was already walking, pulling Tess toward the stairs. "Only two floors up, kid. It's your lucky day." He let them into his room and stood in front of the door, arms crossed over his chest like a sentry. "So talk."

Quickly, concisely Aidan filled him in on the details he felt he could share while Tess sat on the bed rolling her eyes. When he'd finished she waved sarcastically.

"I'm still here, you know."

Vito shot her a seriously ugly glare. "Yeah, and we want to keep it that way." He turned back to Aidan. "Who do you like for this?"

Aidan shook his head. "I can't."

Vito's frustration was palpable. "Because you don't know?"

Because they could be cops. "I have to go." He looked at Tess from the corner of his eye and then back at Vito. "How long are you going to stay, Vito?"

He hesitated. "I've got a few days coming."

"Good." He glanced down at her again. "Clayborn's still out there."

Her spine snapped rigid. "I thought Spinnelli had people picking him up."

"They haven't found him yet. You'll stay with her?"

"Yeah," Vito said grimly. "Tess, how do you get yourself in these situations?"

She surged to her feet and punched Vito's shoulder so hard the man winced. "I didn't do anything here, you asshole."

Aidan was still blinking from the rapidity of her movement and the force of her blow, both distinctly unvictimlike. "I didn't know you had that in you, Doctor."

She gave him a dirty look. "Now that you do, don't forget it. Go. You'll be late. Call me when I can go back in my office. I need to go into the vault and start sorting the records." She lifted a wry brow. "Patrick will want them for his subpoena."

"Who's Patrick?" Vito wanted to know.

"The SA." Aidan pulled on Tess's hand. "I want to talk to you." He pulled her into the hall and shut the door in Vito's scowling face. "I'm starting to feel sorry for Rachel."

Her lips curved. "She's a lucky girl, to have a brother who loves her." She pulled his head down for a short kiss. "Don't keep Spinnelli waiting. He gets impatient."

He slipped his hand under her hair and took the kiss he really wanted, gratified that when he lifted his head she took a long, shaky breath. "So do I." He kissed her again, hard. Possessive. "I'm sorry about this morning. I didn't mean to hurt you."

"It's all right." It was. He could see it in her eyes and his thundering heart eased. He started to back away, then swore. She was in his arms before he could take another breath, her arms around his neck, kissing him like she had that morning in the kitchen and he wondered how he could have ever thought her cold because she was burning him up. Shuddering, he buried his face against her neck.

"Be careful," he whispered fiercely. "Call me if you need me."

"I will. I promise."

He pressed a kiss to her temple. "Have dinner with me tonight."

"What about Vito?"

"Bring him along. As long as he doesn't stay all night."

She shivered. "Will I?"

He nipped her lower lip lightly. "That's up to you. I'm seriously late now. Bye."

Tess pressed the back of her hand to her lips. *Wow.* She'd never been kissed like that. Never. Not by Phillip, damn him to hell. Not by anybody. She took an unsteady step toward the door and it opened before she could knock.

"You were watching through the peephole," she accused Vito and he grinned.

"I always did, kid. How else would I know whose ass to kick for getting too fresh with my sister?" He sobered when she came back in the room. "Mom wants to come."

All the pleasure vanished. "Then let her come."

"She wants you to ask her."

"I did." Too many times in the last five years. "Don't get in the middle of this, Vito."

"I am in the middle of it, Tess."

"Only you," she murmured. Only Vito stood by her, braving their father's wrath. "How are they?" She didn't need to be more specific. "They" were her family.

"Dino's expecting again. It's another boy."

"Poor Molly." That would make five boys for her oldest brother and his wife. Two nephews she'd never seen and three more who couldn't pick her out of a crowd.

"Gino just got a big contract to design a new building. Tino's engaged."

Her heart squeezed. "Is she nice?"

"Yeah." He swallowed hard. "Yeah, she is. Tess, I want you to come home."

Home. The thought made her yearn. "Why?"

"Because I miss you. We all do." He sat on the bed, his eyes closed. "Dad's sick."

Her gut clenched. "How sick?"

"He had a heart attack."

She lifted her chin. "He's had them before."

"This one was bad. He's selling the business."

She turned to the window. "Does he want me to come?" Vito was silent, giving her her answer. She turned back around, her composure restored. "I need to see Flo Ernst this morning. I have a message for her from Harrison. Will you come with me?"

Vito came to his feet. "Sure. Tess, this cop . . ."

"Aidan? He's nice, Vito. Really nice. He loves his mother."

He smiled. "Good. Then I won't have to kill him."

She smiled back. "I'm really glad you're here."

Wednesday, March 15, 8:03 A.M.

Aidan winced when he opened the conference room door to find four pairs of eyes staring. "Sorry," he muttered and slid between Jack and Murphy. "What did I miss?"

"Nothing," Spinnelli said dryly. "But Rick's about to bust, so we'll let him go first."

"I have a lead on one of the cameras." Rick's grin went ear to ear. "The oldest one."

The camera in Tess's shower. The one that had been in the back of his mind all morning. Even as he'd kissed her, caressed her, a small nasty part of his mind had wondered who had seen her. "How?"

"I remembered that model has a switch inside that has to be set, so I checked." Rick held up the camera cover. "There's a partial print on the underside."

Murphy gestured him to hurry. "I'm gettin' old here, Rick."

"We ran the print through AFIS and got a number of matches," Jack said. "Rick remembered one of the names on the list."

"It was a sex pervert that installed cameras in a girls' locker room in a high school," Rick said. "He'd been contracted to run cable through the building and took a sideline for himself. He used this same model camera."

"David Bacon," Spinnelli said, pushing an arrest photo to the middle of the table. "He served three of five years for the locker-room incident. Ended up being classified as kiddie porn because the girls were underage. He got out eight months ago."

"He cried like a baby at his sentencing," Rick said with contempt. "Little shit."

Aidan was staring at Bacon's picture and description, forcing his mind to stick to the logical. "He cried? That doesn't fit." He pulled Tess's handwritten sheet from his pocket. "Tess developed a psych profile last night."

Spinnelli narrowed his eyes. "When did she give you this?"

Aidan kept his face bland. "I saw her this morning before I came in. She gave me the profile then."

Spinnelli nodded, clearly unconvinced. "Uh-huh. What hotel's she in?"

"The Holiday Inn downtown."

"Uh-huh. So what does the profile say, Aidan?"

It appeared that would be all Spinnelli would say on the matter. Aidan let himself relax a little. "She said she hasn't seen this combination of traits in her practice, that it's very rare, especially to see one so focused and successful. He's likely male, based on the number of people killed. He's likely not too young, based on the level of patience and planning he's shown. He's an antisocial voyeur, educated and fond of theatrics. He may be an actor or may go to the theater often— Maybe a season-ticket holder. He knows about voices and impersonations, as well as the technology of surveillance. He knows about medicines, specifically psychotropic drugs, and how to use them to make people suggestible. He understands psychology—he picked three of her most vulnerable patients and customized their torture. Or he knows how to recognize these skills in others and ensure their compliance."

Aidan put the paper on the table so Murphy could see it and continued. "He likes to watch the suffering of others. He probably has a previous history of smaller offenses, although he probably hasn't been caught. He's too smart to be caught. Yet. He also doesn't like to get his hands dirty, but will if called on. He's very goal-oriented and focused. He may own his own business. He's accustomed to delegating and good at it. He's probably not someone who works a menial job." He frowned. "This kind of person would kill his own mother and not lose a minute's sleep if it meant reaching his goal."

"That's complete," Spinnelli said thoughtfully. "She put some time into it."

Aidan thought about her sitting alone in his house with his gun at her side and his dog at her feet, worrying until sheer exhaustion had pushed her into a deep sleep. "She was restless last night. After the day she had, it's no surprise."

"David Bacon laid cable," Murphy said. "He knew how to set up wireless transmissions. That's educated."

"But he worked alone," Rick said. "He liked to watch the girls and know he was the only one who could. It's one of the reasons he only got five years. There was no evidence he had any accomplices or distributed his videos."

"Maybe Bacon's just one of the skilled people he's delegating to," Jack said. "Either way we won't know till we find Bacon."

"We'll find him," Aidan said quietly.

"Well, I've got something, too," Spinnelli offered. "IA broke the Records clerk down and she admitted to checking Adams's and Winslow's files out to Blaine Connell."

Aidan closed his eyes. "No way." They'd never been friends, but Connell had always seemed like a decent guy.

"IA's bringing him in today. We'll get a crack at him after they're done."

"If there's anything left," Jack muttered. "Hell."

Aidan broke the silence. "What about Wallace Clayborn? Have we found him yet?"

Spinnelli shook his head. "I sent out a pair of uniforms last night and they couldn't find him. I gave it to Abe and Mia this morning. Is Tess alone?"

That his brother and his partner would be involved was a comfort. Abe knew his job, as did Mia. They'd leave no stone unturned until Clayborn was found. "No. Her brother came from Philly last night. Apparently her part in Seward's death is big news all over the country and her family was worried."

"I saw it on ESPN last night," Rick offered. "You were on the footage, too, Aidan."

"Don't get a swelled head," Spinnelli said dryly. "What loose ends are dangling?"

Jack scanned his notepad. "I'm still waiting on the serial numbers for the guns you found in Adams's place. If I haven't heard anything by lunch, I'll call."

"We've got the receipts we found in Nicole Rivera's apartment," Murphy said. "Once we find Bacon we can check out the toy store to see if anybody remembers her."

"And we've got to find who had access to all the apartments." Aidan looked at Spinnelli. "Can you get somebody to review the security tapes?"

"Yeah. You guys focus on tracking down David Bacon. I'll take Connell and IA. I'll call you all when we know something. I know Connell. I might be able to believe he passed some records, but I can't believe he'd shoot Nicole Rivera in cold blood. But I've been wrong before. Go and keep me up to date. Oh, and Aidan?"

Aidan turned at the door. "Yeah?"

"Tell Tess we need her to organize those files. Patrick called this morning. He's got a subpoena for her records and wants her to review them with us. While we try to catch this guy we can at least try to block his next move. Tell her I'm sending a uniform to meet her at her office to supervise the cleanup, then take the papers and her thumb drive. Patrick will use her electronic files until the paper records are in order."

"Are you worried she won't hand the files over to you?"

"No, I know she'll do what needs to be done. But we have to be able to document the chain of custody. I don't want any loopholes for sleazy defense attorneys, Aidan. Between you and me, the uniform's really for her safety. I'm worried Clayborn will be watching the office, waiting for her."

The thought of it made him sick. "I'll tell her. Thanks, Marc."

Abe was waiting for him at his desk. "I need to talk to you." He leaned his head close. "Dad reported it."

Aidan's sick stomach pitched even harder. "Is Rachel going to school today?"

"We thought it would look worse if she didn't."

"Probably." He blew a breath up his forehead. "God, Abe. Part of me wishes she'd left well enough alone and never went to check on her friend."

Abe squeezed his shoulder. "I know. She said the same thing. Then she said she wouldn't have been able to look herself in the eye if she'd let it go."

Pride met the nausea half way. "She's a good kid, Abe." He swallowed. "If one of those assholes looks at her wrong . . ."

"I know," Abe said grimly. "Mia and I are off to find Clayborn. Try not to worry."

Aidan rubbed his forehead as Murphy's phone rang. "Murphy must be out smoking. I'm considering taking it up myself. I feel like arrows are coming from all directions."

"I know how you feel."

Aidan knew that Abe did understand. It hadn't been that long ago that Kristen had been the target of angry killers. "Just find Clayborn, okay?"

"We're on it. I'll call you when we find him." Aidan's phone began to ring and Abe raised a brow. "Somebody wants one of you real bad. See you later."

Sinking into his chair, Aidan picked up the phone. "Reagan." He flipped through his Rolodex for the parole office's number. They'd have Bacon's last known address.

"Detective Reagan, my name is Stacy Kersey." The voice was nearly a whisper. "I'm assistant to Lynne Pope, *Chicago On The Town*."

"No comment," Aidan said tersely and started to hang up.

"Wait, dammit!" she snapped, then her voice dropped again. "Listen to me."

"We're not done with your tape." Rivera's final imitation of Tess was evidence.

"It's not about the tape," she hissed. "Lynne Pope just came back from a meeting with some guy claiming to have porn flicks of your shrink on a CD."

Aidan shot to his feet, his pulse spiking. "*What?* Can you keep him there?"

"For a little longer. He's starting to get itchy feet. I'm supposed to be getting fifty grand in cash to pay him for the video. But he won't wait much longer."

"What does this guy look like?"

"Five nine, salt-and-pepper hair. Fifty, maybe. Sleazy."

Bacon. "I'll be there in fifteen minutes. I'm going to send a patrol car to hold him at the door in case he leaves before I get there. Thanks." He ran to Spinnelli's office. "We have a lead on Bacon."

Spinnelli looked up, his eyes narrowing. "Maybe we're finally catching a break here. Go. I'll call Tess and tell her to start on the files."

Aidan found Murphy outside the station's front door taking his last puff. "Come on."

Wednesday, March 15, 8:55 A.M.

"Goddammit to hell." Murphy's oath was savage.

Aidan closed his eyes and fought to get a grip on his own temper. They were five fucking minutes too late. David Bacon was gone, taking his CD with him.

"I'm sorry." Lynne Pope looked devastated. "I tried to keep him here. I should have called 911." She shook her head. "I'm so sorry."

Murphy forced a smile. "You tried and we appreciate it.

Did he say anything before he left? Anything that would let us know how to find him?"

"No. He got fidgety. It was almost like he had radar or something. He started sweating, then jumped up and said he'd be in touch. I called security, but he ran."

"How did he originally contact you, Miss Pope?" Aidan asked, trying not to think about that slimy bastard running around with a CD of Tess.

"He called the switchboard after the broadcast last night. He said he had more information on Dr. Ciccotelli's unethical practices. I met him this morning and he showed me the CD. Said she was a local celebrity now and he wanted fifty grand."

"You could have bought it," Aidan said, studying her angry face. "Why didn't you?"

"I hear cops say they don't like coincidences," she said tightly. "Well, neither do I. Nor do I like being made to look like a fool on camera. I could see the shock in her eyes yesterday, Detective. She's a pawn in whatever the hell's going on here. I won't be."

Aidan gave her his card. "She'd want me to thank you. Call me if he comes back."

Outside Pope's office, Murphy hurried toward the elevator. "Parole Office just opened. Let's get an address for our peeping Tom." He hit the button harder than necessary. "Then we'll get a warrant. Somewhere, something's got to give."

Wednesday, March 15, 9:45 A.M.

"What a mess."

Tess glanced over at Vito who stood outside the vault surveying the ruin. Next to him stood a uniformed officer sent by Spinnelli to supervise the cleanup, but Aidan had told her the real reason for Officer Nolan's presence and it made her feel that much safer. Clayborn would have to get through both Nolan and Vito to attack her. And if he did manage to get her alone, Tess had Aidan's gun in the purse his mother had brought her the night before. "Thank you, Vito. I wouldn't have noticed on my own."

"Be nice to me, kid. I'm on my vacation here." His tone was light, but his face was tight as his eyes paused on the bloodstained paper still on the vault floor.

Tess's heart stuttered painfully. Harrison's blood. She pulled on a pair of plastic gloves and gathered the ruined documents. "I don't think these will be of any use, Officer Nolan. I'll put them in a bag and you can enter them as evidence."

Nolan gave her a curt nod. "That will be fine, Doctor."

He didn't like her, Tess knew. She'd spent so many hours with Aidan and Jack and Murphy and Marc Spinnelli that she'd almost forgotten the rest of the police force still hated her guts. She and Vito worked steadily for nearly an hour before Amy's voice interrupted them. It was a good time for a break.

"Tess?" Amy's face lit up. "Vito! My God, it's good to see you."

He smiled back. "You're looking good, Amy."

"When did you get into town?"

"Last night. I was worried about Tess."

Amy glared. "As were we all. *Somebody* forgot to call to say she was okay."

"I said I was sorry," Tess muttered. "So did you come to harass me or what?"

"I came to see if you were all right." Amy's expression softened. "So are you?"

"I've been better." Her visit with Flo Ernst had not gone well. Still wildly grieving, she'd been given a sedative by her doctor. One of the Ernst sons frostily advised her to come back after the funeral, which would be Saturday. Respecting their grief, she'd pushed aside the hurt and left saying no more. "But I suppose I've been worse." Amy would know better than anyone else, having stood by her through all those times, too.

"I know, honey," Amy said softly. "And you'll get through this like you got through everything else." She looked around. "Where's Denise?"

"In Harrison's office." Tess glanced at the closed door, in her mind seeing the broken furniture, the blood on the corner of his desk. "She's cleaning. I couldn't."

Amy smoothed a hand over Tess's hair. "It's okay. You don't have to be a superwoman every day."

"Dr. Ciccotelli?" A young man wearing the jacket bearing a local courier's name poked his head in the door. "I have a package." He stepped in, bicycle helmet under his arm, a flat cardboard envelope in one hand. "You have to sign for it."

Frowning, Tess did, but Vito stepped up to take the package first. "Let me check this," he said, pocketing the receipt. He felt the envelope. "It's a CD. Were you expecting a delivery?"

She looked at the label. "From Smith Enterprises? No. But I'm always getting samples of textbooks on CDs from companies wanting reviews. Should I open it?"

"I will. Stand back." Stepping to the far corner of the reception area he opened the envelope and pulled out a sheet of paper and a CD. And paled. "Call Reagan. *Now.*"

"What is it?" Tess walked over and frowned when he turned the paper over, hiding it. "Dammit, Vito, let me see it."

She took the page, not sure what she was expecting. Not expecting what she saw.

Frozen, she stared at . . . herself. Full color. Fully nude. A typed line under the picture read "Deposit $100,000 to the account below or the enclosed video will be sold to the media for wide-scale distribution. You have until midnight tonight." Mechanically she handed the page back to Vito, carefully turned on her heel, marched out into the hall where she dropped to her knees and threw up.

Wednesday, March 15, 11:15 A.M.

Aidan was out of the elevator before the doors fully opened, running down the hall to where a uniform stood outside her door. "Where is it?" Aidan demanded.

The uniform, whose name was Nolan, pointed to the edge of the receptionist's desk. "It's there. Delivery guy dropped it by. Made her sign for it and everything."

"Thanks for giving dispatch the company's name," Murphy said. "We were able to send a patrol car to catch up with him when he made his next delivery."

The delivery man waited for them downtown. Neither Aidan nor Murphy expected any more out of him than they'd gotten from the delivery service. The package had been dropped off with a money order that morning. The clerk's description loosely fit Bacon, but it could easily be applied to half the middle-aged men in Chicago.

"The delivery guy looked like a college kid," Nolan said. "I doubt he knew what he had. He would have kept it for himself if he did." Uneasily he looked over his shoulder. "She was totally cooperative about the papers in the vault. I didn't expect that."

Murphy looked inside the office. "Who's been here this morning?"

"Her brother, the receptionist, and her lawyer friend. She got pale and shocky when she saw the CD and her brother wanted to call 911 but she wouldn't let him. The lawyer called their doctor friend who wanted to give her something to calm her down, but she refused. A maintenance person came up to clean the carpet. That's it."

Aidan gave him a brief nod. "Thanks." Inside, Vito stood on the far side of the receptionist's desk. His arms were tightly locked across his chest and a muscle twitched in his cheek as he stared into Tess's office where she sat on the tattered remnants of a sofa looking shell-shocked. Equally horrified, Amy Miller and Jon Carter sat on either side of her, while a young woman hovered in the open doorway to Ernst's office, clearly uneasy. She would be Denise Masterson, Aidan thought, remembering his search of Tess's practice and its employees.

"Do you have any idea how much I want to kill him?" Vito murmured without taking his eyes from Tess.

Aidan exhaled quietly. "Yeah. I do."

Vito's head whipped around, unholy fury burning in his dark eyes. "You knew?"

"Not until this morning. We didn't know he'd sent her a copy."

Vito's eyes slid closed. "Copy. Then there are more."

Murphy cleared his throat. "How close are you to getting those papers in boxes?"

Vito's eyes opened and he blinked, as if just realizing Murphy was there.

"This is my partner, Todd Murphy," Aidan said quietly.

"We'd just gotten started. Get your LT to send somebody to finish the job." Vito's jaw cocked belligerently. "I'm taking her home."

"She can't go back to her apartment," Murphy said, his voice nonconfrontational.

Vito gritted his teeth. "I don't mean that mausoleum on Michigan Avenue. I'm taking her *home*. We'll be on the next flight to Philly."

"No." Tess pushed off the sofa, pausing as if testing the ability of her legs to hold her up. Amy Miller and Jon Carter both stood up behind her, ready to catch her if they didn't. Tess gently pushed Amy's hands away. "I'm fine, Amy." She walked across her office and stood next to Vito, Amy and Jon flanking her from behind. "And I'm not going anywhere, Vito." Her face was pale but her eyes were clear. She lifted her chin and met Aidan's eyes and pride welled within him. "This isn't the same guy."

Aidan knew it, but wanted to hear why she thought so. "Why not?"

"This lacks the coldness, the preparation of the other attacks. This feels more . . . opportunistic in nature. Like one of his flunkies chewed the end of his leash and ran away." She shrugged. "The other attacks were intended to terrify, to subjugate. To exploit sick, vulnerable people until they break. Ultimately the worst this could do is embarrass me. And that's only if I let it. Which I have decided I won't."

"We'll find him, Tess," Aidan said.

"Of course you will. He's the only link to the person who's killed four people. I'm just a piece of this. They should be your focus. I'm okay, Aidan. I wasn't at first, but I am now. Go do your job." Her bravado wilted when he picked up the package that sat on the edge of Denise's desk. "Do you have to take that?"

"It's evidence, honey. But I promise nobody will look at it that doesn't have to." Aidan looked up at Vito. "Are you going back to Philly?"

"You caught the sonofabitch that did this yet?" Still angry, Vito swept his hand wide indicating the ruined office.

Clayborn was still at large. "No, not yet."

"Then I'm staying."

"Then have dinner with us tonight. We can talk more. I'll call you later, Tess." So busy was he with his own thoughts that he was climbing in the passenger side of Murphy's car before he realized his partner hadn't said a word in a long time. "What?"

"Nothing." But Murphy's lips twitched.

"What?"

Murphy glanced over before pulling into traffic. "You called her 'honey.'"

Aidan rolled his eyes. Busted. "So?"

"And she's cooked for you."

Oh yeah. Memories of the morning flooded back and he shifted in his seat. "Just drive, will you?" He looked at his notepad. "Bacon's mother's house is off Cicero." They'd already been to the address Bacon had left with his parole officer, an overworked man who hadn't taken the time to check the fact that the "apartment" was really a pet store in a strip mall.

"What if we don't find him in time?" Murphy asked, all levity gone from his voice. "If one copy of that CD gets out, we can't guarantee Tess it won't be broadcast somewhere. Today or ten years from now. She'll have to live with that. Can you?"

Aidan wasn't sure and that bothered him. "I'm just having dinner with her, Murphy."

Murphy opened his mouth as if he'd say more, then shrugged. "Okay."

Wednesday, March 15, 11:55 A.M.

David Bacon was an innocent man harassed by the police.

It had to be true. Bacon's mother said so from the other side of her screen door. A sour old woman in her seventies, her ragged black hair sported a wide, white stripe down the part and her thin lips were painted bright red. Through the screen door Aidan was struck with the odor of mothballs and cats.

"We're not here to harass him," Murphy assured her. "Can we come in?"

"He's not here," she snapped, holding her body rigid. "And no you may not come in."

"We just came from the address he gave his parole officer, Mrs. Bacon," Aidan said quietly, his eyes searching what he could see of her living room through the screen. "It's a pet store in a strip mall. Right there, that's a violation of his parole."

She paled, leaving two spots of bright rouge on her cheeks. "You can't send him back to prison. It would kill him."

No, that pleasure should be mine. And Vito Ciccotelli's. "Where is he, Mrs. Bacon? Is he living here with you?"

"No, I swear. He moved out." Hurting her feelings in the process, Aidan could see. "He said he needed space. I don't know where he is. Please leave now."

Aidan and Murphy exchanged a glance and Murphy nodded. "I'm afraid you'll have to come with us, Mrs. Bacon," Murphy said.

Her mouth dropped open. "I'm under arrest?"

"No, ma'am." Murphy's voice was deceptively kind. "We'd just like you to come along and answer some questions since your son isn't available to do so."

And so she couldn't call and warn him the cops were on his tail.

Her thin red lips trembled. "But I can't." Weakly she gestured backward. "My cats. Who will take care of them?"

"You shouldn't be gone long, ma'am," Aidan said. "You can leave them some food and water if you like, but we'll need to escort you while you do."

They followed her through her kitchen into the laundry room where she proceeded to fill four small bowls with cat food. The odor was worse in the laundry room, the enormous litter box overflowing.

I think I'm going to pass out, Aidan thought. Holding his breath, his eyes swept the small room, coming to rest on Mrs. Bacon's laundry basket on top of the dryer. Folded neat as a pin were several short-sleeved polo shirts. Men's polo shirts. Sewn above the heart was the logo for WIRES-N-WIDGETS, a local chain of stores offering a wide selection of electronic gadgets. Gently Aidan cleared his throat. Murphy followed his gaze, his lips curving.

"Let's get you a coat, ma'am," Murphy said. "It's cold outside."

Wednesday, March 15, 12:15 P.M.

"More coffee?" the waitress asked from behind the counter. It was an upscale little diner done in a nouveau forties style that brought scenes from the classic old movies to mind. Situated near the Art Institute, it drew an eclectic crowd of businesspeople and academics and was alive with discussion. Nobody paid any attention to a person sitting alone nursing a cup of coffee on a cold afternoon.

Normally this was a place to sit and reflect. Today it was a place to brood.

"Please, but just halfway. Thanks." Something had gone wrong. A loose thread left unsnipped had raveled, threatening the whole plan. A camera in Ciccotelli's bathroom. Who would have considered it? *I should have. I should have checked. I should have killed him.* But that kind of killing required disposing of a body and that left more ends unsnipped. Using Bacon had been a calculated risk. Sometimes risks went wrong.

Now there were films out there whose content was . . .
uncontrolled. *How soon before he tries blackmailing me?* That
thread would have to be snipped. Right away.

The coffee left a bitter taste, but no less bitter than the
knowledge that once again Ciccotelli had landed on her feet.
The cops had formed a protective wall around her. She'd
spent the night with Reagan. Slut. *Don't tease me, Aidan. You
made me remember what it felt like to be wanted, Aidan.* It was
enough to make a person gag.

Reagan was interested. That would have to be nipped in
the bud as well. *And I know the very way to do it.* But first
things first. Bacon needed to be dealt with. Snuffing that sick
sonofabitch would be satisfying.

But even more satisfying would be Ciccotelli's reaction
to her latest loss.

He'd suffered so, moaning for help. Moaning for Ethel.
Begging for mercy, for answers. *Why?* He'd been so pitiful,
his cries stirring the Blades to more violence. The gang boys
had done well. His wounds would show a sustained beating,
but nothing traceable. Some might call their arrangement
blackmail. *I prefer to think of it as a business proposition that
benefited both sides.* The day suddenly seemed less dismal. No
more brooding. There was work to be done.

"Check, please."

Chapter Fourteen

Wednesday, March 15, 3:10 P.M.

Aidan looked up at the store sign with a sigh. It was the third Wires-N-Widgets store in the Chicagoland area. The next nearest store was in Milwaukee, an hour away. "Three strikes and you're out," he murmured and Murphy frowned.

"It could be that the third time's a charm, Aidan."

"Yeah. Cut the smokes and see if you're still so damn chipper." He was discouraged and growing more so. With every hour they didn't have Bacon in custody the chances of some wanker seeing Tess on a Web site went up. He didn't want to have to tell her they'd failed, to see the worry in her eyes.

They went into the store and up to the front counter where a beefy man stood sorting parts. The name tag on his Wires-N-Widgets polo shirt said GUS.

Murphy laid Bacon's picture on the table and Aidan saw

Gus flinch. "Bacon doesn't work here anymore," Gus said and turned back to the pile of tiny parts.

Murphy leaned against the counter. "Why not?"

The man took out a stack of small plastic bags and starting dropping a single part into each bag. "Because the boss fired him." Aidan put his hand on the bags and Gus looked up, pissed. "I have to have these bagged by the end of my damn shift, okay?"

Aidan leaned closer until he was inches from the big man's nose. "This is a homicide investigation, sir. I really don't care if you get your capacitors bagged or not, but I can promise you won't if you don't start talking to us now. Answer the question. Why did your boss fire David Bacon?"

The man's eyes widened. "Homicide? Bacon killed somebody?"

"We didn't say that," Aidan said. "He might know somebody who did."

Gus sighed and dropped his voice. "We don't want any publicity over this."

Aidan and Murphy glanced at each other. "Did he steal something?" Murphy asked.

Gus shook his head. "Worse. We found cameras in the ladies'. Looked into Bacon's record and found out he'd lied on his app. Said he'd never been arrested, but he'd gone to jail for . . ." He leaned forward. "Spying on high school girls," he whispered.

"We know," Murphy said blandly. "Didn't you guys do a background check?"

Gus flushed. "They're expensive," he mumbled and the picture was clearer.

"Your boss cut a corner and now he's afraid his ass is on the line," Aidan said.

Gus gave him a dirty look. "Something like that."

"So when did Bacon get fired?" Murphy asked.

"About a month ago."

"His mother still has all his shirts," Murphy said and Gus grimaced.

"She can keep 'em. Man always smelled like cat piss. We'd never get those shirts clean. My boss just wanted him gone. We didn't want to get sued by any ladies."

"He leave a forwarding address for his paycheck?" Aidan pressed.

"No. Sorry." Gus frowned when they just looked at him. "I'm not lying. My boss said he wasn't going to get his last paycheck and that if he ever set foot in this store again he'd call the cops for sure. Bacon got real pale and scooted faster than if we'd shocked him with a cattle prod. Which we really wish we had."

"I know the feeling," Aidan told him. "Do you have any idea where he lives?"

Gus concentrated. "No. But he came in one day saying he'd had enough of living with his mother and was going to get a place of his own. Spent all morning looking at ads in the paper and making phone calls. Boss docked his pay when he found out."

Aidan felt the hairs on his neck lift. "Do you remember exactly when that was?"

Gus concentrated again, then brightened. "Wait." He rummaged under the counter, coming up with a college basketball schedule. "The second Monday in December." He looked up. "There was a big game that night and some guy came in desperate for a new TV because he was having a party and his TV was broke. I had to help him because Bacon was on the damn phone. Does that help?"

Aidan's smile was grimly relieved. "Tremendously." He gave him a card. "Call us if you remember anything else about Bacon."

Gus looked at the card, then up again. "Now I remember

where I seen you. You're the detective from TV yesterday. You were coming out of Seward's after he killed himself." His eyes narrowed slightly. "Can I have your autograph?"

Murphy was still chuckling over it an hour later as they reviewed Wires-N-Widgets' LUDs for the second Monday in December. Aidan failed to see the humor in his newfound celebrity.

"What is a capacitor, by the way?" Murphy asked. "Those things Gus was bagging."

"It keeps the voltage from changing too fast." Aidan looked at the list of apartments. They were all over the city. It would take hours to check each one. He looked up and Murphy's head was tilted in question. "I took an electrical circuits class as—"

"Part of your degree." Murphy shook his head, smiling. "I know."

Spinnelli walked over and stood over them, a sober frown bending his mustache. "What's so funny?"

Aidan rolled his eyes. "Nothing. We've got a lead on where Bacon might be living." He showed Spinnelli the list of twenty phone numbers Bacon had called looking for an apartment. "We've called a dozen of them so far and none of them remember him."

"He was probably using a different name," Murphy said, totally serious now. "We'll have to show his picture. The places are all over town. This could take a while."

"Split it up," Spinnelli ordered tersely.

Aidan studied his face. "What's happened, Marc?"

Spinnelli opened his mouth to answer just as Abe and his partner Mia Mitchell walked in. Both wore ominous expressions that matched Spinnelli's.

Slowly Aidan stood up, his heart slowing to a hard thud. "Clayborn?"

Abe shook his head. "We followed leads all morning, but he's gone under. We got another call and had to respond."

Aidan's slogging heart took a racing tumble. "Rachel?"

Mia's eyes narrowed. "What's wrong with Rachel?" Abe shook his head harder.

"Nothing. She's fine. Aidan, do you know a man named Hughes?"

Aidan thought, then his eyes slowly raised when his memory clicked. "He's the doorman in Tess's apartment building. Why?"

Mia unzipped her coat and tugged her scarf from her neck. "Because he's dead. He was found in an alley not too far from his apartment, beaten to a pulp."

Aidan lowered himself to sit on the edge of his desk. It was random. It had to be random. But in his heart he knew it was not. "Was he robbed?"

"His wallet was clean except for his license," Abe said. "Somebody wanted him identified, but it would be impossible by his face. He was beaten badly, Aidan, really badly." He drew a breath. "He had two things pinned to his shirt. One was a note printed on a printer. It said 'Be judged by the company you keep.'"

"The second was a newspaper article about Tess," Mia added quietly.

Aidan rubbed his mouth with the back of his hand, the implications too overwhelming to absorb. "He was Tess's friend. This is going to destroy her."

There was quiet for a moment then Spinnelli sighed. "You were right, Aidan. He's not finished yet. But at least we have a motive finally. It's not to get an appeal and it's not to stage suicides for profit."

"It's to destroy Tess," Aidan said quietly. "However he can."

Spinnelli was grim. "And our only leads are a cop who won't talk to IA and Bacon."

Abe's brows came together and he exchanged a look with Mia. "A cop?"

"What was the time of death on the doorman?" Spinnelli asked.

"Ten hours ago," Mia said. "Give or take thirty minutes. Which cop, Marc? Why?"

"A cop who's been in with IA all day, so he couldn't have killed Hughes," Spinnelli answered, without really answering. "So we're down to Bacon." He rapped on the list of apartments with his knuckles. "Go find him."

"We have to go talk to Hughes's wife," Abe said. "She doesn't know yet."

"I need to tell Tess," Aidan said. "I don't want her to hear this on the news."

"And we still need to find Clayborn," Mia added. "What's the priority, Marc?"

Spinnelli considered. "Mia, you take the widow. Abe, you take a few of the apartments, then the two of you get back to searching for Clayborn. I've had calls all day from Ernst's children, demanding to know when their father's killer would be caught." He rubbed his temples. "Apparently Harrison Ernst had friends in high places because the big guys upstairs have been calling, too. Murphy, you take half the list and Aidan, you take what's left over. Tell Tess first, then start looking." His lips tipped up without a shred of humor. "Last one in is a rotten egg."

Wednesday, March 15, 5:10 P.M.

David Bacon slid the deadbolt closed on his apartment door with a grimace. The place would smell like cigarette smoke forever, he feared, shrugging out of his suit coat. It was the carpet. The fibers soaked up the smell like a sponge. Still, it was better than living with his mother. Cigarettes beat mothballs and cat piss any damn day of the week. And he wouldn't have to worry about the carpet for long. Even without Pope's money, Ciccotelli's first blackmail payment would get him an apartment in a better neighborhood. Payments after that would put him on easy street for a long time because this was a horse he intended to ride around the track till it keeled over and died.

He'd taken two steps into his living room when he stopped. Something was different. Dropping his coat, he ran to his computer, his heart was slamming in his throat. Everything. It had been disturbed, the monitor toppled to the floor. "Oh God," he whispered. "Oh no." He'd been robbed.

The laptop had been ripped from its docking station, its keyboard pried away. His hard drive was gone. *Gone.* He forced himself to breathe, to think. It was bad, but not the end of the world. He never left anything on his hard drive, not after the cops used it to put him away last time. Everything of value was on the CDs. His heart stopped. *My God, the CDs. If someone's stolen my CDs . . .*

He ran back to his bathroom and skidded to a stop. His hiding place was still secure. He drew a deep breath, sighing in relief.

And realized the cigarette smell was stronger. Slowly he turned to see the reason why. The cigarette was still lit and held by a gloved hand he hadn't seen in a long time. Bacon frowned, momentarily off balance. "What the hell are you doing here?"

"I came to see you, David."

He froze, staring at the business end of a slim .22. With a silencer. "I don't understand."

"You cheated me. I hired you to do a job, to set up a camera network in Ciccotelli's apartment. You installed a camera on the side. Did you think I wouldn't find out?"

He shook his head, panic sending blood pounding in his brain. "You didn't hire me."

"Of course I did. I just didn't do it in person. Get me the videos."

"No," he said, then gasped when pain streaked down his right arm. Clutching his right bicep with his left hand, he stared at his arm. His right hand had already grown numb, and his left was hot and slick with blood. In disbelief his eyes lifted. "You shot me."

The amused smile sent an icy chill of horror down his back. "Planning to call the cops, David? Somehow I don't think so. They'd come in and search and what would they find? Videos galore. Tsk, tsk. Some are new, but most are the ones you had your mommy hide while you were in a cage. Get them. Now."

"How did you know?" he asked, desperately trying to think of a way out.

"I knew once you saw the hard drive gone you'd run to check your stash. Sherlock Holmes used a similar ploy in *A Scandal in Bohemia*. You really should read more of the classics, David, instead of watching nudie flicks."

He pulled the wallpaper from the wall and cringed at the dry chuckle behind him. "Clever, David. But you always were. Just not clever enough unfortunately. Finish."

With clumsy motions he pulled at the drywall revealing . . . everything. Everything.

"My, my. Haven't we been a busy boy? There have to be . . . How many?"

"Five hundred," he said heavily. It was all over now.

"Five hundred CDs. Must have taken you years, David."

Wednesday, March 15, 5:15 P.M.

Aidan had Tess meet him at his house, so he could tell her the news in a place where she could grieve in private. She waited for him on the passenger side of a car he hadn't seen before, then he realized it was a rental and Vito was at the wheel. She got out of the car and walked up the driveway into the garage, her face numb with dread. Vito followed, his hands full of shopping bags.

She sat down at the kitchen table and Vito set her shopping bags on the floor. Dolly was at alert, her hair raised, a growl in her throat as she assessed Vito.

"Down, Dolly," Aidan said quietly and the dog obeyed. There was no way to sugarcoat what he had to say, so he just said it. "Tess, Mr. Hughes is dead."

The blood drained from her face. "What?"

Aidan crouched in front of her, taking her hands in his. "I'm so sorry, honey."

"He was in an accident?" But her voice trembled and he knew she knew.

"No." He made his voice as gentle as he knew how. "He was beaten to death, Tess." He looked up at Vito and by the horror on his face saw the man already understood. "There's more. You'll hear it sooner or later, so—"

"Just tell me, dammit," she hissed. "Tell me."

"There was a message . . . with the body. 'Be judged by the company you keep.'" He let out a breath. "And a newspaper article about you."

Her hands rose to cover her mouth as it sank in. Her eyes were dry, wide, and full of shocked horror. "Oh my God," she whispered, rocking infinitesimally. "Oh my God."

He drew her into his arms where she sat, unmoving. She didn't fight him, but she didn't accept him, either. She was like a marble statue, frozen. "Tess?" He slipped his hand beneath her hair, cupping her cheek. "Listen to me." He increased the pressure of his fingers on the back of her head until she looked at him, her eyes glazed. "Listen to me," he repeated. "You did not do this. You did not cause this."

She just looked at him. Frustrated and helpless, he looked up at Vito. "I can't stay. I didn't want her to be out in public and hear the news from someone else."

"I appreciate it," Vito said unsteadily. "You catch Clayborn?"

"Not yet. But we do have a lead on the CD. I have to go." But he didn't move, unable to leave her. "Tess," he murmured. "Dammit."

She blinked. "Does Ethel know?"

"One of the detectives is going to tell her now. Mia Mitchell."

Tess nodded. "I know Mia. She'll . . ." She swallowed. "She'll be kind."

Aidan stood, urging her to her feet and she leaned into him. Not an embrace, but a silent gesture of need. Her arms stayed at her sides when his closed around her. He pressed a kiss to her jaw, just above the ribbed collar of her turtleneck sweater. "I have to go."

She nodded stiffly and stepped back. "Where should I go? Back to my apartment?"

"No, not yet. You can stay here, if you want." He glanced over at Vito. "I can put Dolly in the backyard. She can still warn you if someone comes. Otherwise, if you decide to leave she won't let you back in."

"I understand." Vito nodded, still unsteady.

Aidan got to the door, then turned back for a final look. She sat with her eyes closed, her hand on Dolly's neck. She looked fragile.

She opened her eyes and he knew she was not. There was

a steely resolve mixed with the terrible grief. "Go," she said sternly, tears in her voice. "Find him." Her voice broke and the tears spilled from her eyes, streaking her cheeks. "Please."

Wednesday, March 15, 6:45 P.M.

It was done. Joanna Carmichael reread her story one last time before printing it out. She wanted Ciccotelli, but for now she'd make do with one of the flies she'd caught on the flypaper. Perhaps the woman's closest friend would begin to put some pressure on her to give that exclusive. At any rate it was good copy and had already been cleared for approval by the features editor for the weekend edition.

The door opened behind her and she turned to find Keith coming through the door looking tired and worn. He hated his job at the bank. She knew that. He'd turned down a terrific job at a big investment firm in Atlanta to follow her to Chicago where she could pursue her dream out from under the shadow of her famous father and his newspaper. But that his smile didn't reach his eyes wasn't the bank's fault today. It was hers. He was still hurt from Monday morning. "I'm sorry, Keith. I was wrong."

He came over and kissed the top of her head. "I know, baby. It's okay." But it wasn't. She could hear the strain in his voice.

She sent her story to the printer. "You want to grab some supper?"

"I'm tired, Jo. Let's just call for pizza." He stripped off his tie, his eyes narrowing at the first page coming off the printer. "This isn't about Dr. Ciccotelli. Jo, what is this?"

She addressed an e-mail to the features editor and attached the file. "Let's call it subtle influence."

His mouth hardened. "Let's call it extortion. You can't do this, Jo."

She hit SEND. "I just did."

Keith stepped back, his eyes going flat. "I'm not sure who the hell you think you are, but when you decide to return to your senses, let me know." He turned for the door.

"Where are you going?"

"For a walk before I say something I'll live to regret."

Wednesday, March 15, 7:25 P.M.

"Fuck," Murphy muttered. "We're too late *again*."

Aidan stood in the doorway of Bacon's bathroom, his arms locked over his chest looking at the body in the tub with a grim sense of really bad fate. He'd been the one to find the right apartment. It had been the fifth one on his list, an apartment in the refinished basement of an old house owned by a retired couple who had no idea they harbored a sex offender. The husband had recognized Bacon right away, calling him Mr. Ford. Aidan had called in for a warrant and waited for backup, agonizing with every tick of his watch. Murphy arrived at the same time as the warrant, so they went in together.

Bacon's computer had been destroyed, his monitor smashed, his hard drive melted in a bowl of sulfuric acid, if the label on the bottle next to the bowl was accurate. Bacon floated in a tub filled with bloodred water. He'd slit his wrists, the bastard.

A pile of clothes lay on the floor next to the toilet and Aidan gingerly picked up the pants and the shirt. The pants were soaked from water that had spilled from the tub and run across the floor. He sniffed at the clothes. And frowned. "Smell this, Murphy."

Murphy shrugged. "I can't smell anything but cigarette smoke."

"The pants smell like smoke. The shirt doesn't."

Murphy shrugged again. "Sorry." He looked around with a frown. "Why today? Why did he off himself today?"

"I'm wondering the same thing. He thought Tess would pay him blackmail money, so why kill himself today?"

"Excuse me, Detectives." The CSU photographer had arrived and Aidan moved out of the way. "I'll make this quick as possible."

Jack and Rick were right behind the photographer and Rick was already looking around the room shaking his head. "We need to find his stash," Rick said. "These guys always have a video collection and they all have their favorite hidey-holes."

Aidan joined them in the living room. "Can we get anything off that hard drive?"

Rick looked doubtfully at the hard drive soaking in the bowl of acid. "I don't think so. Bacon must have had something pretty damning on that drive. It's how we got him the first time as I recall. He had everything stored on his hard drive. All the video of all those young girls. Without it we wouldn't have been able to get a conviction."

Murphy's gaze was directed to the ceiling. "Let's look for cameras."

"It's unlikely he'll have cameras in here," Jack said. "But we might get lucky and get a picture we can use for a change. It would be ironic."

"And out of type," Rick added. "Bacon likes to watch. Liked, anyway. Being watched would make him feel out of control. But I'll check to make sure."

"For now, we look for his stash," Jack decided. "How big are we talking, Rick?"

"Some of these guys have hundreds of videos. Bacon was at it for a long time."

Hundreds, Aidan thought grimly. *But I only need to find one.* Then he felt guilty. Each video represented a victim, just like Tess. "I'll take his bedroom."

Each of them took a room to search while the ME tech arrived and fished Bacon's body from the tub. Aidan had checked every drawer as well as the mattress and box springs before he opened the closet door. He stared, stunned. Then moved. *"Murphy!"*

"What did you— Damn," Murphy breathed as Aidan lifted a tan coat from the closet, hanger and all. "Nicole Rivera's coat. And the wig, too."

Aidan hung the coat back up. "Why does Bacon have the coat and wig?"

"And the gun."

They turned to see Jack holding a semiautomatic pistol. "Same caliber as the bullet we found in Rivera," Aidan said flatly.

Jack nodded. "It was hidden in the ceiling with some other stuff you need to see."

The other stuff was pictures—copies of the police photos of Cynthia Adams's sister and Avery Winslow's infant son. Lists of Tess Ciccotelli's patients and her personal routine— exercise, shopping, Sunday brunch with her friends. Her preference for the stairs. "Receipts," Aidan murmured. "The original receipts for the doll and the bear."

"And a flash card for a camera." Rick put it on the kitchen table next to the photographs and receipts. "We'll check it out in the lab to see what's on it. And, I found these." Rick pulled two more photographs from the bottom of the stack.

Murphy sighed. "Blaine Connell." It was a night shot, but clearly showed two men. One of them was Connell accepting cash. A second photo, a close-up, showed Connell's hand closing around a stack of bills topped with Ben Franklin's face.

"Do you know the other guy?" Aidan asked and Murphy hesitated, frowning.

Then his eyes widened and he nodded. "Not his name, but I've seen him. He was on the security video of the elevator at Seward's place. He was dressed in maintenance coveralls. Bacon must have hired him." Murphy pulled in a breath. "*Bacon* orchestrated this? All of this?"

Aidan looked at the pictures, the gun. All of it. "It doesn't feel right." It felt . . . anticlimactic. "Why did he? What motive could he have had?"

Jack pushed a piece of paper forward. "It's Bacon's psych evaluation."

Murphy scanned it with a frown. "Tess did Bacon's court evaluation."

"One more thing." Jack held this paper up so that they could all see. "It's a suicide confession. He says he did it."

Wednesday, March 15, 8:15 P.M.

Beside her, Dolly growled and sat up, ears twitching. Tess heard the garage door go up. Aidan was home. He'd have news of the man who'd filmed her. Who might have already sold her pictures to any number of porn sites on the Internet. She could be out there, visible to anyone with an overactive mouse finger and there wasn't a damn thing she could do about it. But even as her gut churned helplessly, she dropped her chin.

It shamed her to be worried about videos when Ethel Hughes's life was truly ruined.

Mr. Hughes. *He was beaten to death.* She could hear Aidan's voice, so very gentle. *Not your fault.* Yeah, right. *Be judged by the company you keep.* Mr. Hughes was dead because he was her friend. Who would be next? Amy? Jon? She'd called them, told them to be careful. Not to go out alone. She hadn't been able to call Ethel, to tell her how sorry she was. Not yet. She would have to, but not yet.

You're a coward, Chick. The truth of it had bile burning her throat. Her friends were in danger, yet here she hid. Doing nothing.

Aidan came through the door, his eyes widening in surprise when Dolly leaped against his chest. Affectionately he scratched the dog's ears, meeting her eyes over Dolly's head. "Where's your brother?"

Tess tapped her lips with her forefinger. "Asleep on your sofa. He'd pulled a double shift before coming out here and then he was up all night worrying about me."

Aidan looked around the doorway to where Vito sprawled on the sofa, snoring softly, his feet dangling off the sofa's edge, Bella curled up on his butt.

"Something smells good." Unbuttoning his overcoat, he walked over to the table, then bent for a closer look, sniffing appreciatively. "Are these cannoli?"

Her mouth tipped up. There was a reverence in his tone that made her heart ease, just a little. "They are. And ravioli, too. All from scratch."

He sampled one of the cannoli, closing his eyes as he swallowed. "My God, these are good. I'm starving. So where did you get the ingredients to make all this stuff?"

"The local market delivers." She waved her hand when he scowled. "I had Vito answer the door. I'm not stupid, Aidan."

"I didn't say you were. How are you, Tess?"

Shrugging, she set about driving the corkscrew into a bottle of red wine she'd bought earlier that afternoon, finding the stabbing, jabbing, and twisting quite cathartic. "You want some? It's good for your heart, you know."

"Is that why you drink it?" he asked.

"Actually it is. My father has a bad heart, so I run three times a week, take an aspirin every morning and a glass of red wine every night." *So I don't end up like him. In more ways than one.* "Do you want some or not, Aidan?"

"Just a little. Did the market deliver the wine, too?"

"This? No. This came from a little wineshop a few blocks from my office. I went by today after I finished cleaning up the vault and swearing at Joanna Carmichael."

His brows went up. "Carmichael came by your office? Why?"

"She still wants an exclusive."

"She hasn't been in her apartment any of the times I've gone by."

"Because she's been following me." Tess thought about the young girl with the innocent looking braid and the predatory gleam in her eyes. "She threatened to do an exposé on my friends. So now I've warned them on two fronts." Exposure and danger. *Because they're my friends.* She'd been trying to keep it from eating her inside all day.

His brows furrowed. "What do your friends have to hide, Tess?"

She shrugged, annoyed at the question. Annoyed that her friends were vulnerable. "Everybody has something they'd prefer stay hidden, Aidan. Even you, I'd imagine."

His eyes shuttered. "So you went shopping?"

A clumsy segue, but she let him have it unchallenged. "I did. I bought some shoes and a present for your mother and some wine." She reapplied herself to the cork, her bad mood rippling. "The woman who runs the wineshop used to be the wife of some high-powered CEO until one day, poof—" She pulled the cork from the bottle with a loud pop. "Her husband says, 'It's over, Marge,' and throws her over for some skinny-assed little bimbo barely out of college." The words came out so bitterly she cringed.

"He cheated on her," Aidan said evenly.

"I suppose I am a little transparent on that score. Anyway, Marge put everything she had into starting her own wineshop." Tess sniffed at the cork. It was good. "I only buy from Marge. I figure she's earned it."

He was studying her steadily. "How are you, Tess?"

Her hands shook as she poured, sending wine sloshing over the glass's rim. "Scared. Wondering who will be next. I feel like such a coward, hiding here."

"Sit down."

She did, sighing when he put his arm around her shoulders and pulled her close. He was strength and warmth at a time when she had too little of either so she let herself lean, resting her head on his shoulder.

"You're not a coward," he murmured in her ear. "Don't ever think that."

"My friends are in danger because . . ." She swallowed hard and forced the words out in a harsh whisper. "Because of the company they keep. And I can't make it stop because I don't even know what I did to start it."

He pressed a kiss to the top of her head, quick and hard. "You didn't do anything. Tess, do you know the name David Bacon?"

She lifted her head, forcing her brain to think. "I think so. He . . . He was one of Eleanor's court evaluations, right about the time she died. It's been almost four years."

"Three years, eight months."

"That sounds about right." She tilted her head, studying him. His eyes had gone flat. "Why?"

"Eleanor was your former partner, right?" he asked instead.

"Yes. She took me under her wing when I was still an undergrad. Groomed me to take her practice. We thought she had a lot more time. She had a stroke—no warning. I took her court evaluations after she died. I do remember David Bacon. Eleanor had done most of the work so I only talked to him once, then I signed off on the report. I never even had to testify in court." She shuddered. "He was creepy."

"You seem to remember him clearly. Was he your first court evaluation?"

"No, I'd done others, but he was my first where I had to work with two branches of law enforcement. The Feds were involved in that one, because . . . Oh my God. He put cameras in a girls' locker room shower. It was kiddie porn because most of them were younger than eighteen and the Feds prosecuted. *He's* the one who put the camera in my shower?"

"It seems so."

She was afraid to ask. "Did . . . did you catch him?"

He nodded soberly and relief flooded her mind. The midnight deadline that had taunted her all day was no more. Bacon wouldn't be selling that video to the media, or anybody else. But something was wrong. "He's dead, isn't he?"

"Very."

"Did you kill him?"

"No."

"I thought this was good news. I'm supposed to feel relieved, right? Why don't I?"

His blue eyes were troubled. "Because it doesn't feel right to me. We found all the evidence that he'd set up Adams and Winslow and Seward. We found the gun that's the same caliber as the one that killed the voice actress. We found the evaluation you signed. We even found evidence that one of the cops in my old precinct was involved."

"That's how he got the police photos," she murmured. "I was wondering. Where did you find all of this evidence?"

"All conveniently hidden behind a ceiling tile."

"Tidy," she agreed. "You don't think he did it."

"No, I don't."

"I only met the man once, Aidan, but from what I remember, he didn't strike me as the kind to be so . . . ruthlessly organized."

He sighed. "I thought so. Tomorrow we'll have to look a little harder at Mr. Bacon. Now I have to go."

"Back to work?"

"No, to my dad's house. I need to talk to Rachel."

"Is she all right?"

"Dad says so, but I want to talk to her." He shrugged. "I need to see her myself."

Tess remembered the way Vito had embraced her this morning, his fear and love palpable, tangible. "I got a thank-you gift for your mother. Will you give it to her?"

"Come with me and give it to her yourself. We'll leave a note for Vito."

Wednesday, March 15, 9:00 P.M.

As sleazy alcoholic has-been PIs went, Destin Lawe was not half bad. He'd done his job, admirably. Now, he was being prematurely retired.

He got into the car looking impressed. "New wheels?"

"Something like that." It really was a shame. Lawe, despite his name, had absolutely no problems skirting or breaking it when necessary. He had been the perfect go-between—an amoral man with gambling debts, liquor bills, and an uncanny ability to catch normally good people doing very bad things. He would be a hard man to replace.

"What's with the raincoat?" Lawe asked, flicking a glance over the ugly mackintosh that had cost way too much money for a one-time use. "The weatherman said it was going to be clear and cold for a few more days."

"I'd say it's going to be getting considerably colder. Did you find her?"

"Of course I did. Though why you wanted a college kid is a mystery to me. Here's her name and address and schedule of classes." He pulled a sheet of paper from his pocket and handed it over while examining the radio on the high-priced Mercedes that had been all too easy to steal. *I haven't lost my touch after all these years.* That it was a newer model than Ciccotelli's just made the find that much sweeter.

The student lived on campus near the shoe store Ciccotelli had visited today. Poor girl. Wrong place, wrong time for her. Lawe had returned the photo of the girl as well. Excellent. Joanna Carmichael had been busy snapping pictures of Ciccotelli all over town, eliminating the need for legwork. "She has bad taste in shoes."

Lawe's eyes froze, his mouth open on an unuttered reply. Even in the dim light of the street lamps it was obvious that every drop of color had drained from his face.

The barrel of a silenced gun had that general effect on people.

"Why?" he asked, his voice hoarse. He thought his movements were stealthy, but his hand going for his weapon was just as obvious as his pallor. A single bullet to his wrist had him screaming, holding his arm in pain. He turned quickly, clawing for the door handle, only to find it gone. He cowered back against the door, breathing hard.

"It's for your own good, really. Blaine Connell is about to talk."

He moaned. "He wouldn't. The cops got nothing on him. I promise."

"Now they do."

His eyes widened as cognition struck. "You gave it to them? Why?"

"Because it was either you or me." The next six shots sank neatly into his heart, the eighth and ninth to his head once he'd fallen forward. "No contest, Mr. Lawe. Given that kind of choice, I'll always choose me."

The mackintosh rolled into a tight little ball, as advertised. That was probably a bonus for campers, who, for reasons forever to remain a mystery, chose to pack their backpacks full of supplies and . . . rough it. The little bloody, balled mackintosh would easily get lost in a busy city Dumpster—*A bonus for me.*

A last look back in the rearview mirror provided a final glimpse of the Mercedes which had not fared nearly as well, its interior soiled beyond reclaim. Hopefully the owners had it fully insured. Because now it was Mr. Lawe's resting place.

In about thirty seconds Mr. Lawe's earthly resting place would approach the temperature of his eternal one. Three . . . two . . . one. Very nice. The blaze lit up the sky briefly, before settling down to a slow, sure burn.

That took care of nearly all the loose ends. Rivera, Bacon, and Lawe. The Blade boys who'd killed Hughes would need to be watched although the chance of one of them succumbing to any weakness was remote at best. But neglect to fully appreciate the loyalty of an employee had nearly allowed Bacon to sink the ship. The cops had found him already. Sooner than expected. Reagan was not to be underestimated.

But they'd found all the right evidence to put their minds at ease and close the case before going on to the next. Pictures, reports, the gun . . . Brilliant to add the gun. *If I do say so myself. And I do.* They'd think they'd solved it. They'd tell Ciccotelli she was safe and she'd think it was true. She might even sleep tonight.

Until the next victim fell. Which would be soon. *Be judged by the company you keep.*

By the time I'm finished no one will stand with her. She will be alone and finally fully vulnerable. Then she'll be mine.

Chapter Fifteen

~

Wednesday, March 15, 9:45 P.M.

What is this?" Aidan's mother's eyes lit up when he walked into her kitchen, then sharpened with interest when Tess came in behind him. Becca and Rachel were sitting at the kitchen table, his mother clipping coupons while Rachel studied chemistry. Aidan put the baked ravioli on the counter and kissed his mother's cheek. "Tess made dinner."

Becca gave Tess a smile. "That was thoughtful of you to think of us, Tess."

Tess held out a box wrapped in foil with a frilly bow. "This is for you, Mrs. Reagan. A thank-you for helping me last night."

"You didn't have to do that!" But her fingers made quick work of the wrapping paper, then she sucked in a delighted breath. "Goodness." She lifted a soft cashmere sweater from the box. She put it down quickly. "It's too expensive. I can't accept this."

"Sure you can," Tess said easily. "It was on sale." She winked conspiratorially. "It's your color, Mrs. Reagan. Go try it on. If it doesn't fit, I have the receipt."

Becca hurried off, leaving Aidan perplexed. "I didn't know she liked cashmere."

Tess clucked her tongue. "I bet you give her pots and pans for Mother's Day, don't you?" She shook her head. "You do. Shame on you, Aidan." Her cell phone rang and her shoulders stiffened. "Not again," she muttered. "One more reporter and I swear to God . . ." She checked the caller ID and relaxed. "It's Vito. He must have woken up and found us gone. Excuse me." She walked into the laundry room, out of sight and Rachel gave him a curious look.

"She cooked in your kitchen?"

"She made cannoli, too, from scratch."

Rachel perked up. "Cannoli? Where is it?"

"At my house. You didn't think I'd bring you any, did you?"

She scowled at him. "Pig. Do you think that sweater was really the same price as one from Wal-Mart?"

Aidan shook his head. "Hell no, but don't tell Mom that. She looked too happy." He sat next to Rachel, studied her face. She looked tired. "Rough day?"

"Yeah. I kept thinking somebody would know it was me that told, but nobody said anything. The cops came during fifth period and took three of the jocks away."

"So Marie told the police who raped her?"

Rachel closed her eyes. "I guess she must have. She wasn't in school again, but word on the street was that her father came in after first period and raised holy hell in the principal's office, so her parents must know now." She opened her eyes, her stare plaintive. "Did I do the right thing, Aidan?"

He hugged her. "Yeah, honey. You did." He hoped he was telling the truth.

Tess came back, her phone in her hand. "Vito wants to talk to you."

"Who's Vito?" he heard Rachel asking as Tess sat down next to her.

"*My* big brother," Tess answered. She tapped Rachel's book. "So what is this?"

"Balancing equations." Rachel grimaced. "I can't figure it out."

Tess bent her head over the book. "A long time ago in a galaxy far, far away I knew how to do this. Let's see if I still can . . ."

Aidan closed the door to the laundry room. "Yeah, Vito? What's up?"

"Your neighbor kid woke me up."

"Twelve-year-old? Freckles? He walks my dog when I'm not home."

"Well, he didn't come to walk the dog. He nearly called the cops when I opened the door. Wouldn't believe I was a houseguest."

"He wants to be a cop," Aidan said with affection. "He's a nice kid."

"Yeah," Vito said a sarcastic laugh. "To you. He only talked to me after I showed him every piece of ID I owned. He said there was a car sitting a few doors down all afternoon. Big guy, shaved head."

Aidan's hair stood up on his neck. Clayborn. "Shit. How did he know Tess was at my house? How did he get my address?"

"I don't know. The kid said he was waiting for you to get home to tell you, but he got caught up in a video game and lost track of time."

"I guess the car isn't there now."

"I've been around the block twice now and I don't see anything. Listen, I have a few errands to run. You'll keep her with you?"

"I won't let her out of my sight. Don't worry."

"Did you catch the scum that sent her that CD?"

"In a manner of speaking. He's dead. Looks like he killed himself."

Vito was quiet for a moment. "Looks like?"

"For now. Let's just say I have a few more questions to answer. Where will you be? Tonight, that is."

"I'm staying in my hotel." Vito's tone changed, going slightly ominous. "Tell Tess I'll pick her up in a few hours. I got her a room there, too, so she can stay with me."

Aidan's lips twitched at the barely veiled warning to keep his hands off Vito's little sister. "I'll tell her." Whether she did Vito's bidding was another thing altogether.

He went back in the kitchen to find Tess and Rachel deep in conversation. Tess had Rachel's pencil and was helping her with her homework.

His mother reappeared, fussing with the collar of the cashmere sweater. "Well?"

Aidan smiled at her. "Tess is right. It's your color, Mom."

A car door slammed outside. "Your father's home," Becca said, frowning. Aidan caught the look she threw Tess just as his father blustered in from outside.

Tess didn't miss Becca Reagan's look, either. She looked up warily as a man came in from outside. He was big like Aidan, his black hair threaded with silver, but his eyes were the same intense blue. Suddenly the kitchen took on a palpable tension.

"Dad," Aidan said. "This is Tess Ciccotelli. Tess, my father, Kyle Reagan."

Kyle Reagan, the retired policeman. Kyle Reagan who at

this very moment scowled at her from beneath bushy gray brows. Tess drew a breath. "It's nice to meet you, sir."

He stood there a moment, then turned to Aidan. "What is she doing here?"

"Kyle!" Becca chided. "That's enough."

With a grunt, he stalked past and headed for the living room. "Don't worry," Rachel said lightly. "He wasn't crazy about Kristen at first, either." She raised a brow at Aidan. "Neither were you."

But Aidan didn't respond. His cheeks were flushed, his jaw tight. "I'll be back."

Tess stood, put a hand on his chest. "Don't, Aidan. It's all right. I won't come between you and your dad."

"No, it's not all right." He went into the living room, his face determined.

"Oh, dear," Becca murmured. "Sit down, Rachel," she added when Rachel stood up to listen at the doorway. Rachel rolled her eyes, but obeyed. The men spoke in low voices, but Tess could pick out a word here and there. Most of what she heard, she understood.

Most importantly she understood Aidan and her father were arguing and she was the cause. And as . . . *interested* as she was in Aidan Reagan, she wasn't about to be the cause of another family rift. Being the cause of her own family's was bad enough. Quietly she shrugged into her coat.

"Thanks for everything, Mrs. Reagan." She squeezed Rachel's shoulder. "You're brother is so proud of you," she murmured. "You did good, kid." Then she marched into the living room where Aidan's father sat in an old recliner, his arms crossed over his chest, his face set in a mutinous frown. Aidan stood before him, feet spread wide, hands on his hips. Their expressions were identical, their harsh voices indistinguishable.

She cleared her throat. "Gentlemen." They quieted, turning to her. "Mr. Reagan, I don't know what you think you know about me, but you've raised honorable children, so I have to believe they learned it from you. I'm not the person you imagine me to be, and if you gave me a chance you'd see that. But I won't be the cause of friction in your family. Trust me, Aidan, it's not worth it. I'll be waiting for you when you're ready to go."

She turned on her heel and walked away, trembling inside but determined not to let it show. She gave Becca a wave before walking through the laundry room and outside where the cold wind whipped at her hair. Aidan's car was parked on the curb. Just a few feet more and—

A hand clenched her hair, yanking her to her toes a second before a hand came over her mouth and a gun to her head. "Don't say a word, Doctor."

Clayborn. Fucking hell. Faced with a gun to her head for the second time in two days, something desperate exploded inside her and she clawed at his face, wrenching from his grip like a wild thing. The sharp rip in her scalp had her eyes stinging but she blinked it away as she got free and took a single running step. He grunted in surprise and grabbed her shoulder in a viselike grip and everything seemed to go on autopilot. She brought the heel of her hand hard up into his nose and, before the shriek of pain crossed his lips, followed it with a sharp knee to his groin.

Breathing like a bellows, she watched him crumple to the ground, his left hand going to his groin, his right still clutching the gun, and with all her weight, crashed the heel of her new boot into his wrist.

She wrenched the gun from his hand and fell on her ass, the cold wet of the ground seeping through her jeans, shocking her into motion. She scrambled backward using her heels for leverage, her cold fingers fumbling with the gun's grip, its trigger. She lurched to her feet and took another stumbling step back.

Clayborn struggled to his knees. Blood gushed from his nose, running down his vinyl jacket. He spat a mouthful of blood to the soggy wet ground. "You fucking cunt," he growled. "You broke my nose. I'm going to kill you for that."

Breathe, Tess. Breathe. She made her hands steady and held the gun with both hands as Vito had taught her so many years ago. Forced her voice to be cool. Collected. Even though her blood was pounding in her ears, deafening her.

"If you come one step closer I swear to God I'll blow your head off." She tossed her hair from her eyes, control returning and with it a cold resolution. "On second thought, come. I'll kill you where you stand, you sonofabitch. For Harrison. Come on. Take a step. I really, really want to kill you."

"You wouldn't," he said, his eyes narrowing. He wiped blood from his face with his sleeve, but it kept gushing from his nose. "You couldn't." Spitting again, he struggled to his feet and she pulled the trigger.

He froze, staring at the ground where the bullet had struck, an inch from his foot.

"You don't think I would?" Her heart was crashing against her ribs and she raised the gun level with his chest. "You ready to bet your life on that? I've had one hell of a day, Mr. Clayborn. So you want to try it, fine. But I warn you, you're betting against the house now. Really, really bad odds."

"Tess? Oh my God. *Dad!*" Aidan slammed out of the house and was at her side in seconds, his gun in his hand. Seconds later Clayborn was on his knees, his hands cuffed behind his back and even still the look he gave her terrified her to her bones. If he'd been free, she'd be dead. It was as simple as that.

"Tess," Aidan said gently. "Put the gun down."

She looked at the gun in her hands, then back at Clayborn. "He killed Harrison."

"I know, honey. And you caught him. He can't hurt you now."

"He killed Harrison," she repeated, the gun still in her hands. Now that Clayborn was on his knees, it pointed at his head.

The door slammed again and she heard a gruff voice commanding Becca to call 911. A minute later a hand gently pried Clayborn's gun from her hands and an arm went around her shoulders.

"Come inside," Kyle Reagan said quietly. "It's all right now."

Tess looked over Clayborn's head and met Aidan's eyes. "Call Abe and Mia. Tell them we found Clayborn."

Aidan nodded. "I will."

Wednesday, March 15, 10:45 P.M.

Aidan's heart was still beating hard as he guided the Camaro into his garage. Even though she now sat safely at his side, he kept seeing her standing in his parents' front yard, pointing Clayborn's gun to the bastard's own head, her hands steady and her face filled with cold resolve.

Afterward, Abe and Mia had arrived to haul Clayborn off and she'd answered their questions with a terse brevity that was wholly uncharacteristic. She'd been angry. She still was. She'd said nothing on their way home, but he could feel her rage still bubbling. Aidan cut the ignition and she leaped from the car and ran inside.

With a quiet sigh Aidan followed, catching up to her in his bedroom where she stood at the foot of his bed with her back to him, ripping at the button of her jeans. Her sweater was already on the floor, leaving her back bare except for the lacy bra he'd already removed once that day. He swallowed back a surge of lust and picked up her sweater, swallowing hard again when he felt the crust of dried blood on her sleeve. Clayborn's blood, which had gushed from his broken nose. It was the second time in two days she'd worn the blood of others. So easily it could have been her own.

She kicked off her muddy jeans, took off toward the bathroom, then stopped abruptly, dropping her chin to her chest. She shuddered out a deep breath. "I know I should thank you for stopping me. I would have killed him if you hadn't stopped me."

This he understood. "You wouldn't have killed him, Tess. Not in cold blood."

She lifted her head, her laugh bitter. "I'd like to think that was true. I taunted him. I told him to try to get me. I wanted to kill him."

His blood ran cold at the thought of her taunting a crazed killer, but he kept his voice even as he dropped her sweater on top of her jeans. "But you didn't. Tess, don't you think I know how you feel? There are times I make a bust and it's all I can do not to rip the perp's head right off his shoulders. That I don't makes me a good cop. That I want to makes me human. You came face to face with the man who killed your friend. If you weren't angry, you wouldn't be normal."

"You sound like a shrink now." She shook her head slowly. "I was standing there . . . and all of the sudden it wasn't just about Harrison. It was . . . all of them. Cynthia and Avery. Gwen and Malcolm." Her voice faltered. "Mr.

Hughes," she whispered. "God, Aidan, he's gone. Because of—"

He grabbed her shoulders and spun her around to face him. "Stop it. Don't you dare say this is because of you."

Her eyes flashed hot. "But it is," she hissed.

In frustration, he tightened his hold on her shoulders. "Dammit, you might have died tonight, Tess."

The heat in her eyes disappeared, leaving behind a haunted fragility that made his own frustration fade away. "Don't you think I know that?" she whispered.

It was the descent from an adrenaline rush after a close call. He'd seen it hundreds of times in hundreds of victims during his career. But this was different. This was Tess. There was fear in her eyes and he wanted it gone. "You're alive," he murmured. Then proved it the best way he knew how, covering her mouth with his.

She didn't back away so he deepened the kiss, his heart pounding harder when after a moment of quiet acceptance she seemed to explode into motion, locking her arms around his neck and lifting on her toes to press her body closer. One kiss became two, then three as his hands slid down the smooth skin of her back, beneath the lace that covered her curves. He cupped her rear end, lifting her higher, tightening his hold when she wriggled against him, humming deep in her throat.

She pulled back far enough to see his face, an almost desperate passion in her eyes. "Tonight, Aidan. Please."

He didn't pretend to misunderstand. "I don't think—" Then his mouth went dry and he couldn't think at all as she stepped back, deftly unclasping her bra and slipping out of her panties. Nude, she stole his breath. Golden skin and . . . curves. Everywhere. His swallow was audible in the quiet of the room. "My God. Tess."

Not taking her eyes from his she pulled his shirt from his

pants, loosening each button with a methodical deliberation that had him nearly hypnotized. Somewhere about halfway up his shirt his senses returned with the urgency of a storm. Fingers fumbling, he managed his belt, his pants, boxers and shoes as she continued her slow progress. With a low laugh he yanked at the last button, shrugging out of his shirt and falling with her to the bed in the same breath. He rolled her to her back, settling between her thighs, anticipation making his heart pound way up in his throat. "Be sure," he said hoarsely.

"Be quiet." She thrust up against him with a roll of her hips, sliding her hands into his hair, pulling him down for the hottest kiss he'd ever had. Her thighs rose to bracket his hips and with a muttered oath he plunged deep, making her arch and cry out.

He stopped, his body tight. "Did I hurt you?"

"No." Her eyes were closed and she drew a deep breath. "It's been a long time." Her hands grasped his back and she settled herself beneath him, drawing him deeper still. "Don't even think about stopping."

Relief made him shudder, the urgent lift of her hips made him move. He watched her face as he did, watched her face tighten, her head toss on his pillow. Watched the way her teeth clamped her bottom lip as her hips bucked harder, meeting each thrust. She felt incredible, but watching her go higher and higher . . . God, he'd never seen anything more erotic, any woman more beautiful. Then her eyes flew open and in their brown depths he saw an urgency and awe that stunned him and he knew this was a place she'd never been before.

"Aidan." It was a muted plea and he knew she was hanging on the edge. Determined that she'd have it all, he slipped his hands beneath her thighs, spread her legs wider, and drove his body deeper, his goal single-minded. Pleasure for her. *For me.*

But he was nearing his limit. Not yet. He bit his lip hard, holding back. And finally, when he thought he couldn't hold back any longer, she arched and came hard, hurling him higher, shoving him over. Groaning her name, he fell.

Wednesday, March 15, 11:35 P.M.

She awoke to his mouth on her breast and arched like a cat, stretching and twisting to fit herself to him. He lay between her legs, his chest hard against her pelvis and it felt good. Not nearly as good as when he'd been inside her, but damn good just the same. Certainly better than the dream from which he'd pulled her. "I was dreaming."

He lifted his head. "I know. You were screaming. Scared the shit out of me." His mouth curved wryly. "You seem to make a habit of doing that."

She feathered the hair at his nape. "I'm sorry."

"So what was the dream, Tess?"

"Same one I've been having every night, just more densely populated." Cynthia, Avery Winslow. The Sewards. Now Harrison and Mr. Hughes. "Do you remember the "Thriller" video, with all those zombies? Well, none of mine were dancing." She pushed her hair out of her face with one hand. "It started Sunday night. It was Cynthia . . . and you were there, too. She was lying there . . ." She grimaced, remembering. "All ripped up, her heart beating in her chest. And you stood over her and grabbed her heart and held it out to me." She swallowed. "Told me to take it."

He looked horrified. "God."

"Yeah. I guess I screamed then, too, because Jon woke me up."

"He was in your apartment?"

She nodded. "He has a key."

He frowned. "Who else has keys to your apartment, Tess?"

"Amy. Robin. I guess Phillip probably still does." She lifted her head from the pillow to stare down at him, not liking the tone of his question. "No way. It's not possible that they had anything to do with this."

"I didn't say they did."

"You thought it."

"That's my job, Tess." His jaw tightened. "I'm supposed to be keeping you safe. Though a fat lot of good I was tonight."

She dropped her head back to the pillow, unwilling to argue with him about her friends. He'd see he was wrong in time. "You kept me from killing the sonofabitch. I suppose I should appreciate that."

"Give it time. Why do so many people have keys to your place, Tess? It's not safe to have that many keys floating around. Somebody had free access to your apartment long enough to place all those cameras."

Dread crept back into her heart. "David Bacon."

"He might have put in the first cameras, but what about the microphones in your jackets? How long have you had them? The jackets."

"Different amounts of time." She swallowed. "It would depend on when I hit the sales. Did you find a microphone in that red jacket I wore on Sunday?"

"Yes."

"I just bought it a month ago. It was a Valentine's Day sale." She closed her eyes. "Somebody's been in my apartment in the last few weeks."

"Maybe not. Have you sent the jackets out to be cleaned?"

"All but the red one. It was brand new. My God, Aidan."

He kissed the hollow between her breasts. "Sshh. We won't worry about it right now. Tell me about your friends."

Her eyes flew open. "No. It's not possible. Don't you think I'd know?" But he said nothing, exasperating her. "I've known Jon since med school. Robin, too. Amy and I have been friends since junior high school, for God's sake."

"Maybe somebody took their key. Made a copy."

She considered that. "That's possible."

"So why do they have keys?"

"Phillip gave them keys when I was sick."

"You mean when you were hurt last year?"

She shook her head, hating the memory. "No, after the con with the chain. I was in the hospital for a few days. Phillip was out of town at a conference, but he came home early. Took me home, put me to bed." She stared at his ceiling. "He'd stand there and watch me like I was going to blow up or something. He didn't do well with sick people."

"What did he do? As a career?"

"He's a doctor, too. I met him in med school along with Jon."

He frowned. "But he isn't good with sick people? Isn't that a job liability?"

"That's why he went into research."

"So how were you sick? Is that what Vito meant when he said you were too skinny?"

"Vito always thinks I'm too skinny."

"You're evading my question, Tess."

She sighed. "I'm lying here naked as a jaybird and you want to talk about me being sick? That's not normal, Aidan."

He nuzzled her breast, kissing close enough to her nipple to make her gasp, far enough away to make her arch. "Tell me what I want to know and I'll pursue other topics."

She laughed. "Is this your normal interrogation technique?"

"Tess," he warned. "I'm serious."

She sighed again. "It's embarrassing, okay? I don't like to talk about it because it's embarrassing. After Phillip brought me home from the hospital I was supposed to recuperate for a week, then go back to work, but every time I got out of bed I'd feel weak and nauseous. I'd go into work and spend seventy-five percent of my day puking my guts up in the bathroom."

"What was wrong?"

She gave him a dark look. "Nothing. I got tested twelve ways to Tuesday and nobody could find any physical reason why I was sick."

"It was psychosomatic, then."

She rolled her eyes. "Posttraumatic stress disorder was what the doctor finally called it. It was humiliating. I was a shrink and it was all in my head. I was too scared to work." She shrugged. "But then it didn't matter anymore because three weeks after that I lost my contract with the court. I didn't have to worry about psycho cons with chains anymore."

"Did it get better?"

She looked up at the ceiling again. "Actually it got a lot worse. Phillip was getting impatient with me. He'd been solicitous as he could be, but he wanted me well. He wanted . . . sex. And I couldn't. I had no energy and I couldn't eat. I could barely dress myself, much less burn up the sheets." She changed the subject. "He was traveling a lot, so he gave Jon and Robin keys. Amy already had a set. They'd come by when I was too weak to go to work. Check on me." She grimaced. "Feed me soup. I really hate soup. Robin's at least tastes good. Amy's was nasty. She's not a good cook."

"I'll remember that. *No soup for you*," he added in a *Seinfeld* Soup Nazi imitation and she chuckled. "So what happened to Dr. Damn-him-to-hell?"

"After a few months of forced abstinence, he decided he'd get some elsewhere." The pain resurfaced, but with less vigor than before. "He had her in my bed."

Aidan was quiet, his eyes steady. "Tacky of him."

She huffed another chuckle. "Yeah. Tackier of her to leave an earring under my pillow and her panties wadded under the sheets at the foot of the bed. Happened when I was at the damn doctor's office. I came home and he was gone. Her perfume wasn't."

"Did you confront him?"

"Yes. He didn't deny it. He just packed up his things and left that night. Never said a word. And I haven't talked to him since. That's all."

"When did you start feeling better?"

"After my honeymoon."

His brows shot up. "Excuse me?"

"The cruise tickets were nonrefundable, so Amy and I drank our way up and down the west coast of Mexico. Somewhere on that trip the nausea passed and when I came back I went back to work. All our friends knew what had happened. You can't cancel a huge wedding two weeks before the date without explaining. Phillip became persona non grata in our little group. Last I heard he had a new girlfriend. Rich bitch from the North Shore."

He smiled. "Tess, you're rich."

"Uh-uh. I'm comfortable. Eleanor was rich. Come next summer, my lease on the apartment expires and I'll be hoofing it from an apartment in a less trendy part of town."

He was frowning again. "Lease?"

"Yep. Eleanor liked to prepay things. She'd paid for her apartment several years out and when she died, she left her remaining months on the lease to me, both the apartment and the Mercedes. On June thirtieth, the clock hits midnight and it all turns to a pumpkin." He looked surprised and that satisfied her. "Told you I wasn't a snob. I'm more of a squatter. With attitude."

He barked out a startled laugh. "Yeah, I guess we saw that tonight. How did you break his nose anyway? He wouldn't say."

She demonstrated, gently pushing the heel of her hand to his nose. "Like this."

He kissed her wrist. "Vito show you how to do that?" he murmured.

She hesitated. "No. Vito showed me how to use a gun."

He pressed his lips to her chin. "You're evading again."

"My dad showed me," she said, annoyed with his persistence. "We lived in a rough neighborhood. My dad wouldn't let me date until I could do the self-defense moves. Although no boy was stupid enough to try anything with me. Not with four big brothers."

"Are they all as big as Vito?"

"About." She sighed. "I miss them. A lot. Vito wants me to come home, permanently." She watched him frown. "My dad is really sick. I don't want it to matter to me, but it does. Seeing you with your parents tonight . . ." She closed her eyes. "I haven't seen my family in a very long time."

"How long?"

"Five years."

"Why?"

"We are estranged."

"Tess."

She lifted a shoulder wearily. "My dad was always very strict. Very Catholic and very strict. We went to mass every Sunday. Excepting Santa Claus and the Tooth Fairy, I honestly believed he'd never lied to me."

"But he did."

"He . . . lied to my mother."

"He cheated on her?"

"Yeah. He and Mom had come to Chicago, visiting. I didn't have Eleanor's place then. Amy and I shared this tiny studio apartment near the hospital where I'd interned so they stayed in a hotel. Mom and I were going shopping." Her mouth tipped sadly. "It's what we did together for fun. We'd gotten all the way to the store when Mom realized she forgot Dad's credit card, so I went back to the hotel to get it for her."

"He was with somebody else."

"A skinny-assed bimbo young enough to be his daughter," she confirmed bitterly. "I think I lost my childhood that day. I'd always been my daddy's girl. Now I have no idea who that man is. He denied he'd done anything wrong, said it was a mistake."

"Could he have been telling the truth?"

Tess tightened her jaw. "She was naked and all over him. I thought that was pretty conclusive. I didn't tell my mother at first, but when I finally did, she believed him. It was a family crisis. Dad was so furious that I'd told, yelling and screaming. He had a coronary. Literally." She swallowed. "I thought he was faking it so I didn't help. I walked away."

"He wasn't faking it."

"No. He'd had a heart attack. Not a bad one, but enough so that his life changed. As did mine. He wouldn't speak to me. His daughter, the doctor, left him to die."

"He's dramatic."

She nodded. "He can be. Anyway, Vito says it's really bad now. He's going to have to sell the business, all his tools. He's a cabinetmaker. One of the last great artisans in Philly. He'd made furniture for the finest families in the city. 'Blue bloods' he'd call them. He thought it was funny that they paid him thousands for a bookcase when they wouldn't look him in the eye on the street. When I was growing up, I hated them."

Understanding lit his eyes. "Because they were snobs."

"I'm not that hard to figure out, Detective."

"Harder than I thought," he said quietly. "But worth the trouble." He covered her mouth with his, tenderly. "I got rushed earlier. I missed a few places."

Reflexively she arched, making him smile. "I didn't mind."

"I think we can do better." He pressed his lips to her throat where the scar marked her flesh and reflexively she pulled away, making him frown. "Don't do that, Tess," he ordered, his tone soft, his words firm. "Don't hide from me."

Phillip had been repulsed. In fact more than half of the scarves she owned had come from him in that month between bringing her home and bringing home someone else. "It's ugly."

"You're beautiful." He kissed her throat, from one side to the other, making her sigh. "Some places," he slid down until his mouth was again at her breast, "more than others. Let me show you."

And he did. And it was better than before. He gave tribute to each part of her body, with his eyes, his hands, and his mouth. And Tess closed her eyes and let him do it all. Let him suckle her breast, first one, then the other until each pull from his lips tugged an answering pulse in her core. She let him kiss his way down her stomach and up her inner thighs and once again he showed her exactly how responsive she could be, dragging desperate pleas from her throat until she was hoarse. He slipped his hands under her bottom and tilted her so that he could stroke deep with his tongue and drive her crazy. He brought her to climax with his mouth, then before her heart had settled, with his clever fingers drove her up and over again, leaving her hollowed out and liquid.

And finally, where he'd plunged hard and fast before, this time he was slow, entering her with a reverence that made her eyes fill even as she moaned with the sheer pleasure of being filled again after so many months alone. He filled her, thick and hard and deeper than she'd ever had before. She blinked, sending tears sliding down her temples and into her hair.

He ceased moving, holding himself perfectly still. "Am I hurting you?" His voice rumbled in his chest, husky and strained.

"No, no. Don't stop." She bent her knees, flanking his hips with her thighs, drawing him even deeper, hearing the quick intake of his breath. "It's just that you feel so good."

He didn't stop. He kept going until she convulsed around him. Until the scream she heard was her own. His face set, feral in its intensity, he lunged a final time and held himself taut inside her as he came, arms shaking, teeth bared.

He collapsed on top of her, knocking the wind from her lungs. His breath beat the hair from her face. He was sweaty and heavy as a rock, but when he tried to move, she wrapped her arms around his back and held him. Felt his heart thundering against her breast. "Not yet. Stay."

He dragged in a rasping breath. "I'm too heavy for you."

In the hall Dolly growled and Aidan lifted his head. A minute later the doorbell rang, sending the dog into a barking frenzy.

"Reagan! Open up."

Tess's eyes widened. "It's Vito. What's he doing here?"

Aidan slid off her, flipping to his back like a landed trout. "Probably making sure I don't do what I just did. I don't have the energy to get up." But Vito started pounding on the door and Dolly's barking grew more frenetic.

"He's going to wake up the neighborhood," Tess hissed. She rolled out of bed and tested her legs, laughing when they felt like rubber. Quickly she pulled on a pair of jeans and Aidan's sweatshirt and went to answer the door.

Vito stood outside, looking all the world like a crazed man. He moved to step inside and Dolly growled, baring her teeth.

"Dolly, down," Aidan commanded softly. "She doesn't like men at night."

Vito ignored him, his hands on Tess's shoulders. "Did he hurt you?"

She blinked. "Who, Aidan?"

"No," he said frantically. "Wallace Clayborn. I tried to call your cell but you didn't answer. I was scared to death." He searched her face. "Your face is red." He rubbed her cheek with his thumb, then his eyes flew to Aidan's stubbled face, darkening. To his credit, Aidan didn't flinch.

She patted Vito's arm. "Come on in. I'll tell you all about Clayborn. You would have been proud of me."

Chapter Sixteen

Thursday, March 16, 6:15 A.M.

"T ess, your cat is in the sink."

Tess rolled over lazily and looked at him standing in front of the sink in the bathroom. Still naked and damp from his shower, Aidan Reagan made a fine picture first thing in the morning. "Turn on the water. She wants to drink from the faucet."

"I thought cats didn't like water."

"She does." She staggered into the bathroom and sat on the edge of the tub, smiling at him as he shooed the cat from the sink and lathered his face. Offended, Bella prissed across the tub and into her lap. "It's your own fault we don't have time for breakfast. Just one more time, you said. A quickie. Yeah."

He grinned. "I didn't hear you complaining a few minutes ago."

She grinned back and it felt so good to do so. "Nope." She

watched him another minute more, petting the purring Bella. And sobered. "What will you do today, Aidan?"

"Tie up all the loose ends on Bacon. See if CSU came up with anything else."

"Because you don't think he did it."

"No. But I've got other cases to close, too."

She remembered the autopsy report she'd seen on his desk. "The little boy."

"Yes. I still can't find his father. And I think his mother knows where he is."

"A father killing his own son." She blew out a breath. "I never get used to those."

"Me, either. So what will you do today?"

"I don't know. Bacon's dead, Clayborn's in jail . . . I'll probably go into the office and start cleaning up. And Harrison's viewing is tonight." Grief resurfaced, painful. "The funeral is Saturday."

"Tell me when it is and I'll go with you."

Warm gratitude softened the sharp edge of her grief. "Thank you. I've got to see Ethel Hughes today. Will you tell her about the note he left on Mr. Hughes's coat?" *Be judged by the company you keep.*

"We'll talk about that this morning. I'll let you know." He dried his face, then turned to face her grimly. "There's something I didn't tell you about yesterday. Come here."

Dread gripped her gut as she stood up, sending Bella to the floor. "Okay."

"Rick was sure Bacon would have kept a stash of videos, but we couldn't find any."

She swallowed. She'd known this, deep down. It had been easier not to think about it. "So the video he took of me is still out there."

"Somewhere. He may have moved them to another hiding place. We have a couple of places to start looking, but it's not a priority for homicide anymore. It'll move to the Electronic Crimes Division. They cover Internet porn and things like that."

She couldn't control the wince. "So, if it does get out . . . Will it matter to you?"

His eyes were solemn. "Some. I don't cheat and I don't share and I guess there's enough macho bullshit in me to care that other guys see what I see. What will you do?"

She attempted a grin. "Make a calendar and schedule a signing tour?"

He chuckled and kissed her lips. "Get dressed. If I don't get you to Vito by seven thirty I'll be late for the morning meeting because I'll be a mashed-up pulp."

Thursday, March 16, 7:30 A.M.

With his arm locked firmly around her waist, Aidan knocked on Vito's door and endured her brother's silent head-to-toe assessment in silence.

"Reagan. Tess."

Tess rolled her eyes and pecked Vito's cheek. "For God's sake, Vito. Stop it." Then she hooked her hand around Aidan's neck and pulled him down for a chaste good-bye kiss. "Now go or you'll be late."

"He can wait another few minutes."

Aidan flinched as Tess's nails dug into his neck. As one they turned to where a very large older man stood, his massive arms crossed over his barrel chest. He was built like a brick, his upper body evidence of years of heavy manual labor. His face was bent in a ferocious scowl, like a father might look at the man who'd been burning up the sheets with his daughter all night long.

"Mr. Ciccotelli." He held out his hand. "I'm Aidan Reagan."

Tess's father just looked at his outstretched hand and the moment grew awkward. With a tired sigh Tess took Aidan's hand in her own. "Dad. I didn't expect you."

He studied her with cool dark eyes and Aidan realized from where her ability had come. "I suppose you didn't," he finally said. "Can we talk, Tess? Privately?"

She looked up at Aidan from the corner of her eye, wary. "Go on. I'll call you."

Aidan stepped back and blew out his own sigh when the door shut in his face, then turned for the stairs. He didn't want to be late a second day in a row.

Thursday, March 16, 7:30 A.M.

Joanna frowned at the inside of her desk drawer. She'd been looking for photo paper to print some of the pictures she'd taken for her exposé on Dr. Jonathan Carter and found half her supply gone. "Keith, have you been printing pictures?"

He didn't look up from tying his tie. "No." Briefcase in hand, he started for the door.

His voice was like ice and she frowned at his back. "I said I was sorry, Keith."

He stopped, his hand on the doorknob. "I'm not sure you understand the meaning of the word, Jo. I'm not even sure who you are anymore. I'll see you tonight."

The door clicked as he closed it quietly. A slam would have been better, but that wasn't the kind of person Keith was. Then she shrugged. He'd come around. He always did. One of Ciccotelli's friends down. Now on to the next fly on the flypaper. She'd already done some digging. She was on to something big. She could feel it.

Thursday, March 16, 7:40 A.M.

Michael Ciccotelli was a forbidding man. From the adjoining room came her mother looking flustered and tired and . . . stuck in the middle.

Tess looked at them both warily. "When did you get in?"

"Last night," her mother answered.

Vito's midnight visit now made sense. Tess sat down. "I don't know what to say."

Her mother fluttered her hands. "You wouldn't come to us, so . . ."

"Gina, sit." Gently her father pushed her mother into a chair, then stood behind her, his big hands on her mother's slender shoulders. "What's going on here, Tess?"

He was pale, his lips colorless. His big hands trembled. "Sit down, Dad."

"I'll sit when I choose. I asked you what's going on. You can start with Reagan."

"He's a nice man. We're . . ." The words escaped her. He'd taken care of her, but that was not the self-supporting image she wished to project. "We're dating," she finally said.

Her father's brows lifted. "I see."

She lifted her own brows. "I'm sure you do," she said coldly.

"Tess," her mother chided and Tess lurched to her feet.

"Why are you here?"

"Don't be rude," Vito muttered.

"Oh, you shut up. I'm not going to let you all brand me a fallen woman. I'm thirty-three years old, for God's sake. And he's the first man I've . . . dated in a year."

"After Phillip." Her father grimaced. "Damn him to hell."

Tess had to bite back a laugh that seemed to come from nowhere. "Aidan calls him 'Dr. Damn-him-to-hell,'" she said and thought her father's lips twitched. A little corner of her heart crumbled and she softened her voice. "Dad, Vito says you're sick. Why did you come all this way?"

He swallowed. "You're in trouble. Your mother wanted to come. So we came."

Her mother looked over her shoulder with a sad shake of her head. "You promised."

He closed his eyes. "All right. I wanted to come. I needed to be sure you were all right. See you with my own eyes." He opened his eyes and she was stunned to see tears there. In all her life she'd never seen her father cry. Never. "You were hurt last year and we couldn't come because we didn't know. You wouldn't tell us. You're in trouble now and we have to hear it on the news. Do you know how that feels, Tess?"

Her mother patted her father's hand. "The news said you told your patients' secrets," she said. "They said you'd been unethical and your license was suspended."

"They're filthy liars," her father uttered, his voice shaking with restrained wrath. He lifted his chin. "You wouldn't do any of that."

Another corner of her heart cracked. "The licensing board did suspend me, Dad. How do you know they're not right?"

He pinned her with his dark eyes. "Because I know you. And I know above all else, you don't lie. I raised you better than that."

"Just like that?" Her own voice was bitter, sarcastic. "You believe me?"

"We've always believed in you, Tess," her mother said softly. "We love you."

Her father sighed. "And I know that things aren't always what they appear to be."

Tess closed her eyes, refusing to be swayed. "I know what I saw, Dad."

"And it looked bad. But Tess, I didn't do anything. That

woman pretended to be a maid and before I knew it she was in my room and . . ."

Tess steeled her spine, the picture all too plain. "I remember. I was there."

He pulled a chair from the little table. "I believe I'll sit now. You always were the difficult one, Tessa. Always asking questions I had no idea how to answer. I always knew you'd be a doctor or a lawyer . . . something big. Something important." He drew a labored breath. "I'm all right. I just get winded sometimes." He steadied himself, meeting her eyes. "But Tessa, you never asked me what happened. I kept expecting you to, but you never did. For years I waited." Her mother took his hand and held it.

"I *saw* what happened," Tess said from between clenched teeth, suddenly unsure of herself and hating her own weakness as much as she'd hated her mother's.

"You saw one piece of it," he insisted. "I kept wondering how, after all the years of your life you could believe that one very bad thing about me. How one moment undid your whole life." He looked away. "And I didn't know anything could hurt so bad."

She looked at her parents' joined hands. And envied their solidarity even as it infuriated her. "Neither did I. I kept expecting you to admit you were wrong like you always told us to do, but you never did." His mouth tightened, but he said nothing. "And you." She looked at her mother's devastated face. "You say you always believed in me, but you didn't. You slapped my face for telling a lie and crawled to him."

Her father turned only his head, staring at her mother in shock. "You struck her?"

"I was angry." She sighed. "I was wrong to strike you, Tess. I was angry and hurt and afraid, too. But I never crawled to your father or anyone. I asked him what happened. And I believed him." Her lips curved humorlessly. "You think I'm a sap."

"I didn't say that." But she'd thought it. She still did.

"Do you think I'm a sap for believing in you now?"

"No." Tess shook her head. "Because I know *I* didn't do anything wrong."

Her father's smile was mirthless. "Isn't it interesting how parallel our paths have become? Because neither did I. If I said I'd never looked at another woman, I'd be lying. But I swear that I have never touched anyone else. Not that day. Not ever."

His comparison struck a chord and Tess faltered, uncertain. "She was all over you, Dad," she whispered.

He met her eyes directly. "She was all over me. I never touched her, Tess."

His voice rang with conviction and truth. He was here . . . and he didn't have to be. He'd believed her, when few others did. Was it possible it was all a misunderstanding? She thought about that day, what she'd seen. The skinny bimbo had wrapped herself around him like a limpet. But had his hands been on her? Tess couldn't remember.

But she did know that never before that day had she caught him in a lie. Not once. He looked terrified, and she became aware that this moment could forever fix or seal the rift. "I should have asked you then. Dad, what happened that day?"

His breath shuddered out of him, his wide shoulders sagging in relief and she realized he hadn't expected blind acceptance, just trust. "She walked right in, Tess. Said she was a gift and I tried to make her leave. Before I knew it, she was stark naked and I had no idea where to put my hands to shove her out the door. She said not to play so hard to get. And five seconds later, you walked in. After you left, I told her that I'd call the cops if she didn't leave. She got huffy. Said she'd been warned I'd be a tough nut, but bail wasn't included in her fee. So she left." He shrugged. "That's all."

That's all. She fought to swallow the lump in her throat as he waited, the agony of expectation on his face and suddenly the truth of that horrible moment was eclipsed by the truth of this one. He'd believed her, this man who'd been her hero. Because he loved her. Could she do less? His face blurred as her eyes filled. "I'm sorry, Dad," she whispered. "Can you forgive me?"

"Come here." He drew her onto his knee and pressed her cheek to his shoulder. "Can we just go on, back to the way things were?"

She breathed in the smell of cedar that always permeated the clothing he wore. Her tears were absorbed by his work shirt and were no more. "That sounds like a plan."

He rested his cheek on the top of her head. "I've missed you, baby."

"I've missed you, too, Daddy. It's been a hard year. A harder week."

"So tell me about it, baby."

Her mother squeezed his shoulder. "First, you lie down. You promised."

"In a minute, Gina," he said sharply, glaring up at her mother.

Shaking her head, her mother disappeared through the door to the adjoining room and returned with an oxygen mask and a portable pump. Tess's eyes widened. "You're on oxygen? And you got on an airplane? Are you insane?"

"I needed to see you," he said, rolling his eyes when her mother fitted the mask to his face. "Now talk to me Tessa." He scowled. "And start with Reagan."

"He saved my life, Dad," she said and watched his face pale beneath the mask. "Breathe." She pressed a kiss to his forehead. "And next time, shake his hand, okay?"

He struggled with a breath. "Okay."

Thursday, March 16, 8:00 A.M.

"So it's closed." Spinnelli looked around the table. "We're done."

Murphy and Aidan sat on one side of the table, SA Patrick Hurst and Spinnelli on the other. Rick and Jack rounded out the other two ends. Nobody looked pleased.

Spinnelli frowned. "Bacon's dead, we have all the pictures, his confession. Clayborn gets arraigned this morning. Tess's life can go back to normal."

"Except that the whole city thinks she's a loose-lipped weasel," Murphy muttered. "I don't know, Marc. It just doesn't feel right."

"Perhaps because you didn't arrest Bacon," Patrick said. "He took away your resolution."

"That's part of it," Aidan conceded, recalling his own helpless fury at seeing Bacon floating dead in the tub. "But it doesn't feel right. I read Bacon's psych evaluation. Tess didn't do the whole evaluation, by the way. She saw him once. The main eval was done by Eleanor Brigham who died before finishing it."

Murphy looked troubled. "Doesn't seem like he could hate her so much based on only a single meeting."

"That's what I was thinking," Aidan said. "Bacon was a drifter with one specific vice—he liked to peep. He never really held a job. There is no ruthless determination, no setting of real goals other than to watch unsuspecting women naked."

"He doesn't fit the profile," Jack said thoughtfully.

"What profile?" Patrick asked.

"Tess's profile," Aidan told him. "Antisocial voyeur. Organized, goal-oriented, and accustomed to delegation. Bacon didn't fit."

"Maybe Tess's profile is wrong," Patrick offered. "She has been distracted."

Aidan shrugged. "It still doesn't explain the timing. Why kill himself now?"

"Maybe he saw the patrol car outside Lynne Pope's office building," Spinnelli said. "He knew we were closing in and panicked."

"This person is cold and calculating, Marc," Aidan argued. "He tortured Adams for more than three weeks. He doesn't seem like the panicking type."

"You say 'doesn't,'" Patrick observed. "You really don't think Bacon is the one."

"I don't." Aidan looked at the evidence, frustrated. "But it's only a feeling."

Spinnelli's face was stern. "Aidan, the fact remains that we have a signed confession. We have all this evidence that points to Bacon. We even have pictures of Hughes dead in that alley on the memory card you found with all the pictures. Unless you have something more than a feeling, we're going to close this case and move on."

"Well, I'm still bothered that we didn't find his stash," Rick remarked.

"Or the camera that took the pictures of Hughes," Jack added. Everybody turned to look at him. "The memory card holding all the pictures of Hughes doesn't fit the digital camera we found in Bacon's apartment. A different camera took those pictures."

"Shit," Spinnelli muttered, now looking very displeased.

"And there's the guy in the picture with Connell," Murphy said. "He's the one who planted the camera in Seward's place. They're damned big loose ends, Marc."

Spinnelli looked at Patrick. "You have all you need to make the appeals go away?"

"The tapes of Tess you found in the Rivera girl's apartment were enough for that. Finding the tan coat and wig yesterday was a bonus."

"All right then," Spinnelli said, holding up his forefinger. "One more day. Go get something concrete. Aidan, stay here." Everybody else walked out, leaving Aidan and Spinnelli alone. "Aidan, I want to be sure this feeling of yours is coming from your gut and not someplace else. I need you thinking with the right head."

Aidan snapped up straight, offended. "That's uncalled for, Marc."

"No, that's my job. You're involved with Tess. She's staying at your house. She's not a suspect, so that's your business. And hers. But I won't have all my resources spent chasing shadows because you're too involved to let this die."

Aidan held back his temper. "The others see the open ends, too."

"Which is why I agreed to give this one more day. You have other cases on your plate, Aidan. Make sure you remember that."

Aidan's nod was curt. "Yes, sir."

Thursday, March 16, 8:15 A.M.

Tess closed the adjoining door to her father's hotel room. "He's asleep now."

He was, but not the robust snoring sleep she remembered from her youth. His sleep was frail, his massive chest taking shallow breaths. During her internship she'd done a round in cardiology. She remembered the gray skin, the struggle to breathe. The hopelessness of the patients as their hearts gave out and left them waiting to die.

Her father would be one of those patients, very soon. Sorrow surged like a mighty wave, bringing with it a hopelessness of her own. "I had no idea it was this bad," she whispered, then turned to where her mother and Vito sat by the window, sipping coffee. Her mother's face was calm, but the torment in her eyes told the bitter truth.

"He wouldn't let me tell you. God knows you come by your stubbornness honestly."

Tess sat on Vito's bed, drained. "He says he's on the list for a transplant."

"He is." Gina shrugged. "But at his age . . ." She looked away, blinking hard.

Vito squeezed her hand. "Mom, don't. Please don't cry."

Gina aimed a look a Tess. "When he saw you on the news . . . It caused him pain."

"I'm sorry."

Gina shook her head. "It's done. He's been doing a lot of brooding lately, thinking about the two of you. Sometimes, when he thinks no one is around, he cries."

Tess's eyes filled, her throat burned. "Stop," she whispered hoarsely.

"I'm sorry." Quietly her mother sipped her coffee. "I don't mean to make you feel worse. I just want you to know how things are. The doctors say he could live a year or six months. His doctor would be very angry to know that he's here right now."

"He shouldn't have come," Tess whispered.

"Nothing on earth could have kept him from getting on that plane, Tess. He needed to fix things. He'd allowed it to go on long enough." With a deep breath, her mother put her cup aside and stood up. "What he told you today was the absolute truth."

Tess nodded. "I know. But you believed him right away and I didn't."

Gina's laugh was harsh. "No, I didn't."

Tess frowned up at her mother. "I don't understand. You . . ."

"I know what I said. And I know what I did. I've had to live with it for the last five years. I knew something terrible had happened that day. You came back to the store to get me and your face was whiter than a bleached sheet. But you didn't tell me then."

"I didn't know what to do. I didn't want to hurt you."

"I know. What you don't know is that I knew about the woman before I finally pried it out of you a month later."

"I don't understand," she said again.

Her mother walked to the window. "Did you know that high-priced hookers carry business cards? Later I found her card in the pocket of your father's pants. I told myself it was nothing, that she was probably just a new client and that you'd been feeling sick like you'd claimed. When I finally got you to tell me what you'd seen . . . I don't know what came over me. I did a terrible thing and I've regretted it since that day.

"I struck you and called you a liar, then confronted your father with the lies you'd told. He confirmed them, though. He told me some cock-and-bull story about a woman who showed up in our hotel room and took off all her clothes. That he'd never touched her. And like a good wife, I told him I believed him."

"But you didn't," Tess murmured.

Gina threw a look over her shoulder. "What self-respecting woman would?"

"Mom?" Vito's face was shocked.

She sighed. "I know. After I'd confronted your father, Tess, he confronted you."

"I remember." Her mother had asked her to come home, said they needed to talk. That request now made sense. "He had his first heart attack that day."

Her face tightened. "I took care of him, hating him every minute. Hating myself for hating him and for what I'd done to you. Finally when he was well enough, I told him I was going to my sister's house for a break. I came here instead."

Tess's eyes widened. "Here, to Chicago? You never told me."

"I didn't want anyone to know. I still had the business card and I found the woman." Gina turned from the window. "She remembered your father and confirmed every word he said. After he threw her out of our hotel room that day she called her agency. They called the original client who apologized and said her gift was for a man in the same room one floor up. I went to the agency and they showed me the receipt from the client."

Tess let out a breath, relieved and at the same time struck by a horrible sadness. "It was a mistake. I lost five years because of a mistake." She narrowed her stinging eyes at her mother. "For God's sake, why didn't you *tell* me?"

For a minute Gina said nothing. Then very quietly, "Because then I'd have to admit that I hadn't believed him, either. And every time I looked in his eyes, I knew I could never do that. It meant too much for him to believe I had."

"So why tell her now?" Vito asked unsteadily.

"Because she'd beat herself up because she should have believed him, like I did," she answered as if Tess weren't sitting right there. "That she'd been wrong and sent your father to his grave with her stubbornness." She smiled at Tess sadly. "Right?"

Tess nodded, the lump still clogging her throat. "Yes."

"You were always your father's girl, Tess, more than mine. These last five years, being at odds with you . . . it's nearly killed him and that's no exaggeration. But just because you're Michael's doesn't mean I understand or love you any less. When he made his peace with you, I knew I needed to, too. My apology is harder to make, because unlike your father who did nothing wrong, I was very wrong. I'm sorry, Tess."

There was a long period of quiet in which Vito hung his head and Gina and Tess just looked at each other.

"You know, Mom, I'm not sure if I should feel gratitude to you for trying to make me feel better or fury for keeping this secret for so long," Tess murmured and Vito lifted his head, giving her a silent, weary look of sorrow.

"I suppose both are in order," her mother said evenly.

"Truth of the matter is, before today, I might not have believed you anyway. After today, I didn't need you to believe it. So somewhere, it all evens out."

Her eyes were drawn to her father's door. "I feel like I should stay here . . . watch him breathe . . . Something."

"He wouldn't want you to do that. He'll be awake when you come back."

Tess looked at Vito. "I have an office to clean and a license to fight for. Bacon is dead and Clayborn is in custody, so you don't have to stay if you don't want to. You've been away from your job for too long already, Vito."

Vito shook his head. "Reagan didn't believe Bacon is responsible for the killings. He didn't say so, but I could tell."

Tess's chest grew heavy. "No, he didn't believe it. There's something you should know. The man they found dead yesterday put cameras in my office and apartment."

Gina nodded. "Which was how they knew about your patients. You told us that."

Tess raised her eyes to the ceiling. "What I didn't tell you is that he put a camera in my bathroom. In . . . in my shower."

Gina's coffee cup clattered to the table. "Oh my God." It was barely a whisper.

"Yeah. Well. Yesterday he threatened to sell . . . video of me to the media."

"Then I'm glad he's dead," her mother said viciously.

"But the police never found his files. The original video files."

Vito frowned. "Reagan said Bacon destroyed his own hard drive."

"He did. But they expected to find a collection, and didn't. These pictures of me might get out. We need to prepare Dad in case they do. It won't be good for his heart."

"Hold off, Tess," Vito advised. "They might find them."

Tess stood up. "All right, I will. Now I'm going to clean my office and go buy the groceries to make tonight's dinner. Will you help me cook it, Mom?"

Gina nodded graciously, aware of the extended olive branch and accepting it. "I don't think you need my help, Tess, but I will just the same."

Thursday, March 16, 8:45 A.M.

"You guys sure know how to show a girl a good time," Julia VanderBeck remarked when Aidan and Murphy walked into the morgue. "Never a dull moment."

"Did Bacon's autopsy tell you anything?" Aidan asked, impatient.

Julia smiled wryly. "Mr. Bacon told me a great many things. If you hadn't come down I would have called you. Come, take a look."

She flipped the sheet from Bacon's body and Aidan felt another jolt of rage at the man himself, and at the fact that he'd escaped justice in death. But he pushed it back and made himself listen to Murphy's placid voice.

"Cause of death?"

"Let's just say your Bacon could be nicknamed 'Rasputin.'" She manipulated Bacon's arms, positioning them so that the long red lacerations up his inner arm were visible. "He was cut, probably by the boxcutter you found on the corner of the tub."

Aidan tilted his head. "Was cut?"

She nodded. "Was cut. He didn't do this to himself, even though you're supposed to think he did. Look at his arms. The cuts are straight up and down. Now, normally this means the victim really wants a successful suicide, if there is such a thing."

"But?" Murphy asked and Julia smiled.

"Your boy is left-handed." She lifted his left hand. "Calluses on his middle finger from writing. So I'd expect to see the slice on his right arm to be deeper and straighter. He'd use his dominant hand first, left hand to right arm, to get the biggest impact. Normally the slice on the other arm isn't so straight, isn't fully connected because he's in pain and his right hand will already be feeling numb and it's not his dominant hand anyway. It'll start and stop. And it isn't as deep."

"But Bacon's don't follow pattern," Aidan said.

"Nope. The slices are exactly the same depth, and I've never seen that before. I wondered how could somebody slice a full-grown man that neatly without him fighting back, but I didn't see any defensive wounds."

"He was unconscious when he was cut," Murphy mused.

"I don't think so. Do you remember the tox report on Cynthia Adams?"

"Magic mushrooms," Aidan answered. "Psylo . . ."

"Psylocybins," Julia supplied. "Bacon's blood doesn't have any, but I did find something from a different plant. Ingested, it causes paralysis, localized to certain joints. Inhaling speeds and spreads the effect. I think he was conscious the whole time he was being sliced up—and I think he felt everything."

"Good," Aidan said grimly and Julia half smiled.

"I agree with you on that one, Aidan. At some point he lost enough blood that he lost consciousness and he slid down into the water. Based on the amount of water in the tub and Bacon's size and weight, I wouldn't have expected him to sink so that his head was submerged. But his lungs were filled with water and blood."

"Somebody held him down," Aidan said slowly.

"I'd say so. But his injuries don't stop there. Look." She adjusted Bacon's right arm to show his shoulder. "At some point during the day he was grazed by a bullet."

"Shot, cut, poisoned, and drowned." Murphy shook his head. "You're right. Rasputin he is. So which one killed him?"

"Officially? The drowning most likely. But boys, this guy did not kill himself."

Chapter Seventeen

~~~

Thursday, March 16, 9:35 A.M.

Jack met Aidan and Murphy at Bacon's apartment. "Rick says we need to keep looking for his video stash, that he's got to have one here somewhere."

"We will. But first let's figure out what the hell happened here." Aidan walked back to the bathroom and stood in the doorway. "Shot, cut, poisoned, and drowned. How?"

"We know the drowning was last," Murphy said. "The poisoning was before the cutting or the knife strokes wouldn't have been so neat. That leaves the shooting."

Aidan considered the scenario. "I think the shooting happened first."

"Why?" Murphy asked.

"Remember when we found his clothes yesterday?"

"Right here." Murphy pointed to his feet. "Shirt, tie, pants, boxers, and socks. His suit coat was in the living room."

"His coat smelled like mothballs and cigarette smoke."

"Like his mother's house."

"But not cat piss. I hadn't thought of that. I can't imagine a suit being stored in that house without picking up some of the cat odor. His Wires-N-Widgets shirts sure did."

"We found boxes of clothes in the living room yesterday," Jack said. "Heavy mothball odor. Didn't smell anything like cat pee."

"He's got a storage unit," Murphy said, nodding. "But why the shooting first?"

"Because his suit also smelled like sweat, but his shirt smelled like a combination of cigarette smoke and fabric softener."

Murphy's brows went up. "It was a clean shirt."

"Man's got a nose," Jack chuckled. "I, on the other hand, have an eye. Look there."

Aidan followed the line of Jack's pointing finger, over to the far bathroom wall. "A hole." They hadn't seen it the day before, sidetracked with the planted evidence.

Jack pushed past them and inspected the small hole. "Could have been a bullet. If it was, somebody's dug it out. Nothing there now but crumbled drywall." He turned back and looked at Murphy. "Step into the hall." Murphy did and Jack stood in the doorway, his back to the door hinges. "I'm Bacon and you've got the gun," he said to Murphy and traced an imaginary trajectory in the air. "Based on the height of that hole in the wall and Bacon's height and where it hit him on the shoulder, you were standing close to where you are now. And you're shorter than Bacon. By about two to four inches. Bacon was five ten. You're five six, five eight, tops."

Aidan smiled grimly. "So we have an antisocial voyeur with a Napoleon complex. Okay, you come up behind Bacon. You shoot him in the arm? Why?"

"To force him into the tub or to force him to inhale the poison?" Murphy said.

"Or both." Aidan. "You're shot in the right shoulder, Jack. What do you do?"

Jack clapped his left hand over his right shoulder. "Ouch," he deadpanned.

Aidan chuckled. "And now you have a bloody left hand."

Jack nodded. "I'll get the Luminol."

Thirty minutes later, Jack turned off the lights, revealing the glow of shoe prints on the floor and a fully formed handprint on the wall between the toilet and the sink.

Aidan hovered his shoe above the footprint on the floor. "I'm a thirteen. This is a size nine, maybe?"

"About," Jack said. "They look like dress shoes. So our guy is about five eight with a size nine foot. It's a start. I'm curious about the handprint." The bathroom had a wallpaper border with blue flowers. Above the border was painted drywall, below, solid blue wallpaper. The handprint was on the lower half. "If I'm Bacon and I'm staggering, my bloody hand's going to hit higher, above the border. So let's see why it doesn't."

Jack ran a metal file under the flowered border and gently tugged at the solid wallpaper until it came loose as a sheet. "It's not glued down," Murphy said.

Jack looked over his shoulder. "The corners are worn. Somebody's done this a lot."

Aidan's pulse kicked up a notch. "His stash of videos." Tess would be saved all kinds of embarrassment. "Hurry, Jack."

"You want it done fast or you want it done right?"

"I want it done both," Aidan retorted.

"He sounds like Spinnelli," Jack threw back and Murphy laughed.

"He does at that. Hurry, Jack."

Jack stuck his finger through a hole in the wall. "Turn on the light, Aidan." Jack pulled away a drywall panel, two by three feet, exposing wooden joists.

"Well?" Aidan asked when Jack shone his flashlight around.

Jack turned around, shaking his head. "It's empty."

Aidan dropped his chin, disappointment palpable. "I don't want to have to tell her this." Once again he wished he could bring Bacon to life so he could kill him himself.

Jack sighed. "She's a big girl. She can handle more than you give her credit for."

Aidan straightened his shoulders, remembering the truth of that statement. Tess was a strong woman. He only hoped he was as strong. "You're right." His mouth tipped up sadly. "She said if the videos got out she'd make a calendar and do a tour."

Jack ran his tongue around his teeth. "I ain't touchin' that with a ten-foot pole, Reagan. I value my marriage and," he looked pointedly at Aidan's fists, "my face."

Murphy coughed. "Let's finish this. Kid Sherlock," he added dryly.

"Okay. I'm Bacon." Aidan focused. "I come home from peddling to Lynne Pope—and I'm waiting for Tess to pay me a hundred grand. I'm surprised by a visitor." He looked at Murphy, understanding dawning. "The killer came for Bacon's video stash."

"And he came prepared. Left all that tidy evidence stuck up in the ceiling where we'd be sure to look for cameras. What're in those videos that our boy's afraid of?"

"We need to find out. So you say, 'Take me to your videos' and I say 'Go to hell.' "

"I shoot at you to make you show me. Graze your arm. 'Show me,' I say."

Jack tapped the wall. "Your hands are bloody when you do."

Murphy pointed to the tub. "'Now get in the tub,' I say because I still have my gun."

"I do, and you make me inhale the poison."

"We found cigarette stubs in the tub." Jack said. "I'll get them analyzed ASAP."

Aidan nodded. "I can't move, so you cut me, turn on the water, watch me bleed."

"But it takes too long or I'm just a cruel bastard," Murphy finished. "So I hold your head under until you're dead and leave your body for the stupid cops to find."

Aidan stared at the tub. "Then you clean the wall, replace the shirt and plant the evidence to throw the stupid cops off the trail. Leaving you free to plan your next murder." He turned to Murphy grimly. "The company you keep."

Thursday, March 16, 11:00 A.M.

"Wow." Murphy whistled as he walked through the door of Tess's office. "Clayborn sure did a number on this place."

"I know," Aidan said grimly. "Last night he nearly did a number on Tess."

Murphy's lips twitched. "I would like to have seen him when she was done with him."

Denise, the receptionist, came out of Harrison's office carrying a box of trash. She did a double-take when she saw them, her eyes flickering. "Can I help you?"

"We're here to see Tess," Aidan said, studying her. Denise had been surprised to see them. Surprised and a little afraid. And Aidan wondered why.

"She's been in her office all morning." With her head she motioned to the door that stood slightly ajar. "Go on in."

Aidan pushed at the door, revealing Tess standing in the middle of the room, a clipboard in her hand and her hair held up in a ponytail that made her look young and sexy at the same time. She turned, momentary alarm giving way to pleasure.

"Aidan! And Murphy, too," she added when Murphy pretended to pout.

"You've made some progress," Aidan noticed.

"We cleared out the broken furniture at least." She held out her arm from which a little camera dangled. "I'm taking notes for my insurance claim."

"Are you here alone?" Aidan asked, frowning.

"Denise is in Harrison's office. Vito's downstairs with the guys who hauled away the big stuff. Jon came by." She smiled. "Robin sent soup."

Aidan smiled back. "No soup for you."

She laughed softly, her cheeks going a little pinker and he knew she was remembering the night before, when he'd said the same thing while lying on top of her, her thighs hugging his hips, her breasts brushing his face every time he turned his head. He shifted his weight, trying to adjust the sudden pressure against his fly.

She cleared her throat. "Amy brought a plant. She has a green thumb, but I'll probably kill the damn thing." She bit her lip. "So what's happened?"

"Bacon didn't kill himself, Tess," Aidan answered. "He was murdered."

Her breath eased out slowly. "I see. Then . . . we're not done, are we?"

"No. I want you to be careful. On your guard. Never alone, you understand?"

"I thought it was too good to be true. So did you. I'll tell Amy and Jon and Robin to be back on alert."

Aidan wanted to kiss the scared frown from her mouth. "And you'll tell Vito."

"Tell me what?" Vito asked, coming up behind them.

"That the saga continues. Camera-boy was murdered. My friends are still at risk."

Vito scowled. "Terrific. So what the hell are you guys doing about this?"

"Investigating," Aidan said calmly. "When are you leaving?"

Vito's grin was really just a baring of teeth. "Not soon enough for you, Ace."

Tess rolled her eyes. "Vito. Aidan, my parents want to meet you tonight. Can I use your kitchen? I'm cooking."

He wanted to touch her so bad he could taste it, but Vito's glare kept his hands in his pockets. "You still have the key?"

"Yeah. Will Dolly eat me?"

"Probably not. If she growls at you, go get Rachel. She gets home from school at three. I'll meet you back at my house at seven, okay?"

"Make it eight." Her eyes shadowed. "Harrison's viewing is at seven."

"I'll go with you. Now we need to go." He threw a look at Vito. "Investigate."

Walking toward the elevator, Murphy gave him an amused side glance. "Parents?"

"Just donate my life insurance to a worthy charity, okay, Murphy?"

Murphy laughed. "Okay, Ace."

Thursday, March 16, 11:00 A.M.

Andrew Poston was the son of a local circuit court judge and was therefore already out on secured bond while the other boys who'd raped Marie Koutrell, the ones from poorer families, still languished in the county jail. He'd given a very curt "not guilty" to the judge at his arraignment and was heard muttering that if he caught the person who'd turned him in, he'd rip them apart with his bare hands.

Poston had very big hands, so his threat certainly was not an idle one. His lawyer had advised him to keep his mouth shut and Poston responded with a few creative places his lawyer might shove his advice. All in all, the kid had a certain style. He might be a formidable force in a few years, as long as he could keep his ass out of jail. Which might be a difficult proposition. The victim had named him specifically. That alone wouldn't be so bad—there were a half dozen guys who'd swear it was consensual. But another witness had independently, anonymously corroborated that identification, saying he was in the victim's house, drunk, wild, and making unwanted sexual advances toward the victim.

That anonymous witness had to go or Andrew Poston could very realistically find himself with a felony record. One little night of fun with a slut who'd asked for it could ruin a young man's life. So the witness had to go.

Of course that the witness was also the fastest way to Aidan Reagan was pure luck. Kismet. Really good karma. Because Aidan Reagan had to go. He was too close to Ciccotelli. For the first time since her fiancé left her, she was . . . having sex.

It had to stop. Reagan had to go. Killing a cop was dangerous and would not go unnoticed or unpunished. Scaring him away was a more palatable solution.

He was home now, Andrew and his father, the judge. Pulling into the driveway in a Lexus SUV. Mrs. Poston met them at the door, a worried expression on her face and a padded envelope in her hand.

It had been delivered that very morning, addressed to Andrew. Of course if his mother had opened it, the impact would have been spoiled. She would have reported the contents. Or maybe not. At any rate Andrew had the envelope in his hands and based on the feed coming from the microphone inside the envelope's padding, he was opening it, finding the CD with the Post-it note attached. "Play me," it said. There was a long pause. The recording was poor, unclear, but it would tell him everything he wanted to know. A violent, rather creative curse exploded from Andrews's lips. He'd found it. Excellent. There was more scuffling, then the boy spoke.

"Hey. It's me," he said, his voice muffled. "I know who turned me in . . . Rachel Reagan. Little bitch, spying on us." He listened, then laughed. "You're right there. She would have been a hell of lot better than Marie. Do me a favor, okay? Show her my appreciation for her phone call to the cops. Make sure she knows that we know it was her and if she doesn't back down, she'll be sorry. And do it today. Thanks, buddy. I'd do it myself, but I've got to keep low key for a few days till all this blows over."

A blast of painfully loud hard rock music followed, signaling the end of his conversation. The cacophony ceased with the flick of a switch inside the car. The wheels were in motion, figurative and literal. A touch to the gas pedal sent the car rolling down the Postons' street toward the main road. It was time to get back to work. And time to tune into the local news to see if Marge Hooper had been discovered yet.

Ciccotelli would truly be distraught by the news. *Excellent*. She'd lost a friend in Hughes, an acquaintance in Hooper. Soon she'd lose Reagan, her lover.

There would be no way he'd stay with her when he learned his sister's safety was at risk. Once young Rachel was properly warned by Poston's friends, Detective Reagan would get a message threatening far worse harm to his sister because of the company he kept. Being a smart man, he'd choose the right path.

The next strike would be far more remote. A perfect stranger who just happened to be unlucky enough to come into casual contact with Tess Ciccotelli. It would drive her crazy. She'd feel so guilty. She'd be afraid to leave her apartment. Afraid to say "boo" to another living soul. A delightful thought.

Of course the coup de grâce would be closer to home. Family. The choices had become wider with the arrival of her brother and parents from Philly. It was an unexpected development. One of those dual-edged swords. On one hand, her family issues had been resolved, so she was no longer alone in a big city. This was bad. On the other hand, it made for delicious irony. Just when her family is reunited, they bite the dust. So which one? Her brother or her parents? Which would hurt her the most?

But first . . . One stranger coming up.

Thursday, March 16, 12:15 P.M.

"This isn't right," Tess murmured, standing outside Dr. Fenwick's licensing board office, Vito at her side. "They know I haven't done anything wrong, but they insist on this suspension. It makes me look even guiltier."

"We should have brought Amy," Vito said. "She could have cut through all this shit."

"You're right. I just didn't think they'd be so unfair." Next time Tess wouldn't attempt to talk to Fenwick without a lawyer. It seemed that was the only thing the man understood. "Let's go. Dad should be awake and ready for lunch." She passed the elevator on her way to the stairs.

"Dr. Ciccotelli?"

She stiffened at the voice behind her, her hand on the doorknob.

"Reporters," Vito growled softly. "Go, now."

"Wait." It was a young woman, professionally dressed. "Are you Dr. Ciccotelli?"

"I am," Tess replied. "Who are you?"

The woman held a thick sheaf of papers, her face blank. "You're served, ma'am."

Stunned, Tess accepted the papers, then skimmed the top page. "I'm being sued."

Vito grabbed the paper. "By who?" Quickly he read the page. "Your patients are suing because you turned the records over to the police." He looked up, frowning. "You were subpoenaed. You didn't have a choice."

She took the papers back and laughed hollowly. "Pain and suffering. Five million dollars. This won't stand, but it will still cost me to make it go away."

"How did they know you gave up the records?"

Tess shook her head. "I don't know. It wasn't on the news. Hell. What next?"

And if on cue, her cell phone rang, a local number she didn't recognize. Tempted not to answer, she wondered if it could be her mother calling from the hotel and answered anyway. "Ciccotelli."

"Tess? It's Rachel." The girl sounded strange. Detached. "I . . . I need your help. It's an emergency."

Tess listened to her stammered request, then took the stairs at a run. "Hurry, Vito."

Thursday, March 16, 1:30 P.M.

Aidan looked up when the brown bag dropped on his desk. Spinnelli stood looking down, his expression wry. "Congratulations."

Aidan opened the bag, sniffed. "Baklava. I'm touched, Marc," he said dryly.

"I'm told it's your favorite bribe." His smile was brief, then he sobered. "Your feeling about Bacon was right. And you were also right that my comment earlier was uncalled for. You've shown considerable restraint and focus under the circumstances."

Aidan's cheeks warmed. Then he shrugged. "You were partly right anyway. Part of it is my personal interest in this case." He pointed to a stack of papers. "I haven't touched the Danny Morris case in two days. His father could be in Mexico by now."

"He's not. He's hiding somewhere. He'll come out soon enough."

"You sound sure about that."

Spinnelli sat on the corner of his desk. "I am. Danny's father didn't give a shit about him. He was a possession, a thing to be controlled. He won't believe anyone else will give a shit, either. But you do and when he comes out of his sewer, you'll be waiting. On your way home tonight, check his haunts. You keep showing up and his friends will get nervous. Somebody will talk."

"Thanks. That helps." He'd been feeling guilty for neglecting that precious child's case.

Spinnelli crossed his arms over his chest. "So what do you have, Aidan?"

"When we found Bacon's hidey-hole empty at his apartment, we called Rick. Rick said a lot of times these guys have backup copies. Murphy's at Bacon's storage unit now. We figured both of us didn't need to be there to search. I came back to start working the connection of David Bacon and Nicole Rivera to our guy."

"Good work," Spinnelli said. "Finding the storage unit."

"It wasn't rocket science. Once we got the warrant for his

mother's house, we found the receipts for the storage unit in her kitchen drawer." Aidan sniffed at his sleeve and winced. "I'm never going to get this suit clean."

Spinnelli chuckled. "I didn't want to say anything but you might want to go home and change before you pick up Tess tonight." His gaze sharpened. "So what connections have you made?"

Aidan looked at his stacks of paper in disgust. "None yet. Rivera was an actress and a waitress. Bacon was an ex-con selling widgets for a living. I've checked their phone records and bank statements and nothing crosses. The only thing they had in common was that they needed money, but Rivera had to leave her old apartment for one in a lousy part of town because she didn't have enough money to pay the rent. If she was getting cash from our boy on the side, she wasn't using it for her bills. I'm meeting Rivera's old roommate later. I'm hoping to get some information out of her."

"Keep me up to date."

When Spinnelli was gone, Abe came over, papers in his hand. "I'm finishing the paperwork on Clayborn." He grinned. "Tess did a number on him, Aidan. He looked like he'd gone a round with the champ."

Aidan shook his head. "I'm not sure I've ever been so scared in my life."

"That feeling I can understand. Look, Mia and I worked Clayborn for hours last night. He finally admitted why he didn't want his records shared." Abe rolled his eyes. "He'd applied to the police academy and didn't want his psychiatric history to jeopardize his chances."

Aidan cringed. "Surely the personality profile would have weeded him out."

"One can only hope. The other thing we tried to figure out was how he knew Tess was with you at Mom and Dad's house. Clayborn finally said he'd been called on the phone.

Somebody told him to look at your house. Even gave him the address. He wouldn't say who, but I pulled his cell and home LUDs. There's one number that's a disposable cell and I had a thought. Do you have any of Tess's LUDs?"

Aidan riffled though his stack of papers until he found her office LUDs. "She only got one call on her home phone—that first night with Cynthia Adams. The other two came on her office phones." He glared up at Abe. "She wouldn't let us tap her office line. Patient confidentiality."

"Your boy knows that," Abe said. "Exploits her ethics."

Aidan compared Clayborn's LUDs to Tess's, his pulse hiking up. "One match. This is the call she got about Seward. Nicole Rivera made that call." He looked up at Abe. "We never found any cell phones in Rivera's apartment."

"Her killer took them."

"Along with the coat and wig. This is the same disposable cell phone number. Sonofabitch. He told Clayborn where she was."

"We hadn't released Clayborn's name to the press, Aidan. It was on the scanner, though. We had an APB out."

Aidan gritted his teeth. "Then he knows she's with me. He dangled bloody meat in front of Clayborn. Son of a fuck-ing bitch. He always gets somebody else to do his dirty work." He dropped his eyes back to the LUDs of Tess's office phone. And frowned. "I didn't notice this before. I was so busy looking at calls in, I didn't look at calls out."

Abe stood behind him, leaning over his shoulder. "You mean that call to 911?"

"Yeah. Tess got the call about Seward at three fifteen. She said she ran out and told Denise to call 911."

"Denise is the receptionist?"

"Yeah." His frown deepening, Aidan found Tess's cell phone LUDs. "She called me at three twenty-two, seven minutes later."

Abe straightened. "But Denise didn't call 911 until ten minutes after Tess hung up."

Aidan looked up over his shoulder. "Tess said she didn't know why the cops took so long to get to Seward's. She hadn't planned to intervene, but Seward had a gun to his wife's head. She expected the cops to get there before she did."

"And they would have if Denise had called as soon as she was supposed to. Why didn't she call right away?"

Aidan considered the receptionist in his mind. She had access to all of Tess's files, to her patients. Not only their histories, but their addresses, phone numbers. She'd been there when the courier had delivered the CD, so she knew about Bacon's unauthorized films. She hadn't been able to meet his eyes earlier in the day when he and Murphy had dropped by to tell Tess about Bacon's murder.

Aidan spread the papers in the stack across his desk, scanning them. "Denise Masterson. I checked her already. She doesn't have a record." He quickly scanned the only information he had on Masterson. "She's worked for them for five years now. Before that she was in college. No major debts. She drives a ten-year-old car and shares an apartment with a roommate. That's all I know." He puffed out his cheeks. "I've got to leave here in an hour to meet with Nicole Rivera's old roommate. Afterward I'll swing by and talk to Denise's."

"You could ask Tess."

"Ask Tess what?"

Tess watched both men spin around, surprise on their faces. From behind, they looked nearly identical, broad backs in white shirts and black trousers. Identical dark heads, identical shoulder holsters. But Tess thought she'd be able to detect Aidan in a roomful of identical men. She'd run her hands over that back the night before. Now she'd have to give him some very bad news.

Aidan's eyes narrowed. "What's wrong?"

"Sit down. Both of you."

"Tess—"

She held up her hand. "Please." Aidan sat in the chair, Abe on the desk. Both wore identical wary expressions. "It's Rachel." Both jumped to their feet, color draining from their faces. With a silent sigh, she looked up at them. "She's not injured badly."

"Where is she?" Aidan's voice was lethal. "Tess, don't play games with us."

"Do I look like I'm playing a damn game?" she asked sharply. "Sit your asses down. This is why she didn't call you two to start with." Slowly they sat again. "She's waiting in the hall with Vito. She called Kristen and her other sister-in-law, but got voice mail. She didn't want you or your parents to see her the way she is, and I gave her my number last night when I was helping her with her homework. She wanted me to meet her at your house and help her clean up before you saw her."

Aidan swallowed hard, still pale. "You didn't, did you? We'll need . . . evidence."

"I took her to the ER, not," she said when they tensed, "because it was that bad. She needed a few stitches, that's all. I called a cop who took a report and took some pictures. Then I brought her straight here." She crouched next to Aidan's chair and took his hand. "Somebody beat her up, tore her clothes. It looks a whole lot worse than it is. They didn't assault her in any other way. Do you understand me?"

Stiffly he nodded. "Who?"

"Two boys from her school. Now she's been through hell this afternoon. Do not make it worse. Wipe that look off your face." She looked up at Abe. "You, too. You both look like you're going to kill. She's afraid you'll lose your cool and get in trouble and lose your jobs."

Abe drew a breath and forced his face to relax. "Go get her."

Realizing she was making it worse, Tess hurried back to where Rachel waited with Vito, Tess's new coat around her shoulders, the collar pulled up around her ears. "They're as prepared as they're gonna be, kid," she said. "Let's get this over with."

"They're going to be so mad," Rachel whispered, her lips trembling.

"Of course they are. They have a right to be mad, but they're good men. They won't do anything stupid." She took Rachel's arm and led her into the bullpen where both stood, waiting. One look at her face had their fists clenched.

Rachel tried to smile. "It's really not as bad as it looks." And thanks to a little ice and some basic first aid, she didn't look nearly as bad as she had.

Aidan forced a tight smile. "I don't know, squirt. You look pretty bad." He rolled his chair away from his desk. "Sit down." She did, gingerly. "Talk to us."

"I got caught up in a rush in one of the stairwells at school. Looking back, I think they planned it, because all of a sudden the bell rang and the crowd scattered. They grabbed me from behind and covered my eyes. I fought, but they were a lot bigger."

Both Aidan and Abe grew even paler and Rachel shuddered. "I thought they would do to me what they did to Marie, but they didn't. They stuffed a rag in my mouth and hit me. Ripped my shirt and smashed my face against a brick wall. Then told me to count to fifty before getting up. I didn't go to the office because they would have called Mom and Dad and I didn't want them to worry. So I slipped out the emergency exit and started walking."

Aidan wiped his palms on his pants legs. "Didn't the alarm go off?"

"It's rigged. Kids use it for skipping all the time."

"Did they say anything, Rachel?" Abe asked.

She shrugged. "That I should have kept my mouth shut. Called me names."

Abe gently lifted her chin. "Do you think you could identify them?"

"Yeah." Rachel nodded grimly. "I do, because later I saw them. When you catch them, I'll do the lineup."

"She gave the names to the cop who took the report," Tess said. "The boys are being picked up by squad cars as we speak."

Aidan's smile was unsteady. "That's my girl." He touched his finger to the edge of the bandage over her eyebrow. "How many stitches, kid?"

"Only three."

"Hell, you got more than that ice-skating last year. That was, what, nine?"

"Eleven." She blew out a relieved breath. "You're calmer than I thought you'd be."

Aidan's smile dimmed. "I'm a damned good actor, squirt."

"Why didn't you call us, honey?" Abe asked.

She looked at Abe, then back at Aidan. "Because it looked a whole lot worse. I didn't want to make Mom and Dad upset so I started walking to your house." She looked away. "I know it was stupid to walk by myself, but I wasn't thinking too clearly."

"It's okay," Aidan said. "Happens to the best of us. When did you see them?"

"I looked back and saw them following me and that's when I got really scared." Her smile was grim. "I think they thought I was going to talk and they freaked. They chased me but I ran fast. I got to your house and released the hound." The last was said in a cultured affectation that was meant to make them smile, but it fell flat in the gravity of the situation. "Dolly scared the shit out them," she finished. "It was very cool."

Aidan's smile was feral. "Did she get either of them?"

"No." Rachel's lips curved and a smile rose to her eyes. "But one of them had to go home and change his pants. Dolly was amazing. I tried calling Kristen and Ruth, but got their voice mail. Tess gave me her number for homework questions last night, so I called her. She's a doctor. I figured she'd know what to do."

"How did you get her stitched up without a parent?" Abe asked. "She's a minor."

Tess glanced down at Rachel. "I stitched her up myself. Before Tuesday I had privileges at County, so I have a badge and nobody asked any questions. And I did a rotation in the ER there during my internship, so I know where things are kept. The hospital isn't responsible. Only me." She gave Rachel a wink. "But if your folks decide to sue me, they'll have to stand in line."

Aidan frowned. "What's that supposed to mean?"

"Three of my patients are suing me personally for pain and suffering for having their records released to you." Her lips quirked humorlessly. "If I had money before, Aidan, I got none now." She brushed her hand over Rachel's head. "Show them the rest, sweetie. They're going to see it sooner or later."

With a sigh, Rachel folded down her collar. Her thick black hair, which had hung halfway down her back was now a jagged mess, barely reaching her nape. "It actually feels kind of good," she said lightly. "I must have lost five pounds of hair."

Stricken, Aidan touched the tip of her shorn hair. "Oh, honey, I'm sorry."

"Stop it," Rachel said brusquely, taking Aidan's hands in

hers. "It's hair, Aidan. Just hair. Besides, I already have an appointment to fix it."

Tess nodded. "One of Robin's waiters moonlights as a hairdresser. He'll make you mahvelous, dahling. A good cut, some highlights . . ."

Rachel patted Aidan's hands. "I'll come out of this better than I went in."

"Sounds like you took care of things pretty well, Tess," Abe commented. "Just one more thing. Which cop did you call to take her statement?" Tess looked across the bullpen to the empty desk next to Abe's with a lifted brow and Abe sighed. "I should have known something was up when she took a long lunch. Where is Mia now?"

"She got another call just as we were leaving the ER. That wasn't more than twenty minutes ago. I asked her not to call you until I had a chance to talk to you. She said for you to call her when you're ready."

"Then I guess I've got someplace to be." Abe brushed his thumb against Rachel's bruised face. "Next time, call us. We're big boys, kid. We know how not to erupt."

"Okay." Now that it was over, Rachel's blue eyes filled. "I'm sorry." Abe crouched in front of her chair and pulled her into his arms, smoothing his hands up and down her back. "Oh, Abe, I was so scared."

"I know. But you were so brave. Don't be quite so brave again though, okay?"

With a shudder she nodded and Abe gave her back a final pat before standing up and pulling Tess to his chest. He kissed the top of her head. "Thank you," he said and let her go with an unsteady grin. "When things settle down, I want you to teach her whatever you did to Clayborn last night. Very, very cool, Tess."

"I will. Now go. Mia's waiting for you."

Aidan sat on the edge of his desk and folded his arms over

his chest. "So what am I going to do with you, squirt? I've got some calls to make."

"We can take her home," Tess said. "Vito and me."

Aidan saw Vito standing over against the wall, as if for the first time realizing he was there. "Thank you. I—" His phone rang and Tess admired the long lean lines of his body as he reached to answer it. "Reagan . . . Yes." His eyes darted to hers and his face went even paler than before. "Get Spinnelli," he mouthed. Tess ran but by the time she returned with Spinnelli, Aidan had hung up the phone and was quickly dialing again, demanding the call be traced.

Spinnelli's eyes were glued to Rachel. "My God. What happened?"

Tess was watching Aidan's face, dread rising to choke her. He was visibly shaken but he said nothing, wouldn't meet her eyes. "Aidan? Who was that? What did they say?" She tugged on his arm. "Aidan? Look at me, dammit."

Slowly he did, holding her gaze as seconds ticked and the muscle in his taut jaw twitched. Then his eyes flicked to Rachel and stayed there.

And Tess knew. Covering her mouth, she lurched back. "No." She thought about the way she'd found Rachel, bruised and bleeding and scared. It was bad enough when she thought it had been retribution for Rachel's anonymous tip. She swallowed back the bile that burned her throat. "Be judged by the company you keep?" she whispered.

Aidan nodded.

"Holy hell," Spinnelli muttered. He pulled Murphy's chair around their desks. "Sit down, Tess, before you faint. And who are you?"

"Vito Ciccotelli." Behind her Vito's voice was rough, his hands tight on her shoulders as he pushed her into the chair. "Philadelphia PD. I'm her brother."

Spinnelli pinched his lips together hard. "I'll call your dad to pick you up, Rachel."

"No." Rachel shook her head. "'Be judged by the company you keep'? What does that mean?"

"It means that you were hurt because you know me," Tess said woodenly. "You're not the first."

She shook her head again. "Those boys were friends of those asshole jocks that raped Marie. That had nothing to do with you."

Tess turned her head to look into the girl's blue eyes. "And how do you think they found out it was you, Rachel?"

Rachel opened her mouth, closed it again as Tess's meaning sank in. "All those people . . . They died just because they *knew* you?" she asked, wide-eyed. Horrified. "Your doctor friend, too?"

Tess nodded, her mind spinning, her body numb. "And my doorman friend."

Spinnelli hesitated. "Tess."

Her eyes flew up to meet his. He shook his head sadly and Tess felt her heart stumble and stop. Her lips didn't want to form the word. "Who?"

"Do you know a Marge Hooper?"

She blinked slowly, unable, unwilling to comprehend. "She owns the wineshop."

"I'm so sorry, Tess. Mia called right before you came to get me. She's at the scene now, Abe's on his way."

The room started to spin and she closed her eyes, focusing on the strength of Vito's hands on her shoulders. "How?"

Spinnelli cleared his throat. "I don't think—"

She opened her eyes and stared fiercely into Spinnelli's face. "Goddammit to hell," she hissed. "You tell me, Marc."

He flicked a glance at Rachel who still sat, stunned. "Not here. Not now. Rachel, I'm going to call your father to come get you."

Aidan stood up, his face once again unreadable. "I'll take her home, Marc," he said grimly. "I have to go out anyway. Come on, Rachel."

Rachel stood up unsteadily, Aidan's hand supporting her arm. She started to shrug out of Tess's coat, but Tess shook her head. "Keep the coat," she said and looked up at Aidan's flat eyes. "I owed your brother one anyway."

He said nothing, just nodded once and walked away.

Numb, Tess didn't move. He was gone. Without a word. But what could he have said? *Bye, Tess, thanks for a night of mind blowing sex but you nearly got my sister killed?* He'd be justified. She couldn't even blame him for going. Just by being seen with her, he'd risked his family, his sister. Everyone else who'd been targeted was dead. Rachel could have been, too. Nothing else mattered except that girl's safety.

Not even your heart, Tess? Not even that.

"That sonofabitch," Vito muttered. "I'd like to . . ."

"Vito, stop. What else could he do? We'll just score another one for the bad guy," she murmured. "He's made all my patients fear me. Now the people I care about are afraid of me, too."

Vito crouched beside her, taking her cold hand in his warm ones. "Come home with me, Tess. Where you belong."

"I can't. Not until this is over. I'm not going to run and hide." She looked up at Spinnelli. "Tell me about Marge."

"Her throat was slit sometime between midnight and four this morning."

She closed her eyes, then opened them, unable to look at the picture her mind conjured. "She has two children, Marc. They're both away at college."

Spinnelli's face was kind. "We'll find them and tell them. Tess, about Aidan. He didn't mean to be abrupt. He had a shock and so have you."

She stood up on shaky legs. "Vito, I'm ready to go now. Take me back to Aidan's."

Vito's tight jaw dropped. "After that? After he treated you like that?"

She nodded. "I think I should get my things," she said and he relaxed a fraction. "My clothes and Bella. If the hotel won't let me keep Bella there, then maybe Amy can watch her until I can get back into my place."

"Tess, don't do anything hasty," Spinnelli said. "Please."

Ignoring his plea, she squared her shoulders and looked up at him. "Marc, somebody watching me knew that Rachel was involved in the report of that rape to the police. This has gone beyond trashing my professional reputation or whatever other motives you think this sick bastard may have had. Somebody wants to hurt me and they don't care who else has to pay in the process." She sighed. "And I can't think of anybody that hates me that much."

Chapter Eighteen

Thursday, March 16, 2:00 P.M.

Aidan pulled into traffic, his cell phone to his ear. "Kristen?"

"Aidan." Kristen sounded hassled. "I'm eye-ball deep today. Is this fast?"

"Rachel's hurt." Beside him, Rachel stared out the car window, shaking her head.

"Oh, my God." The activity in the background abruptly ceased. "How bad?"

"A few stitches. I'm taking her home now." A task he dreaded. He hated the look he'd see on his parents' faces—the worry and the fear.

And the blame. They wouldn't mean to, but he and Abe had promised their father she'd be safe. It had been a stupid promise to make. "Can you tell me if any of the guys she turned in are out on bail?"

He could hear her keyboard clacking. "Just one of them.

Andrew Poston was released on bail this morning. Andrew is a judge's son. This is going to be ugly, Aidan."

"I don't give a damn whose son he is. I want a warrant for Poston's house."

"Aidan . . ." Kristen hesitated. "You shouldn't be involved. This isn't your department."

"I got a call right after Tess brought Rachel to me, Kristen. The caller said the next time my sister would get worse if I didn't change the company I keep."

Kristen's little gasp echoed between them. "Abe told me about the doorman and the note. Was the caller male or female?"

"I couldn't tell. The voice was distorted."

Kristen sighed. "All right. I'll try to get you a warrant. Promise me you'll take Murphy."

"I will, thanks. I have another call coming in." He pushed a button. "Reagan."

"It's Murphy. We found them."

It took Aidan a second. "Bacon's videos? You found them? All of them?"

"They're probably his backup set. He's got them all organized by year. Women and . . . kids. God." Murphy sounded ill. "I've never seen anything like it."

"Murphy, the ones of . . ."

"Of Tess?" he asked, understanding. "I'll get a police-woman to view those."

"Thanks. Meet me at my house and I'll bring you up to speed. We've got a lot to do and I promised Tess I'd go with her to Harrison Ernst's viewing tonight." He slipped his phone in his pocket and glanced at Rachel who was staring at him wide-eyed. "What?"

"You're going out with her tonight? With Tess?"

"It's not a date. It's a viewing, but yes, I'm going with her tonight. Why?"

"Because you just walked out like you never planned to see her again."

"That's ridiculous. She didn't think that."

"Yeah, she did, Aidan. I saw her face when you walked away. It wasn't like it was even her fault or anything and you got all broody and mad. I didn't know what to say to her. She'd been so nice to me and you were mad at her."

"I wasn't mad at her. She knows better than to think that," he protested.

"I know what I see. I'd call her if I were you or she might get away. She's a whole lot nicer than Shelley, Aidan. Shelley looked down on us. Tess . . . she fits right in."

"How do you know? You've spent less than four total hours with her."

Rachel's look was coolly adult. "She talked to me last night and today about her family. Partly to take my mind off the pain when she was stitching me, but partly because I think she needed to talk to somebody. It's funny. I never thought that shrinks needed to talk to people, too. Her family seems just like us. Except that her dad's sick, you know. She just found out her dad needs a heart transplant or he'll die."

Aidan's own heart clenched. "Poor Tess. On top of everything else."

"Call her, Aidan. Don't let her get away or I'll kick your ass. Better yet, I'll have her do it. That was pretty amazing, what she did to that guy last night."

Yeah, it was amazing. And after he'd finishing having the shit scared out of him, he'd found it incredibly arousing, the sex better than any he'd ever had before. Tess was most definitely not what he'd first labeled her to be. "How'd you get so smart, kid?"

Rachel smiled at him and he wondered when she'd grown up. "Good genes."

Thursday, March 16, 2:55 P.M.

"Tess, what is *taking* you so long?" Vito boomed from the kitchen.

"I can't get Bella in the carrier." Tess sat on the edge of Aidan's bed, drained. She looked at the bedding she and Aidan had all but destroyed in the four times they'd . . . Right here and now she could be honest with herself. They'd had really good sex. And maybe, when all this was over and she was no longer a threat to the safety of anyone around her, they might have really good sex again.

But from where she was sitting right now, that didn't look likely. He'd walked away like she was a plague carrier. For all intents, that's exactly what she was. But of course everything looked worse when you were having the day from hell.

Marge Hooper's had been considerably worse. Marge was dead. It started to sink in on the ride to Aidan's. They hadn't really been friends, more like acquaintances. But she was dead, the message clear. Nobody Tess knew was exempt.

"This has been a really shitty day, Bella," Tess told the cat, who sat poised to run again. Her parents' revelations, being sued, stitching up Rachel Reagan, then watching Aidan walk away . . . And looming over it all was Marge and Mr. Hughes and Harrison. "I didn't think after yesterday it could get much worse. I was wrong." She stood up. "So stop being a pain in the ass and come here so I can get out of here." She reached, only to have the cat escape again, nimbly climbing to the top shelf of the bookshelves that filled an entire wall of Aidan's bedroom. Every shelf was bowed, loaded with books.

Angry male voices distracted her and she could hear Aidan and Vito arguing in the kitchen. With a tired shake of her head, Tess left them to it. They were big boys, after all.

And she had to catch her cat. Standing on her toes, she grabbed onto the highest shelf and felt for Bella's collar just as Aidan appeared in the doorway, looking furious.

"What the hell are you doing?"

"I'm trying to catch my damn cat," she bit out. "And it's not going well."

"Tess— *Hell.*" She felt the shelf give and his hands grab her at the same time her fingers closed around Bella's collar, then everything seemed to tumble. Bella jumped and the shelf pulled from the wall, sending fifty books crashing to the floor. The cat prissed away, unhurt, but perturbed. Leaving Tess standing with the cat's collar in her hand, her heart going a mile a minute because Aidan's arm had banded across her stomach, pulling her off her feet and against his hard body.

"Are you all right?" he asked, his voice throaty and rough.

"I'm confused, Aidan," she said quietly. "What do you want from me?"

"I don't know yet." He turned her in his arms, cupped her face. "I know I don't want you to go. Not like this. If you need to go back to your parents, that's one thing. But don't go because of what I said."

"You didn't say anything. That was the problem." She shook her head wearily. "This doesn't really change anything. What about Rachel?"

"She's home and safe with my folks." He huffed mirthlessly. "She was right, the squirt. She said I'd hurt you and I never meant to. I promise you that. I figured you'd . . ." He shrugged. "Understand how I was feeling. I wasn't mad at you, Tess."

"Who were you mad at then?"

"The situation. Myself. I was supposed to protect her and I didn't. But I wasn't mad at you. You're not responsible for any of this."

"You're not just saying that so I'll stay and cook for you?"

One side of his mouth bent up. "Now that you mention it, all the cannoli is gone." He kissed her softly and she melted into him. "Stay with me, Tess."

"I will, if you do something for me."

He glanced at the bed. "I can't. Murphy's coming in a few minutes."

Her lips curved. "That wasn't what I meant. Aidan, I'm a psychiatrist, not a mind reader. You do understand the difference, don't you?"

His thumbs stroked her mouth. "I'm still on the bed. Sorry."

She chuckled. "You are single-minded." Sobering she frowned. "I don't know how you feel if you don't tell me, Aidan. My job is to get people to talk to me so I can figure out what's going on in their mind. You don't talk to me."

"I talk all the time."

"Not about what's important. I told you everything about me, but you put me off."

"You want me to talk . . . right now?"

"Not right now. But definitely later. Why did you come back here?"

"I have to meet Murphy. We're going to go search the house of one of the assholes at Rachel's school. Then I have an appointment across town with a witness." He kissed her hard. "I'll be back in time to take you to Ernst's viewing."

Tess's gripped the front of his shirt, holding him in place when he tried to step away. "You're also the company I keep, Aidan," she said fiercely.

"I know. I'll be careful."

"I've been trying to think of who can hate me this much. I can't."

"I know, Tess."

"I was thinking he might come to Harrison's viewing tonight." Her fingers tightened. "But if I go, every person there will be a target. If I go shopping, they're a target. You're a target. Your family. My family." She closed her eyes. "It's starting to drive me crazy."

"That's what they want to do," he murmured. "We won't let them." He kissed her again, slow and serious this time, leaving them both breathing hard. "Now I've got to go. Walk me out and lock the door."

She walked him to the front door and waved as he got into Murphy's car, her glands still pumping. She closed the door and turned to find Vito scowling at her. "Don't," she said. "Just don't."

He followed her into the kitchen. "He must have done some smooth talking in there," Vito said sarcastically and Tess slapped the cat collar on the counter.

"What is your problem, Vito? Just spit it out."

"Fine. You've known this guy for three days."

She started peeling tomatoes with a vengeance. "Four, but you've made your point. I'm a slut that falls into bed too soon. You've been thinking it. You might as well say it."

"Fine. It's too soon."

Tess waved the paring knife under his nose. "You sleep with women you've only known a few days. And don't tell me you don't."

Vito glared. "Not lately."

"So go get some! Maybe it'll sweeten you up!" She put down the knife and calmed herself. "Vito, it's none of your business, but I love you and what you think about me matters so I'll tell you anyway. I've been with four guys in my life. Four. I made all of them wait a hell of a long time, except for Aidan. It wasn't about him. It was about me. What I needed. Right now, he's what I need. So be nice to him. For me."

"Doesn't it matter that he tried to hurt you?"

"When? In the police station? That was a misunderstanding."

"You let a misunderstanding with Dad keep you away for five years, Tess. This guy waltzes in and all of a sudden you're living with him. He hurts you and you forgive him just like that." He snapped his fingers in the air.

"Maybe my misunderstanding with Dad taught me a few things. I lost a lot of years. And I'll be honest with you. I've been lonely since Phillip. I missed having someone. I don't think that's so wrong."

Vito leaned against the wall, his shoulders slumping. "I don't want him to hurt you."

"If he does, I'll survive." Bella sauntered in and Tess scooped her up. "Here, hold her. I need to put this back on." She grabbed the collar and pulled at the buckle.

Then stopped. And stared. "Oh my God."

Vito stooped to stare with her, then looked up, his eyes narrowed and angry.

She put the collar on the counter and ran out the front door to the street, dialing her cell frantically. "Aidan? I know how he found out about Rachel."

Thursday, March 16, 3:15 P.M.

Kristen was waiting for them in front of Poston's house, warrant in hand. "What's wrong?" she asked, seeing the scowls on their faces.

"Tess's damn cat was wired for sound," Aidan muttered. "Rachel held the cat in her lap the entire time she told me everything. That's how he knew. Why are you here?"

"Andrew Poston Senior is a judge. Patrick called it preemptive damage control."

Mrs. Poston was waiting at the door, her face filled with dread. "What is it?"

"We're here with a search warrant, Mrs. Poston," Kristen said, following Aidan and Murphy up the stairs. "You'll find it all in order."

Aidan shoved at Andrew's bedroom door. "It's locked. Let us in, Andrew." When the boy didn't respond, Aidan shoved his shoulder into the door. Cracking wood was followed by Mrs. Poston's cry of outrage as Aidan burst into Andrew's room where the boy stood, a CD in his hands.

"Hand it over," Aidan demanded.

"No." Andrew snapped the CD in two, the crack loud as a gunshot. His startled look changed to a sly grin. "I've been right here since my lawyer sprang me this morning."

Aidan looked at the broken CD in the boy's hands and the smug smile on his face and tamped back his temper, knowing that ripping the kid's fucking face off would jeopardize this case and his career. Still, for Rachel, it might almost be worth it. "You do realize that whoever sent you that CD is responsible for the deaths of eight people. When you become dispensable, that number could go up by one." Andrew's grin faded and Mrs. Poston gasped.

Andrew tossed his head back, arrogant. "I can take care of myself."

"Like you took care of that girl Monday night? Like you took care of Rachel Reagan?" Murphy asked, his anger barely masked.

"The girls wanted it. I don't need to force myself on anyone. And I never touched that Reagan bitch. If she says so, she's a dirty liar. I was here. All day. Right, Mom?"

His mother wrung her hands. "Yes, he was. I called my husband. He's on his way."

"That's fine, Mrs. Poston," Aidan said mildly. "Just fine. Tell your husband he can meet us at the police station. Being a judge, I'm sure he's familiar with it. Oh, you know, Murphy, we never got a chance to introduce ourselves to young Poston here. This is Detective Murphy. Over there is States Attorney Kristen Reagan. And I'm Detective Reagan." The punk's face paled, a gratifying sight to see. "Let's go, kid."

"Where?" His bravado was largely diminished.

"Downtown with us," Aidan said. "For now, we'll call it obstruction. Once this is all sorted out, then we'll see what else we can tack on."

Thursday, March 16, 4:00 P.M.

"Can you fix it?" Aidan asked after Rick had examined the CD pieces for several silent minutes. He, Murphy, and Spinnelli had been quiet as long as they'd been able.

"So that it'll play like a CD again? No. Doesn't mean I can't recover some of the data. It'll take me a little while."

"How long?" Spinnelli asked impatiently.

"A few days? It's like putting Humpty Dumpty together. And I may not find anything."

"Get started," Spinnelli ordered. "What about the microphone in the cat's collar?"

Rick shrugged. "Similar to the ones we found in Tess's clothes. It was transmitting using your wireless Internet connection, Aidan. You need to get a better firewall. I had Jack's guys do a sweep of your house. We didn't find any other devices."

"Thanks." Aidan didn't want to think about what the microphone had picked up the night before. Neither he nor Tess had been overly quiet in the . . . throes of passion.

Rick gathered the CD fragments carefully. "I'll call you when I have something."

Murphy slumped when the door closed behind Rick. "It could be a dead end."

"You always say I'm the pessimist," Aidan said. "Maybe he'll find something good. We've still got the Poston kid in Interview. What do you want to do with the little prick?"

Spinnelli scowled. "For now, I have to release him to his parents. I don't want to charge him with anything until we know what's on the CD. We picked up the two boys who hurt Rachel, by the way. As enforcers go, they didn't do a very good job. Nearly every kid in school knew they'd gotten cold feet afterward and tried to follow her." His mustache twitched. "Your dog has apparently taken on legendary proportions, Aidan. She's a two-hundred pound mastiff who took a bite out of their asses as they ran crying."

"Good. I wish Dolly had taken a chunk out of their—" A knock at the conference room door had him turning. One of the clerks stuck her head in, papers in her hand.

"Aidan, I got the LUDs you requested."

"Thanks, Lori. Denise Masterson's LUDs," he told Spinnelli and Murphy.

"Denise Masterson is Tess's receptionist," Murphy explained to Spinnelli.

"The one that didn't call 911 right away yesterday?"

"She's the one." Aidan ran his finger down the page while Lori waited. "Here it is. A call made one minute after Tess left for Seward's on Tuesday. Lasted eight and a half minutes." He looked up. "Can you do a reverse lookup on this number?"

"Already did." Lori's brows went up. "It's the features editor at the *National Eye*."

Aidan blinked. "A tabloid? Tess's secretary called a tabloid instead of 911?"

"You want me to run a check on her bank accounts?" Lori asked.

"Yeah. As soon as you can. Thanks." He turned back to

Spinnelli and Murphy. "That's why it took the cops so long to get there. If they'd gotten there sooner maybe Malcolm Seward's wife would still be alive."

"Bring her in," Spinnelli said. "Let her wonder what she's going to be charged with."

"She had access to all the patient files, Marc." Aidan mulled the loose ends in his mind. "Our guy had to know that Bacon made the videos—that's why he killed him."

Murphy scowled. "Denise was there when Tess got that blackmail CD from Bacon, so she knew about the cameras. She could be an accessory, maybe unconsciously."

"Bring her in," Spinnelli said again. "And ask Tess to come down and observe. She knows this woman. Maybe she can help us get at her motives."

Thursday, March 16, 5:05 P.M.

Through the glass, Tess stared at Denise Masterson who was sitting at the interrogation room table, nervously twisting the rings on her fingers. Tess looked up at Aidan's profile, disbelieving. "You guys can't be serious. Denise? She's no killer."

Beside her Aidan was unsmiling. "Maybe she didn't kill anybody, but it looks like she sold information to the *Eye*. If she's willing to sell information to a tabloid, maybe she sold it to somebody else. Somebody had to have access to your office, Tess, to plant all the cameras and mikes. If she didn't, maybe she let them in. For a fee."

"You're sure she sold to the *Eye*?"

"She deposited ten thousand in her checking account this morning, Tess," Murphy said quietly. "You give her a raise recently?"

She sighed. "Not ten thousand dollars. Shit. Go ahead."

Spinnelli joined Tess as Aidan and Murphy moved into the little room where she herself had sat just days before. Aidan sat on the corner of the table nearest Denise, arms crossed over his chest. Murphy made himself comfortable in the chair next to her.

"How much money do you make, Miss Masterson?" Aidan began.

Denise blinked once. "I . . . I don't think that's any of your business."

"Aidan," Murphy chided gently. "You already know how much she makes." He aimed a benign smile at Denise. "We checked before we picked you up."

Her eyes flicked up to Aidan's face before returning to Murphy. "Then why ask?"

Murphy kept smiling. "We were hoping you'd tell us where the ten thousand dollars came from—you know, the money that appeared in your account this morning."

She paled. "It was a gift. I was worried that with Dr. Ernst's death and Dr. Ciccotelli's losing her license that I'd lose my job. My aunt gave me the money."

"Generous aunt." Aidan leaned a little closer. "What's her name?"

Again Denise licked her lips. "Lila Timmons."

Tess glanced at Spinnelli before returning her attention to the woman she thought she'd known. "Lila Timmons was one of our patients. She died last year. Was that the best name she could come up with?"

"Unlike you, some people fold under pressure, Tess," Spinnelli said.

Aidan was writing the name on his notepad. "We'll check her out." He sat and stared at her, saying nothing more. Tess remembered when he'd used the same tactic on her and despite her contempt for what Denise had done, she felt a tug of pity.

After a minute of bearing Aidan's stare, Denise dropped her eyes. "Can I go now?"

"You're not under arrest, Miss Masterson. But I do have one question before you do." Aidan put a picture on the table and Tess cringed. It was Gwen Seward's autopsy photo. Denise's hand came up to cover her mouth, muffling a horrified whimper.

"Miss Masterson, I just wanted you to see what was happening to Gwen Seward while you were on the phone to the *National Eye*. She won't have an open casket. There's not enough of her head left."

Denise gagged and threw up in the trash can Murphy had set next to her foot.

Aidan pushed harder. "Gwen Seward might still be alive if you'd called 911 the way Dr. Ciccotelli asked you to do."

Denise covered her face with her hands. "I didn't kill her. Her husband did."

Aidan pulled her hands from her face and held the picture in front of her eyes. "Because you didn't call 911. Why did you wait ten minutes, Denise?"

Denise clenched her eyes closed. "Take it away. Please don't make me look at it."

"Tell me why you waited ten minutes."

"All the others were already dead. I didn't think there was a rush."

Aidan shook his head as if to clear it. "Are you telling us that you called the tabloid first because you thought Malcolm Seward was already dead?"

Denise nodded, trembling. "They called me that morning and told me they'd pay me ten thousand dollars for a scoop."

Tess frowned. "The *Eye* didn't get the scoop, Marc. There were twenty reporters outside Seward's on Tuesday, so they shouldn't have paid her anything at all." Her gut clenched. "Oh my God. She was there when the courier brought the

CD." She clutched Spinnelli's arm. "Find out if that's the scoop she sold them."

Spinnelli patted her arm. "Give Aidan and Murphy another few minutes with her."

"So you sold Dr. Ciccotelli out," Aidan was saying.

Denise lifted her chin. "I did nothing illegal. My lawyer told me so."

"Who is your lawyer, Miss Masterson?" Murphy asked, his tone still mild despite the contempt Tess could see in his eyes. "He may have given you bad information."

"Can I go now?"

"In a minute." Aidan drew another photo from the folder.

"Who is that man?" Tess asked.

"He's the one we saw going into Seward's apartment," Spinnelli murmured.

"I know him," Tess said and watched Denise's eyes flicker. "And so does she."

Spinnelli's head whipped around. "Who is he?"

"I don't remember," Tess said. "Not yet."

Denise was shaking her head. "I don't know him. I've never seen him before."

"Oh, come on, Denise," Aidan said, his tone mocking. "Did he pay you, too?"

Denise's eyes narrowed. "No."

"Ask her about the CD," Tess said. *And if she's told anyone, I'll kill her myself.*

Spinnelli leaned his head in and motioned for Murphy to come, then whispered in his ear. Murphy nodded and returned to Denise. "We're curious, Miss Masterson. First of all, I want to reestablish where that ill-gotten money came from. Did it come from Lila Timmons who has been dead for a year or from the *National Eye*?"

Denise clenched her teeth. "I told you it was the *Eye*. And not illegal."

"Okay. Just crossing my 't's.'" Murphy smiled. "Now tell me why they paid you ten grand for a story that was yesterday's news just an hour later? Seward was no scoop."

Denise swallowed hard. "I'm going home."

Murphy and Aidan exchanged a glance and Tess could see that Aidan had quickly picked up the ball. "You told them about the videos of Dr. Ciccotelli, didn't you?" Aidan demanded, standing up, his hands on his hips.

Denise paused, her hand on the doorknob and Tess's stomach pulled inside out. "And if I did? That wasn't illegal, either."

"No, just despicable," Aidan spat out. "How could you?"

Denise turned, her face twisted and angry. "Because I needed the money. Because she pays me next to nothing. Because she has a fancy apartment and a Mercedes while I drive a ten-year-old bucket of rust. Eleanor picked her up out of the gutter and made her. Did she do the same? Did she ask me if I wanted to be part of the practice?"

"I don't recall seeing a medical degree on your résumé, Miss Masterson," Aidan asked coldly. "Or a PhD. So what purpose could you have served?"

Denise was trembling, her cheeks mottled red. "I have a degree. If they'd wanted to bad enough, they could have done something. I've been waiting for her and the old man to do the decent thing for years, but they treat me like some kind of *secretary*."

"You *are* a secretary, Miss Masterson," Murphy said mildly.

Aidan walked over to her, his expression one of disdain. "If I were your employer I'd fire your ass. But if you choose not to show up for work tomorrow, that's fine by me. You, too, Murphy?"

Murphy pushed his lips into a lazy pout. "Fine with me. I'll escort you out."

When they'd gone, Aidan came into the back room where Tess stood shaking her head in disbelief. "Harrison and I paid her twenty percent more than the city average for receptionists with her experience. And we paid her health benefits, too. I even offered to help her go back to school."

"So what did she mean, Eleanor pulled you up?" Spinnelli asked.

Tess sighed. "I met Eleanor when I was in college. Amy and I were temping to earn money for school and the agency sent me to Eleanor and Harrison. They liked me and offered me a job. I couldn't work all the time because I was in school, but I worked whenever I could. I did all the filing after hours and on weekends."

"That doesn't sound terribly significant," Aidan said with a frown.

Tess drew a breath. "And . . . Eleanor put me through medical school."

Aidan blinked. "Wow."

"Not for free. It was a loan and I worked to pay it off at bank interest rates, after I graduated. It let me focus on med school. I didn't have to work long hours to pay tuition. I'd paid off eighty percent of the loan when she died. Her will forgave the rest."

"Why would Eleanor give you such a loan?" Spinnelli asked.

"Eleanor used a walker. I helped her get around. Did errands for her. I didn't do it for the money. I did it because she was a kind person and I liked her. And I learned so much from her . . ." Her throat thickened. "And from Harrison. They brought me into the practice when I got my license. When Eleanor died, I thought Harrison would bring in somebody else, but he'd become attached to me, too, he said, and asked me to stay." She lifted her chin. "But they didn't make me. They helped me make myself."

Aidan frowned. "How did Denise know that story? Was it common knowledge?"

"I don't know. My friends at the time knew. Phillip knew, because I told him. Why?"

"Because it's a little seed that has made your receptionist hate you."

"I still can't see Denise planning all those suicides. Frankly, she's not that bright."

"But she knew the guy in the picture," Spinnelli said. "The one who installed cameras in Seward's place. Maybe he put them in your place, too."

She thought about it rationally. "You're right. She must have been the one to let him in, even if she didn't know what he was doing. I hate to believe she did know." Tess rubbed her temples and peered up at Aidan. "You think Phillip was involved."

Aidan met her gaze steadily. "Haven't you thought so?"

"I guess so. Again, I can't see him doing this, but I didn't see Denise being so angry either. I didn't exactly like her, but I didn't *not* trust her, if that makes sense."

Aidan's cell phone rang. "Murphy? . . . She did? Good. Call me when she stops." He closed his phone. "Murphy's following her. She made a phone call from a public phone across the street. I'll have the number traced."

Tess studied the picture Aidan had shown Denise. "I've seen this guy before, but I don't remember where. Can you make me a copy? Maybe it will jar my memory."

Aidan led her toward the door. "I will. Listen, I have one more stop to make before I come home. If I'm late, wait for me. Don't go out alone. How are you getting home?"

"Vito's waiting downstairs. Aidan, I need to warn the people that know me."

"You can warn your friends to be a little more careful. Just don't mention the note."

" 'Be judged by the company you keep,' " Tess said bitterly. "I won't."

Chapter Nineteen

Thursday, March 16, 7:15 P.M.

Aidan slid his arm around her as she hesitated at the funeral home door. "Ready?"

Tess nodded, fast and hard. "Yeah, I think so." But she trembled.

"Let's get it over with. Then we'll go home and let your father poke me with sticks."

She chuckled, his intention. "He will not poke you with sticks. I hope."

A man in black pointed toward a room filled with men in suits and women in tasteful dresses. *A veritable who's who of Chicago society,* Aidan thought, recognizing a number of them from the black-tie affairs Shelley's stepfather used to host.

A stillness fell throughout the room when they entered, conversations stalling until finally the only sound was the classical music piped in through the speakers. A frail-looking woman stood to one side of the mahogany casket, flanked by Harrison's children.

"You want me to go up there with you?" Aidan murmured.

"No, stay here. I have something to tell her but I won't be long." She hugged Flo, whispering in her ear and Flo went still, tears rolling down her face even as her mouth trembled in a smile. Tess came back to where he was standing, her own eyes wet.

"What did you tell her?" Aidan asked, slipping his hand under her hair.

"I told her Harrison's last words were that he loved her. She knew it, but she needed to hear it."

"I'm glad then." Looking over her head he scanned the room. "Do you see anyone you know here?"

She looked around. "I see lots of people I know, but nobody who hates me."

"Let's stay a little longer," he murmured in her ear. "I want to see who shows up. I'll stay back here and watch. You mingle."

Who showed up first was Murphy, his wrinkled suit making him look like Columbo at a country club. "Did you trace Denise's call?"

Aidan glanced over to where Tess stood, talking with the mayor. The mayor. Hell. Shades of Shelley. Just being around all these bigwigs was making him nervous. He focused on Murphy's question. "Yeah. She called a company named Brewer, Inc. It's listed as a beer importer."

"Interesting, because after she made the call, Denise went straight to an apartment that wasn't hers, but nobody was home. I talked to the landlady and she says it belongs to some guy named Lawe. She says he's a PI and identified his picture."

"Why would Denise go to see a PI? A lawyer maybe, but a PI?"

"Don't know. The landlady said she saw Lawe yesterday morning, but he hadn't been back since then. She has a package for him and he hasn't come to claim it."

"Maybe he went away for a few days."

"Maybe. Except I got an itchy feeling so I called the morgue. They just brought in one man, same size and general shape as the PI. Except he's charbroiled."

Aidan flinched. "Ouch. Nasty."

"Yeah, the stolen car he was in caught on fire, but the locals have real fast emergency response, so they put it out before it turned him to ash. Arson found remnants of a small pipe bomb hooked up to a manual timer. His chest was full of lead, same caliber as the gun that shot Bacon. Julia wasn't in the morgue, but Johnson said they'd rush a dental match to prove the charbroiled guy is Lawe."

"Tess has seen him before. She can't remember where."

"Maybe with Denise. The landlady thought Lawe and Masterson were an item."

"Let's talk to Blaine Connell first thing in the morning and see if this yanks any more out of him. I found out what Bacon and Nicole Rivera had in common."

Murphy's brows went up. "Dish, boy," he said and Aidan chuckled.

"Nicole's brother is in jail, waiting trial. Nicole's roommate said she was saving every penny for a lawyer for him instead of the putz they sent from Legal Aid."

"So both Bacon and Rivera were acquainted with the legal system," Murphy said thoughtfully. "And speaking of the legal system, look who's here."

"Jon Carter and Amy Miller." With a second man Aidan didn't know. "Let's mingle."

"Detective Reagan." Jon Carter shook his hand soberly.

"Dr. Carter. This is my partner, Detective Murphy."

"I remember you," Jon said. "You visited Tess in the hospital last year."

Murphy shook his hand. "That's right. Did you know Dr. Ernst?"

"We all did. Poor Flo. I can't imagine what she's going through. But mostly we're here for Tess." His jaw tightened, his face growing dark. "It's a unified 'fuck you' to whoever's doing this. They think that we'd leave her? That's not going to happen."

"Jon," the other man murmured. "Not here. It's not the place."

Jon gave himself a shake, visibly forcing himself to calm. "I'm sorry. It's just that this whole thing has me so damn mad. You do remember Amy, don't you, Detective?"

"Of course," Aidan said, noting the way Jon's cheeks had grown red and the vein throbbed at his temple. The man was furious and controlling it well. "It's nice that you all came for Tess. This has been a hard day for her."

"A hard week," Amy corrected sadly. "It's nice to see you again, Detectives. Thanks for taking such good care of Tess. She's not an easy person to care for."

"You can say that again," the second man said and held out his hand. "We haven't met. I'm Robin Archer. I've known Tess a long time."

Aidan's eyes widened as he shook the man's hand. "You're Robin?"

Jon's mouth curved in wry amusement. "I told you Tess and I were only friends."

Aidan cleared his throat. "So you did. I hear you make soup, Mr. Archer."

Robin grinned engagingly. "She hates it, I know. That's why I keep bringing it."

Aidan blew out a breath. "Well."

Jon sucked in one cheek. "Well." Then he sobered. "What have you found out, Detective? Tess told us today that the man you'd thought had done it, didn't."

"We've got some strong leads. I'll let you know something as soon as I can. Dr. Carter, can I talk to you for a moment?" Aidan took him aside. "Since you told me about her father, I wanted you to know he was in town and they are talking."

Jon sighed. "She told me. She also said he's got heart disease. She'll need support in the months ahead. To get him back, and now this . . . Poor Tess."

"I have some other questions, if you don't mind. Can you tell me about Phillip?"

Jon's brows bent. "You think he's involved in this?"

"I have to ask the questions. This is somebody with a very personal grudge."

"But Phillip?" Jon sighed. "He and Tess met in med school. He was only part of our group because of Tess. The rest of us didn't like him too much, but we never let Tess know. I never saw the attraction, but she seemed to love him. I always thought it was because he was so unlike her father. Her dad's dramatic and loud and Phillip wasn't either of those things."

"Was he violent?"

"Phillip?" Jon seemed genuinely astonished. "Never that I saw. He was controlled. Fastidious. Tess found out he'd been cheating, two weeks before the big day. Man never even denied it. Just packed his bag and walked away."

"That's what Tess said," Aidan said thoughtfully and Jon's astonishment grew.

"She told you about Phillip? It took TNT for me to get that much out of her."

But she'd told him easily as he'd held her in his arms. Tonight, he'd do the same. Trust her with the things that hurt. "Do you know who the woman was?"

"No. Phillip and I never talked. He's rather . . . conservatively tied. I don't have his home address, but he works at the Kinsale Cancer Institute."

"And his last name?" Aidan's smile was wry. "I know him only as 'Dr. Damn-him-to-hell.' "

Jon laughed softly. "I like that better. It's Parks. Phillip Parks."

"One last question. You mentioned your group—who else is in it?"

His eyes widened. "You can't possibly . . . I suppose you have to. Even me. Well, it used to be bigger, but people have moved on. Tess and me and Robin and Amy, of course. Gen Lake, Rhonda Perez, but neither of them come often any-more."

"Who's left the group in the last . . . six months?"

Something flickered in Jon's eyes. "Jim Swanson."

"Why did he leave?"

John hesitated. "He went to Africa to do a tour with Doc-tors Without Borders."

There was more to that story, Aidan could tell. "Sud-denly?"

"He said he'd been thinking about it for a while. Seemed sudden to the rest of us."

He was sure Jon knew more, but decided to press from a different angle. He'd ask Tess later. "Thank you, Dr. Carter. I appreciate the information."

"You can ask me anything, Detective. After Robin, Tess is my best friend."

Thursday, March 16, 10:45 P.M.

"Come here, Tess." Her father patted the cushion of Aidan's sofa and she curled up next to him, her head on his shoulder.

"So, was it good? The ziti?" She'd planned a more elaborate meal, but going down to the police station this afternoon had forced her to throw together an old standby.

"Nearly as good as your mother's," he said loud enough for her mother to hear in the kitchen. Then whispered, "Just as good. So where is your young man?"

"Still out on call." The call had shaken Aidan. For almost two hours she'd been trying not to think about who it could be this time. "It happens when you're dating a cop."

"He seemed . . . nice." The word was grudgingly uttered, but made Tess smile.

"He is nice." She listened to him breathe. "Dad, don't take this wrong, but go home."

His shoulders tightened. "Why?"

"Because you need to be close to your doctors."

"Uh-huh." He kissed the top of her head. "Why, Tessa? I can handle the truth."

She sighed. "Because you're not safe here. Three of my friends are dead. Aidan's sister was hurt this afternoon. I just got you back. I don't want to see you get hurt, too."

"If you come with me, I'll go."

Tess frowned at him. "That's not fair."

He shrugged. "So sue me. That's the deal, Tess. I'll go home if you do."

"You're going home because you should be near your cardiologist. I'm staying here because I am home." And it was odd that the picture that flashed in her mind was this very room. Living in Eleanor's apartment had been wonderful, but Aidan's house felt like a home. "Plus, I've got Aidan to watch out for me."

"And I've got Vito, so we're at an impasse. Did you say you made cannoli?"

She laughed. "You're a stubborn man."

"I know." He pushed to his feet. "It was nice seeing Amy again. Almost like old times." Amy had stopped by after Harrison's viewing and shared their dinner. Seeing all their faces around the table really *had* felt like old times.

"She didn't have to stay away because I did," Tess said.

Her father pulled the cover off the cannoli. "She didn't."

"Michael!" Gina came to her feet and snatched the plate from his hands. "He's not supposed to have that," she added more gently.

"One won't hurt." He looked at her mother with puppy dog eyes. "Tess made them."

"What do you mean, Amy didn't stay away?" Tess asked.

"No," her mother insisted and put the dessert away.

Her father sighed. "Amy came home every Thanksgiving. I thought you knew."

Tess shook her head. "I didn't. I spent Thanksgiving with the Spinnellis. Amy said she was spending it with friends from law school."

"She didn't want to hurt you, Tess," Vito said uneasily, then backed up when Dolly sat up and growled. "That dog is a menace."

"No, she's just telling us Aidan is home." A few seconds later she heard the garage door. Her stomach rolled, worrying about who he'd discovered dead, a note pinned to their coat. "Excuse me." She slipped into the garage, needing a minute alone with him.

Aidan got out of his car and his shoulders sagged when he saw her. "Tess."

"Who was it?"

His mouth twisted. "Danny Morris's mother."

"The little boy," she murmured. "His mother was killed?"

Even from ten feet away she could see the cold anger in his eyes. "Killed herself. She left a note. Said she felt guilty that she hadn't protected him. That I was right."

She wanted to go to him but sensed he needed to be alone. "About what?"

He dropped his chin to his chest. "I knew she knew where the father was. Monday night, after the asshole's pal hit me in the bar, I went to her house. Told her she was protecting a monster. Asked her what kind of mother would do that." He looked up, his eyes anguished. "I pushed her too hard."

"No, Aidan, you didn't." Unable to stay back any longer, she put her arms around his shoulders, pulled his head to the curve of her neck. "You didn't tell her anything she didn't already know. And if she hadn't cared about her son, nothing you said would have made any difference. Did she tell where you could find her husband in the note?"

His head lifted, their eyes inches apart. "Yeah, she did, but he wasn't at any of the spots. How did you know?"

"I've seen it before. A person will often try to set things right before they take that final step. Sounds like she tried."

His jaw tightened. "She should have stayed alive to testify against her husband."

"You would have," she said quietly and his eyes flashed.

"I wouldn't have allowed some bastard to murder my son."

"Not everybody does the right thing, Aidan. And not everyone is strong." She kissed him, tenderly. "I'm sorry."

Wearily he dropped his head back to her shoulder. "Do you know a Sylvia Arness?"

She shook her head, dread again descending to grip her gut. "No."

He straightened, grasping her upper arms. "You don't? Are you sure?"

"I'm sure." Her heart was pounding now, so hard it hurt. "Why?"

His grip tightened. "African American woman, age twenty-three?"

"No. Aidan, tell me why."

"Because she's dead. Howard and Brooks from our unit responded just as I was leaving the Morris scene. They called me when they found the note pinned to her coat."

Her throat closed. "Be judged by the company you keep?"

"Yes. You're sure you don't know her? Sylvia Arness was the name on her ID."

Slowly she shook her head. "Maybe it's a copycat."

"Maybe. Will you come downtown and take a look at her so we'll know for sure?"

Woodenly she nodded. "Of course. I have to tell my folks I'm leaving."

He stopped at the door. "You'll give your father a . . . scare looking like that."

Heart attack. He'd been about to say "heart attack" and checked himself. Drawing herself tall, she closed her eyes and focused. When her eyes opened, he nodded. "Better. He'll still know something's wrong, but it won't scare him."

"Thank you," she murmured. "I wasn't thinking."

"You're entitled." He pushed open the door and greeted her waiting family with a tired smile. "I'm sorry I was gone so long. It was another case."

Tess came into the kitchen behind him and met Vito's eyes, saw he understood.

"Dad, it's getting late," he said. "Let's go back to the hotel."

Michael sat down in the kitchen chair, his jaw cocked stubbornly. "I'm not blind and I'm certainly not stupid. Tell me the truth, Tess."

She squeezed Aidan's hand. "Thanks for trying," she murmured, then looked at her father. "Dad, Aidan did have to go out on another case. But as he was leaving it, something else came up that may or may not be related to me. I have to go help them out. Please go with Vito. You need to rest. I'll call you, I promise."

Michael rose, his chin lifted. "You won't let her out of your sight, Reagan?"

Aidan shook his head. "I promise."

Thursday, March 16, 11:20 P.M.

Spinnelli and Murphy met them at the morgue.

"If this is a copycat, this could get ugly very fast," Spinnelli said.

"I want to know how a copycat would know about the message," Murphy grumbled. "We kept that out of the press. Until now. The crowd around Arness saw it."

Tess's body was rigid against Aidan's side. "Let's get this over with."

Johnson was waiting next to the metal table on which lay a person covered with a sheet. "She was shot at nine-fifteen. It looks like it was point-blank. The bullet was heavy caliber, probably a forty-five. It entered in her back, right at her heart and tore straight through." His expression was kind. "If she felt any pain, it wasn't more than a minute."

"But she would have been afraid," Tess murmured, her eyes fixed to the sheet and Aidan knew in her mind she was there with the woman as she faced her death. It was what she did. She entered her patients' minds with them, lived their fears. Because she cared. It was an odd place to have that realization, standing in front of a corpse.

"The gunshot brought people running. There was a lot of confusion, so nobody saw anything," Aidan said. "CSU is still combing the scene."

"Wait." Murphy held up his hand. "When he shot Rivera

it was a twenty-two and Julia thought he'd used a silencer. Why use a forty-five at a time when people were around?"

"He wanted her to be found quickly," Aidan said.

"But he took the time to pin the note to her coat, knowing people were coming." Spinnelli's mustache bunched in a frown. "That hardly sounds like our careful killer."

Tess straightened her spine. "Please, can we just go ahead? I'm ready."

Aidan squeezed her waist as Johnson pulled back the sheet, exposing the woman to her shoulders and for a moment Tess just stared.

"I've never seen . . ." She stopped. "Wait. Where was she found?"

"On the UI campus. She's a—"

"Student there," Tess finished for him, her voice nearly toneless, the color draining from her face. Johnson quickly pushed over a chair and he and Aidan lowered her to it. Tess moistened her lips. "I said 'hello.' That's all."

Aidan crouched down to look up into her face. "When?"

"Yesterday. I needed new boots. Because you had all my clothes and my shoes."

Spinnelli gently squeezed her shoulder. "You met her in the shoe store?"

Stunned, she nodded.

"How did you know she was a student?" Murphy asked.

"She . . . she was flirting with Vito. The girls always flirt with Vito. I'd picked out my boots and was going to the register and she was behind me. I said 'hello.' After we left, I teased Vito and he said she was just a college kid. She'd told him so. I only said 'hello.'" She barely inhaled, her breaths were so rapid and shallow. "That's all." Her hand covered her mouth, her eyes far away. "And now she's dead. Oh my God. How can I warn people I don't even know?"

Aidan knew how. "It's time we took the offensive. Tomorrow I'll call Lynne Pope at *Chicago On The Town*. We owe her a favor and I'll give her an exclusive."

"You're gonna be a star, Ace," Murphy said, tongue in cheek.

Aidan gripped Tess's knee. "Are you okay with this? Everyone will know."

She looked so lost his heart nearly broke. "Nobody will want to talk to me," she murmured. "They'll hide when I walk down the street." Then her eyes lifted to Sylvia Arness's face and her lips firmed. "But they'll stay alive. Do you have Pope's card?"

Aidan pulled it from his wallet. "Tess, I'll talk to her."

"No, I will. I have a few things of my own to say to this asshole. I'm taking my life back. He thinks he's going to drive me into a closet, make me curl up like a baby and . . . snivel. Well, he's wrong. Johnson, I need to use your phone."

"I won't let you do this," Aidan said, blocking her path. "You'll make him so angry that he'll come after you."

She sucked in one cheek and stared up at him defiantly. "I have a hell of lot more protection than she did." She thumbed back at Sylvia's body. "I have all of you. She didn't have anybody. And neither will the next person. And goddammit, there better not *be* a next person. Let him come after me. We'll be ready."

Friday, March 17, 2:35 A.M.

Tess sat down on the edge of Aidan's bed. "It was nice of Lynne to meet us." She and her cameraman had filmed the entire segment while Aidan paced in the wings.

The look he threw over his shoulder was wry. "She'll get a decent share once this airs tomorrow." He pulled off his tie, tossed it on his dresser. "I'd say it was a win-win."

Tied in knots, she fought the urge to get up and pace as he undid each button of his shirt. "She said she'd air it on *Good Morning, Chicago* and *Chicago On The Town* with teasers at noon," she said, knowing she was babbling, unable to stop herself. He shrugged out of his shirt and her mouth went dry. Clothed, the man was lethally handsome. Bared . . .

"Yes, she did." He looked over at her carefully. "Tess, are you nervous?"

She closed her eyes, now embarrassed as well. "Yes."

He sat next to her and pulled her against his side. "Why?"

"I just called a killer a 'spineless coward' and challenged him to come after me."

He chuckled, once. "*Now* you think about that?" He kissed the top of her head. "You did what you needed to do, Tess. I don't like it, either, but something's got to give."

The whirlwind inside her began to change, slowing to something harder and deeper. "I don't want to go to any more funerals, Aidan."

"I know. We'll find him soon, and all this will be over."

She lifted her head, met his eyes. "And then what?"

He didn't pretend to misunderstand. "I don't know. What do you want, Tess?"

She considered her answer as carefully as he'd asked the question. Her response could set the pace for their entire relationship—because they did have a relationship. Born in fear, it didn't have to continue that way. Maybe that was why she was so nervous. "I want a home and somebody to love me."

"You want a husband."

There was a kind of wistfulness to his words that made her throat hurt. "Yeah." She drew a breath. "And if that scares you away, it would be better to know that now."

"It doesn't scare me, Tess, at least not the way you mean."

"Then how? Talk to me, Aidan."

He grimaced. "I'm trying to. I guess I'm not doing a good job of it."

She touched her lips to his lightly. "Would it help if you lay down on the couch?" Splaying her hand against his hairy chest, she gently pushed him to his back so that he lay half on the bed, his bare feet still solidly on the floor. She came down on her side next to him, propping herself on her elbow. "Relax."

He looked at her from the corner of his eyes, wary. "Okay."

"You're not relaxed." Slowly she fanned her hand across his chest, enjoying the way the coarse hair tickled her palm.

"That's not making me more relaxed, Tess," he said dryly.

Her hand stopped. "Sorry. Who was Shelley, Aidan? And how did she hurt you?"

His eyes slid closed. "For a while, she was my best friend. Or I thought she was."

"Hurts inflicted by a friend can be twice as hard to heal."

"When I was a kid, my best friend was Jason Rich." He paused and his thumb began to stroke the back of her hand. "Me and Jason, we were tight. And trouble." His lips quirked. "Did you know that green army men melt in a saucepan on a high flame?"

"No, but I did play with Vito's G.I. Joe. Joe had the hots for my Malibu Barbie. I think I would have been mad that you ruined my saucepan."

"My mother was." He was quiet, thinking. "When we were ten, Shelley moved in next door. Her mom was divorced and that was a big hairy deal in our neighborhood."

"Mine, too. So did Shelley join the army soldier melt-down mission?"

"No. See, Shelley had eyes for Jason and I was a third wheel."

"Kind of like I feel when I'm at Jon and Robin's," she said lightly.

One blue eye opened. "You could have told me about Robin."

"You didn't ask." She sobered. "And it's never been important to me. They're my friends. Did Jason and Shelley stay your friends?"

"Sure, but everything changed when we hit puberty. Jason and Shelley were inseparable. Shelley got pregnant when we were seventeen. She and Jason eloped."

"Oh, dear," Tess murmured.

"Shelley's mom was married again by then and moderately comfortable. She moved and gave the old house to Shelley and Jason." He sighed. "Then Shelley lost the baby. But she didn't want to be divorced like her mom had been and she did love Jason, so they stayed together. I decided to be a cop like my dad and brother. So Jason did, too. I went on patrol. Jason went to Narcotics." He shook his head. "He got caught 'appropriating' evidence for personal use. He got fired. Shelley was distraught. Jason was . . ." He pursed his lips. "Suicidal."

Her heart was pounding harder. "Oh, no."

"But he was thoughtful, my pal Jason. He didn't want Shelley to find him dead. So he came to my apartment instead." His throat worked as he swallowed hard. "He took a lot of pills. Washed them down with a fifth of Jack Daniel's. And went to sleep. I came home from my shift twelve hours later and he was dead."

"How cruel of him." Her voice was harder than she'd intended it to be.

He opened his eyes. "I thought you had sympathy for suicides."

"I have pity for the emotional trauma or mental illness that drives people to suicide. I have sympathy for the ones they leave behind. I have respect for the ones who get help. Jason had a life and wasted it. And he took you down with him. That's despicable."

His eyes flickered. "I always felt the same way and wondered if I should."

"I would if somebody I cared about took their own life. Unless of course they were too mentally ill to stop themselves. Was he?"

"I don't know. I guess I never will. But Shelley was devastated. She had no income, no life insurance. No pension. No education. No one to lean on."

"Except you."

"Except me. We got close. I'd always had a thing for her when we were kids, but she was always Jason's girl. Now she was mine. I was happy."

"And guilty because you were happy at your friend's expense?"

"A little. Yeah. Anyway, I asked Shelley to marry me and she said yes. I'd saved some and bought her a reasonably sized ring."

"Did she like the ring?"

"Said she did. But she didn't show it off to our friends. Once she hinted at a bigger rock and I refused. I couldn't afford it and that was that. But her mother's new husband made a fortune when his business went IPO. Her mother bought Shelley a bigger ring."

"Oh dear."

"Yeah. It was the first big fight we had. It wasn't the last. Stepdad was dripping in cash and generous with it. Shelley got new dresses, furs. Then she said she wanted a house in North Shore." His jaw tightened. "Daddy was going to help."

A blow to his pride. "And you said no."

"Damn straight I said no. Asshole looked down at me every chance he got."

That explained a great deal. "So what was the straw that broke the camel's back?"

"Daddy offered me a job." The sneer hardened his voice. "I wouldn't take it and Shelley pouted. Said I could make three times a cop's salary. Cop's salary," he spat it out. "She said it just like that. Like it was something to be ashamed of."

Tess tried never to judge the motives of patients' families that she'd never met. But this man wasn't a patient. He was her lover, and he was hurting. "She didn't love you if she would have changed you. And she didn't know you if she thought she could have."

His chest expanded as he drew a slow deep breath. "Thank you."

She wriggled her fingers until they twined with his. "And?"

"That's all."

No, it wasn't. But it was clear that was all he planned to say. "Okay."

He opened one eye. "Okay? That's all?"

She gave him a wry smile. "You want me to pout? Not my style." She snuggled her head on his shoulder. "There is one thing I would like to get out in the open, though."

He stiffened. "What?"

"Harold Green."

Abruptly he sat up, leaving her lying on her side staring at his broad back. "No."

Tess flinched. "Why not?"

"Because . . ." He stood up and walked to the window. "Because I don't want to talk about him. It was an accident, nothing more. End of conversation."

"That's what you told your father last night."

"Tess, let it go. Please."

"I can't. If you won't talk, will you listen?"

"Can I stop you?" he asked curtly.

She tried not to be hurt. "Yes. Just tell me no and I'll go to sleep."

"I did tell you no and we're still talking about it." His voice was like ice.

"Fair enough." And she tried to keep her voice even. "It's late, Aidan. Let's go to sleep." With a helpless backward glance, she went into the bathroom and shut the door.

Chapter Twenty

∽

Friday, March 17, 2:55 A.M.

Tess emerged from the bathroom wearing one of Aidan's shirts, startled to find he hadn't moved. "Is someone out there?" she asked and he shook his head.

"No. Dolly would let us know if there were."

"Come to bed, Aidan. I promise I'll let you sleep." She slid between the sheets and flipped off the light, leaving them in semidarkness. His profile was stark, his fists on his hips as he studied something outside only he could see.

"I found her," he said suddenly, roughly. "The third little girl."

Tess sat up. The third little girl Harold Green had so viciously killed. "I know. Murphy told me the first night. I'm sorry."

"She was eviscerated. Did you know that?"

She swallowed. "Yes." It had been horrific. The pictures of all three children brutalized so senselessly seemed to mock the decency of anyone who looked at them. But looking was necessary to treat the man who'd inflicted such hideous wounds.

"We thought she was still alive," he said. "Green said she was still alive."

"In Harold Green's mind, she was."

"Bullshit," he hissed. "Harold Green was a stinking murderer."

It was better to face it head on. "And I let him go?"

He said nothing, which was everything, of course. She tried not to feel hurt, but it was hard. So she fell back into the familiar and talked to him as she would a patient, never forgetting she sat on his bed wearing one of his button-up shirts and nothing else. "Aidan, what did you do when you found her? The third little girl?"

His throat worked. "I dropped to my knees and sobbed like a damn baby."

"I'm sure you weren't the only one," she murmured.

"She was only six years old." He choked on the words. "Goddammit to hell. I didn't want to remember her, but that night, seeing that woman all open like that . . ."

Cynthia Adams. A suicide, covered by a man on whom suicide had left a personal scar. And still he'd cared enough to try to find Cynthia's killer. "And I let him go," she said again and he shuddered in a breath.

"It was a mistake," he said, a little too desperately. "You've made the right calls on so many others. You're entitled to one mistake."

She understood where he was coming from, but was unsure how to show him he was wrong. "Did you ever see the movie *The Sixth Sense*?" she asked suddenly and his head whipped around, his eyes wet. Appalled.

"You're talking about a *movie*?"

She nodded, her voice calm despite the tension coiling in

her gut. "Yes. Did you? It's the one where the little boy sees ghosts all around him."

"I've seen it," he bit out. "Four stars."

"The scariest part was that he saw ghosts in the day when it's supposed to be safe."

"Is this going somewhere, Doctor?" he asked acidly.

"Yes. Harold Green didn't see ghosts, Aidan. He saw demons, and not just at night in his dreams. They were everywhere, watching him all day, every day and every night, wherever he went, waiting to pounce and eat him. They had fangs that dripped blood. It turned out the demons were precious children. But he couldn't see the difference."

"Of course he said that," he spat. "He'd say anything to keep from going to prison."

"There are all kinds of prisons, Aidan. Have you been to a psychiatric hospital?"

"No."

"When this is over, I'd like you to come with me to one. Green is constantly sedated so that he can't hurt the staff. He is in a fog where only strong meds keep the demons at bay, and still he sees them. He screams and thrashes and they have to restrain him to the bed for his own safety. He cries and rants, because he's so damn terrified. His entire existence comes down to what he sees and can't change. He's all alone."

"His rich parents don't go to visit him?" Aidan asked bitterly.

How could I have missed that? "Money means power, but in Harold Green's case, it means little. His mother comes to visit sometimes, but the visits have become rarer over time. She keeps hoping he'll improve, that he'll go back to being the man she knew. The son she loved. That despite everything, she still loves. But the days go by and he's trapped in that prison in his mind, afraid and alone." She drew a breath and slowly let it out. "Sometimes . . ." She shook her head, her eyes filling with hot tears.

He stood rigid, then slowly turned so that he finally looked at her and not the window. "Sometimes what, Tess?" he asked quietly.

She was ashamed of what she was about to say, but needed him to understand. "Sometimes when I see him, so afraid and tortured, I think it would be better if he just died. And sometimes . . ." She looked away. "Sometimes I think about being the one to do it. And I'm never certain if it would be because I'm being merciful or vengeful.

"I held his fate in my hands in that courtroom, Aidan, and I spared him, because he wasn't competent to stand trial and the law says he can't be convicted of his crimes. But I saw what he did, and *dammit*—" Her voice broke and she resolutely steadied it. "I saw the eyes of the mothers of the children. And the wife of the cop he strangled. And I hated Harold Green. But I did what I needed to do." She closed her eyes, sending the tears down her cheeks. "And given the same circumstances, I'd do it again."

Aidan stood there, her tears wrenching at his heart. She was a woman who did the right thing when it was the hardest thing. Once he'd thought her cold, but now he knew that she cared too much and only her iron will hid that from others, allowing her to do her job. That he could understand, having to do one's job when it ripped at the heart. They had a great deal more in common than he'd originally believed. And somewhere deep in his bruised heart, something bloomed. For now, he'd let it be simple respect.

"I'm sorry. I didn't understand." He sat next to her. "Don't cry anymore, please."

She gritted her teeth on a sob. "I can't stop seeing that woman's face in my mind— Sylvia Arness. She should be going to parties and going to classes, but she's dead."

He wiped her wet cheeks with his thumb. "Because some sick bastard knows this is the best way to you. We won't let him win, Tess." The sob broke loose and he pulled her into his arms, rubbing his hands on her back, kissing her as her weeping grew more intense, until the only way he knew to stop it was with his mouth.

He pulled her face from his chest and covered her mouth with his, hard and insistent. For a few seconds she struggled, then surged to her knees, returning the kiss with a desperate, bruising force, her hands on his chest, her fingers threading through his hair there. Her fingertips teased his nipples, yanking a growl from his throat.

He lunged from the bed, jerking her to her feet, working the buttons of the shirt she wore, swearing when they wouldn't budge from their holes, finally ripping until buttons flew and her breasts were filling his hands. Her hands were busy at his waist and suddenly his pants were around his ankles and he kicked them away. She shoved his shorts down next, leaving him naked, while his shirt was still draped over her shoulders. He started to push it away, but stopped, startled when she switched on the light.

Her hair was tousled from his hands, her lips swollen from his mouth and her cheeks streaked from her tears. But her eyes burned and he trembled where he stood.

"I didn't get to see you last night," she said. "I want to see you." She pushed him to the bed and straddled his waist, leaning over him to press his hands to the pillow beside his head when he reached for her. "No," she whispered. "Tonight it's mine. Let me."

The air trapped in his lungs, he nodded, understanding that this was about control. Her life had been slowly taken apart, piece by piece, pounded to rubble. This was hers.

She slid down his chest, her mouth busily kissing its way south and his hips arched in reflexive response. She stopped, her lips a breath away from his twitching cock and he groaned her name. "Tess."

"Sshh. Let me." Her fingertips traced the length of him, making him flinch. "Let me." Then her tongue followed the path her fingers had taken and he groaned again.

"Please." He arched helplessly. Begging her. "Please."

But nothing happened and he finally lifted on his elbows to look down at her. She was examining him intently, her expression curiously analytical. Turning only her head, she met his eyes, her mouth unsmiling. "I've never done this before."

His body froze. *Don't stop. Please don't change your mind,* he thought frantically.

She licked her lips. "Tell me if I do something you don't like."

Thank you, God, he thought, then he couldn't think at all because her mouth closed over him, hot and wet and so damn good. He closed his eyes and let himself feel. Let himself be drawn away from the ugliness of reality to all that mattered—this woman and the unspeakable pleasure that had him catching his breath, arching his hips higher, harder. He clasped his hands around her head and showed her how he liked it then let them drop with a groan as she picked up the rhythm without losing a beat.

His groan set her body on fire. She'd brought him pleasure and spiked her own. Shivers and tingles raced across her skin and the hot throbbing between her legs was unbearable. She wanted, no, *needed* like she'd never needed before. It had never been like this, never this frantic race to completion, never this craving to be filled. Sex had always been something she just did. Enjoyable, but not necessary.

Being with this man was necessary. Making him groan was more imperative than taking her next breath so she changed her angle, increased the pressure of her mouth, and gently cupped him in the palm of her hand.

With a strangled cry his magnificent body arched and froze, leaving him supported by only his heels and the back of his head. Pleased, feeling powerful and utterly female, she released him and pushed him back to the mattress. Straddling him, she dropped kisses up his body. His hands gripped her rear, kneading convulsively.

His eyes opened and stole her breath. "Let me have you now." Not waiting for her answer he rolled them and in one hard stroke was inside her, filling her to bursting. Her cry mixed with his groan and he held her eyes as he held his body rigidly still. "I didn't want to want you," he said hoarsely, his thrusts punctuating every other word. "I didn't want to care about you. But I do. Understand that."

"I understand." She arched, murmuring wordless sounds of pleasure as he kissed her throat. Then he opened his mouth over her scar, sucking hard, and she understood he sought to leave his own mark over the one she despised. Her pounding heart squeezed painfully. "Aidan."

The pleasure became intense, too intense. Sensation began to coil, her muscles contracting around him and his thrusts became harder, faster, the coil inside her tighter and tighter, her grip on his hands tighter and tighter and she was afraid. Afraid that she'd never get there and terrified of what would happen if she did.

"Let it happen," he breathed in her ear as if he'd read her very thoughts. "Let go. Let me see you. Feel you. Please, Tess."

"Aidan." It was a whimper, a plea, then finally, finally exultation as the coil suddenly sprang free, sending fire through her body. She jerked against him and moaned, dimly aware that he'd found his own release, his body going stiff, his head thrown back in a wracking ecstasy that was utterly silent.

His weight dropped onto her, their hands still joined.

Their bodies still joined. Her chest hurt. Her throat hurt. She felt more incredible than she'd ever felt in her life. "Oh."

His chest heaved once. It might have been a laugh.

They lay like that for what seemed like forever until he released her hands, pushed himself on his elbows and looked down at her, his face sober. "I didn't mean for this to happen like this tonight."

She blinked. "What?"

"I didn't mean to go so hard, so fast. I'd planned to seduce you slowly, but after what you did . . . There was no way."

She smiled, kissed his stubbled chin. "I guess I was being uncooperative again."

He didn't smile back. "Why did you do it?"

"You mean . . . ? You know." She couldn't finish, her cheeks heating, her eyes skittering away. "You must think I'm silly, not to be able to say it."

"I think it was the most incredible thing ever I've felt," he said quietly.

She tried not to beam. "Really?"

His mouth turned up in an indulgent smile. "Really. So why, Tess? Why with me?"

"I never wanted to before," she answered truthfully. "Then with you, last night . . ." She sighed. "I'm not going to be coy. I know I'm attractive. I know men look at me. But Phillip gave my confidence a beating. You made me feel beautiful. Desirable. I wanted you to feel the same way." She shrugged, awkward. "You can't understand."

He looked down at her, his gaze intense in the low light of his bedside lamp. "You don't know what I understand, Tess." With that he reached up and snapped off the light and drew the blankets over them. In the darkness he rolled them so that her cheek was pressed against his chest, his arms around her, the solid beat of his heart in her ear.

Her breathing became slow and deep and she was almost

asleep when he spoke again, his voice vibrating against her cheek. "After that day . . . when I found the third girl . . . I came home and Shelley pounced. I was so devastated and she used that to try to talk me into leaving the force."

She brushed the coarse hair on his chest with her fingertips, glad the woman wasn't here. She'd slap her face. "That was selfish."

His laugh was harsh. "At the end I had no idea what I'd seen in her at the beginning. All I know is that I was so hollowed out . . . so angry . . . I wanted to strike her. I had my hand in the air and—I stopped myself midswing. Then I gave her an ultimatum. Ask me about working for her stepfather again and I'd leave. And I meant it."

He was quiet a long time. Finally she asked, "Did you? Leave?"

"Not then. She got better for a little while and I honestly thought we could make it work out. I didn't leave until the day you testified in court. At Green's trial. I was so furious with you . . . I'd taken the day off to go to court. After all of the cops got up and walked out of the courtroom to protest you, I went home. I needed someone that day and Shelley should have been the one."

A sense of foreboding crept into her heart. "And?"

"And I walked in on her and another man. In our bed."

She drew a breath and said the only thing that came to mind. The same thing he'd said to her the night before. "How tacky."

His chuckle was grim. "Touché. She saw me standing there. He was . . . busy. To this day I don't think he knew I was there. But she sure as hell did. She just looked at me over his shoulder. Raised her eyebrows. And that was all. I walked away and never went back. Kristen went back for my clothes when she wasn't home. I'd brought her to see this place because I wanted to buy it, but she'd turned her nose up at it. So two weeks later I bought this house, threw down some roots. She threw down her own. She'll marry him in a few weeks. He works for Daddy and she got her house on the North Shore." He sighed. "So now you know it all."

"Thank you for trusting me."

His grin flashed. "Thank you for . . . you know. It was damn good for a beginner."

Her eyes widened. "You said it was the best you'd ever had."

"I wasn't lying. It just seems that being your first try, there's nowhere to go but up."

Her lips twitched. "Or down, as it were. Go to sleep, Aidan. It will be morning soon."

Friday, March 17, 7:30 A.M.

"That bitch." Joanna stood in front of the television, her mouth open, her fists on her hips. Tess Ciccotelli filled the screen, her face by turns nervous, sad, and artfully sincere. Then the camera panned back. "She's talking to Lynne Pope."

Keith looked up from his morning paper with a frown. "Jo, stop this now. She's not going to give you your story. Get over it and move on."

She glared at him over her shoulder. "Thank you, Mr. Supportive."

"Grow up, Jo." He folded his paper. "I got a call yesterday afternoon from a bank in Atlanta. They want me to start working for them first of next month. It's a huge opportunity. Jo, I want to go home. I thought if you had a reason to go it would change your mind."

"You have a reason to go," she said angrily. "It's your career. Your life."

"Which I thought was yours, too," he said quietly. "I haven't given them an answer yet. I'm going to get dressed for work now. We can talk about it tonight."

She watched him go, furious. She didn't want to talk about it. She was staying and getting that damn byline if it was the last damn thing she did. She turned toward the kitchen when a photo on the TV screen caught her eye.

"Sylvia Arness was shot point-blank with a high-caliber weapon. Police are currently investigating. Witnesses say they heard the gunshot and found the body. Pinned to the woman's coat was a note reading 'Be judged by the company you keep.' Police refuse to comment on the meaning of the message. We'll keep you informed . . ."

Slowly Joanna sat down at her computer and clicked until she brought up the photos she'd taken of Ciccotelli Wednesday afternoon. There was the wineshop, the sweater store, the florist, the shoe store . . . *Here it is.* The dead woman in a single frame with Ciccotelli. They'd barely spoken for a moment. And now the woman was dead. A chill ran down her spine. *My God.* Her stomach clenching, she paged back until she came to the wineshop, another thought connecting. She compared the grainy photo on page four of today's *Bulletin* with her own photo. "Marge Hooper, fifty-three, a victim of a robbery at her wineshop," the *Bulletin*'s caption read. It was the same woman.

She paged through the rest of her photos, her lungs holding the same breath. The doorman was in her pictures, too. *Three dead.* All pictures she had taken. She thought back to the missing photo paper. Someone had been in her files. Her blood went cold.

Call the police, Jo. Now. She realized her hand was trembling as she reached for the phone and jumped like she'd been shot herself when it suddenly rang. "Hello?"

"Miss Carmichael? My name is Dr. Kelsey Chin from the

Women's Clinic in Lexington, Kentucky. I understand you called yesterday."

Her hands still shaking, Joanna skimmed her notepad until she found the name that had come up as part of what she now termed her "flypaper research." "Dr. Chin. Thank you for returning my call. I'm researching a story and I'm hoping you can help."

Friday, March 17, 7:30 A.M.

Aidan had dropped Tess off at her parents' hotel room door twenty minutes before—just in time to see her interview with Lynne Pope. Her father sat very still when Pope's piece ended. Her mother sat next to him, holding his hand. Vito paced. Tess sighed.

"They aren't lying when they say the camera adds ten pounds," she said lightly and cringed when three pairs of furious eyes turned on her.

"Are you sure that was wise, Tess?" her mother asked. "Baiting him like that?"

"Of course it wasn't wise," Vito exploded. "Where the hell was Reagan when this interview was taking place?"

"Pacing, just like you're doing now. Last night they found another body. Vito, do you remember the young girl that flirted with you in the shoe store?"

Vito's face drained of color. "She's dead? That was what last night was about? You didn't even know her. He's killing perfect strangers now?"

Tess nodded. "I have to make sure nobody else is caught unaware. I thought that Lynne Pope did a sensitive job with the interview."

Her father stood, his skin gray. "Who have you made so

angry that they'd do this? My God. They killed a perfect stranger."

Tess bit back the annoyance at his choice of words. "I don't know, Dad. The police have thoroughly checked patients who I evaluated for the court."

"Have you given them a list of patients from your practice?"

"They have the list, yes. Honestly, I doubt any of my patients could conceive of such a convoluted scheme, or be organized enough to carry it out if they did. This is a personality type I'm not sure I've ever seen before. Dad, lie down. You look terrible."

He sat on the bed. "I don't feel well," he admitted. "Gina, can you get my pills?"

Tess gently pushed him to his back, lifting his feet to the bed. "Rest. I'm being careful, Dad. I promise." She and Vito went into Vito's adjoining room and she let her shoulders sag. "He needs to be home."

"He won't go until you do," Vito muttered. "Tess, please just come home. At least until this is over. At home, on my turf I can protect you."

Tess shook her head. "You still don't get it, Vito. This is all about me. If I went to Philly, so would he. Then we'd just be moving the problem to a different city. Aidan and Murphy have some leads. I trust them." She rubbed his arm. "Don't you?"

He sank into a chair. "I feel so helpless. I've got to go back to work soon. They've been cool about the leave, but I've been gone three days now."

Tess laid her cheek on his head. "It has to end soon, Vito. Before anybody else dies." Within her pocket her cell rang and dread chilled. "I don't want to answer that."

"It might be Reagan. Answer it."

Tess pulled the phone from her pocket. It was Amy. "Hey."

"Tess? It's Amy. Where are you?"

The chill became ice at the tone of Amy's voice. "With Vito at the hotel. Why?"

"It's the *Eye*. They're accusing you of doing the videos voluntarily." Amy hesitated. "You're on the front page, Tess."

Denise. Goddamn her to hell. "Denise sold the story," she bit out. "I swear to God I want to . . ." She drew a breath. "How bad is it?"

"Bad. Real bad. They . . . They have a picture on page two. It's the one that came on the blackmail note, Tess. I'm sorry."

Bile rose to choke her and blindly Tess handed the phone to Vito and sank onto the bed, her eyes unfocused on her hands. She heard Vito demand an explanation, heard his hissed curse. Then he was kneeling before her, clasping her hands in his.

"What can I do?" he asked, his voice low and miserable.

Tess sat for a long moment considering her response. "I could ask you to kill the bitch. But that would be illegal." She made a decision, and once made, stood up resolutely. "You can drive me to the courthouse. There's a lawyer I want to see."

Friday, March 17, 7:30 A.M.

So, she's gone on the offensive. I didn't think she'd have the nerve. Every eye in the coffee shop was fixed on the broadcast and sympathy for Ciccotelli ran high. But every person murmured that if they saw her they'd cross to the other side of the street. It would be harder to take out even strangers now. Perhaps the cat-and-mouse had played itself out. The remaining loose end had been effectively snipped.

It was time for the coup de grâce. And then . . . ultimate satisfaction.

The waitress walked over with a full pot of coffee. "Refill?"

"Please. And then the check. . . ."

Friday, March 17, 8:15 A.M.

Blaine Connell looked like he hadn't slept in days. His union rep was by his side at Spinnelli's conference room table, looking arrogant and confrontational. Spinnelli and Patrick stood to one side while Aidan and Murphy took the chairs at the table. The black suit from IA lurked in the corner, wary and watchful.

Murphy slid the photo of Connell accepting money from Lawe across the table and Connell stiffened. "We've been through this," the union rep inserted. "Officer Connell says he doesn't know that man. This photograph is a clear fabrication."

"We know his name is Destin Lawe," Murphy said levelly. "He's a PI. He's dead."

Aidan watched Connell's shoulders relax slightly. "He threatened you, Blaine?" Connell's eyes flickered. He had a family, Aidan knew. "Sandra or the boys?"

Again the flicker, stronger this time and Aidan sighed. "Blaine, you were a good cop. You can still be a good man. Ten people are dead. If Lawe was threatening your family, he can't hurt them anymore. Help us, Blaine. Tell us where you met him. We've got to find a connection between Lawe and this killer or more people will die."

Connell whispered in the union rep's ear. "He wants immunity," the rep said.

Patrick frowned. "It depends on what he's done. I can't give blanket immunity."

The union rep stood up. "Then we're done here. Come on, Blaine."

Aidan began to line up the pictures of the dead. "Arness. Hooper. Hughes. Malcolm and Gwen Seward. Winslow. Adams." Connell flinched, but sat, his lips firm.

The union rep tugged on his shoulder. "Let's go, Blaine."

Aidan kept going. "They were the innocents. Look at the accomplices. Our boy doesn't like loose ends. David Bacon. Nicole Rivera. Destin Lawe." Connell blanched at Lawe's charred corpse. "None of them came to us. To our knowledge they remained faithful till the bitter end. Do you think you're exempt? If you thought Lawe was the biggest threat to your wife and kids, think again. You are a loose end, Blaine."

"Let's go, Blaine."

Connell pulled away. "He came to me. Said he needed a favor, a few crime scene photos. Said it would bring down the shrink that set Preston's killer free."

"Dr. Ciccotelli," Murphy said and Connell jerked a bitter nod.

"She's the one. Bitch has ice in her veins."

Aidan remembered her anguish the night before, her wrenching sobs. He should feel anger on her behalf. But instead he just felt sad. "No, she doesn't," he said.

Connell's lips thinned. "You're sleeping with her, Reagan, so you're hardly an authority on the subject. She'd better be a ten on technique, because that's what you traded your reputation for." He sneered. "The *Eye* had a teaser shot at the top of page two. I guess we can all see what's flushed your conscience down the fucking toilet."

Now Aidan's temper boiled. Feeling Murphy tense beside him, Aidan stared at the table, then when he was calm again, he looked back up at Connell. "How did Lawe contact you?"

Connell looked away. "He caught me coming out of the courthouse, then later he called from a pay phone to set up the drop. Down by the warehouses on the lake."

"Do you remember the days?" Murphy asked.

"December fourteenth outside the courthouse. The seventeenth for the drop."

"You sound certain of those dates," Murphy said. "Why?"

Connell looked away. "I just remember them, that's all."

Aidan stood up. "Maybe because that's the day you flushed your conscience down the fucking toilet," he said tightly. Murphy rose and touched his shoulder.

"It's not worth it, Aidan," Murphy murmured and Aidan drew a breath.

"I know." He said nothing more until the four of them had reached his and Murphy's desks and Aidan sank in his chair. "I wanted to smash that sneer off his damn face."

"But you didn't," Spinnelli said. "Good job."

"What will you do next?" Patrick asked.

"Follow up on those dates," Murphy answered. "See if anything pops."

"And we'll pay a visit to Tess's ex-fiancé, Dr. Phillip Parks." Aidan checked his watch. "He should be getting into his office in the next half hour."

"What will you do with Connell?" Spinnelli asked.

Patrick looked troubled. "It's evidence tampering. I'm going to push for his termination. No pension. Beyond that, I'll let you know." He went back into the conference room where Connell, his union rep and IA waited.

"I saw Tess's segment on *Good Morning, Chicago*," Spinnelli said. "She looked confident and sympathetic. Hopefully when this is over Pope will bring her back on. Then the public won't cross the street every time she passes. Don't worry about the tabloid, Aidan. These things blow over in a matter of days."

Spinnelli closed himself in his office and Murphy sat down at his desk. "He's right about the *Eye*, Aidan. It seems bad now, but it will blow over."

Aidan's teeth clenched. "Did you see it?"

Murphy hesitated. "Yeah. The picture is cropped so it doesn't really show anything, but the story is packed with innuendo. I would have told you but I thought you'd seen it."

Aidan shook his head. "I don't want to. I guess that makes me a coward."

"It makes you human, Aidan. So how's Rachel this morning?"

"Staying home from school today."

Murphy winced. "Stitches sore?"

Aidan chuckled, thinking about her desperate phone call at 6:00 A.M. "Actually it was her hair. All that bravado about it being 'just hair' kind of disappeared when she woke up and looked in the mirror. Tess is supposed to take her to that hairdresser friend of hers this afternoon so by tonight she'll be chic and sassy again."

He dropped his eyes to the records that one of the clerks had left on his desk, determined not to let the *Eye* derail his focus. Lawe was listed as president of Brewer, Inc., his apartment rented in the corporation's name, as were his utilities, his car, even his credit cards. He had three different banks in town. Probably had money offshore as well. All three local banks showed safe-deposit boxes, which they'd check after visiting Dr. Damn-him-to-hell. He'd wondered if he'd be able to hold his temper with Dr. Damn, but his confrontation with Blaine Connell left no doubt. If he could refrain from punching Connell's lights out after that crack about Tess, he could handle anything.

Aidan frowned to himself. So the *Eye* had a picture of her. It had to have come from Masterson. And that *was* illegal. He'd make sure little Denise did some time. He hadn't known about the picture until it slithered out of Connell's mouth. Aidan wondered if Tess had seen it. If she was all right. She'd been frank with Lynne Pope the night before, stating on camera that she had been photographed against her knowledge. So the *Eye*'s little bomb had either considerably less sizzle for being scooped, or would have record sales because of the publicity.

Either way, she was strong enough to deal with this. *So I will be, too.*

"So, is she?" Murphy asked out of the blue and Aidan looked up. Murphy's eyes were fixed assiduously on his own desk, his pen scratching on his notepad.

"Is who what?"

"Tess. A ten."

Aidan blinked, then a slow grin spread up his face. "She's not even on the chart."

"That's kind of what I thought."

Murphy's rueful acceptance had him chuckling. "So, Murphy, are you ready to visit Dr. Damn-him-to-hell?"

"What the hell? Let's go."

Chapter Twenty-one

∼

Friday, March 17, 9:30 A.M.

Kristen's smile lit up her face when Tess peeked in her office. "Come in. Sit."

"I won't stay long." Tess's smile was wry. "*You* still have a career."

Kristen's smile dimmed. "You will, too, when this is all over."

"Maybe not. Have you seen this?" She held out the *Eye* and watched as Kristen's eyes narrowed and her cheeks grew red.

"Son of a bitch," she bit out. "Where did they get this?"

"From my secretary." Tess looked up at the ceiling. "I'm having a hard time with my professional confidence right now. This woman despised me and I never saw it."

"I do know how you feel. I ate dinner every night with a killer and never knew. Sometimes people only let you see the face they want you to see. Even psychiatrists."

"All I know is that I'm damned tired of being worried, which is why I'm here. Last night I started taking my life back with that interview." And with what went on afterward. Just thinking about how Aidan responded in bed made her heart race. Thinking about how he'd respond to the picture in the *Eye* was making her ill. "I'm pressing charges against my secretary and the newspaper. I need you to recommend a lawyer."

"Good for you, Tess. But why not Amy Miller? You've been friends for a long time."

"That's why. When I thought I needed her for criminal defense we had a big argument because we didn't agree on my cooperation with the police. I hurt her and she hurt me and I don't want to risk that friendship. Oh, and the attorney will need to defend me in civil court, too. I'm being sued by my former clients. Pain and suffering."

Kristen grimaced. "Is there any silver in that cloud?"

"You're asking about Aidan."

She grinned. "And trying to be discreet about it. Well?"

"We'll see. I don't know what he'll say about that." She pointed to the paper.

"He's a good guy, Tess. He's more . . . volatile than Abe, but deep down, they come from solid stock. You made quite an impression on their dad, by the way. Kyle's telling everybody that you're the best girl street fighter he's ever seen."

Tess rolled her eyes. "Wonderful. What an endorsement."

"From Kyle Reagan, it is. It's respect, and for the Reagans, that's everything."

"I hope it's enough. I'm tired. I haven't gotten any sleep the past few nights."

Kristen's grin grew. "Oh, yeah?"

Tess's cheeks heated. "I'm leaving now and going home to take a nap."

"Go back to Aidan's and sleep. Things will be better when you wake up."

Friday, March 17, 10:15 A.M.

"Well, this doesn't look good," Murphy said as Aidan stopped the car next to Parks's apartment building. Three squad cars and an ambulance were parked on the curb.

"I'm thinking three strikes, you're out this time, partner. I think we're too late again."

"I'm thinking you might be right," Murphy agreed grimly. "Always a bridesmaid . . ."

Parks's door on the sixth floor was easy to find—it was the one with uniforms standing guard outside. Inside were two detectives from their unit, Howard and Brooks, and ME Johnson. Kneeling on the floor, Johnson looked up when they came in.

"I had a feeling you guys would be showing up soon."

Howard looked at them with surprise. "Who is he to you?"

"Tess Ciccotelli's ex-fiancé," Murphy told them. "We were coming to question him this morning. Damn. This is the third time we've arrived too late."

"This is getting old," Aidan muttered in agreement. "How and when?"

"Three bullets to the lower abdomen, a fourth in the head," Johnson said. "The ab shots were probably taken from a few feet away. The last one was right to his head, probably for insurance. Time was twelve fifty-six."

"And twelve seconds," Brooks added sourly.

"He wore a pocket watch," Howard explained. "Haven't seen one of those in years. Got hit by one of the bullets to his gut. Looks like he'd just come in the door. We've got building security pulling up the tapes as we speak. You guys want this case, or what?"

Murphy puffed his cheeks and blew out a breath. "We've got a full plate right now."

Jack came in looking disgruntled. "I was planning to take the day off, guys."

Aidan looked at Dr. Damn-him-to-hell lying sprawled on his back, the carpet soaked with his blood. "I hate to tell Tess about this. Parks was scum, but . . ." He narrowed his eyes. "Murphy, I asked Carter about Parks last night. Five hours later, he's dead."

"Carter?" Murphy looked skeptical. "He's Tess's friend."

"With a key to her apartment and his own surgical tools."

"The cuts on Bacon's arms." Murphy scowled. "And knowledge of meds. All right, we'll take this case off your hands, boys. Shit."

"Detectives?" A middle-aged man poked his head in the door. "I've pulled the security discs for last night. Lobby and first- and sixth-floor elevator cameras."

Aidan stopped at the door. "You coming, Jack?"

Jack stood in the middle of the room frowning. "No, I'm going to go over this room with tweezers. He had to have left something behind."

The manager led them to his control room. "This is video of the sixth-floor elevator. I cued it to ten minutes after Parks was shot." He hit a button and Aidan caught his breath.

"Damn." A figure in a tan coat and a black wig stepped into the elevator, keeping her face carefully averted. "That can't be Tess."

"Of course it can't," Murphy said. "But just for kicks, tell me why."

"Number one, she's got claustrophobia. She would never have taken the elevator, she'd have taken the stairs. Number two, she was with me." Brooks and Howard exchanged a glance. "With me, Lynne Pope, and her cameraman," he added darkly. "She was in the middle of that damn interview at one this morning."

"That's a pretty tight alibi," Howard agreed.

"Looks like somebody got a two-for-one discount at Coat-n-Wigs 'R' Us," Murphy murmured. "Let's take a look at the lobby video."

The security manager hit a few more buttons. "Same time frame."

Murphy stepped closer. "Can you freeze the frame? Aidan, look at the shoes."

Aidan squinted. "Wingtips. Looks the same size we saw in Bacon's bathroom."

"Shoulders look a little wide, too," Brooks offered. "Look at the way the coat stretches at the back. Could be a guy in women's clothes."

"Carter is too tall," Murphy said, then lifted a brow. "But his boy Robin isn't. Archer's about, what, Aidan? Five eight?"

Aidan's pulse started to race. "Let's go."

Friday, March 17, 10:30 A.M.

Tess dropped her purse on Aidan's kitchen table. "Vito, you don't have to stay with me. Dolly is here and Aidan left his gun."

Vito scowled. "Like that's supposed to make me go? Think again, Tess."

"Suit yourself. I'm going to sleep for a little while before I take Rachel to get her hair fixed this afternoon. What will you do?"

"Find a book to read. Reagan certainly has enough of them."

"He just finished his bachelor's degree. I don't know what in."

Vito's brows dipped a fraction of an inch. "Psychology."

Tess stopped in the doorway and turned to stare at him. "What?"

"His degree is in psychology. I thought you knew."

A different distress filled her. They had a common bond and he'd kept it hidden. "No, I didn't."

Vito sighed. "I imagine your having an MD after your name made him feel . . . odd, so he didn't tell you. Don't feel too bad, Tess. It's a guy thing."

"How do you know about his degree?"

"I asked him last night before he got that call. He told me and Dad and Amy while you and Mom finished making dinner." Vito was looking at her intently. "He's been taking classes for years, trying to figure out his niche. I got the impression something pushed him into psychology, although he's got at least four minors. You should ask."

His friend Jason's suicide guided his choice. But that was Aidan's private hurt, one he'd shared with her alone and she hoarded it away. "That explains all the books." She felt both proud of his accomplishments and deprived because he hadn't told her himself.

"You wish he'd told you himself," Vito observed. "I'm telling you he's a guy. There aren't many of us who can get past having his woman be higher on the food chain."

His woman. It left her with a warm feeling. "Do you think he can get past it?"

"Time will tell. What do you think?"

"I know what I want to think. I want to think he can and that he will." Inexplicably her eyes filled with tears. "I think I need to sleep."

Vito wrapped his arms around her. "Tess, things happen we can't explain. And every so often, a good thing comes from the bad. Maybe Reagan is your good thing."

"I hate that my picture's in the paper," she whispered. "I hate it for him and for me."

"I know. But you'll get through this. Now go sleep. It'll be better when you wake up."

Friday, March 17, 11:15 A.M.

"Detectives." Robin Archer opened the door of a tasteful three-story brownstone, the surprise on his face quickly becoming concern. "What's happened?"

"We need to talk to you and Dr. Carter," Aidan said, his voice flat. "Is he home?"

"Yes." Brows crunched, Robin let them in. "This way. Jon, the detectives are here."

Jon was standing when they entered the solarium, a video game controller dangling from one hand. He took one look at their faces and his color drained away. "Tess?"

"She's fine. She's with Vito," Aidan said. "Dr. Carter, I need to ask you some questions. Would you and Mr. Archer come downtown with us?"

Jon and Robin exchanged a look. "Can we not talk here?" Jon replied.

Aidan and Murphy had agreed not to press the issue if they said no. They weren't close to getting a warrant for their arrest. "You and I can talk here. Mr. Archer and my partner can go . . . where?"

"Come with me," Robin said quietly. "We'll go in the kitchen."

"What's this about, Reagan?" Jon asked sharply when they were alone.

"Where were you last night, Dr. Carter? After you left the viewing?"

Jon sat down. "We went out to dinner. Morton's."

Aidan lifted a brow. "Not the Blue Lemon?"

"Sometimes Robin likes to eat other people's food. We left the restaurant at about eleven thirty. I assume that was going to be your next question."

"It was. And then?"

"We went to the movie theater. *Umbrellas of Cherbourg*. It's French. Quite moving."

"I've seen it. Four stars. Kind of late to be going to the movies, isn't it?"

"One of the benefits of living in the city, Detective. Robin closes up the bistro around midnight every night and my hours are irregular. I'm sure there is someone at both the restaurant and the theater who can vouch for our movements."

Aidan's heart sank. So close. But he had no doubt that their alibi would be confirmed. "We'll be sure to check."

Jon nodded. "I've answered your questions. Will you tell me what this is about?"

"Phillip Parks is dead.'"

Shock had Jon's eyes widening. "Oh my God. When?"

"About midnight. We'd just talked about him a few hours before. I had to ask."

"I understand. Does Tess know?"

"Not yet. Dr. Carter, you don't have to let us do this, but

we'd appreciate being able to check your closet. Yours and Mr. Archer's."

"What are you looking for?" He shook his head. "You can't tell me. I understand."

Thirty minutes later Aidan and Murphy regrouped. Jon and Robin sat in the solarium, a uniformed officer standing at the door.

"Nothing," Aidan muttered. "Carter has nothing out of the ordinary in his closet."

"Archer wears loafers, not wingtips," Murphy said. "A half size bigger than the shoe from Bacon's bathroom."

"I called the theater. They're not open yet, but I found ticket stubs in Carter's pants pockets. They saw *Umbrellas.*" His cell phone rang. "Reagan."

"Aidan, it's Lori. You got a phone call from Africa a few minutes ago. A Dr. Trucco from Doctors Without Borders. He said you e-mailed him about a Jim Swanson."

He had the night before, after bringing Tess home from that interview. "What did he say?"

"That Dr. Swanson never came to Chad. Trucco said he received a letter from Swanson saying he'd changed his mind, that he was staying in Chicago."

"I see. Thanks, Lori. I appreciate it." He hung up and turned to Murphy. "Swanson never went to Africa."

"Did you ask Tess about him?"

"Didn't have a chance. Let's see if Carter knows more than he let on last night." They joined the two men in the solarium and sat down. "We're sorry we had to do this."

"We understand," Jon murmured.

"No, we don't," Robin protested. "Why did you come here? We haven't seen Parks since he and Tess broke up."

"Let's rewind a little, back to last night," Murphy said. "Dr. Carter, you told my partner that one of your group left the city to join Doctors Without Borders."

"Jim. Jim Swanson. He went to Chad."

Aidan shook his head. "No, he didn't."

Carter and Archer shared a puzzled glance. "Yes, he did," Robin insisted. "We got a postcard from him about six weeks after he left."

"I just heard from the clinic where he was supposed to report. He never did. The director received a letter from him saying he'd changed his mind."

Robin left the room, returning with a card. "My niece collects stamps, so I saved it."

Aidan turned it over. "It's a generic card from your hospital, Dr. Carter."

"He took a stack of them. He wasn't sure what kind of supplies he'd be able to get over there. But the stamp says 'Chad.' In French."

"Dr. Carter." Aidan waited until the man met his eyes. "I'm telling you that Swanson never arrived. If you know more about Swanson, this would be a good time to tell us."

"Tell them, Jon," Robin murmured. "They need to know."

Jon looked down, then back up with a sigh. "I honestly thought he was out of the country. Jim had a thing for Tess. Apparently he always did, but she was with Parks. When she threw Parks out, Jim was ecstatic. I guessed, but I don't think anyone else knew. He waited about six months, then made his move. Spilled his guts."

"And she said?" Aidan asked.

"She said that he was her friend and no more. He was devastated. He couldn't stay in Chicago. He announced at the next Sunday brunch that he'd decided to go to Africa. We were all stunned, of course. It seemed to come out of nowhere. But I saw Tess's face. She wasn't stunned. She was horrified. But neither of them said a word."

"So how do you know about it?" Murphy asked.

"The night before he left he showed up on our doorstep, drunk." Robin took up the story. "Poured his heart out, poor guy."

"I was trying to sober him up," Jon remembered. "He had a plane to catch the next day. But when he was finished I understood why he had to go. He really loved her and it was totally one-sided. I can't imagine how much that hurt."

Aidan couldn't imagine it, either. Tess Ciccotelli was a woman who made men take second, third, and fourth looks. To fantasize. But to really love her and not have her . . . It could make a man bitter. Vengeful. "So what did you do?"

"I drove him home, put him to bed, and set his alarm. I called later, just to make sure the alarm woke him. He never answered and a month later everybody in the group got a letter saying he was settled in and doing fine. I didn't hear any more until that postcard and nothing since."

"Do you have a picture of Swanson?" Murphy asked.

Jon thought. "No, but Tess does. On the wall in her living room. It was taken at the Lemon, at the last brunch before Jim left."

Aidan nodded. "I've seen it. It's right next to the pen-and-ink sketch of the beach her brother Tino did. But everybody's sitting down in the picture. How tall is Swanson?"

"About my height," Robin said. "Five eight, maybe five nine."

Yes. "And when did he leave? Can you remember an exact date?"

Jon frowned at Robin. "It was a few weeks before Christmas. December tenth?"

"It was the tenth," Robin confirmed. "I'd just finished decorating the Lemon."

Aidan glanced at Murphy, saw his partner's small nod. Swanson had left town just days before Lawe made contact with Blaine Connell for the first time. The two were connected. He could feel it. "Dr. Carter, did you mention our conversation to anyone?"

"Robin and I discussed it at dinner, but not at the viewing. You never said not to."

Aidan sighed. "Somebody knew we suspected Parks because he's very dead."

Murphy cleared his throat. "Can you bring us the clothes you wore last night?"

Jon started. "Oh, no. You think— Of course you do. I was bugged like Tess."

When Jon returned with the garments Aidan and Murphy were standing at the door. "Did Swanson have a key to Tess's apartment?" Murphy asked.

"I don't think so." Jon handed over the coats and took the receipt Aidan had prepared. "Listen, Detectives, Jim may have been lovelorn, but he wasn't twisted. I can't see him doing all this."

"Well, somebody's doing it," Aidan said tightly. "And right now Swanson's the best lead we've got. Thanks for the help, gentlemen."

Friday, March 17, 12:15 P.M.

Tess's cell phone woke her. Groggy, she groped for it, dislodging Bella from her butt with a swat. "Yeah?"

"Tess, it's Amy. Wake up."

The urgency in Amy's voice got her moving. Quickly she sat up. "What's wrong?"

"Vito called me. Your dad's in the ER, Tess. I'm on my way to get you."

Tess's heart stopped. "What happened?"

"He had a heart attack, honey. A bad one. Your mom called Vito. He didn't want to wake you if he didn't need to, but it's a lot worse than he thought."

"Oh God, oh God." Tess jumped from the bed, disoriented. "I need my shoes. Damn, where are my shoes? Where are you?"

"Just turning on to Aidan's street. Meet me outside and I'll drive you to the hospital."

Tess flew, her heart pounding now. *Hold on, Dad.* Amy's car was sitting in the driveway and Tess hurriedly climbed in. "Let's roll." Amy drove while Tess tried to catch her breath with no success. "I can't breathe. Dammit. I need to call Aidan." She fumbled her cell phone, her fingers feeling thick and clumsy.

Amy pulled to the curb. "Tess, you need to calm down."

"Why are you stopping? Drive, dammit."

"Give me your phone. I'll dial. You relax or you'll have a heart attack." She reached over for the phone, her hand closing over Tess's. "You'll upset him if you go in like this. Calm down. Here, let me help. My massage therapist hits this pressure point on me."

Tess closed her eyes and tried to breathe, knowing Amy was right. She'd kill her father rushing to his side this upset. Amy's fingers kneaded her neck, pressing hard on the corded tendons along her spine. "Feels good," Tess murmured.

Then she winced at the pinch at the curve of her neck. "Ow. That hurt."

"It's a pressure point. Puts you right to sleep like a baby," Amy soothed. "Sleep, Tess. When you wake up, everything will be fine. You'll see."

Tess's eyes grew heavy and she sank back against the car seat. The car started moving again as she slipped into warm darkness.

Friday, March 17, 2:15 *P.M*

"I've got something." Aidan stood so he could see Murphy over the small mountain of paper covering their desks. They'd taken papers from all three of Lawe's safe-deposit boxes. Aidan had been sorting for the last hour while Murphy tried to find some trace of Jim Swanson.

Murphy crossed to his side of the desk. "Looks like his ledger."

"It is. I see dates and in most cases, customers. He's got the payment for each job noted, but the actual job itself is kind of a code. This guy made damn good money."

"Yeah, but he's snap, crackle, popped, so hell of a lot of good his money is now."

"Thank you for the visual. You finding anything?"

"Nothing so far. If Jim Swanson's in this country, he's not using credit cards and he hasn't filed a tax return this year. His parents died when he was in college and none of his extended family's heard from him in years. Seems like he was a loner."

"Well, I'll keep plugging through this ledger and—" His phone rang. "Reagan."

"Hello?" It was a whisper. Female. Scared. "Are you looking for Dan Morris?"

Aidan cupped the phone. "It's about Danny Morris's

father." He cleared his throat. "Yes, ma'am. Do you know where he is?"

"He's here. In my apartment. If he knew I was calling." There was a loud crash in the background. "Oh, no. I have to go. Don't. Please." The last two words were a shrill cry and the line went dead. Aidan pulled up the reverse lookup registry and typed in the number on the caller ID. "It's in South Side." He looked at the pile of paperwork, then at Murphy who nodded.

"Let's go get Morris so we can get back to this."

Friday, March 17, 2:45 P.M

The apartment was empty. Not a stick of furniture. Not a soul in sight.

"What the hell?" Aidan muttered.

"You're sure about the address, Detective?" the SWAT leader asked.

"I double-checked it," Murphy said. "The call came from this apartment."

A uniform in body armor came back from the bedroom. "There's a phone back there, plugged into the wall. Nothing else in the room."

"That's because they just moved out." The manager stepped inside, frowning.

"We've been duped," Aidan said grimly. "This is a wild goose chase."

"Then we must be getting close," Murphy said.

Aidan's cell phone rang and his heart skipped a beat when he saw Rachel's cell phone ID. "Aidan." Her voice was high and thin. "Please come home."

"Rachel, honey, calm down. What's wrong?"

"Tess was supposed to pick me up to get my hair done. She didn't come, so we called her cell but she didn't answer." Dread began to claw its way through his belly.

"She's probably with Vito." *Please, let her be with Vito.* "Did you call him?"

Murphy whipped around, alarm on his face. "Tess?"

"Vito's here. At your house." Rachel's breath was hitching and suddenly, so was his own. "Aidan, we found him at the bottom of the basement stairs outside. He's hurt. Bad. Mom's with him now. I called 911, but please . . ." Her voice broke. "Please come home. We've searched everywhere. Tess is gone."

Aidan was running, hearing Murphy calling Spinnelli. "We're on our way to Aidan's house," Murphy said. "Have Jack Unger meet us there."

Friday, March 17, 3:00 P.M

It was pitch dark. *I can't see.* Panicked, Tess tried to move but her limbs refused to respond. *Sleep, Tess.* Amy was telling her to sleep. Now, or before? She tried to focus. She'd been sleeping. *Am I still sleeping?* She didn't think so. It hurt too much.

She hurt. Her head. Her throat. Her back . . . *Something's wrong with my back. I can't move. Car accident? Was that it? Where am I? Where is Amy?*

Aidan. She'd been trying to call Aidan. *Why?* It was important. She knew it was important. *Focus. Think.* She tried to grab on to reality. But clarity hovered just beyond reach as her mind began sliding back toward the warm nothing. She fought, but it was like strong hands, pulling her down. Dragging her under. *No, please, not again.*

Friday, March 17, 3:15 P.M.

Vito was sitting at Aidan's kitchen table when he and Murphy burst in the door. Spinnelli stood by the stove looking grim and Dolly barked frantically from somewhere in back of the house. Flanked by Rachel and his mother, Vito's face was white as a sheet. An EMT tended to a gash on the back of his head. Bruises on his forehead and cheek lent the only color to his face.

Vito lifted his eyes to Aidan, terrified and helpless. "She's gone," he said, his voice a toneless whisper that turned Aidan's gut to water.

Spinnelli cleared his throat. "We've got an all-points out for her. There's no evidence of forced entry. She either let somebody in, or she left on her own."

"Dolly wouldn't have let anybody in the house," Aidan said, his lungs unable to take in enough air. "For God's sake, Vito, what happened?"

"Your dog was growling." He winced when the EMT began to bandage his head. "I went outside to investigate. Had my gun out and went around back. The next thing I knew I was at the bottom of the stairs to the basement. My gun was gone and your mother was there." He closed his eyes. "And Tess was gone. I called Jon and Amy and Robin while Rachel called 911. Nobody has seen her."

Aidan's basement was a walk-up, the back door leading to a concrete stairwell that started five feet below ground level. "It's soggy outside. Did he leave any footprints?"

"He did." Jack came up from the basement. "We're taking an impression. The shoe looks like it could be the same one you saw on the person leaving Parks's place."

Vito's head swung from Aidan to Jack and back again. "Phillip Parks?"

"He's dead." Aidan pulled out a chair and sank into it, suddenly so weary. "He was shot to death last night. When did this happen, Vito?"

"About noon. Tess had gone to sleep . . . She was so upset by that damn picture in the paper . . . I told her everything would be better when she woke up."

A thought struck and Aidan frowned at Vito. "Why aren't you dead?" He waved away his mother's outraged gasp. "I mean all the other people that cross him end up dead. Why did he spare you?"

Vito covered his face. "I don't know. God, how am I going to tell my parents? I was supposed to keep her safe. This is going to kill my father."

Aidan rubbed his forehead. "I can't think." His mother rose to stand behind his chair, her hands firm on his shoulders. He leaned his head back against her, grateful for her quiet strength. "I just can't think."

"Aidan, why don't you stay here?" Murphy said gently. "I'll go back to the office and pick up where we left off before we were sidetracked by that wild goose chase."

Aidan pushed himself to his feet. "I'll go, too. I'll go crazy sitting here."

Vito rose as well, unsteady on his feet, but his dark eyes were clear. "Let me help. I haven't asked, you know I've stayed out of your way. But goddammit, you have to let me help." He glared at the EMT. "I'm not going to a hospital."

The EMT backed up, palms out. "Okay."

"Your parents are going to need you, Vito," Aidan said.

"I'll get them and bring them to our house," his mother said.

Aidan kissed her forehead. "Thanks, Mom. Vito, if you're coming, come."

A cell phone jangled and all hands went to their pockets.

"It's me," Vito said. He listened and sank back into the

chair. "When? . . . Stay where you are. I'll be right there."
He closed his phone, his body still. "That was my mother,"
he said, again so tonelessly Aidan's hair stood on end. "She
went to do some shopping because my father was asleep.
When she came back, he was gone."

Chapter Twenty-two

Friday, March 17, 5:00 P.M.

It was dark. And she still couldn't move. *I'm paralyzed.* But if she was paralyzed she shouldn't feel pain. She shouldn't feel anything and she did. Her body hurt, head to toe. Gradually her senses adjusted. It wasn't dark, her eyes were covered with a blindfold. *And I'm not paralyzed.* Her hands and feet were tied, her mouth gagged.

Tied. Gagged. *He has me.* She was terrified. *And alone.*

Her back ached from the cramped position in which she was forced. She heard a weak groan to her right. *I'm not alone.* But she was still terrified.

Her head throbbed and her heart beat so hard it hurt. She drew a breath through her nose and smelled wet rotting earth. *Was she outside?* No, it wasn't cold enough. *What happened?* The last thing she remembered was being in the car with Amy. Where was Amy? Did she hurt, too? Was that Amy's moan she'd heard?

A door opened and Tess stiffened. Waiting. Footsteps padded across the hard floor. Again she heard the low moan to her right and above her a tsking sound.

"So you're awake, old man."

At the sound of the familiar voice Tess's racing heart stopped, shock sending her body convulsing on a shudder. Disbelief surged. No. It wasn't possible. It was another voice imitation. Or a nightmare. *Please, let this be a nightmare.* A terrible nightmare. But a very real toe kicked her aching back, drawing a very real moan from her throat.

"You're awake, too. Looks like our little family reunion is about to begin."

The blindfold cut into her skin as it tightened, then abruptly loosened and Tess found herself staring up into the eyes she'd trusted for so many years. Now they sparkled brilliantly. Wickedly. Insanely. Horror gripped her and she simply couldn't look away. *Dear God.*

Amy's smile turned her blood to ice. "I told you when you woke up everything would be fine. See? Daddy is here."

Numbly, Tess rolled her head sideways. Her father lay curled next to her, his eyes closed, his head less than a foot away. Her eyes skittered up, around. This room was a closet. A tiny little closet. A cold sweat shivered down her body and nausea built. What felt like a groan in her throat came out a whimper and once again Amy smiled.

"It is a little room. You're probably wondering what's going to happen to you now."

Tess could only stare.

"You're thinking *She's insane.*" Amy grabbed her hair and jerked her face up, her eyes now flat and cold. She shook her hard. "Aren't you?" She threw Tess's head back and it hit the floor with a thud Tess more heard than felt. She felt . . . dissociated. Floaty.

"The tranquilizer's still wearing off. You know, all that worry about your heart, all that exercise, the aspirin, the glass of red wine a day? Not necessary. You're strong as an ox. If that tranq didn't kill you, nothing will." She opened the door then laughed. "No, wait. I will. But I want you totally coherent when I do. I want you to feel everything." She closed the door, leaving Tess stunned. Defenseless. Terrified.

Her father moaned. *I have to get him out of here. He'll die.* Then a horrified laugh scraped her throat. *Of course he will. So will I.*

Friday, March 17, 5:15 P.M.

Aidan looked at the conference room whiteboard, aware of every one of the five hours she'd been gone. The board was covered with names of customers he'd found in Lawe's ledger. All were corporations that made nothing, served no purpose other than to link to other corporations that made nothing. Arrows pointed in every direction.

In the middle of it all was Deering, which linked to Davis, which linked to Turner and back to Deering. The elaborate labyrinth of corporate entities smacked of money laundering, of someone with assets or activities to hide. Who was Lawe's customer?

The elaborate labyrinth did not tell them where to find Tess. Vito and Jon and Amy frantically called every hour and each time he had to tell them the same thing. *She's still missing. We're still working on it.* He'd never felt so desperately helpless in his life.

"What the hell is that?" Murphy demanded behind him. He came into the conference room and stared at the board, his normally placid face hard and angry.

"I take it you can't find Swanson."

Murphy's jaw twitched. "Not a trace. Customs has no record of him leaving the country. I checked with a stamp expert who said the stamp from Chad is sold in collector packets on eBay. The postmark is a fake. Nobody has seen Swanson. He's either dead or gone under." He closed his eyes. "Sorry. It's just that it's been five hours."

Aidan shoved back the fear that was clawing its way up his throat. "I know."

"So what the hell is this? Looks like Madden's Monday night play-by-play."

"These are the corporations listed as Lawe's customers. I checked all the individuals in his ledger and most of them were divorce cases, so I assumed Lawe was looking for assets or doing surveillance for custody disputes. These corporations are suspicious because it's the perfect way for a person to operate under the radar."

"It's a shell game," Murphy said.

"Exactly. A and B partner to form company C, which hires and pays Lawe. I can't find a single individual on the officer's roster. But Deering is the main entity."

Spinnelli and Jack came in and frowned at the board. "Nothing?" Spinnelli asked.

"Nothing," Aidan confirmed bitterly. "It's driving me insane."

"Well, here's something new for you," Jack said. "I examined Dr. Carter's coat, the one he wore to the viewing yesterday." He held out his hand and in his palm was another sewn-in needle-sized microphone. "I went back to his place and checked the rest of the clothes in his and Archer's closets. This was the only one that was wired."

"Then he was there last night," Murphy said. "At the viewing."

"There's a few more things you should see. One of my guys found this in Parks's apartment." It was a small plastic bag that held a hair. "It's not Parks's fiancé's. I've established that. It could belong to his maid. I'm checking. It appears to be a woman's hair. There is evidence of chemical color. Highlighting."

Aidan stared at the hair, his mind speeding ahead. "But the shoes."

"We examined the plaster casts we took of the footprints outside your back door, Aidan. The outline perfectly matches the shoeprints we found on Bacon's bathroom floor. But the pattern in these new footprints isn't consistent. The depth changes from front to back, side to side with every step, like the feet inside the shoes slipped around. And, the person who left the prints weighed between one twenty and one thirty-five."

"Not a man," Spinnelli said. "A woman. Masterson?"

"Denise Masterson fits that description, but she wasn't at the viewing last night, at least not while we were there," Murphy said while Aidan thought about the night before, the people he'd seen. A snippet of conversation stood out in his mind.

"She's a difficult person to care for," Aidan murmured.

Jack frowned. "What?"

"Amy Miller said that about Tess last night at the viewing. I thought she meant Tess was hard to take care *of.*" He was reluctant to believe where his mind was headed.

"She's the right height, right weight," Murphy said quietly, voicing Aidan's thoughts aloud. "Her blonde hair is streaked blonder."

"But they've been friends for twenty years. She took care of Tess when she was sick, defended her when she thought we suspected her. She and Amy are practically family. But she does have a key to Tess's apartment, and access to her office, too." He rubbed his temples. "She's been calling me every hour, asking if there is any news. Why? Why would she do this? It doesn't make sense."

"Can we tie her to Rivera or Bacon?" Spinnelli asked tightly. "Or Lawe? We need to be able to tie her to more than just Tess to get a warrant."

Aidan rose, every muscle tensed. "If there's a link we'll find it. For now, let's check her apartment. She could have Tess there. I'll go right now."

Spinnelli held him back. "No. Not you."

Desperation clawed, but he controlled it. "I won't do anything stupid."

"Not knowingly. But if it is Miller, she's smart. If she suspects we're on to her she could go under and then we won't find Tess. Let's at least get her in here where we can watch her while we get a search warrant for her place. I'll call her, tell her we have a lead and ask her to come in and look at some mug shots. You find a link."

"What about Swanson?" Murphy asked. "Should we stop looking for him?"

Spinnelli pursed his lips. "You're sure Swanson wasn't at the viewing last night?"

"I checked the funeral home video we made," Murphy said. "He wasn't there."

Spinnelli nodded. "Then focus on Miller. Find me a link."

"Bacon was an ex-con," Aidan said. "Rivera's brother's in jail waiting trial, and Miller's a defense attorney."

"That's a place to start," Spinnelli said. "Call me when you find something."

In thirty minutes Spinnelli was back. "Miller's not answering her home phone or her office phone. Do you have a cell number?"

"No. Tess had it programmed into her cell phone. I have Jon Carter's numbers, though." From his wallet Aidan pulled the emergency list Jon had given him the day Malcolm

Seward nearly killed Tess. "This time of day he's probably at the hospital."

Spinnelli hesitated. "I don't want him tipping Miller off."

"I don't think he would, Marc," Murphy said thoughtfully.

Aidan stared at the paper in his hand, remembering the afternoon Carter had written it. "I agree. In fact, I think we should bring him in. He knows Amy. Knows her habits. We have to get inside her head to know what she's going to do next."

Spinnelli nodded stiffly. "All right. Call him. But ask him to come here. We tell him *here*. And since we're bringing in the people who know Miller best, let's get Vito Ciccotelli and his mother in here. He's got to be going crazy sitting on his hands."

Friday, March 17, 6:00 P.M.

The stage was set. All the actors in place. But there was a sense of dissatisfaction. The end would come all too soon. So much planning, so much anticipation required a longer, more meaningful payout. Ciccotelli's life could be ended with a simple bullet to the head. Either of the Ciccotellis in fact. It would probably be safer that way.

But far less satisfying. *I'll play with her for just a little longer. Make it last a little longer. Because when it's over, there will be nothing.* The future loomed, empty and desolate. Because of her. Because of Tess Ciccotelli. Goddamn her to hell.

Rage pulsed and visions of Ciccotelli's body, torn and mutilated taunted. Beckoned. Not yet. *Get control of yourself. Sit down and get control of yourself.*

The computer chair was the only place to sit, but from there the computer screen called. It was better than magic. It was access. Total and complete access to anyone, anytime. Access was information. Information was power. And power was everything.

There were microphones to check. Fewer now that Ciccotelli's apartment and office had been swept clean. But the upside was that Ciccotelli no longer occupied either place. She was in essence, homeless. Jobless. It made losing the access worthwhile.

That the police had found the devices was an expected outcome. What had been unanticipated was Ciccotelli's discovery of the mike in the cat's collar. Bad luck there.

The recording quality had been poor, the cat's purring a source of interference, but the information obtained had been of the highest quality, little Rachel's anonymous tip to the police and Reagan's concern over finding a little boy's killer perhaps the most useful. It had only taken a few discreetly placed calls to find out who the little boy was and his father's name. A call to a female client with something to hide guaranteed a series of randomly placed phone calls luring Reagan to various points around the city where the boy's father would allegedly be.

He'd figure it out quickly, but wouldn't be able to resist any of the calls on the off-chance it could be real. People with scruples were so easy to manipulate.

Now Joanna Carmichael was another story. Hers was one of the few devices that remained, but the mike worked elegantly. The girl had done a good job, tailing Ciccotelli. Her threat to expose Ciccotelli's friends had been alarming at first, but so far, she'd done nothing more in depth than the amateurish exposé on Jon Carter. Unfortunately the buzz would do nothing more than boost business at Robin's bistro.

And, thinking of Jon and Robin, it was likely the police had found the video at Parks's apartment and even now suspected the pair. Parks had been a loose end that desperately needed snipping and there had been no time to lure him away to a safe place. The shoes had been a clever ploy and combined with the calls luring Reagan to the far sides of the city should throw the police off for a while. When all was said and done, most of the bastards in blue couldn't find their asses with both hands. Although Reagan and Murphy were a little smarter than most and unflaggingly loyal to boot.

That kind of loyalty never ceased to mystify. Saps, all of them.

The file holding feed from Joanna's home phone was open now. Six telephone calls had passed in and out of Joanna's phone since Wednesday. A mouse click had the tape rolling. The first five calls were of no consequence, but the sixth . . .

"Joanna Carmichael, this is Kelsey Chin."

A jolt of shock permeated. She'd found Chin. Chin, who knew things. Private things. Joanna had made an appointment to see Chin . . . this morning. Like Bacon, Joanna now had unauthorized information. Like Bacon, Joanna would have to go.

Friday, March 17, 6:10 P.M.

Murphy hung up his phone. "Guess who defended David Bacon?"

Aidan didn't look up from the list of people who'd visited Nicole Rivera's brother in jail. Amy Miller was nowhere in sight. "Arthur somebody from Legal Aid. I checked that."

"But guess who Arthur the Legal Aid guy took the case

from when she excused herself for conflict of interest in the middle of the case?"

Now he looked up. "Amy Miller?"

"None other. Arthur said she got as far as filing the motions when Eleanor Brigham was assigned the case. Because Miller knew Eleanor through Tess, she asked the judge to excuse her. At the time Arthur thought it was because she had a full caseload."

Aidan's pulse spiked. Finally, something they could use. "It's a strong link. She knew Bacon's talents. She put him on her contact list for future use."

Murphy picked up the phone. "I'll call Patrick."

"You have something then?"

Aidan twisted in his chair to where Vito Ciccotelli stood with his mother in the doorway, Spinnelli just behind them. Vito looked terrible and Aidan's heart bent in sympathy. He had a harder time with Gina Ciccotelli. On the way to the viewing the night before, Tess had told him of her reconciliation with her father. She'd also related her mother's role in the whole terrible misunderstanding. Aidan didn't think he could be as forgiving. Still, his own mother had taught him respect and he came to his feet.

"We may," Aidan confirmed. "Sit, please. We'd wanted to bring you two together with Jon Carter, but he's in surgery for the next hour." Aidan pulled out a chair for Tess's mother, then straightened to meet Vito's dark eyes, so like Tess's he once again had to press the fear back. "It's a woman," he said directly. "We think it's Amy Miller."

Gina gasped, her hand flying to cover her heart. "No. That's simply not possible. She's like my own daughter. She'd never hurt Tess."

But Vito sat very still. "I don't know, Mom. I think she would."

"Why, Vito?" Murphy asked. "What do you know?"

"Nothing specific," he murmured. "Just a feeling I've had for years. I didn't want to have it, so I told myself I was wrong." His mouth twisted. "I should have listened to myself. You know Amy lived with us from the time she was fifteen."

"Tess said they were like sisters," Aidan said, "but no. I didn't know she lived with you. Why did she?"

"Because her father was murdered. Amy's father and my father were business partners and good friends. Amy's mom had died . . . oh, a long time before."

"When Amy was two," Gina whispered. "She killed herself."

Vito frowned. "You never told us that."

"Amy's father never wanted her to know, so we never told her. We took her in. Made her our own. Vito, you're wrong. Amy can't be involved in this."

"How was her father murdered?" Aidan asked tightly.

"He and his fiancé were stabbed in a robbery." Vito dropped his eyes. "Amy was assaulted. Raped." Vito paused meaningfully. "She said. They arrested a neighbor kid."

"Leon Vanneti," Gina said, her voice trembling. "He was a no-good boy. Ran wild with those motorcycle boys." She swallowed hard. "You always said he was innocent."

"Because I thought he was."

"You said 'she said,'" Murphy observed. "Why?"

"I knew Leon. He was wild, but he wasn't bad. But the hospital did an exam. Found semen and some bruising. It all came out at the trial."

"Along with the bloody knife they found under his bed," Gina snapped. "Vito, how can you say these things?"

"Because it didn't make sense. Leon wasn't stupid. He would have hidden his tracks. He said he'd never touched her but the jury didn't believe him. Bad-looking motorcycle dude versus a sweet little girl. There was no DNA analysis because it was about seven years too early. Now Leon's serving a life sentence."

"And Amy became a defense attorney," Murphy mused. "Being a victim, I would have thought she'd go the opposite way and prosecute."

Amy's career motives were something to consider. Aidan tucked the thought away. "Why did you think Amy could hurt Tess?"

Vito shrugged uneasily. "It was more of a feeling. Tess was the only one of us to have her own room, because she was the only girl, but she was thrilled to share with Amy when she came to live with us. Amy wanted her own room. Made a hell of a fuss. She always wanted special treatment."

"She'd just lost her parents," Gina protested.

"So you said," Vito said. "Many times. Then things would go missing. Little things, nothing big. And there was the crawl space thing."

Gina shook her head, desperation in the gesture. "An accident. Vito, please."

"What crawl space thing?" Aidan asked, but he thought he knew.

"When she was sixteen, Tess got locked in the crawl space under the house where we grew up." Vito said. "It's small and dark, and—"

"That's why she never takes the elevator," Aidan murmured and Vito nodded.

"We'd gone away for a long weekend. Tess and Amy were supposed to go to a friend's, but Amy changed her mind and came back to go with us. Apparently Tess followed her but got locked in the crawl space. She was down there for three days. No food or water. She'd pounded her hands to a pulp and scratched until her fingernails were broken to the quick."

Aidan flinched. "God."

"Amy claimed that she didn't know Tess had decided to come home and go with us. But it was hard to blame Amy. She felt terrible. Nursed Tess for days."

Gina pushed away from the table. "Vito, this is wrong." Her arms crossed over her chest, she paced angrily. Then stopped abruptly in front of the whiteboard, her entire expression flattening in shock. "What is this?" Her question was hoarse.

Aidan got up and walked to the board. Her hand shook as her finger tentatively touched one of the corporations' names. Deering. The key entity.

"This name. I've seen it before." She turned to look at Vito, her eyes filled with horrified realization. "It was the customer that hired that woman."

That woman. Realization hit Aidan like a brick as Vito surged to his feet. Amy. Again. Tess's and her father's estrangement had been no misunderstanding. No accident. A fury bubbled from deep within him.

"What woman?" Murphy asked.

Aidan evenly, quickly, told the story.

"The one that's ripped our family in two for five fucking years," Vito fumed. "That conniving bitch. Amy wanted Tess out of the picture so she deliberately set Dad up."

"While she came to our Thanksgiving table and sat in Tess's chair." Gina's eyes filled with tears.

"And it worked for five years." Wearily Aidan rubbed his head.

"Phillip Parks," Murphy said behind him, very quietly and Aidan knew.

"Amy was Parks's other woman."

Murphy nodded. "When we questioned Parks he might have told us, exposing her."

Aidan sank into his chair. "She's been systematically ruining Tess's life for years."

"Why did Amy's mother kill herself?" Spinnelli asked.

"She was paranoid schizophrenic." Gina was trembling uncontrollably. "We watched Amy so carefully. We knew it was inherited sometimes. But Amy always seemed so normal. So happy. We didn't want to scare her so we never told her."

Vito closed his eyes. "God."

"Did Tess know this?" Aidan demanded and Gina shook her head.

"It was Amy's father's wish that nobody ever know. So we kept it hidden."

The phone on the conference room table rang and Murphy snapped it up. "Thanks," he said and hung up. "Patrick says he'll meet us at Miller's with the warrant. Let's go."

Friday, March 17, 6:45 P.M.

Sometimes the best approach was to hide in plain sight. A brisk knock brought a man to the door. The boyfriend... what was his name? Keith. Must remember the details. But the boyfriend was not the desired party. Joanna Carmichael was.

"Can I help you?" he asked with a deep drawl.

"I'm here to meet with Miss Carmichael regarding her ongoing investigative piece."

Keith's jaw tightened. "Oh," he said flatly. "That. Well, she's not home right now. You'll have to come back later." He started to shut the door, then his eyes widened with shock as he stared at the pistol, complete with a silencer.

"Now where is that Southern hospitality I've heard so much about? Invite me in."

He backed up at a suspicious angle, hitting a desk that sat just inside the door, his hands behind his back. He moved quickly, but ultimately not quickly enough. His knees hit the floor before he could point the gun he'd pulled from the drawer, a red stain quickly spreading across the front of his starched white shirt. It was just as well. He'd been a dead man from the moment he'd opened the door. He'd just sped up the timetable when he'd pulled the gun. Foolish, really.

He probably wouldn't have had the guts to use it anyway. He fell forward, his gun slipping from his grasp to lie harmlessly on the carpet. It would make a charming souvenir. The floorplan of this place was much like Cynthia Adams's apartment, ten floors up. Carmichael would be home soon. The closet would be a reasonable place—

The boom of Keith's gun shook the air in the same moment that pain speared, hot and sharp. And then pain gave way to shock. *He shot me. My arm.* He propped himself up on his elbows, the gun held unsteadily in both hands. A grim smile stamped on his mouth. The sonofabitch really did have the guts after all.

"Fuck you," he rasped. Then he collapsed, trapping the gun beneath him.

Shock gave way to fear. Run. *Run.* A second passed before her feet obeyed. The stairwell was closer. *Run. Down one floor, now two. Breathe.* The sleeve of the tan coat had a neat hole around which blood had already soaked.

Carefully she took it off and walked out onto the tenth floor, the coat draped to cover the wound. The elevator came quickly and with no further ado, descended quickly to the lobby. From there, walking out as cool as a cucumber was no issue at all.

Friday, March 17, 7:00 P.M.

She wasn't here. Aidan stood in the middle of Amy Miller's living room watching Jack's team look for anything that might indicate Tess had been here. But there was nothing. Nothing. And he felt true fear. Cold. Debilitating. Paralyzing in its intensity.

Tess and her father weren't here. Neither was Amy. Fury bubbled up and he silently clenched his fists at his sides. Made himself take a deep breath. Losing his temper wouldn't bring Tess back safely. Understanding Amy would bring Tess back. Figuring out Amy's next step before she made it would bring Tess back.

I'm not a mind reader, Tess had said. Suddenly, fiercely, Aidan wished that he was. He needed to be. Needed to get inside Amy's head.

Don't be a mind reader. Be a cop. Do your job like you do every day. The fist that clenched his gut eased, just enough to get his focus back. *Get inside her head.* Aidan did a slow turn around the room, examining the movie posters that covered the walls. "She's a collector," he murmured, vaguely surprised. It was a rather eclectic collection, spanning the 1930s to the 1990s. Some movies were classics, others more obscure.

All had a common theme. His heart started to thud. "Murphy! Come here."

Murphy came from the kitchen holding two glass jars, one in each hand. "What?" He looked up and whistled. "These must be worth a mint."

"They are, but it's not the money. It's the meaning. Look." He started at the end of one wall, pointing. "*Double Indemnity* with Barbara Stanwyck."

"I've never seen it," Murphy said.

"Woman uses a man to kill her husband and gets away with it. *All About Eve.*"

Murphy's eyes were bright. "Anne Baxter plays another manipulative bitch. They're all movies where women win."

Aidan stared at the poster that was centered on one wall

and the last piece of the puzzle fell into place. His heart was racing now. "Murphy, listen." He read off the actresses' names. "Stanwyck, Turner, Davis, Baxter."

Murphy's eyes widened. "The corporations you had on the white board." He scanned the posters. "But Deering was the name in the middle. I don't see that."

Aidan tapped the poster in the middle. "This one is from *Hush, Hush Sweet Charlotte.* Olivia de Havilland drives her 'friend' Bette Davis insane. De Havilland's character's name was Miriam Deering. Each one of these movies is about a woman manipulating either men or other women. It's a fucking road map. She must have thought she was so damn clever. Tess would have seen the posters a million times."

"And she never suspected a thing. Amy taunted her with the information and Tess never suspected. How much are these posters worth, Aidan?"

"If they're original? Close to two hundred grand total."

"You took a film appreciation class when you were getting your degree, didn't you?"

"Yeah," Aidan said flatly. The thrill of cracking the code had quickly cooled. "Hell of a lot of good it does me now. What does any of this have to do with where Miller is right now?"

Murphy clasped his shoulder and gave him an encouraging squeeze. "Try to relax your mind, Aidan. Think about what we know, not about what we don't. Think about this. Two hundred grand is a lot of cash to plunk down for wall decor. I looked at Miller's 1040 for last year and she only declared sixty in income. The rent on this apartment is consistent with that. The posters aren't."

Aidan lifted his brows. "Earlier, you said you were surprised she didn't become a prosecutor. If you're looking for shady minions to do your bidding . . ."

"As a defense attorney, she has access to all the bad guys she needs to do any little thing she wants done." Murphy looked around the living room. "You know the one thing I expected to see was a big computer system. When Rick showed us all the cameras I had a vision of this James Bond-like console that had ten monitors and covered a whole wall. There's no computer here. Not even a monitor."

"She probably has a laptop."

"Probably, but she had all this footage to watch. Cameras in Tess's apartment, her office, Cynthia Adams's apartment . . . I can't imagine her spending the time watching one feed at a time, especially since she still puts in time on her job. She's got to have at least two or three monitors, Aidan. Otherwise, it's not logistically possible."

Aidan nodded grimly. "Then she's got another place where she plays. I'll check into any real-estate holdings of her corporations, starting with Deering."

"Aidan, Murphy," Jack called from the bedroom urgently. "Come and see."

Aidan stopped short at the sight. The armoire doors were thrown back, revealing dozens of pictures. One face was common to all. "Swanson," Aidan murmured.

Vito stood at the foot of Amy's bed, his head bent under a frilly pink canopy. "There are more under here," he said flatly.

Aidan and Murphy bent close to the pictures on the armoire. Many were group photos. "This was taken at Robin Archer's bistro. Tess has one just like it." But closer inspection had his gut clenching once again. "She's cut Tess out of this picture."

"Out of all the pictures," Murphy murmured. "Looks like Swanson sat next to Tess every chance he got. Miller is obsessed with this guy."

Aidan glanced at Vito. "Swanson went missing three months ago."

"I was thinking he was dead, but if Miller was stalking

him and he felt threatened, he might have used the Doctors Without Borders ruse to disappear," Murphy said.

"Look at these," was all Vito said and stepped back from the bed.

Aidan stuck his head under the canopy and blinked. "Holy shit." The entire area of the canopy was filled with more pictures of Swanson in various stages of undress. "Looks like he was in his bedroom when she took these through the window."

"I went by his last known address yesterday." Murphy frowned. "The bedroom faced the street. These pictures would have had to be taken from an apartment across the street." He lifted a brow. "It could be where she plays."

Aidan felt a little lift of hope. "Let's get over there."

"I'll call Spinnelli. He can start checking addresses. Get us a warrant."

"Wait. Before you go . . ." Standing in the bedroom closet doorway, Jack held up a pair of wingtips. "Right size. Blood on the laces." He turned them over. "No mud on the soles. We'll test to see if the blood is Bacon's."

"Then she had two pairs of shoes," Murphy mused. "Those and the ones she wore this afternoon when she hit Vito."

"She has a whole hell of a lot more than that." Jack stepped back. "Take a look."

Two large suitcases lay opened on the floor, filled with men's clothes. "The luggage tag says 'Jim Swanson,'" Jack said. "His wallet's there, with his driver's license, a plane ticket to Chad, and his passport. And this, wrapped in a shirt." It was a butcher knife, crusted dark brown.

Aidan's blood went cold. "He's dead then. She killed him."

"But why?" Murphy asked. "Why would she do that?"

"She was obsessed with Swanson," Aidan said, his stomach still pitching. "The night before he left he got drunk, remember? He went to Jon Carter's, spilled his guts." He glanced over at Vito. "Swanson was in love with Tess, but she'd turned him down. It was why he went to Africa."

Vito's eyes widened. "This is that guy? She told me that it had happened. Never told me the guy's name. She says I'm the only one she told. She felt guilty as hell."

"So let's play this out." Aidan pointed to himself. "I'm Amy. Murphy, you're Swanson. You've come home from Carter's and you're drunk and despondent. Not fleet on your feet. Meanwhile, I'm pining for you. Have all these pictures of you. You're leaving tomorrow and I may never see you again. I go to you and . . . what? Pledge my love?"

"She might." Murphy nodded. "But I say 'No way. I love Tess.' You get mad. What happened when she got mad, Vito? Really mad?"

Vito paled. "I only saw her really mad once. She'd been stood up by some date for a school dance. The guy got a better offer from a more popular girl. She completely trashed her room, throwing things . . ." He swallowed. "She slashed up the dress she was supposed to have worn along with the mattress on her bed. She begged me to help her get the ripped mattress out of her room before Mom and Dad found out. She said she cut the mattress by mistake, but they were gouges, like she'd stabbed it. If my parents had only told us about her mother . . . I never would have kept that secret."

"She'd be horrified when she saw what she'd done. She loved him and she killed him," Murphy said slowly. "And in her mind, it's all Tess's fault."

"This was the trigger that changed this from a habitual torment to focused vendetta." Aidan drew a deep breath. "She wanted to strip everything from Tess. Her career, her credibility." *Her life.* He couldn't bring himself to say those words.

"You," Murphy added. "You were supposed to leave when Rachel was threatened."

"But you didn't," Vito said unsteadily. "Thank you."

Aidan remembered the look on Tess's face when she thought he had. He'd thought she'd known what was in his mind. He'd thought she'd figured him out, all nice and tidy because that's what she did. She analyzed and diagnosed. Helped suicidal people at their most vulnerable. Blocked killers and rapists from using insanity to escape justice. And she was very good at what she did.

He'd thought such skill would be ingrained, reflexive, something she did with everyone. But it seemed the people she cared about were not subject to such scrutiny. Because she cared openly and without reservation, she expected the same. It had left her vulnerable to those whose motives were selfish or brutal. Phillip Parks. Denise Masterson. Amy Miller.

"Jack." One of the CSU techs came back, a brown envelope in his hand.

Jack pulled out a stack of postcards and a sheet of stamps from Chad. "They're already written," Jack said. "She planned to send these out every few months."

"She must have written the letter to the clinic's director," Murphy added. "To cover up what she'd done. Let's check out the apartments across from Swanson's old place."

"And any other real estate held by the Deering corporation." Aidan was almost out the door when his cell phone rang.

"Reagan, this is Jon Carter. I just got out of surgery and got my messages. One was from you and one was from Amy Miller."

Aidan stopped short. "What did she say?"

"It was a strange message. She said she needed my help, that it was an emergency. She said she'd been with a client, a young kid who panicked and shot her. She wants to meet me so I can stitch her up because she doesn't want the GSW reported. Said she didn't want this kid's life ruined because he made a mistake."

"Where is she supposed to meet you?"

"I told her I'd meet her at my house in thirty minutes. I called you because as I was standing in surgery, I kept thinking about last night. Amy held my coat while I gave my condolences to Flo Ernst. I hope I'm wrong, but I won't take a chance with Tess's life."

"We're on our way, Jon. We'll be at your house in fifteen minutes."

"Then I was right." He sounded weary.

"Yeah." Aidan drew a breath. "You were right."

Friday, March 17, 7:30 P.M.

"Tess?" It was a weak moan, barely audible.

Tess lifted her head and squinted in the darkness, so relieved. Her father was conscious. Alive. Cautiously she rolled to her side and met his eyes. His hands and feet were also tied, but for some reason Amy hadn't gagged him.

Amy. It was so unbelievable. Until she started stringing things together. *The crawl space.* She'd been so shell-shocked at the time and Amy had been so solicitous. Just as she'd been after the con with the chain. She brought me soup. Nasty soup. Tess had always thought Amy was just a terrible cook. Now the six weeks she spent weak and vomiting began to make more sense. *She poisoned me.* What a bitch. But why?

Because she's insane, Tess. And Tess had learned that sometimes that was the only reason anybody needed. But Amy's anger had changed. Before Cynthia Adams, her anger had never been lethal. Just . . . mean. What changed?

Tentatively she nudged her father's knee with her own.

"Tess," he whispered. "You're alive."

For how long? She nudged him again, giving comfort, seeking it at the same time.

"I have a knife in my pocket," he murmured. "My whittling knife. Can you get it?"

His whittling knife. He'd always been ready to carve her a knickknack of some kind when she was small, keeping the knife in the holster pocket of his carpenter pants. She could see it in her mind's eye. Now if only she could reach it with her bound hands.

Friday, March 17, 7:30 P.M.

Joanna headed for her apartment building with a spring in her step. Her visit to Lexington had been eye-opening, Dr. Chin's information a springboard for what had become a piece of serious journalism. She hadn't gotten Ciccotelli's exclusive, but what she had gotten on the doctor's best friend might be better. She couldn't wait to tell Keith.

She'd done it. She'd finally done it. A byline of her own. And nothing like the frothy piece she'd written on Jon Carter's alternate lifestyle that would appear in the society gossip page. This was hard-hitting journalism. It was page one. Above the fold.

Finally. And Cyrus Bremin wouldn't scoop her on this one. She had the editor's promise. But the man had promised before and given her story away, so she'd have to wait and see. Still, she rounded the corner with a grin on her face.

The grin faded and her step faltered as her building came into view. For the second time in a week an ambulance was on her curb. She sprinted the last block. Where before she'd been excited at the prospect of reporting Cynthia Adams's suicide, now she felt dread.

She caught up with a cop. "I live in this building. What's happened?"

He looked at her face, his eyes narrowed. "What's your name?"

"Joanna Carmichael."

His eyes went flat. "We've been looking for you. Come with me."

No. Dread mounted as he led her to the elevator and up to her floor. *No.* The door to her apartment was open. People were inside. Not people. More cops. *Keith.*

She was stopped a few feet from the door by a tall dark man and a smaller blonde woman. The man put a hand on her shoulder. "Miss Carmichael?" Numbly she nodded.

"I'm Detective Mitchell and this is my partner Detective Reagan," the woman said. "Can you tell us where you were an hour ago?"

Her heart slowed to next to nothing. The tall dark one was the brother of Ciccotelli's cop boyfriend. "With my editor at the *Bulletin.* Why?"

The woman looked her straight in the eye. "We have bad news for you."

The woman's words were drowned out by the squeak of gurney wheels. It bore a body bag. "Keith?" She started after the gurney, panic sending everything else to the back of her mind. The voice she heard screaming was her own. *"Keith."*

Chapter Twenty-three

Friday, March 17, 7:30 P.M.

The bleeding had nearly stopped on its own and it didn't throb as badly as it had when the wound was fresh. Still, it needed to be stitched or it would rip open again. Jon would be here soon. He'd stitch her up and Ciccotelli's torture could commence.

Jon's empty driveway was visible through binoculars from a block away. As was the low-slung Camaro creeping down the road, a block in the other direction.

Aidan Reagan's car. It took a full moment for the shock to sink in. Jon Carter had reported her. *They suspect.* Impossible. The shoes had been such a clever ploy. They were supposed to suspect Robin Archer, but he remained at home even after a morning visit by police. *Now they suspect me.* But how?

And importantly, what next? The wound needed to be attended to. Ciccotelli would have to do it. *I hope her father is still alive, because only a gun to his head will force her to* do the job properly. Once the stitches were in place, Ciccotelli and her father would have to die. Quickly and far less painfully than planned. *I have to get away.* Far away.

Friday, March 17, 8:15 P.M.

"She must have seen us." Aidan threw his coat on his desk in disgust.

"We waited for forty-five minutes," Murphy told Spinnelli. "She never showed up."

Spinnelli sighed. "We know how Miller got shot. We got a call right after you left for her apartment. Joanna Carmichael's boyfriend was found dead in his apartment. The boyfriend was lying on his own gun, which had been fired once. And we found photos on their PC. Apparently Carmichael had been taking pictures of Tess all over town."

Another dead person. *Damn.* "Tess said Carmichael had been following her."

"Well, she'd done a damn fine job of stalking. We found pictures of Marge Hooper and Sylvia Arness and half a dozen other people that Tess met that day. Carmichael told Abe and Mia that she'd suspected someone may have been in her files, but she'd gotten 'distracted' by a story. So it looks like Miller's walking around with a bullet hole."

"Carmichael got too close to Miller," Murphy murmured. "What was the story?"

"She hasn't said. Mia says Carmichael kept muttering 'above the fold.'"

"So her boyfriend pays for her obsession with Tess and an exclusive with his life." Aidan sighed. "Did you find anything at Swanson's old apartment?"

"It was rented two months ago by a young couple," Spinnelli said. "So Miller's not there now. But before that, it was rented by Deering, Inc."

So close. But still, no help. "Have we run a search on Deering's holdings?"

"Lori's doing it now. We should have something in an hour or so. I had Denise Masterson picked up again. She asked to call her lawyer and guess who he was?"

"Destin Lawe," Murphy said and Spinnelli nodded.

"She was very unhappy to learn that he's dead. He'd told her he was a lawyer."

"Which was why she called him as soon as we let her go yesterday," Murphy said.

"We also got three more calls reporting sightings of Danny Morris's father. All fake."

"She knows we'll follow every lead. Damn the bitch," Murphy hissed.

Aidan was ready to scream. "None of this helps us find Tess."

"We've got an APB out for Miller," Spinnelli said patiently. "Aidan, we're dead in the water until Lori's done with that records search. Use this time to recharge." He narrowed his eyes. "That's an order. Once you get that printout of real-estate holdings, you'll be off like a rocket. I want you focused when you do."

Aidan made himself leave the bullpen, running into Rick on his way to the elevator.

"I've been looking for you," Rick said. "I have something." When Aidan looked blank, Rick frowned. "The CD that the Poston kid smashed. I have something."

New energy surged to give him the lift he'd been needing. "Let's go look."

Friday, March 17, 8:15 P.M.

Tess nearly laughed. It was a damn ludicrous request. "You want me to do *what?*"

Amy didn't smile. "Here's a sterilized needle and some thread." She bared her forearm, revealing ripped skin. "Stitch it up." She held her gun in her left hand, the barrel pressed to Michael's temple. "Don't make me flinch. My left hand's not so steady."

Tess sobered instantly. "All right. Just don't hurt him."

"She'll kill me anyway. Don't help her." He grunted when Amy kicked his stomach.

"Shut up, old man."

"It's all right, Dad," Tess murmured, then met Amy's eyes. "I can't help you with my hands tied." After an hour of contortion, she'd managed to retrieve her father's whittling knife from his holster pocket. With her hands tied behind her back, the only place she could reach to hide the knife was inside the back waistband of her jeans. At the moment it was sheathed and totally useless. But when Amy freed her hands . . .

Amy took her own knife, a large butcher variety, and cut the ropes that bound her hands. "One false move and your father won't need to worry about his heart anymore."

"This will hurt," Tess warned. "I don't have anything to deaden the pain."

Amy smirked, her eyes sweeping the shelves of the little room in which they were being held. "I do, but there's no way in hell I'm letting you use it on me."

Battling the nausea that went with the tiny little room, Tess noticed all the plants and bottles lining the shelves. Most were mushrooms and another piece of the puzzle fell into place. "Hallucinogens. You used these on my patients."

Amy held out her arm. "Shut up and stitch."

Tess shook her head. "I'm getting nauseous in here. I'm afraid I'll botch the job."

"It's a risk I'm willing to take," Amy said dryly. "Get started."

Tess threaded the needle. "Did you use these drugs on my patients?"

Amy made an impatient sound. "Yes, I did."

Tess made a neat stitch and Amy hissed in pain. "Did you put them in my soup?"

"Of course. It seemed like the perfect time to separate you from Phil."

Tess made a few more stitches. "Did you sleep with him? With Phillip?"

Amy's smile was nasty. "Of course. And took pictures of the grand event. They were enough to convince Phil to walk away from you. I couldn't let you get married."

"Why not?"

"Because then you'd be happy. I couldn't have planned Green or the con with the chain any better if I'd tried. But I could run with the aftermath."

"I thought I was losing my mind," Tess murmured, thinking of the weeks she'd been too weak to go into work and wondering if her mind was rejecting her career.

Amy chuckled good-naturedly. "I know. By the way, I really did mean that you looked like a dime-store hooker on Sunday."

Tess tightened her jaw. "I know. Eleanor was right about you. She never liked you."

Amy's arm tightened beneath Tess's hands. "Bitch. She paid, too."

Tess looked up. "What?"

"She was always doing things for you. Giving things to you."

Tess remembered their shock at Eleanor's sudden death. "You killed Eleanor and made it look like a stroke."

"I did." Her lips thinned. "The skin on her neck was so wrinkled the ME never even saw the little mark the needle left behind."

"But they didn't find any drugs."

"The beauty of air, Tess."

Dully, Tess dropped her eyes back to the stitches. "You injected her with air."

"The old man was supposed to throw you out on your ass."

"But that didn't happen," Tess murmured, so many things clearer now.

"You landed on your feet," Amy said bitterly. "Like you always do." She shook her head hard. "Did," she corrected. "Your charmed life will end tonight."

Tess was coming to the end of her stitches and her feet were still tied. "What are you going to do to us?"

"Shoot you. It's like a big circle. I started out with you because I killed my father. And now I'll finish by killing yours."

Tess bobbled a stitch, making Amy swear. Michael looked up, his eyes mere slits. "You killed your own father? Why?"

Amy's face hardened. "He was getting married. I didn't want him to. She had five children and they were all going to overrun *my* house. Take *my* things." Her chuckle was ugly. "Hell of it was, I ended up with *your* five children, so it wasn't any better."

"You framed Leon," Tess murmured, taking her time over the last few stitches.

"It was easy to do." Her face darkened. "Framing you should have been so easy."

"Why wasn't it?" Tess asked.

"I was afraid the cops would miss the important clues so I left too many."

"You did too good a job," Tess murmured, playing the game.

"I did," Amy replied, pleased. "Now framing your old man was a piece of cake."

Tess gritted her teeth. Amy had set that up, too. "You had me fooled."

"The great psychiatrist. No better than anyone else. You see what you want to see." Amy flexed her fingers. "You did a good job. For that the old man will go quickly."

Tess knew it was now or never. She whipped her father's knife from her waistband and while Amy was inspecting her stitches, Tess struck, slicing deep into Amy's uninjured arm. Letting out a piercing howl, Amy swung the gun upward and Tess treated her to the same move she'd used on Clayborn. Amy screamed, blood gushing from her nose and Tess threw herself into Amy's body, knocking her against one of the walls. Pots on the shelves above teetered and Amy was momentarily stunned.

Tess grabbed Amy's gun with one hand and sawed at the ropes around her ankles with the other. She stood, the gun in her hand while Amy sneered. "You won't do it."

Tess knew Amy was at least partly right. This woman had been her closest friend. And it had been entirely one-sided the entire time. Still, Tess couldn't see herself pulling the trigger, taking Amy's life. The woman she'd loved like a sister was mentally ill. She'd spared Harold Green. Did she owe Amy any less? "I don't want to kill you, Amy. But I will if I have to. Stand up and don't touch my father or I swear I will kill you."

Amy stood up. "Such a little bitty room, Tess. I don't think you've got enough air."

Tess gritted her teeth. "I seem to be doing very well, despite my fear." And to her surprise that was true. "Now

move. Away from my father." Amy moved a few feet closer
to the door, her eyes watchful. Tess knew Amy was just waiting for her to blink. "That's far enough. Dad, I can't take my
eyes off her to untie you."

"It's all right, Tess." He was so weak. "Just get help."

"Move, Amy. We're going to make a phone call and this
time I get to talk for myself."

Friday, March 17, 8:20 P.M.

Aidan, Murphy, and Spinnelli stared at the photos Rick had
spread across the table. "The missing slivers of the CD trans-
late to missing bands across the width of the picture," Rick
explained.

"You found pictures?" Aidan asked. "I was expecting an
audio file."

"Oh." Rick shook his head to clear it. "I've been looking
at this too long. I did find an audio file, but just pieces. Like a
cell phone conversation that keeps going in and out. But
there's enough to nail Poston for sure. While I was looking
for the audio segments, I found some picture files, buried
deep. She must have tried to wipe this disc clean with a gov-
ernment wipe. That only erases the data if you wipe it seven
times and even then, data's been known to stick around. See
if the pictures mean anything."

The picture was of a wall, with pictures. Pen-and-ink pictures of a beach. He'd seen this wall before. His heart leaped
into his throat. "This is Tess's living room."

Murphy grabbed one of the pictures. "You're kidding."

Aidan looked up. "She did the same thing with Tess that
she did with Swanson. These were taken from outside Tess's
apartment. That's where she plays."

Murphy nodded excitedly. "From the building across the street. But that building's got forty apartments on the street side. Can you project the apartment from the angle?"

"Maybe," Rick said. "The resolution's poor, but I can guess."

Spinnelli knocked on the table to get their attention. "We need to know which specific apartment to get a warrant. You can't just guess."

Aidan picked up the phone. "Lori, do you have that real-estate list for Deering yet?"

Two minutes later Lori brought the printouts and Aidan ran his finger down the list. "She owns twenty apartments. But only one across from Tess. Let's go."

Friday, March 17, 8:45 P.M.

"Stop now," Tess said and Amy stopped, a mocking smile on her face.

"And if I don't?"

Tess fired a shot, letting the bullet fly close to Amy's head. "Then I'll shoot you."

Amy's face turned a mottled red. "You bitch. You've always had it all."

"And now I'll have you in jail. Which is where you tried to send me."

"And I would have if it hadn't been for those damn cops."

"You sound like the villains in *Scooby-Doo*," Tess said and Amy's scowl deepened. "So much for classic films." She looked around, but to her dismay saw no phone.

"No phone," Amy said smugly. "Just the Internet. Now what?"

"Come with me. We're knocking on some doors. I'm sure

somebody in this building has a phone." She waved Amy in front of her, motioning her toward the door. "Go."

Instead Amy charged. Tess flew backward, flat against the glass patio door and Amy wrested the gun away. Bleeding and bruised, Amy stood, pointing the gun at Tess's heart. "Now *you* move. Out on the terrace. Full circle with your dad, full circle with you. This all started when your patient jumped. Now the headlines will have you jumping as well. Open the door."

"No." Tess knew the moment she was on the terrace that she was dead.

Amy unlocked the door and pushed it open, letting in the cold night air. She grabbed Tess's hair in one hand, with the other pressed the gun to her temple. "I said go. Now." She dragged Tess to the balcony and pushed her so that she leaned over the edge. Tess cried out when the butt of the gun came down against the small of her back. Instinctively she moved to get away from the pain, throwing off her center of gravity and Amy pushed.

Sending Tess over the edge.

"Police!" Aidan stepped aside to let the SWAT team break down the door and Aidan's heart dropped to his feet. On the balcony Amy stood. Alone. Barely visible were two hands, hanging on to the ledge for dear life. *Tess.* Aidan ran forward only to have Amy Miller turn, her eyes wild and insane.

"Everybody leaves or I'll shoot her hands," she threatened calmly. "And she'll fall, twelve stories. If she doesn't die, she'll wish she had and so will you."

Murphy was behind him. "On three, Aidan," he said softly. "One, two,—"

Three. Both he and Murphy shot simultaneously, the force of their combined fire to her torso sending Amy over the edge. Not waiting to check where she landed, Aidan ran, and he and Murphy dragged Tess back to safety. She was white-faced and panting, in too much shock to say a word.

Aidan swung her into his arms and carried her back into the living room.

"She's on the pavement," Murphy said from the balcony. "She's dead."

"Full circle," Tess murmured. "Like Cynthia."

Aidan thought he'd never put Tess down as long as he lived. Seeing her two small hands clutching the edge of the balcony had driven more than twenty years from his life.

Tess struggled to her feet. "My father. Call 911. He needs oxygen."

So did she, Aidan thought, but supported her as she ran to a back room where Michael Ciccotelli lay, still bound and pale. He looked up and closed his eyes in relief. "You're alive. I heard the gunshots."

Tess dropped to her knees and searched for the knife to cut his bonds. Tears were pouring from her eyes and Aidan didn't think she was even aware of them. Her hands were shaking, making the knife a danger. "She's dead, Dad. Amy's dead."

"Tess." Aidan crouched down, took the knife from her hands. "Sit and breathe." Quickly he cut Michael's bonds and helped the older man straighten his limbs. "You're both going to a hospital and you will not argue. Agreed?"

Michael looked at Tess. "I'll go if you do."

She nodded, her hand over her mouth. "Okay."

"Tess? Dad?" Vito skidded to a stop in the open doorway. "Oh, my God, Tess." He dropped to his knees beside her, grabbing her in his arms. "Spinnelli called me and I got here when you were still hanging off the balcony. I thought you'd fall." His arms tightened and he rocked her hard.

Michael's eyes grew wide. "You were hanging from the balcony? Dear God."

"I thought I'd have a heart attack," Vito said fervently. "Mom and I stood there. We couldn't breathe. And then Amy went over the side and Reagan pulled you back over." He looked up unsteadily, meet Aidan's eyes. "Thank you."

Aidan managed a nod. "It's okay. I'm not sure I'll ever breathe again, either." He blew out a breath and drew in another experimentally. "I guess I can."

Tess gently pulled from Vito's arms and turned into Aidan's. She put her head on his shoulder. "I don't think I've ever been so glad to see anyone as I was when you looked over that balcony." She touched her lips to his. "Thank you."

Aidan buried his face in the curve of her neck and shuddered. It was over. Finally over. "You're welcome. Let's get you checked out, then let's go home."

She tilted his head up, smiled into his eyes. "I'm not cooking tonight, Detective."

His laugh was strangled. "It's okay. I got no spit to swallow anything you'd make. Maybe tomorrow."

"Tomorrow it is."

Saturday, March 18, 8:30 A.M.

Tess gingerly stepped from the elevator at Aidan's floor, her heart racing. She stood for a moment and drew a deep breath.

"Still hate elevators, Tess?"

She looked up to find Marc Spinnelli studying her with a kind smile, a coffee cup in one hand. "Yeah, but I think I might hate heights just a little more now."

He grinned. "I'd say you'd have a right to that phobia, Doctor." He slid his arm around her shoulders. "I didn't get a chance to talk to you last night. Are you all right?"

"I'm fine. Sore, but fine." She'd woken in Aidan's bed an

hour before. He'd been gone already, a note on his pillow. "Sleep in," he'd ordered, but this morning she needed answers. She needed *him*. "Is Aidan here?"

He nodded, understanding. "In the conference room. I'll walk you."

Five pairs of eyes looked up when she came in. Jack, Rick, Patrick, and Murphy. And Aidan. He stood up, a frown bending his brow. "I told you to sleep."

"I couldn't." She held out the morning *Bulletin*. "Did you see this?"

Aidan sighed. "Yeah, we did. Sit down, Tess."

She took the chair he offered and spread the paper out, once again staring at the bold black type. The headline read DEFENSE ATTORNEY A KILLER. Under the bold print were two stories. The first was the bigger one, byline Cyrus Bremin. It detailed Amy's role in the killing spree of the last week, culminating with Phillip Parks and Keith Brandon. Their pictures stared up from the page and Tess could only feel sadness. Her own picture was included, next to a grainy photo of her hanging from the balcony. That picture left her stomach raw and turbulent. She'd dreamed about it the night before, her fingers slowly slipping from the balcony as horns blared from the traffic below. But she hadn't been asleep. It was just her memory playing that one horrific moment again and again. But she was alive. Thirteen others were not.

The second story was smaller, but just as shocking. Amy had been working for several powerful families in Chicago, earning blood money as she helped them put any employees who'd displeased them in prison. Invariably those employees were killed, sending an effective message to anyone considering a betrayal. Apparently among these employees, Amy Miller was associated with certain doom. Somehow Joanna Carmichael had uncovered this. And it had cost her boyfriend his life.

"She finally got her byline," Tess murmured. "Carmichael, that is."

"At a price," Aidan returned quietly. "Are you all right?"

Yes, she started to answer, then stared at the front page. "No. I'm not."

"How's your father, Tess?" Murphy asked.

"Stable." She managed a ghost of a smile. "Crotchety. He wants to go home." Her smile faded. "He wants me to go with him."

Something flashed in Aidan's eyes, but he just smiled. "We'll talk about that when everything's settled down. Have you eaten?"

"Your mother made me." Tess had woken to the smell of eggs and bacon and the easy smile of Becca Reagan, which seemed to take the edge off the worst of situations. Tess had spent the evening before in the hospital where she was examined and released quickly. Her father had been admitted, of course. Vito and her mother still sat by his side. But her father had insisted she go home. Get some sleep. Home was Aidan's house.

"What did you find out last night?"

"That everything in Carmichael's article is true. And more."

"She set up innocent men," Patrick said harshly. "A few I prosecuted. If the police got too close to one of the family's crimes, the family brought her in. She'd set up a scapegoat, arrange for the evidence to be found. And 'defend' the poor bastard so that he never had a chance at justice." He clenched his jaw, contempt in his eyes. "And I never suspected a thing. Neither did Kristen. Before we worried about appeals because of you. Now we're dealing with possible reversals of every case she defended."

"Ironic," Tess murmured.

"Nicole Rivera's brother was one of those innocent men,"

Aidan said. "She chose the boy because she believed Rivera was the best choice to imitate you. She set Miguel Rivera up for murder, then extorted his sister."

"The boy is free?" Tess asked.

Aidan nodded. "Last night."

"But his sister is dead," Murphy said flatly. "He has no one."

"Because Amy killed her." Tess closed her eyes. "And all those other people. And I still don't know why, other than that she hated me." The silence around the table was uncomfortable and awkward. Tess looked at their faces. "Tell me. Now."

"It was Jim Swanson, Tess," Aidan said gently. "She was obsessed with him."

"But he wanted me." She frowned. "He left three months ago for Africa. Is that what triggered all of this?" Aidan's eyes flickered and Tess knew. "He's dead, isn't he?"

"I'm sorry, Tess. Swanson never showed up at the clinic in Chad. We found his things in Amy's closet, a knife with dried blood of his type. She must have killed him in a rage. Then blamed you."

"She's hated me, all these years." Her mouth twisted bitterly. "Hell of a shrink I turned out to be. A killer at my front door and I never knew."

"Her mother was schizophrenic, Tess," Murphy said. "Your mom can tell you more, but it looks like Amy's been on the edge for years. Just smart enough to hide it from everyone. Including you."

"It's just been recently that her sanity started to slip beyond her grasp." Aidan squeezed her hand. "She couldn't hide it anymore."

"My mother knew?" Tess fought to swallow. "She knew?"

"She knew Amy's mother was sick, Tess. She had no idea Amy was, too."

Stiffly Tess nodded. "It doesn't matter. She poisoned me, you know. In my soup."

From across the table Jack grimaced. "The mushrooms? Julia thought as much."

"And she slept with Phillip."

"We figured that," Murphy said.

Tess nodded again, rolling the mental tape of the night before in her mind. "And she killed her father." But to her surprise, no one looked shocked. "You knew this, too?"

"Vito suspected. Apparently a neighborhood boy was charged."

"Leon Vanneti." Tess frowned. "He was innocent, like Vito said. But it's just my word. There's still no proof." Her eyes widened. "She said Leon raped her. They didn't do DNA then, but if they still have evidence maybe they can clear him now."

"I'll make the calls this morning," Spinnelli promised. "At least we can set one thing right."

Tess sighed. "She killed Eleanor, too."

This raised a few eyebrows. "Really?" Murphy asked. "How did she do that?"

"She injected her with air. Because Eleanor had been kind to me."

Spinnelli cleared his throat. "We do have some good news for you, Tess. Rick?"

"We found Bacon's original files in the apartment last night," Rick said. "Along with the one CD labeled with your name. Lynne Pope was able to identify it as the label she saw the day Bacon tried to sell it to her. So at least all the copies are accounted for."

Relief nearly made her head swim. "I didn't want to be so worried, but I was."

Spinnelli patted her shoulder. "Well, you don't have to be."

"Do you know why Amy wanted Bacon's files so badly?"

"I've had a policewoman viewing the footage since we got the CDs from Bacon's storage locker. She saw Amy taking bottles from your medicine cabinet."

"The bottles she planted in Cynthia's apartment."

Aidan shrugged. "It seems like a small thing for her to worry about, but I suppose she was worried Bacon would blackmail her since he was blackmailing you."

"That about wraps it up," Spinnelli said, "unless you have any other questions."

Tess looked at the newspaper again, her eyes skittering from the photo of herself dangling from the balcony. "I would like to know how Carmichael discovered all this."

Aidan held out his hand. "Let's pay her a visit, then I'll take you to see your father."

Aidan buckled her seat belt. She sat quietly, her hands folded in her lap, her face pale with the frail, vulnerable look of a traumatized child. He didn't speak until they were well away from the police station. "You should be home in bed."

"I couldn't sleep, Aidan."

He knew that. She'd lain beside him during the night, her body stiff and frozen, tears seeping from her eyes until he'd finally given them both what they needed. She'd responded with a ferocity that still left his skin tingling from head to toe. God help him, he wanted to feel that same way again. Right now. Instead, he kept his voice gentle. "You could have taken one of the sleeping pills Jon prescribed."

"After yesterday I think I've had enough tranquilizers for my lifetime." Her smile was strained. "But thank you. I'll be all right, Aidan. It will just take some time."

"I've got time, Tess."

Her serious eyes were like a punch to his overactive system. "Good."

"I have one other piece of good news. Do you remember that friend of Danny Morris's father?"

"The one you hurt your hand trying to arrest?"

"Yeah. I stopped by his apartment on my way into work this morning. Guess who was sleeping it off on the couch?"

Her eyes narrowed in satisfaction. "You arrested the father."

"He was trying to get away, but he was too disoriented to do anything but stagger. He'll be charged with murder."

Her nod was sober. "Good." Then she looked away, and he thought he understood how she felt when he'd closed himself to her.

"Tess, talk to me. Tell me what's bothering you." He pulled the car into an empty parking lot and hooked a finger under her chin. Her throat worked as she fought to control the tears, but still they rolled down her face. "Please talk to me."

"I would have killed her, Aidan. She was like my sister and I would have killed her."

He narrowed his eyes. "She deserved to die, Tess. She killed so many."

"She was sick." She swallowed hard. "And I never helped her."

He sighed. After everything, he was a cop. And she was a doctor. "You know what I realized yesterday afternoon, standing in her apartment? That one of the things I'd been afraid of was that you would worm your way into my mind, take away my privacy. Then I realized that you don't do that with the people you care about the most. It left you vulnerable with Amy, with Phillip. But it puts you on equal footing with me."

She blinked at him. "So I'm inept with my loved ones . . . which is good."

He ran his tongue over his teeth. "Essentially, yes."

Her lips curved. "That's so sweet." She wiped at her eyes. "I'm a mess."

"You're beautiful. Tess, the night before last, I asked you what you wanted. You said it was what you'd always wanted. Somebody to love you."

She lifted her chin. "And you said it didn't scare you away."

"It didn't. It doesn't. You never asked me what I wanted that night."

She bit her lower lip. "So? What do you want, Aidan?"

He hesitated, self-conscious. "I always wanted a woman like my mom."

She smiled. "Somebody to cook for you?"

"There is that. But more of what she's been to my dad all these years. He'd come home, tired and worn and upset over something that had happened on his shift. And she'd be there. She'd always . . . just be there. And she loves him for who he is."

"I can see that. She's a good person, Aidan."

"So are you, Tess." He took her hand, pressed it against his lips. "I think I was afraid that you would do more than just be there. That you'd analyze and judge and maybe tell me I was crazy, because sometimes that's how I feel."

"I wouldn't do that." Her mouth quirked up. "Apparently, I'm inept."

"Only in that. In everything else, you're quite the expert. Let's talk to Carmichael."

Saturday, March 18, 9:45 A.M.

Carmichael was standing on the curb outside her apartment, a suitcase in her hand. She was pale, dark circles shadowing her eyes. She didn't look happy to see them.

"Miss Carmichael?" Tess said. "I was so sorry to hear about your friend."

Joanna eyed her head to toe, speculative, yet detached. "I should say the same."

But she didn't, Tess realized. "I'd like to speak with you."

She looked down the street. "I'm going to the airport. I have only a few minutes."

Tess nodded. "That should be enough. I want to know how you discovered Amy Miller had been working for organized crime families."

A mirthless smile bent Joanna's mouth. "It really wasn't that difficult. I was looking for dirt. I found it. Your friend Jon's story was little, but your friend Amy's . . . Real big. I knew she hung with the doctors that met at the Blue Lemon every second Sunday and I wondered why all those doctors and one lone lawyer. That's when I found she'd gone to med school in Kentucky while you were in med school here in Chicago."

"We couldn't get into the same school," Tess told Aidan. "She dropped out because she couldn't stand the cadaver dissections. Ironic, isn't it?"

"She didn't drop out, Dr. Ciccotelli. She was expelled, or she would have been if she hadn't managed to get some incriminating photos with one of her professors."

Tess blinked. "She was nothing if not predictable."

"I tracked down one of her old roommates through the dean's secretary at the med school. Apparently she hadn't liked Miller and had no hesitation in pointing me in the right direction. I caught up with Kelsey Chin, who is now a doctor in Lexington. She told me about the expulsion and the pictures. She said that Miller had tried to enlist her help in taking the photos, then went to their other roommate when she said no."

"So how did you find out about the organized crime?" Aidan asked impatiently.

Joanna's

"I wondered at the ethics of someone who could do such a thing. Plus, she lost a lot of cases, yet still she had the money for clothes and cruises."

"Actually, I paid for the cruise," Tess said.

Joanna's smile was bitter. "Then I guess I just lucked out, because that made me check her client list. From there it was just connecting the dots." A cab stopped at the curb. "And now I've got to go. I'm flying home to bury Keith."

"And then?" Tess asked.

"I'll be back." Her bitter smile twisted. "I got a promotion. Big raise. I've learned to be careful what I wish for." She got into the cab without a backward glance.

The cab disappeared around the corner. "I don't know if I feel sorry for her, Aidan."

He put her back in his car. "She's got to live with what she's done. She pulled the tiger's tail and her boyfriend paid the ultimate price." He climbed in beside her and squeezed her hand. "There was nothing you could have done, Tess."

Tess drew a shaky breath. "I know. And maybe that's the hardest part to face."

"Look . . . I know this cop who has a bachelor's degree in psychology and whose couch is available for a moderate fee."

Tess laughed and it felt good. "Moderate?"

"Oh, all right. I'll give you my advice on the barter system."

"What barter did you have in mind?"

He pulled away from the curb. "If you have to ask, you're not as smart as I thought."

"I did say I wasn't a mind reader, Detective."

He grinned. "So you did. I guess I'll just have to spell it out for you later. For now, I'll take you to your father. He'll be waiting for you."

Epilogue

Philadelphia, Saturday, October 28, 7:25 P.M.

"He's having a good time," Tess said, a catch in her voice.

Michael Ciccotelli was dancing with his wife, who for once wasn't telling him not to overdo it. Tess's wedding day was a day to be overdone, everyone living it as if it might be the last time the Ciccotelli family gathered together. It was bittersweet, but Tess had come to peace with her father's condition even as they all hoped for a donor.

Aidan stood behind her, his arms around her waist, his feet completely covered by the six-foot train of her grandmother's satin gown. "Yes, he is. Are you?"

She shivered as he brushed kisses against her bare neck. "It's getting better."

"I can guarantee it will get better tomorrow." They'd rejected a cruise as too "Phillip" and a European vacation as too "Shelley" for their honeymoon, opting to spend a week at the Jersey shore. Then they'd return to Chicago for a party at the Lemon with all their friends, although most of them were right here with them now. Aidan's family was here, Rachel and Kristen as bridesmaids. Abe was his best man and even Murphy had agreed to don a tux as an usher. Vito looked right at home in his tux, and at the moment was trying to fend off a determined young woman. As Tess always said, all the girls flirted with Vito.

At Vito's side was his friend Leon who had been released months before after DNA testing proved he had not raped Amy Miller. With Tess's testimony and Amy's mental illness, Leon's entire conviction had been overturned. It was good to see justice prevail.

Jack and Julia were here, as were Robin and Jon and Patrick and Flo Ernst and Ethel Hughes, and even Lynne Pope who planned to show a clip of the wedding on *Chicago On The Town*. Closure, she'd said. Which of course it was.

The rest of the hall was filled with more Ciccotellis than Aidan could count. Right now Michael Ciccotelli was approaching, his face a picture of paternal pride. "It's my father-daughter dance, Tessa. You'll have to let her go, Reagan."

Aidan obliged and noticed he wasn't the only one wiping his eyes when Michael swept his daughter onto the dance floor. They made a beautiful pair. When the DJ had played the final strains, Tess leaned over and whispered in her father's ear. Michael delivered her back to Aidan, his smile gone wry. "You'll take care of her," he said.

Tess rolled her eyes. "She can take care of herself."

Ignoring her, Aidan said, "With my life," which seemed to please his new father-in-law. Michael walked to his wife and sat in a chair before she nagged him to. "What did you tell him out there?"

"That he has to stick around for the next family function. No checking out allowed."

Aidan narrowed his eyes. "And what might that family function be?"

"A christening."

His narrowed eyes popped wide. "Tess?"

She laughed. "No, I'm not. But I intend to be very soon. I know this cop, see, whose therapy couch could be used for something far more exciting than therapy."

"Really?"

"Oh, yes. And I'm told his fees are moderate."

"Downright cheap."

"Then what are we waiting for?"

Aidan kissed her soundly, drawing hoots from everyone close enough to see. "I'm not waiting for anything anymore. I have it all right here."

About the Author

RITA Award-winning author Karen Rose has always loved books. Jo Marsh from *Little Women* and Nancy Drew were close childhood friends. She was introduced to suspense and horror at the tender age of eight when she accidentally read Poe's "The Pit and the Pendulum" and was afraid to go to sleep for years, which explains a lot . . .

After earning her degree in chemical engineering from the University of Maryland, Karen married her high school sweetheart. She started writing when characters started popping up in her head and simply wouldn't be quiet. Now she enjoys making other people afraid to go to sleep! When she's not writing, she teaches high school. She lives in sunny Florida with her husband and their daughters.

Karen was honored and totally thrilled to receive the Romance Writers of America's highest award in 2005—the RITA for Best Romantic Suspense for *I'm Watching You* (Warner Books, 2004).

Visit Karen's Web site at www.karenrosebooks.com for more information on Karen, her books, and upcoming events. She loves to hear from readers, so please contact her at karen@karenrosebooks.com.

"Rose is making her mark on the suspense genre."

—*Romantic Times BOOKclub Magazine*

Turn this page for more of the heart-pounding excitement that only Karen Rose can deliver!

COUNT TO TEN

available in mass market in early 2007.

Chapter One

Chicago, Saturday, November 25, 11:45 p.m.

A branch slapped the window and Caitlin Burnette's jaw clenched. "It's just the wind," she muttered. "Don't be such a baby." Still, the howling outside was unsettling, and being alone in the Doughertys' creaky old house wasn't helping. She dropped her eyes back to the statistics book that was responsible for her being alone on a Saturday night. She should be with her friends. There was a party at TriEpsilon that sure as hell would have been more fun than this. Noisier, too. Which was why she was here, studying the most boring subject in the quiet of a boring old house instead of in her sorority house with a party going on all around her room.

Her stat professor had scheduled an exam for Monday morning. If she failed it, she'd fail the semester. If she failed one more class, her father would take away her car, sell it, and use the money to take her mother to the Bahamas. He'd already made up the for sale sign for the windshield, the bastard. Mom had bought a new bathing suit, so sure were they that she'd fall on her face. .

Caitlin ground her teeth. She'd show them. She'd pass that damn test if it killed her. And if she didn't, she had nearly enough money in savings to buy the damn car herself or maybe even a better one. The money the Doughertys were paying her to take care of their cat would put her over the top and—

A different noise had her chin jerking up, her eyes narrowing. What the hell? It came from downstairs. It sounded like… a chair scraping against the hardwood floor.

Call the police.

She had her hand on the phone, but she drew a breath and made herself calm down. *It's probably just the cat.* She'd look pretty stupid calling the police about a twenty-pound, overly pampered Persian. Plus, she really wasn't supposed to be here right now. Mrs. Dougherty had been clear about that. She was not to "stay over." She was not to "have parties." She was not to "use the phone." She was to feed the cat and change the litter box, period. The Doughertys might get mad and refuse to pay her if they found out she was here. Caitlin sighed. Besides, word would get back to her dad and wouldn't he just have a field day with that? All over a stupid fluffy cat named Percy of all things.

Still, it didn't hurt to be careful. Quietly Caitlin pulled the small gun from Mrs. Dougherty's nightstand drawer and disengaged the safety. She'd found the gun when she was looking for a pen. It was a .22, just like what she'd shot dozens of times at the range. She descended the stairs, the gun pressed against the back of her leg. It was pitch black, but she was afraid to turn on a light. *Stop this, Caitlin. Call the cops.* But her feet kept moving, soundless on the carpet, until two steps from the bottom, a stair creaked. She stopped short, her heart pounding, and listened hard.

And heard humming. There was somebody in the house and they were *humming*.

The screech of something heavy being dragged across the floor drowned out the humming. She smelled gas.

Get out. Get help. She lurched forward, stumbling when her feet hit the hardwood floor at the base of the stairs. She fell to her knees, and the gun flew from her hand, skittering across the floor. Loudly.

The humming stopped. Desperately she made a move for the gun, grasping for it in the dark, her hands frantically patting at the cold hardwood. She found the gun and scrambled to her feet. *Get out. Get out. Get out.*

She'd taken two steps toward the door when she was hit from behind, knocked to her knees. She tried to scream, but she couldn't breathe. Together they slid a few feet before he pushed her to her stomach. He was lying on top of her. He was heavy. *God, please.* She struggled, but he was just too heavy. In a second he twisted the gun from her hand. His breath was beating hot and hard against her ear. Then his breathing slowed, and she could feel him grow hard. *Not that. Please, God.*

She clenched her eyes closed as he thrust his hips hard, his intentions clear.

"You weren't supposed to be here." His voice was deep, but it was fake. Like a bad Darth Vader imitation. Caitlin focused, determined to remember every last detail so that when she got away, she could tell the police.

"Please don't hurt me," she whispered.

He hesitated. She could feel him take a breath and hold it. Time stood still. Finally he let the breath out.

Then he laughed.

Sunday, November 26, 1:10 a.m.

Reed Solliday moved through the gathered crowd, listening. Watching their faces as the house across the street burned. It was an older middle-class neighborhood and the people standing outside in the cold seemed to know each other. They stood in shock and disbelief, murmuring their fear that the wind would spread the flames to their own homes. Three older women stood to one side, gnarled hands clasped, their worried faces illuminated by the remains of the fire that had taken two companies more than thirty minutes to bring under control. This fire was too hot, too high, too many places within the house to feel like an accidental fire.

Despite their shock, this was the time to interview the onlookers, before they had time to share stories. Even in groups of people with nothing to hide, shared stories became homogenized stories in which relevant details could be lost.

Arsonists could go free. And making sure that didn't happen was Reed's job.

"Ladies?" He approached the three women, his shield in his hand. "My name is Lieutenant Solliday."

All three women gave him the once-over. "You're a policeman?" the middle one asked. She looked to be about seventy and tiny enough that Reed was surprised the wind hadn't blown her away. Her white hair was tightly rolled in curlers, and her flannel nightgown hung past the hem of her woolen coat, dragging on the frosty ground.

"Fire marshal," Reed answered. "Can I get your names?"

"I'm Emily Richter, and this is Janice Kimbrough and Darlene Desmond."

Reed glanced at the ladies over his notepad as he took down their names. "You all know this neighborhood well?"

Richter sniffed. "I've lived here for almost fifty years."

"Who lives in that house, ma'am?"

"The Doughertys used to live there. Joe and Laura. But Laura passed away and Joe retired to Florida. His son and daughter-in-law live there now. Sold it to 'em cheap, Joe did. Brought down all the property values in the neighborhood."

"But they're not home now," Janice Kimbrough added. "They went to Florida to see Joe for Thanksgiving."

"So nobody was in the house?" It was what the men had been told on arriving.

"Not unless they got home early," Janice said.

"But they didn't." Richter said firmly. "Their fancy truck is too tall for the garage, so they park it in the driveway. It's not there, so they're not home yet."

"Have you ladies seen anybody hanging around that doesn't belong?"

"I saw a girl going in and out yesterday," Richter said. "Joe's son said they'd hired somebody to feed the cat." She sniffed again. "In the old days Joe would have given us his key and a bag of cat food, but his son changed all the locks. Hired some kid."

The hair on Reed's neck stood on end. Call it instinct. Call it whatever. But something felt very bad about all this. "A kid?"

"A college girl," Darlene Desmond supplied. "Joe's daughter-in-law told me she wasn't going to be living in. Just coming in three times a day and feeding the cat. The girl's the daughter of somebody she knows from work."

Reed looked over his shoulder. They'd pretty well knocked the fire down. But if there was anybody in there . . . "I'd appreciate it if you could get me Joe Dougherty's phone number in Florida. Thanks, ladies, you've been a big help." He jogged across the street to where Captain Larry Fletcher stood next to the rig, a radio in one hand. "Larry."

"Reed." Larry was frowning at the burning house. "Somebody made this fire."

"I think so, too."

"So what did you find out from the old ladies?"

"The owners are out of town, but they hired a college kid to watch the cat."

Larry's head whipped around, his jaw clenched. "Hell, why didn't anybody say anything? They said nobody was home. The owners were out of town."

"They said the kid wasn't supposed to live in. What did you find in the garage?"

Larry closed his eyes briefly. "A new BMW and an old Chevy. Both burned, but the Chevy's a total loss. There were a few explosions in the garage after the first big one in the kitchen. The Chevy could have belonged to the girl. I'll send a pair in to look for her."

"I'll keep canvassing the crowd. Let me go in as soon as I can."

It had been a nice house, Reed thought an hour later as he walked through what was now a ruined shell. What the fire didn't get, the water would, was the general rule. In this case, the fire got nearly everything. It would be daylight soon, and he'd be able to get a better view with the sun shining through the holes the boys had chopped to vent the roof. For now, he flashed a high-powered light on the walls, looking for the burn lines.

He stopped and turned to the firefighter who'd manned the inside line. "Where was it burning when you got here?"

Brian Mahoney shook his head. "Where wasn't it? There were flames in the kitchen, the garage, the upstairs bedroom, and the living room. We got as far as the living room when the ceiling started to crumble and I got my guys out. Just in time, too. Kitchen ceiling caved. We focused on keeping it from spreading to the other houses after that."

Reed looked straight up through what had been two stories, an attic, and a roof and saw stars in the sky. They could have four different points of origin. Some bastard wanted to be sure this place burned. "Nobody hurt?"

Brian shrugged. "Minor burns on the probie, but he'll be okay. One of the guys got some smoke. Captain sent them both to the ER to get checked out. Listen, Reed, I came back in to look for the girl, but there was still too much smoke. If she was here . . ."

"I know," Reed said grimly. He started moving again. "I know."

"Reed!" It was Larry, standing in the kitchen next to an overturned table.

Immediately Reed noted the stove pulled away from the wall. "You guys pull that stove out?" he asked.

"Not us," Brian answered. "We didn't get close enough to this room to touch anything. You're thinking he used the gas to start this thing?"

"Maybe. But he had to have used something else in the other rooms. You guys see any gas cans upstairs?"

"No, but it doesn't mean they weren't there. It was blacker than night in there."

Reed looked over at Larry, who continued to stare down at his feet. "Larry?"

Larry's shoulders sagged. "She's here."

Reed gritted his teeth and moved to Larry's side. He shone his light down, dreading what he'd see. And drew a breath. "Goddammit."

This wasn't a case of smoke inhalation. This body was charred beyond recognition.

"Dammit," Brian echoed, tightly furious. "Do you know who she was?"

Reed shined the light around the body, trying to see what he'd have to move to get it free. "Not yet. I got the number of the old owner of this place from the ladies across the street. Joe Dougherty, Sr. His son, Joe Jr., lives here now. Joe Sr. said Joe Jr. and his wife went on a chartered fishing boat twenty miles off the Florida coast for the weekend. He doesn't expect him back until Monday morning. He did tell me his daughter-in-law works for a legal firm downtown. Supposedly the girl they'd hired is the daughter of one of the wife's officemates. I'll see if I can locate her parents." He sighed when Larry continued to stare at the body on the floor. "You didn't know she was here, Larry."

"My daughter's in college," Larry returned, his voice rough.

And mine will be soon enough, Reed thought, then banished the thought from his mind. Thoughts like that would drive a man crazy. "I'll get the medical examiner's office out here," he said. "Then I'll be back at first light. You look like shit, Larry. Both of you do. Go back to the station and get some rest."

Larry nodded dully. "You forgot to say 'sir.' " It was an attempt at levity that fell miserably flat. "You never said 'sir,' not in all the years you rode with me."

They'd been good years. Larry was one of the best captains he'd ever had. "Sir," Reed corrected himself gently. He pulled Larry's arm, making him move away from the charred obscenity that had once housed a young woman's soul. "Go get some rest, Larry. You too, Brian. I'll let you know what I find."

Sunday, November 26, 2:30 a.m.

A criminal always returns to the scene of his crime. Which was why he hadn't. He would do the unexpected. He would not be caught. He was sitting in his car, miles away, the heater keeping him cozy, his police scanner keeping him in touch. The firemen had put out the fire already. Took two companies this time, a testament to his success. The house was a total loss. By now they'd found the surprise in the kitchen. Bet that shocked the shit out of them. He switched off his scanner and smiled.

No. It wasn't just a smile. It was a grin. He felt . . . renewed. Bullet-proof. King of the whole damn world. In the past, he'd so wanted to burn up the people in their houses, to see them in pain, to hear them beg him not to hurt them, but something had held him back. Misplaced mercy, perhaps. So he'd made himself content with torching the houses when nobody was sure to be home. But his mercy wouldn't be misplaced any more.

Mercy was earned, and nobody on his list had earned it. Tonight had opened his eyes to a lot of things.

Tonight was like . . . a gift from Fate. He'd been watching the Dougherty house. The old man and his wife weren't home. The big truck hadn't been in the driveway for almost a week. He'd broken in, started setting up just as he had in the other houses. Then he'd heard the thump on the stairs. Shocked the hell out him. But it had only been a girl. Miss Caitlin Burnette. Tiny little thing. Easily overcome. His grin turned wolfish. He'd nearly forgotten how good it could feel when they said no. God, what a rush.

He needed to feel it again. Soon. His thoughts twisted abruptly. To *her*. Leanne. Bigger and clumsier than Caitlin Burnette and not nearly as pretty. Leanne actually thought *she* could do the breaking up. That he'd sit back and let her treat him like shit. *She actually thinks she can tell me no.* Maybe a little of what he'd given Caitlin would teach Leanne a lesson. He'd have to plan it carefully. *Too obvious a move would point the finger back at me.* And he was much too smart to ever allow that to happen. He'd think about it. Half the fun was in thinking about it. Planning it. He'd consider all the risks, all the things that could go wrong, and come up with a plan for each one.

For now, he had bigger fish to fry . . . so to speak. He'd been out of the race for a while now. He had some catching up to do. He patted his pocket. He was armed now, thanks to little Miss Caitlin. That should make things easier should he run into any more unexpected barriers. He'd barely started on the list of houses he'd burn. Then there were the businesses, which would offer a different challenge. And as for Leanne . . . He pulled his car away from the curb with grim determination. She'd get hers. He'd make sure of it. He'd teach her that she couldn't tell him no.

Nobody would tell him no ever again.

Chapter Two

Monday, November 27, 6:45 a.m

Daddy!"

The shout, accompanied by the banging on his bedroom door, sent the tie tack in Reed's hand skittering to the floor and under his dresser. He sighed. "Come on in, Beth."

The door exploded, admitting both twelve-year-old Beth and her twelve-week-old sheepdog, which took a running leap, landing in the middle of Reed's bed.

"Schmuck, no." Beth yanked on his collar, pulling him across the sheets to the floor where he sat, his puppy tongue sticking out just far enough to make him too cute to punish.

Hands on his hips, Reed stared in dismay at the muddy streaks Schmuck left behind. "I just changed my sheets, Beth. I told you to wipe his paws before you brought him in the house. The back yard is a mud bath."

Beth's lips twitched. "Well, his paws are clean now. I'll wash the sheets again. But first I need lunch money, Dad. The bus is coming soon."

Reed pulled his wallet from his back pocket. "Didn't I just give you lunch money a few days ago?"

Beth shrugged, her hand out. "You want me to go hungry, or what?"

He shot her an overly patient look. "I want you to help me find my tie-tack. It rolled under the dresser."

Beth dropped to her knees and felt for the tie-tack. "Here it is." She dropped it in his palm, and he handed her a twenty.

"Try to make it last for at least two weeks, okay?"

She wrinkled her nose, and in that moment she looked so much like her mother that his heart squeezed. Mary used to look just like that when he suggested she try some new food she'd never eaten before. For all her creative flair, Mary had been a creature of habit.

Beth folded the bill and slid in down into the pockets of jeans that hadn't seemed that tight before. "Two weeks? You've gotta be kidding."

"Do I look like I'm kidding?" He looked her up and down. "Your jeans are too tight, Bethie," he said, and she got that look on her face. Damn, he hated that look. It seemed to have appeared about the same time as the pimples and the mood swings. Reed's younger sister Lauren had informed him in a dark whisper that his baby was no longer a baby. God. PMS. He wasn't ready for this. But it didn't seem to matter. His baby was almost a teenager. She'd be going off to college any day now.

His mind flitted to the young woman they'd found in the rubble of the Dougherty house. If she was the college house sitter, she wasn't much older than Beth, and Reed still didn't know her name. He hadn't heard from Joe Dougherty, Jr. or his wife yet, so he'd have to start with the wife's personal records. Once he found out where Dougherty's wife worked, he could narrow down the parents of the dead girl.

Beth spoke, her acidic tone piercing his thoughts. "Are you saying these pants make me look fat?"

Reed sucked in his cheeks. There was no good answer to this question. "No. Not even close. You're not fat. You're healthy. You're perfect. You do not need to lose weight.

Her eyes rolled, her tone became longsuffering. "I'm not going anorexic, Dad."

"Good." He let out the breath he'd been holding. "I'm just saying we need to go shopping for bigger jeans." He smiled weakly. "You're growing too fast, baby. Don't you like the idea of new clothes?" The tie-tack rolled in his clumsy fingers, which were no longer as dexterous as they once had been. "I thought all girls loved shopping."

Quickly Beth took over the task of fixing the tie tack and smoothing his tie with a practiced hand. The look he hated disappeared, replaced by a wicked grin that made her dark eyes sparkle. "I *love* shopping. You could go with me and we could make an afternoon of it. I bet we could spend six hours in Marshall Fields alone. Sweaters and jeans and skirts. And shoes! Just think of it."

Reed shuddered, the picture abundantly clear. "Now you're just being mean."

She laughed. "Revenge for the fat comment. So you want to go shopping, Daddy?"

He shuddered again. "Frankly, a root-canal without Novocain seems less painful. Can Aunt Lauren take you?"

"I'll ask her." Beth leaned up and kissed his cheek. "Thanks for the lunch money, Daddy. Gotta go."

Reed watched her dart away, the sloppy pup at her heels. The front door slammed as Beth headed out, the sheets on his bed still muddy from the dog she'd begged him to buy for her twelfth birthday. He knew if he wanted to sleep on clean sheets tonight, he'd best change them himself. But the smell of coffee tickled his nose. She'd remembered to flip the switch on the coffee machine, so he'd cut her slack on the puppy prints. She was a good kid.

Reed would sell his soul to make sure she stayed that way. He glanced over at the picture on his nightstand. Mary serenely stared back as she had for ten years. Sitting on the edge of his bed, he picked up the picture and dusted the frame with the cuff of his shirt. Mary would have enjoyed Beth's coming of age, the shopping trips, the "talk." He doubted even the "look" would have fazed her. Once he would have damned the world that his wife hadn't had the chance to find out. Today . . . Precisely he set the picture back on the nightstand so that it once again covered the dust-free strip of wood. After ten years, the rage had become a sad acceptance. What was, was. Shrugging into his suit coat, he shook himself. If he didn't hit the road soon, traffic would make him late. *Coffee, Solliday, then get moving.*

He was pulling out of his garage when his cell phone rang. "Solliday."

"Lieutenant Solliday?" The voice was frantic. "This is Joseph Dougherty. I just got back from a charter fishing trip, and my dad said you called."

Joe, Jr. at last. He put the car in park and pulled out his notepad. "Mr. Dougherty. I'm sorry to have to contact you this way."

There was a heavy sigh. "Then it's true? My house is gone?"

That was the understatement of the year. "It's true. Mr. Dougherty, we found a body in the kitchen."

There was a beat of silence. "*What?*"

"Yes, sir. It appears to be a woman. The neighbors said you had somebody watching your house."

"Y-yes. Her name is Burnette. Caitlin Burnette. She's supposed to be very responsible." Panic had taken the man's voice a little higher. "She's dead?"

Reed thought of the charred body and swallowed his sigh. *Yes, she's very dead.* "We're assuming the body we found was your house-sitter, but we'll have to investigate before we're certain. Do you have her parents' names?"

"My . . ." He cleared his throat. "My wife does. I'll get them and call you back."

Reed tossed his phone to the passenger seat, only to have it ring again. Caller ID this time was the morgue. When it rains . . . "Solliday."

"Reed, it's Sam Barrington." The new medical examiner. Barrington had taken over when the old ME went on extended maternity leave. The old ME had been efficient, astute, and personable. Barrington . . . well, he was efficient and astute.

"Hey, Sam. I'm on my way into the office. What do you have?"

"Victim's a woman, early twenties. Best I can tell, she was five-two, five three."

Barrington wasn't the type to call with such basic information. There had to be more. "And?"

"Well, before I started to cut, I did an initial x-ray of the body and I'm glad I did. I expected to see the skull in fractured fragments."

Which was the general way of things. When bodies were subjected to that kind of heat, the skulls sometimes just exploded from the pressure. "But you didn't."

"No, because the bullet hole in her skull vented all the pressure. Reed, this is a homicide."

Reed let his head drop back against the headrest. "Crap. This changes everything." Now he had to share. He got the arson, the cops got the body. Too many damn cooks in the kitchen.

"Thought you'd want to know," Sam said briskly. "I'm going to start the autopsy right away, so you can come by anytime this morning."

"Thanks. I will." He put his car in gear and pulled onto his quiet tree-lined street. It had been a while since he'd worked with Homicide, but he thought Marc Spinnelli was still the lieutenant there. Marc was a straight shooter. Reed only hoped the detective Spinnelli assigned wouldn't be a prima donna asshole.

SSIHM LIBRARY/
RESOURCE CENTER
610 W. ELM AVE.
MONROE, MICHIGAN 48162